EIGHT MINUTES IDLE

Also by Matt Thorne

Tourist

EIGHT MINUTES IDLE

Matt Thorne

SCEPTRE

Copyright © Matt Thorne 1999

First published in 1999 by Hodder and Stoughton
A division of Hodder Headline PLC
A Sceptre book

The right of Matt Thorne to be identified as the Author of the Work
has been asserted by him in accordance with the Copyright,
Designs and Patents Act 1988.

10 9 8 7 6 5 4 3 2 1

British Library C.I.P.
A CIP catalogue record for this title is available from the British Library.

ISBN 0340 73882 0

Typeset by Palimpsest Book Production Limited,
Polmont, Stirlingshire
Printed and bound in Great Britain by
Clays Ltd, St Ives plc

Hodder and Stoughton
A division of Hodder Headline PLC
338 Euston Road
London NW1 3BH

For My Father

Part One

Office Romance

1

Some days having a job seems the most decadent pursuit imaginable. I sit at my desk filled with gratitude towards the team leaders and line managers, my fellow employees and the company's clients: everyone involved in the maintenance of this air-conditioned alternative to gainful unemployment. I grin to myself as I log on, happy in the knowledge that while my peers are watching films and starting bands, reading books and writing theses, I alone am about to enjoy a day of true idleness, tapping numbers into my keyboard and talking on the telephone.

I've always wanted to work in an office. As a child I'd stare at the billboards on the way to school, memorising the dimensions of each new development: 550×210. 180×715. Metre after metre of available space. I couldn't wait to have my own work station, my own ID card, my own square of sectioned-off carpet. It didn't matter what I did. Success has never been an issue. All I've ever wanted is an excuse to put on a tie.

The man next to me is normally named Gordon. From nine to five, however, he's known as the Car Insurance King. Whenever anyone phones the agency with a Car Insurance enquiry, they're instantly transferred to Gordon. The tablets Gordon takes have two unfortunate side-effects. He gets scratching fits and he talks to himself. The other members of my team (Ian, Adrienne and Teri: with only five members, we're the smallest team in the office) have tried several methods to work out what he's saying. The most successful to date was when Ian plugged his headphones into the back of Gordon's *Aspect*, trusting the small microphone the Car Insurance King speaks into when answering calls would be powerful enough to pick up his idle-time soliloquy.

It was only a relative success. Ian could confirm Gordon pronounces human words, but the lapses in transmission prevented him from discerning whether they are spoken in any logical order. In spite of my encouragement, Ian has so far proved reluctant to repeat this experiment.

When Ian first came here, it was impossible to get anything out of him. He'd accepted work as a necessary privation, but saw no reason why he should socialise with his fellow inmates. My few attempts to begin conversations were scuppered by my ignorance of football, an interest that led him into an unlikely office-only friendship with Gordon, consolidated during the four fifteen-minute fag breaks which punctuate our working day. (Not smoking also threatened to isolate me from the rest of my team, and I now sit alongside them at the smoking table, the stink of their cigarettes spoiling my sandwiches.) Just when I'd decided my friendships at work would be limited to arguments with Adrienne and the odd smile from Teri, Ian approached me at the company's monthly karaoke evening. At first I feared he wanted us to do a duet, but instead he started slagging off the two line managers up on stage doing a shaky version of 'Shiny Happy People'. As we talked, I soon realised that we'd been spending our weekends in the same clubs, dancing to the same music and talking to people two links away from one another. We agreed to go out together the following Friday.

Over the next few weekends, I discovered that Ian had managed to cut down boozing after work, but still allowed himself a Blackthorn breakfast every morning, pouring two cans of cider into a bowl and drinking them through a straw to heighten the effect. He told me he's always thought of himself as a hellraiser, especially since his short spell in a juvenile detention centre. When he told me this I started to get worried. Not because I thought he'd beat me up, but because I have similar *form*, and usually enjoy telling people this at the start of any prospective friendship as an excuse to hide in the corner should any violent encounter arise. I've often thought it's worth my twelve quid a week not to have to fight again, but now I worried that Ian would sense I wasn't a real hard man and call my bluff. Instead he commiserated with me about the injustice of my fine and explained that he'd been sent away for breaking his stepfather's jaw after watching him beat up his mother for the zillionth time. The nobility of his crime embarrassed me, and when he asked what I'd been done for, all I could do was shrug and say, 'You know. Stuff.' He hasn't mentioned it since.

The hardest part of being a good employee is trying to shut down your senses. It's easy to convince them you're competent, but the truly superlative worker is the one who has no interest in the world beyond their work-station. Like Gordon. Concentrating during a call is no problem, but once you're into more than three minutes of idle time, it's impossible to stop your eyes exploring the rest of the office.

Most mornings are busy enough to postpone this curiosity until mid-afternoon. The light on your *Aspect* glows yellow when you've got calls waiting, and will quickly turn red if you don't hit *Ready* the moment each dialler hangs up. Enough red lights and you'll be monitored, a procedure most employees are eager to avoid. On Wednesdays, however, everything slows. To get through these empty mid-week mornings, I focus my attention on the area behind reception. Three purple screens section off a small square where the limited human intercourse of Quick Kall Ltd takes place. It's here that people are reprimanded, disciplined, dismissed. It's from here that people are escorted out of the building. From here calls are monitored, and it's on this desk that employee reports are written. This is the private space where line managers hide to gossip and joke, taking bets on who'll be next to go.

Whenever I watch this area, I'm convinced they're talking about me. Their anxious looks in my direction prove I'm the one being monitored, and the horror in their eyes lets me know that they not only listen in to my calls, but also spend their evenings watching my life outside the office on giant video screens. Usually I can dismiss this as paranoia. This morning, it seems I'm right.

The team leader approaches my desk.

'Can I have a word with you please, Daniel?'

I follow her across to the area behind reception. The team leader is wearing her usual work suit, a burgundy jacket and matching skirt so stiffly formal it could be a uniform. Her face reminds me of a Peanuts character, usually Peppermint Patty but occasionally Lucy or Charlie Brown himself. She looks at me.

'I've just had a phonecall from the hospital. Your father's had an accident.'

I don't know what to say. 'Is it serious?'

'I think so. The nurse said he's been asking for you. Would you like the afternoon off?'

She watches me. I try to gauge what's expected. I'm reluctant to lose a day's pay and feel happy to work at least until lunchtime, but worry that appearing unemotional might be equally detrimental to my career.

'Thank you,' I tell her. 'That's very kind of you.'

I swagger into the hospital, determined not to be upset. As I am to learn over the next few weeks, only the doctors and nurses can keep up this demeanour for any length of time. The moment I see my father lying on a trolley, a white blanket wrapped around his battered body, I immediately lose all my verve. The first thing that strikes me is the smell. Not the hospital smell, but the smell of my father. He smells scared. I stand at the end of the bed.

'Hello Dad.'

'OK, Dan?' he asks. His eyes don't look right. A nurse stands alongside him, writing onto a clipboard with a blue biro. Her black hair is pulled back into a ponytail.

'Do you want to take that side?' she asks, stepping onto the wheel-release.

Dad looks up. 'Don't let him do it. You should see him with the shopping.'

The nurse laughs and we wheel him across the tiled floor. She leads in front and I push from behind, the wobbling wheels dragging us to the left.

'I don't think I'm the best nurse for your father,' she says. 'He seems a little timid.'

'What happened to him?'

'A direct hit. He went up in the air, came down headfirst onto the car's windscreen and bounced off into the path of another car. The second driver stopped inches away from his head.'

I look down at Dad's forehead. He has a circular cut around his left temple, small black crusts giving way to gooey red in the centre. The nurse drags the trolley into a small sectioned-off square that backs onto a fire exit. She hands me a translucent plastic jug.

'He'll probably need this in a minute.'

She ducks back behind the curtain. Dad reaches beneath his blankets and looks me in the eye.

'You'll help me, won't you? I can't move.'

'OK.'

He holds my gaze. 'I know you hate this sort of thing but I'll do it for you one day. You'll have to flop me inside.'

I scoop the jug along his legs. 'Be careful,' he warns, and I realise I'll have to pull the blanket back. Dad stares straight ahead, nervous about the nurse returning. I balance the jug between his thighs and reach down. My fingers find his penis and guide it inside the neck of the container.

'What'd it feel like?' I asked. 'Getting hit.'

'I don't know. I've got a twenty-minute blackout.' He shuffles anxiously. 'Please. You have to tilt it.'

He tries to move the jug. I press it into his stomach. The skin beneath it whitens. Dad holds his breath, twitches his penis, and releases a stream of urine against the inside of the jug. 'Tilt it. Tilt it,' he orders. 'Hold it downwards.'

I follow his instructions, hoping it won't spill onto his stomach. Dad seems to sense the jug filling and stills his arc.

'Finished?'

He nods. I slowly stand the jug up. A final spasm splashes piss across my fingers. I sigh, and avoid his eye as I carry his urine away. I spot the nurse who wheeled Dad over, and raise the jug in her direction. She points to the room next to his trolley. On the wall inside is a poster of a white-haired professor holding up a conical flask of urine. He's gazing admiringly at the golden fluid, with the word *Eureka!* printed alongside his mouth. A second poster shows a tribe of gorillas. Each gorilla holds a bottled sample. There is no caption. I can see why the professor is funny, but the primates perplex me. Are they holding their own urine? Are they supposed to represent doctors? Patients? Or is the joke more subtle, based on the odd juxtaposition?

I dry my hands and return to Dad. He's talking to a doctor. When the doctor notices me, he asks: 'Are you a friend of the patient?'

I nod. Dad looks hurt.

'He's my son.'

'Son. Right.' The doctor's face changes and he extends his hand. I shake it, then sit in the corner and listen to him ask Dad about his health. He perks up considerably when Dad tells him he doesn't drink or smoke, as if there's now a possibility he might live. The doctor's brown hair is shaved around the nape of his neck, with a floppy (but controlled) fringe. He's wearing cream chinos, brown shoes and a Ben Sherman shirt with a button-down collar. His aggressive good health makes me think how comforting it must be to have this man for a friend. Most doctors I've met have been creepily misanthropic, their pallid bodies suggesting they boil themselves in carbolic soap. If I knew this doctor I would stick to the same diet he followed, meet him for squash three times a week, and seek his advice on the most trivial of medical problems.

I couldn't imagine him suffering from anything, and suspected he probably saw existence as an ongoing challenge to live as long as possible. Of course, I knew he was probably administering himself injections and addicted to barbiturates.

'I'm not going to lie to you, Steve,' he says. 'I wish it was all good news but I'm afraid it isn't. You've got two serious fractures, one in your leg and the other in your elbow. The second one is more worrying because we're not sure how far the split has gone. I'll have to look at your X-rays to know for sure, but I think we'll have to take some bone from your leg and graft it into your elbow.'

The doctor looks at Dad. Most men'd appreciate such a straight-talking physician. Or at the very least be shamed out of self-pity. But no doctor's going to make my dad take this like a man.

'Will I have a scar?'

He laughs. 'I'm afraid so. But it shouldn't be too disfiguring.'

Dad doesn't laugh. He has the same stubborn look he gets when telling me about his depressions. Somewhere along the line he's come up with the ridiculous idea that his feelings are important, and it's too late to persuade him otherwise. The doctor's waiting for a matey joke, but Dad remains defiantly downcast. The doctor shrugs and leaves. Dad calls me over.

'Is there a bag under the trolley?'

'What sort of bag?'

'They put all my stuff in a white bag.'

'Is this it?'

He nods. 'Find my wallet.'

I look through the bag. His suit's shredded, but not that bloody. The wallet's in an unsealed brown envelope, along with his car keys and broken gold glasses. I rest the wallet on his blanketed chest.

'I need you to do something for me.'

'I know,' I said, 'I'll find her.'

He looks surprised. 'Who?'

'Mum. I've got some numbers I can try.'

'No. There's someone else.'

'Another woman?'

He sighs. 'Not exactly. Put the wallet in my hands.'

He thumbs through his cards until he finds a folded piece of graph paper. He's about to hand it to me when a policeman pushes through the curtain.

'Mr Thomas?'

'Yes.'

'We've got statements from the driver and the witnesses, and we want to hear your version.'

'I don't have one.'

'I see. There's only really one confusion. Were you on the way to the cashpoint, or coming back?'

'He must have been going everso fast. To send me up in the air like that.'

The policeman laughs. 'You'd be surprised, sir. It doesn't take much.'

'Daniel, how much money's in my wallet?'

'Thirty quid.'

'Then I was coming back.'

I follow the policeman behind the curtain. He explains that Dad's entitled to see any of the information they've collected. He writes down the name and address of the driver and hands it to me. *Ted Davis. 9, Engine Road.* I stare at the name and try to picture someone driving into Dad.

'Was it his fault?'

'The first witness says your Dad was hit on the left side, the second says it was the right. The third says a black man held up the Bristol & West.'

He laughs. I watch him walk past a man with a spiralling gash around his left eye, then return to Dad. He's holding out a piece of graph paper. It's a list of seven phone numbers, each coupled with a woman's Christian name.

'Who are these people?'

Dad grimaces. 'I'm in too much pain to explain. Just call each of the numbers and tell them what's happened.'

'OK.'

'Keep it simple, OK? And go easy, some of them might be a bit temperamental.'

By mid-afternoon, they've decided to save Dad's operation for tomorrow. I stay with him until he's settled in Ward Seven, then he tells me to go home.

'OK.' I pat his chest. 'I'll sort out things with your college. Think of this as a rest.'

He pulls himself up and looks at me. 'You know I'm not going to be able to afford next month's rent.'

'That's OK,' I tell him, 'I'll handle it.'

A word about money. I never read anything without thinking about how everything's paid for, so I'll explain that right at the beginning. I earn one hundred and ten pounds a week after tax. I pay twelve pounds to a former girlfriend (the GBH thing), twenty-five pounds to NatWest, and ten pounds to the Midland. I share a flat with my father, and my half of the rent (including community charge, water, electricity and heating, but not the TV licence, which we don't pay) comes to forty pounds. That leaves me twenty-three pounds to live on. Very occasionally I manage it. Most weeks I don't.

The flat I share with my father isn't really a flat. It's not quite a bedsit either. It's a long, thin room about twenty-five feet in length, but only about seven feet in width. My father sleeps in the far left-hand corner. I sleep in the right. I've always felt that there's something nightmarish about looking up and seeing my father stretching away into the distance. He, on the other hand, loves it. He says we're like the Likely Lads, but I can't help thinking Steptoe and Son is nearer the mark.

On the bus ride home, I wonder how I'm going to be able to pay the rent. There doesn't seem any way I can manage it on my own, and I suppose the sensible answer would be to get someone to take over Dad's half of the room. But I can't see someone who doesn't know me agreeing to live in such close proximity. Especially when

11

there are much better places for the same money. It shouldn't be that hard to contact Mum, but after everything that's happened I can't see her giving me money to bail out Dad.

Maybe Mr Farnell will understand.

To get to our room you have to follow a small muddy lane and then climb a rusted metal staircase which takes you up to where we live without disturbing the landlord in the house below. This staircase is guarded by a fat ginger tom I've befriended by feeding him cod chunks broken off from the fish and chips I bring home almost every night. (At weekends, we go to the Chinese.) Tonight tom sees I don't have any food and jumps down into the pile of rotten mattresses beneath the staircase where he watches me fiddle with the slipped doorlock for a full five minutes.

Our room is one of four. The other three are empty. When we first came here, Dad and I took a room each. Two rentdays later we realised we couldn't afford to live separately. The landlord's in no hurry to fill the remaining rooms, maybe because ours is the only one without a dripping ceiling. Having the floor to ourselves means that we get unlimited use of the kitchen and bathroom. It also means he sees no urgent need to fix the washing machine, fridge or toilet (which can only be flushed by pulling a shoelace tied to the rod inside).

Even though I've just left him in his hospital bed, I still expect Dad to arrive home any minute. It's been a long, draining day, and I haven't yet had time to analyse how I feel about this change in my life. I know tomorrow I'll be able to think about the upside of having the flat to myself, but for now, it's hard to get past the fear of being forced to fend for myself. I also know if I stay up much longer I'll give my worries time to metamorphose into the type of night terrors that'll control my brain until morning. So I turn out the lights and proceed directly to bed, hoping my mental exhaustion will be strong enough to take immediate anaesthetic effect.

2

Schools and universities must be the last two places in England where people try to avoid reading. All day I see people using books to make their days less monotonous, from the secretaries reading Grisham and Ludlum on the bus to the pretentious temps shocked to discover that carrying a copy of Nietzche isn't the surefire conversation starter it was at university.

My own book this morning is one of my father's, taken from the small pile that surround his bed. Dad's one of these people who believe it's better to know a few books intimately than to read indiscriminately. He has little time for fiction, and his library consists mainly of blue-spined Pelicans he amassed in the late sixties. The titles span the full range of social sciences, from *Political Ideas* and *Man and the Vertebrates* to *Using and Abusing Your Child* and *Hypnosis: Fact and Fiction*. It's hard to discern what prompted this uncharacteristic spurt of autodidactism. Maybe Dad was swept up in some kind of intellectual revolution that was cut short when my birth forced him into an electronics job.

I've decided to read all these Pelicans before Dad gets out of hospital, hoping they'll help me grasp the peculiar tenets that underpin his current thinking. I'm starting with Dr Michael Young's

Rise of the Meritocracy, an essay on education and equality. I've got a hunch that the equation on the back cover (IQ + effort = MERIT) might be the key to Dad's philosophy. If I get through these books before Dad gets through physiotherapy, I'll turn my hand to the C plus plus programming he teaches his students at the technical college. Once I've mastered that, I'm sure I'll understand him.

Not that I'm mocking my Dad's mental ability. My own choice of reading material is hardly intellectual. Usually I only read books for the story, preferring detective novels and science-fiction. I tend to see the world in this way, imagining my life as a complex mystery filled with red herrings or an exploration through fantastic terrain. When I watch films, I think about death. When I read books, I contemplate physical decay. In most of the sci-fi sagas I've read, there's been an underlying preoccupation with the frailty of the body, and Dad's accident has brought this theme back into my mind. I remember one interplanetary tetralogy where the hero lost another limb in each new volume. I found this slow disintegration fascinating, imagining the mental summing up that must follow every loss. It reminded me of that feeling when you accidentally bend the cover of a new book and you force yourself to keep looking at the imperfection until you assimilate it into your perception of the book. It also made me wonder (and this was the consideration that returned with Dad's accident) how much of my body I'm prepared to lose. Between you and me, I think I'd be happier being just a brain, and I find physical disability much less distressing than mental collapse.

I always sit towards the back of the lower deck, on the seat above the wheel arch. This gives me a good vantage point to observe the other passengers who fill the bus as it makes its way to the Centre. I feel unusually at home during this early-morning run, entranced by the down-at-heel boredom of the women who surround me. (It's almost always all women. The men take the top deck or drive.) I have a particular fetish for their tights and shoes, which seem to wear more quickly than their skirts and blouses. The crinkled toes of my favourite woman's blue leather shoes are like two smiling faces that promise me it'll be a good day.

The team leader beckons to me as I enter the office, her smile almost sympathetic.

'Come over to the desk, Daniel.'

She takes me behind the screens and tells me to sit down. I stare at her purple work jacket, trying to imagine her without it. She flicks her hair from her face and looks at me.

'How's your father?'

'OK. He's broken his leg and his elbow.'

'Elbow? That sounds nasty. Are you going to need more time off?'

'I suppose so, but I don't want to take it. I need the money.'

She smiles. 'Are you having financial problems then?'

I look at her warily, worried I might be talking myself out of my job. Offering sympathy, after all, is a good way to assess someone's mental state.

'I live with my dad. While he's in hospital, I'll have to pay the rent on my own.'

I check her lips, expecting a smile. But she just nods and waits for me to continue. There's so much empathy in this department. Everyone here is making do. And we have the grace not to question each other's resignation.

'Can you work in the evenings?'

'Some.'

'What about weekends?'

'Probably.'

She opens a drawer and lays two printed grids on the table. 'Well, I've got the timesheets here, and you're welcome to take on some overtime.' She stands up. 'Decide what you can do and I'll pencil it in.'

Ian, Teri and I have a long-standing agreement. While, on the whole, conversation is encouraged, it is also understood that entertaining your co-workers can be as draining as coping with callers. So if anyone's lucky enough to achieve a state of silent reverie, their musings are allowed to pass uninterrupted. On the other side of the table, no such rules are observed, with Adrienne going on at everyone while Gordon whispers to himself.

Ian nods at me. I sit down. The Suggestions Book lies open on my desk.

Daniel Day Lewis
Pierce Brosnan
Val Kilmer
Ronnie O'Sullivan

'What's this?'

'We might be getting a new team leader,' Adrienne tells me. 'Those are my recommendations. Feel free to add your own.'

'What's happening to Alice?'

'She's exploring other career options.'

'Such as?'

'Screwing management.'

'Who?'

'Dunno. Someone upstairs.'

I like Adrienne. Tuesdays, Fridays and Saturdays she DJs at The Pentangle, which makes up most of my social life. She always starts each week by bringing in flyers for everyone, even though Ian and I are the only ones who ever turn up. She plays a mix she'd never get away with in a proper club, but nevertheless manages to sum up the exact mood of every week. Although she always sticks to the same basic tracks, the subtlest variations in her set-list can alter the actions of everyone present, deciding whether the worried sixteen-year-old goes home with the hairdresser from London, or halting a fight between two angry hod-carriers. I waste whole afternoons watching Adrienne, wondering which tunes are playing in her head as she moves around the office, and build up courage to ask her about the French hip hop she usually ends with.

The other great thing about Adrienne is that she can mend anything. For a certain number of pints, she'll take on any job you offer her. Half a pint will pay for most minor tailoring. Six pints, plus parts, will get your sink fixed. A hundred pints and she'll build you a summerhouse. At first I fretted about the kind of relationship I was encouraging by giving her my washing, but somehow she makes the transaction seem perfectly appropriate, and I now rely on her to solve all my problems with haberdashery and hardware.

I sit down and log on, ten minutes late. I still need to find my headset and set up my screens, so I let Ian take the calls a little longer. Finally settled, I uncap my ballpoint and hit *Ready*.

Hello, Angel Cruises appears on my screen, alerting me to which company I'm pretending to represent. I recite this salutation and the caller replies, 'Hello, yes, we went on one of your cruises last summer and we enjoyed it so much that we're thinking about taking another one.'

'OK. Would you be going next year, the year after, in five to ten years, or . . .'

'I shouldn't think it'd be until after the millennium.'

'I see. Are you interested in the Caribbean Cruise or the Round the World trip?'

'Caribbean.'

I take his details, and two more calls, then put someone on hold while I ask Ian, 'Are you going tonight?'

'Yeah. You?'

'Hopefully. I'll have to pop in and see Dad first. How many calls do you reckon I could get away with?'

'Personal?'

'Yeah.'

'Three, maybe. If they're not to the same number.'

'Could I do one on your password?'

'Sure. What's the problem?'

'No problem. I've just got to tell some people about my Dad.'

'OK, log off and we'll swap numbers.'

I can tell Gordon's listening to us. Making private calls is a sackable offence at Quick Kall Ltd, and I'm sure his automaton mind can't cope with such flagrant rule-breaking. His usual head-jiggling's become even more spasmodic, and I'm worried it's going to flip off his neck completely. But we can trust him not to shop us: he's had first-hand experience of office politic's unfair twists. Being a good team player is a complex business.

I dial. *Marilyn 67***** The phone rings fifteen times before I hang up. I make a note alongside her number, then try *Brittany*. Who are these women? Six rings, and the message clicks in: *Hi, Brittany and Roger can't make it to the phone right now, but if you'd like to leave your name and number, they'll get back to you a. s. a. p.*

'This is a message for Brittany. Steve Thomas has been involved in an accident. He's broken his leg and his elbow and he's going to be out of action for the next few weeks.'

Teri touches my arm. 'You shouldn't be so blunt. It can come as a shock to hear someone you know's been involved in an accident.'

Teri speaks so rarely that I always assume everything she says springs from her own experience. Her reproach makes me feel guilty, as if I've delivered upsetting news to her instead of some stranger's ansaphone.

'I have to be blunt. I don't know who these women are.'

'So why are you calling them?'

'Dad asked me to.'

Ian leans over. 'How many numbers are there?'

'Seven.'

'Are they call girls?' Adrienne asks, hidden behind her work station.

'I've no idea. He's never brought any of them home.'

'There you are then.'

'Nothing wrong with that,' says Ian, 'fair play to the man.'

The team leader's watching us, clearly troubled by the group conversation. Teri straightens the crumpled graph paper.

'I'll do one, if you like.'

'OK, try number three. Diane.'

She keys in the number. I call woman four, *Valerie*. The phone rings. I'm about to cut the line when a voice says, 'Hello?'

'Hello, my name's Daniel Thomas. I'm Steve's son.'

She pauses, then, 'Yes?'

'Dad's been, um, involved in an accident.'

'What sort of accident?'

'Nothing serious. He's all right and everything.'

'Where is he?'

'He's broken his leg.'

'Where is he?'

'And his elbow.'

'Where is he?'

'But he's OK, there's no . . .'

'Tell me where he is.' The voice is angry and upset. I now realise Teri was right, and wish she could take over this conversation. I still have no idea who these numbers belong to. Surely a call girl wouldn't get this emotional.

'He's at St Hilda's. Ward Seven.'

'Tell him I'm on my way.'

'I'm at work, actually. I'm not supposed to make personal calls.'

'Tell him I'm on my way.'

She hangs up.

The identity of these seven strangers is still the primary topic of conversation during our first break. All five members of our team sit together on the left-hand side of a long plastic table, staring out at the rest of the smoking room like a row of High Court judges. Dorothy Richardson writes somewhere that it's more harmonious for couples to sit alongside, rather than opposite, each other, but we are not couples, and I'm sure even Dorothy would be disturbed by our row of grim visages.

'Perhaps he's a Satanist,' Adrienne suggests.

'My dad?'

'I don't see why not. Seven's a Satanic number, isn't it?'

'It's five, not seven. It's the number of points on a pentangle,' Ian tells her. 'Besides, if you count his dad, it wouldn't be seven, would it? There's eight of 'em.'

'What about that Bram Stoker book? That thing about the seven stars, what's that about?'

'I don't think he is a Satanist,' I offer, although knowing my dad, it's hard to be sure.

'Well, maybe it's a Snow White thing. Perhaps they're all midgets.'

'He does like fairy tales. He sleeps on a big pile of old mattresses, like the Princess and the pea.'

'Why don't you meet one of them?' Teri suggests. 'Then you could ask.'

'You're all assuming they know about one another. What if he's having seven different affairs?'

'He'd have told you, wouldn't he?' says Ian. 'He wouldn't want you giving the game away.'

'I don't know. Perhaps he takes my discretion for granted. He's in a lot of pain, and probably isn't thinking that clearly.' I swallowed. 'Do you think I should call the hospital?'

Gordon stops jiggering and says, 'That'd probably be a good idea.'

I don't have time to get home and change, so I go straight to the hospital before the club. I stuffed my jacket and *The Rise of the Meritocracy* in the locker at work, and without my tie I don't look too intimidating. The nurse at the front desk is the one I called earlier, and she tells me that Dad's had two visitors so far.

'Did you ask him if they knew about each other?'

Her face is disapproving. 'He doesn't care, apparently.'

'Can I see him?'

'Of course, but bear in mind that he's still coming around from the operation. A lot of what he says will probably be rubbish.'

I thank her, and walk down to Dad's ward. The TV blares at maximum volume, Channel Four news audible from the corridor. I take a red plastic chair from the pile by the door.

'I hear you've already had some visitors.'

'Oh Dan,' Dad moans, 'I'm not up to explaining now. I've just had eight hours of surgery.'

'But it's not just my curiosity. I've got to explain to the nurses.'

'I've spoken to them,' he says wearily.

'And the people at work. They've got you down as some sort of superstud.'

He smiles, but doesn't reply.

'How are you, anyway?'

'It's horrible. I've been unconscious for eight hours, and now I've got that noise hammering in my skull.'

I look at the television. A decrepit-looking man with thick glasses and a ragged grey beard sits opposite it, perched up on pillows and obviously engrossed.

'Have you eaten yet?'

He shakes his head. 'No, I'm starving. But I'm going to have a sleep first.'

'Do you want me to go?'

'In a minute. I'm sorry, Dan, I really can't concentrate.'

'It's OK. You've been through a lot.'

He nods. 'He must have been going everso fast, mustn't he?'

'You know what that road's like. They tear up and down it like a racetrack.'

I didn't expect to get out of the hospital so early, and still have ninety minutes before the club opens. It's not long enough to get home and back, so I chat to the nurses for a bit and then head down to the fish and chip restaurant behind the Hippodrome. Most of the actors performing here come across to this restaurant for their dinner, and the waitresses always squint at you as if trying to work out whether you're famous. I order fish and chips and sit in the back room, under the montage of posters from pantos gone by.

After dinner I walk to the furthest cashpoint, trying to kill time. I've got ten pounds left of this week's money (if I forget about Dad's share of the rent, a problem I've decided not to think about for the moment), and Ian owes me three pints from a bet last week, so at least tonight's taken care of, although the rest of the week's looking a bit dodgy. I suppose I'll just have to talk to Mr Farnell.

Ian always arrives early, so I don't have to wait too long on my own. Before he shows up, I watch Adrienne, who starts DJ-ing even before the club opens. She's put her hair up tonight, a long brown plait swinging between her headphones. She looks quite attractive when she's concentrating, her lips pressed tight as she tries to match her BPMs. But I'm too intimidated by Adrienne to genuinely fancy her. I need at least a hint of possible success before I fall for someone.

'All right, mate?' Ian asks, sitting alongside me at our usual table. 'She's looking fit tonight, isn't she?'

'I was just thinking that. Do you suppose she's found a man?'

'Nah, we'd have heard about it. Perhaps she's after someone. You'll have to watch yourself.'

I laugh.

'No, really,' he insists, 'I reckon hearing about your dad's made her curious. She wants to see if it runs in the family.'

'He wouldn't tell me anything, you know. And I really pestered him.'

'Your father's clearly a gentleman. What d'you want to drink?'

Spending time at The Pentangle isn't that different from being in work. I sit alongside Ian, watching Adrienne. Our conversations here are equally limited, only now due to the music instead of our respective tasks. Drinking beer makes things pleasanter, of course, but it doesn't help me escape the sense of restriction.

At about ten thirty, Adrienne takes a break from the decks. Usually she only strays as far as the bar and back, but tonight she comes over to where we're sitting and lowers herself onto the empty stool.

'Not dancing?'

'We're saving ourselves,' Ian tells her, 'we never get up before midnight.'

'What if a girl asked you?'

'It'd never happen.'

'It's happening now.'

Adrienne holds Ian's gaze. He looks at me and nods towards the dancefloor. I follow them across to an empty space near the front. I wonder if I should tell Adrienne how much I like her dress. It's black, of course, but short and sporty. A nice change from her usual funeral fashion.

Ian's taking the piss, putting his arms across our shoulders and using this support to swing between us. Adrienne smiles and tries to dance seriously, evil-eyeing her stand-in as he fluffs a mix. It feels good to be dancing with my workmates, and I want Ian to stop mucking about so Adrienne will stay with us. He notices her irritation and starts dancing normally, a self-effacing, shrugging shuffle. His skull shines under the lights, almost blue beneath his closely cropped hair.

Adrienne accompanies us for three tracks, before another fluffed intro sends her angrily back to her podium. Ian seems happy to keep dancing, grinning at me as the tempo increases. I wave at Adrienne and she smiles back, holding her headphones to her left ear as she sets up the next record.

I leave earlier than usual, too anxious to enjoy myself. I can't afford my usual taxi so I walk home, feeling as if the emotion of the last few days is finally catching up with me. It takes a good hour to walk back from the Centre, and by the time I get home even the fat ginger tom is asleep.

3

Lonely? Or Just bored?

I hate adverts. They always destroy the mood. It's hard enough convincing myself that cable-hunting for free snippets of sex TV is a rational act without husky-voiced invitations to dial a chatline. I spend all day on the phone. Calling *Sexspeak* is the last thing I want to do when I get home. It's almost as bad as the presenters on *Television X* promising *our films are hot enough to keep you lads up all night*. Helen Gibson is a far more reassuring hostess, keeping things dignified even during the *Spot-the-Bot* slot. She treats every guest as an equal, talking about *the business* as if softcore pornography is a feminist-capitalist cartel.

Get connected. Call the Gay Network now. No thanks. I usually begin with the first half of *The Sex Files* on *UK Living*. The programme's wistfulness seems defiantly English, even if the format's nicked from America. Its presenters are like characters in a Muriel Spark novel, trapped in a structural puzzle they have no hope of escaping. And like Spark characters they remain cheerfully game, ignoring their context. After thirty minutes of retired vicars thumbing through rubbermags, I'm ready to move up to *L!VE TV's Sex Show* (AKA Turned-on TV) with the aforementioned Helen

G. Tonight she's talking about an American 'boob cruise' where a hundred and twenty men go to Barbados with thirty topless models. By now, I feel at one with the guests, enjoying the frank conversations and the nautical three-minute thrill. After the ad break, I usually change to the *Adult Channel's Dish of the Day* (although sometimes the Dish is a dick, in which case I flip forward to the *Ten Minute Teaser* on *Television X*). Tonight, it's a Dish.

Dish of the Day starts with an image of a tabletop. The model's name appears on the dinner plate, between the knife and fork. I've never really thought about this arrangement before. Odd the way writing helps you see clearly. Tonight a blonde in red underwear is dancing to Dylan's 'It's All Over Now, Baby Blue'. This seems a startling change from the usual pervy synthpop, and suggests some frustrated sound engineer's trying to fuck with me. Dylan's hectoring voice glosses the woman's actions in the same hypocritical manner as a *Sun* editorial. Adding this song to these images seems like ingratitude, and once again forces me to wonder what I'm doing. I suppose I should applaud the pornographer's *Verfremdungssekt*, but that's hardly what I've tuned in for.

After *Dish of the Day*, it's back to *L!VE TV* for *Exotica Erotica*. The producers of this programme have bought up a seemingly inexhaustible supply of European sex films, added incidental music and split them into thirty-minute segments. As upsetting as this must sound to the true cineaste, it's perfect for video vultures like me. If I'm watching a film on television, I can rarely concentrate for more than half an hour, and if I switch off a video I'm unlikely to come back to it. This way I get just enough narrative to send me to sleep, with the added attraction of erotic images to candycoat my dreams.

Tonight's film is called *Quiet Days in Clichy*. For the first five minutes it seems innocuous enough, a reasonably budgeted fantasy about two writers coming to Paris. But as the writers stumble from one brothel to the next, I realise these actors are not the usual non-stars of low-grade pornography, but, Good God, Andrew McCarthy and Nigel Havers. The latter I can just about understand making a film like this, but Andrew *McCarthy*? You're asking me to accept the star of *Weekend at Bernie's* and *Pretty in Pink* as a marauding Brooklyn sex-fiend?

I turn up the volume, paying more attention than usual and wondering which writer McCarthy's supposed to be playing. The little round glasses make him look like Joyce, but surely they can't be attempting to pass Joyce off as an American? Is he Miller? Hemingway? And who's Havers? At one point McCarthy launches into a monologue on Dostoevsky, but this doesn't make things any clearer. Finally, someone addresses him. 'Hello, Joe.' Joe who? Now I'm really confused. The plot's a kind of X-rated two men and a little lady thing, with McCarthy and Havers being left a child by a dead prostitute. The child's called Colette. The Colette? Christ, this is fascinating.

I spoke to Farnell today. I knew he wouldn't simply accept my excuses, but I didn't expect him to come up with an immediate solution. He listened to me explain that I'd started working longer hours, but it'd be a while before I could afford both halves of the rent, and then rubbed his beard and said: 'So, basically, you need someone to take over your father's share of the rent for a month or so?'

I nodded. He grinned.

'I know just the man.'

Sharing with a stranger is totally different to living with Dad. What if my new room-mate is fastidious, and objects to my mess? Or messy himself, messier than me? Messy with food. I don't mind scattered clothes, but can't cope with rotting meat and dirty plates.

I turn off the television and take another look at Dad's side of the room. I've already cleared all the books and letters, and pushed his disk-boxes beneath my bed, but don't feel ready to handle his clothes. I took most of his T-shirts and pants into the hospital, but I'm not sure what to do with what's left. I sit on his mattress and pick up a shoe. It's a grey slip-on, with a man-made upper and a thick off-white sole. I stare at the brown line around the heel of the insole and wonder why I feel so guilty about handling Dad's possessions.

He has a lot of shoes, an obvious anxiety for a man with no sense of smell. Dad's greatest terrors: clothes, food and shit. He lives in constant fear of bodily odour, drinking gone-off milk and stepping in dog-dirt. As a child he was acutely aware of his sweating feet, but unable to imagine how bad they might smell, and terrified of taking off his only pair in public in case someone said something. Now he buys a new pair almost every time we go shopping, letting them pile up around his bed.

I go to the kitchen and fetch a black bin-liner, thinking it's best to stuff everything away without thinking about it. I'll have it all laundered and get Adrienne to iron it later. Once the bag's full, I dump it on my side of the room, beneath the plain brown table that supports my stereo. Then I disconnect the computer, deciding I can always get someone to help me put it back together once my guest has gone. The keyboard and computer slide under my bed, but there's no room for the monitor so I hide it at the bottom of the wardrobe under an old linen shirt.

The last part of my operation is also the most unsettling. I know from experience that Dad likes to hide things, and I don't want some stranger uncovering his secrets. So I lift up the mattresses and pull them away from the wall. Thankfully, the only things he's hidden are words, with two hard-backed notebooks stored between the mattresses. Relieved, I straighten the bed and put the notebooks with his social science volumes on the other side of the room.

I'm expecting diaries, but as I flip through the two notebooks, I realise they're actually minutes from a series of meetings. They must be something to do with the college, although the personal nature of what's recorded makes me wonder what sort of class they might be describing. I can see why he's hidden them, but as the names are replaced with initials, and there are several different types of handwriting (some hard to read), it's hard to put it all together. I also feel guilty about snooping, and decide to abandon any serious study. Besides, it's almost one o'clock and I have work tomorrow.

4

I awake at five to nine. I've missed the bus that gets me in early, the bus that arrives just in time, and the bus that makes me ten minutes late. I ought to phone in and make something up, but the nearest phone's at the Texaco, and if I walk there I'll miss the next bus as well. I could always say I had to see Dad, but I don't want to jeopardise the sympathy I usually get when I use that excuse. I'll have to make a direct appeal to the team leader, like Ian did when he found out his girlfriend had been unfaithful.

I hate being late. It'd be much less stressful if I could resign myself to getting in trouble, but I can't help gripping the handle of the seat in front of me, pushing it forward as if my urgency can make the bus go faster. The other passengers are also distinctly unappealing, with none of the solidarity you get on the eight o'clock.

As soon as the bus swings into my stop, I jump from the doorway and race along the tarmacked bridge to Quick Kall's offices. I check my inside pocket. No ID card. Any possibility of my arrival passing unnoticed has now gone. I sprint up the front steps and into reception, leaving a smeared handprint on the glass door.

'I've forgotten my pass,' I announce breathlessly. 'Could you buzz up? Floor seven.'

I hover by the desk, hoping that it's Adrienne or Ian who get sent down to rescue me. After a few anxious minutes, I see the stiff suit of the team leader, her skin looking tanned behind the brown glass. She walks me to the lift.

'Are you OK, Dan?'

'I'm sorry I'm late. I overslept. All this stuff with Dad has left me shattered.'

'Don't worry. It happens to all of us. It's just a shame it should happen on the day of your appraisal.'

I breathe deeply, reminding myself that she's never been renowned for her tact, and that her comment is not intended to upset me. As far as she's concerned, it *is* a shame, that's all.

The team leader wears her ID card on a chain around her neck. You have to be at least a team leader before you qualify for a chain. I once considered buying my own chain from an army surplus store, just to see what they'd say. 'Where d'you get that chain? Did you steal it?' 'No, I bought it. It's my chain.' 'You can't just go and buy a chain. Chains have to be earned. What you've done is like buying a medal of honour and calling yourself a soldier. Wait till you've seen some action. Then you'll get your chain.' Team leaders also get to have a small polaroid picture of themselves laminated onto the back of their pass, while us grunts are expected to give ours up at a moment's notice. No wonder I've misplaced my pass. It means nothing to me.

Her mouth looks serious as she holds her card to the magnetic pad alongside the doorway, lowering her head so the chain doesn't pull tight around her neck. Once we're inside the call-centre, she returns to her desk and I approach my table, stopping briefly by the water-cooler to siphon myself a drink.

My appraisal takes place at ten thirty, when everyone else is on their break. The team leader takes me into Conference Room 3 and arranges herself behind the desk. She seems to suffer some kind of neurosis about putting her legs beneath a table, always setting her chair a short distance away from any furniture. Maybe she just likes people looking up her skirt.

It must be so much nicer to work in rooms like this, with the freedom to pull the blinds on the rest of the office and air-conditioning you can regulate. I watch the sunlight as it swirls the room's dust-motes, before settling on the underside of the team leader's chin. It looks like a small yellow beard. It's strange to see the sun. A mild winter has shaded imperceptibly into a dreary spring, keeping the sky grey for the last six months. It's not that cold, but not warm either. Suit weather, if you don't mind damp shoulders after a shower.

The sun heads for my face next, and I enjoy a moment of warmed lethargy before she starts to speak. So much of work is like being at school, and this moment feels like facing an antagonistic teacher and knowing that no matter what I'm about to be reprimanded for, I'm at the centre of a system that only allows her to get to me by following predetermined rules, and as I'm not worried about doing well, there's little she can threaten me with.

'Do you set yourself goals, Daniel?'

'In what sense?'

'Well, for example, when you log off your stats at the end of the day, do you say to yourself, I've taken a hundred calls today, tomorrow I'll try to take one hundred and ten?'

'Sometimes, but I do try to prioritise meeting the caller's needs over meeting a self-imposed numerical target.'

She stares at me. 'And what do you see as the callers' needs?'

'It depends. Information.'

'Information, good. What about the salutation?'

'What about it?'

'If you receive a call for *Angel Cruises*, how do you answer it?'

'Hello, *Angel Cruises*, how can I help you?'

'Can?'

'Pardon?'

'You'd say "how *can* I help you?"'

'Yes.'

'Not *may?*'

'What?'

'You wouldn't say "how *may* I help you?"'

'What's the difference?'

'There's a great difference, both grammatically and semantically. I realise this *may* sound pedantic, but *Angel Cruises* are paying you to use that salutation. They have specified the exact words that are to be spoken, and the slightest change could adversely effect their business. Do you appreciate what I'm saying?'

I nod.

'Good. Now what I've got to say next is awkward for me, so I think it'd be best if I'm frank with you.'

'OK.'

'Basically, I've had word from above that our team is the worst in the call-centre. Now, I realise that you can turn round to me and say, "If we're the worst team, what does that say about our team leader," but that won't solve anything.'

'Worst in what way?'

'In every way. Call-response efficiency for one, as well as the longest combined idle-time of any team in the office, but worst of all, they don't think you work well as a group.'

'I see.'

She sighs. 'Quick Kall Ltd prides itself on being a very forward-thinking organisation, and one of the guiding principles behind our success is that we're prepared to treat all our workers as individuals. Creativity, for example, is always respected, and you are given opportunities to express your talents through dress-down day or the work-station decoration competitions. We're also aware that every team is different. The Banks and Building Societies team, for example, are very chatty, and consequently, their call-response stats are frequently lower than those for any other team, but they have a huge positive influence on office goodwill. Our team, however, has bad stats and a detrimental effect on the atmosphere of the office.'

'How?'

'I don't know. There's something wrong with the dynamic.

The managers think you might work better if there were only four of you.'

'Why?'

'Have you read Cordwinder Bird's *Office Numerology*? It suggests that success in business is all down to the numbers. Four is a positive number, five is . . . well, they've given me a fortnight to decide who should go.'

She smiles at me from beneath her fringe. 'Of course, I'm not supposed to tell you this, and I'd appreciate it if you didn't share this information with the other members of the team.'

'OK.'

'Thank you. I've told you this because I know you're going through a difficult time, and couldn't cope with being laid off right now. But I also need you to tell me something in return.' She opens the desk and lays two stats print-outs on the table. 'Both Ian and Teri made outgoing calls on Tuesday. As you are aware, outgoing calls pertaining to business matters are permissible, and no doubt if I was to confront them, they'd claim this was the case. I could call these numbers and ask if these people do have business with any of their clients, but then I'd have to tell them that we're an agency, something I'm forbidden to do. So it'd make things a lot easier if you could tell me whether you overheard either Ian or Teri making personal calls yesterday.'

She waits. I swallow.

'Teri.'

'Pardon?'

I stare at her. 'Don't make me say it again.'

She stands up. 'Thank you, Daniel. You've been very helpful.'

The others are returning from their break as I walk back to my desk. Ian asks me how it went and I tell him about us being the worst team in the office. He laughs, and tells Adrienne, who makes me repeat it. Everyone wants to discuss this, but I'm feeling too guilty to explain further. I'm glad I didn't betray Ian. I realise it'd be better if I hadn't betrayed anyone, but I don't feel the same responsibility towards Teri. Which is ironic, because now I'm responsible for her losing her job.

The team leader beckons to Ian. 'My turn,' he says, standing up. 'You seen this?'

He passes me the Suggestions Book. For some time now, Adrienne has been compiling Gordon's Log, an imaginary journal detailing the interior life of our least socially adept team member. I've never been convinced this is a good idea, and as I'm sure this kind of group persecution would tip Gordon over the edge, it seems a bit risky to trust he's not going to read it. I try not to attract his attention as I look over the latest entry:

Gordon's Log 5/3/9 —
I feel it's my Duty to recount a v. strange Experience that happened to me last night. After eating dinner with Mother as usual (three fish-fingers, Alphabites and Tesco's own brand baked beans), I retired to the Lounge to watch the 'Victoria Wood – As Seen on TV (Series Two)' Video that my Auntie gave me for my 31st birthday. While I was enjoying Mrs Great Suprendo's unique brand of Social Comedy, I nevertheless began to feel a little restless, and wondered if it was too late for a little trip into the Centre. Assuring Mum that I'd be back on the last Bus, I changed into my tightest blue Levi's and a plain White Shirt, and headed down to the Bus Stop. I spent the early part of the evening on a solitary pub crawl along Queens Street, favouring the hostelries frequented by the City's young Actors and Artistes. Eventually, I started chatting to a charming young man called Darren, who invited me to accompany him to an impromptu Garden Party on the nearby Common. When I asked him if it wasn't a little late for such a Gathering, he assured me that all the most distinguished Garden Parties took place after Midnight as a way of ensuring that they wouldn't be gate-crashed by the General Public. I immediately saw the logic of this Statement and agreed to accompany him. I have to Confess, Dear Diary, that I was

feeling a little the worse for wear by this stage, and I'm afraid I lost consciousness shortly after arriving at the Common.

The following Morning I awoke feeling battered and weary after spending the night sleeping on wet grass. I felt particularly tender around my Legs and Backside and, most curious of all, I felt as if I had a bruised Throat. As I rubbed my Adam's Apple, I had a sudden recollection of some foreign, twitching thing being forced into my Mouth. Oh my God, I thought, did I really swallow a CROW?

'What d'you reckon?' Adrienne asks as my eyes come up from the page.

'You're wasting your talent. There's magazines in London that'd pay good money for this sort of thing.'

She laughs. 'Did she really say we're the worst team in the office?'

'She'll tell you too. Wait and see.'

On Friday evenings, the team heads down to The Friar, Quick Call's local pub. I usually avoid this session, returning home to change before going to The Pentangle with Ian. Today, however, I trail along with the others, wanting to postpone meeting my new room-mate as long as possible. We find a table on the other side of the room to the team leaders, and Gordon goes up to buy a round.

Adrienne smiles at me as Gordon fiddles with his money, unwrapping a small plastic bag of change and counting the coins onto the bar. I know he looks stupid, but let's just review today. First I betray Teri for doing me a favour, and now I'm laughing at Gordon for buying me a drink. I bet they're glad to be my friends.

Ian's hardly spoken to me since his assessment. He seemed amused about us being the worst team, so I can only assume the team leader's singled out his individual work for criticism. Or maybe, a paranoid voice suggests, I've been naive believing that my job's safe, and the team leader's asked everyone who they saw making personal calls in a perverse test of team loyalty. I can't imagine Ian betraying anyone, but being asked in the first place would make him furious.

'I must say I feel really motivated now,' Adrienne tells us. 'That little pep-talk's made me determined to do well.'

Gordon places the drinks on the table. 'I can't believe we're that bad. I reckon they've said that to all the teams.'

'She's such a bitch,' Teri hisses, surprising everyone.

Adrienne laughs. 'I can't fault that assessment.'

Teri takes her drink. 'It wasn't that long ago she was on the same team as me. She thinks she's really fucking something since she moved up. Just cause she fucked herself into a job.'

Adrienne grins at Teri. 'Maybe we should give it a go.'

She grimaces. 'Have you seen her boyfriend?'

Adrienne shakes her head.

'I've been watching her since she came here,' Teri continues. 'The bloke she's seeing now moved up just before her. We were all on the Emergency Contraception line together, before any of you came here. She didn't even talk to him before he became management. She's just a slut.'

No one says anything. Teri's never even raised her voice before, and everyone's waiting to see what she'll say next. Apart from her reticence, the main reason Teri gets ignored is because she's so much smaller than the rest of us. Even Adrienne is almost six foot, and always wears her black boots with the two-inch heels. But every time Teri speaks up, I think about how she's not that bad looking beneath her heavy brown hair.

'Let's change the subject,' Ian suggests.

After Ian's decree, the conversation is limited. He talks to Gordon about football, and I ask Teri what sort of crank calls they got on the Contraception line, but I can tell everyone's been hurt by today's appraisal, and none of us are ready to think about anything else. If this *is* a motivational exercise, it has, at least, brought us together as a group. Usually Friday evenings are a time when we quietly shut off, preparing ourselves for a weekend away from each other's faces.

Tonight, however, our injured pride makes us reluctant to give up this company, and I can tell no one wants to think about their failure alone. So when Adrienne asks Teri and Gordon if they're coming to The Pentangle, for the first time ever, they say yes.

Gordon goes to the payphone to call his mother. I remember today's entry in Gordon's Log, and worry about taking responsibility for him. Adrienne's satire is so well observed that I have trouble separating the fictional Gordon from the real thing. At every company karaoke evening, he gets dangerously drunk and has to be sent home in a Quick Kall taxi. I'm worried about taking responsibility for him, especially in a nightclub. I feel angry at Adrienne for creating this situation. After all, she gets to observe the action from the safety of her DJ booth.

We leave The Friar and head across the bridge towards the city Centre. I've never gone out into the city with my team before, and I can tell everyone's excited. It's as if we've all been studying for an exam we've just been told we have no chance of passing, and now we're making up for all the months we've wasted studying.

Our first stop is the row of cashpoints along Stone Street. I watch the others check their balances and guiltily pocket their twenty pounds. Teri grins at me. Tonight is already illicit. None of us can afford this, and although I no longer have to stump up the full rent, I still haven't made the last two weeks' bank or GBH payments.

Ian stands on the edge of the kerb, rocking back on his heels as he waits for us to regroup. Adrienne goes ahead and leads us down Stone Street to the Centre. A man in an orange polyester shirt notices us all coming down the pavement together and crosses to the other side. It's hard to imagine anyone seeing us as intimidating, especially as any other week I'd be the one walking alone.

'What sort of music is it?' Gordon asks, tilting his head to one side.

'All sorts, Gordon. Ask Adrienne. I'm sure she'll play something you'll like.'

*   *   *

Adrienne tells us to wait outside while she gets permission to let us in early. The owners of The Pentangle are an Italian family who couldn't sustain the restaurant they'd opened and were persuaded to convert it into a nightclub. For the first few weeks they watched in horror as their plush carpets were worn smooth by dancing feet, but now they seem happy about the arrangement, eagerly greeting Adrienne and smiling at us as we traipse in.

Ian and I head straight for our usual table, pulling over two extra chairs so Teri and Gordon can sit with us. Gordon's reluctant to give up his jacket, and keeps looking round as if he's about to go home any minute. I stare at his flickering lips, wondering what he's saying about this place. A woman comes down from upstairs and installs herself behind the bar. It's my round.

I ask my workmates what they want to drink and walk up to order it. The barmaid smiles broadly when I offer payment.

'No charge,' she says, 'not for friends of Ms Tyler's.'

I laugh, but she insists, pushing my hand away. Maybe I don't have to feel guilty about tonight after all.

We're all pretty wasted when Teri slips off her chair. Everyone laughs at her, putting it down to drunken clumsiness. But as she rights her chair, Teri complains: 'She's taking the piss.'

'Who?'

'What's she doing? Stalking us?'

I follow her line of vision and see our team leader putting her padded black jacket into the cloakroom. Her casual clothes are as defiantly plain as her work uniform, the sort of thing someone might wear around the house, but not to a club, even a place as unpretentious as The Pentangle. Her white T-shirt hangs shapelessly around her body, making her breasts look both absurdly prominent and deliberately unsexy. Her grey leggings look as if someone's spent months stretching them out of shape before letting her wear them. I turn to Teri: 'Is that her boyfriend?'

Teri nods. 'Disgusting, isn't he?'

He is. Like most fat men, his trousers hang downwards, the two sides of his shirt struggling to cover a small diamond of white flesh above his waistband. His mouth is neither jolly nor kindly, but set in a petulant frown. His clothes are as disgusting as the team leader's, his satorial inelegance the only thing that connects him to her. His white trainers are tied with thick neon laces, the bulbous tongues pulled back to reveal two inches of white nylon sock before his grey suit begins. Thick-lensed, grey-framed glasses complete the management look, giving him something to poke at with piggy fingers during boring board meetings.

Ian takes his coat. 'Sorry, Dan, I'm going home. I can't make small talk with her.'

He leaves us and pushes through the dancefloor, heading towards Adrienne to tell her about the unwanted arrivals. I understand Ian's irritation, but I don't want to be the only one responsible for Gordon.

'She must know Adrienne DJs here,' Teri insists. 'It's not the sort of place you end up in accidentally.'

'I'd have thought she'd prefer somewhere more mainstream. Ritzy's or Club IQ.'

'Fat Bastard looks nervous. D'you think she dragged him here?'

'Of course. It's a statement, isn't it? She's trying to pretend she's one of us.'

Teri's a lot more fun now she's got a few drinks inside her, and I wonder why she hasn't come out with us before. Her eyes remain fixed on the couple, watching them huddle just inside the doorway, clinging to each other and looking out of place. I've never seen anyone not fitting in at The Pentangle, a club where even Gordon can pass unridiculed. But these two are too anxious, frowning at the music and clearly uncertain how to behave. The team leader keeps glancing in our direction, coming over after sending her boyfriend to the bar. Gordon stands up and pulls out a seat for her.

'You don't mind me joining you, do you?' she asks. 'I don't want to spoil your evening.'

'It's fine,' he assures her, looking round defiantly at the rest of us. Gordon once told me that all his superiors knew he ought to be at least a line manager, and the only reason he was still on our team was because he was so good at taking calls. Whenever he's with the team leader, he always talks to her about the specifics of Quick Call's operation, acting as if they're on the same level. No doubt he sees tonight as the perfect opportunity to further his cause, and feels unconcerned about alienating Teri and me.

Her boyfriend returns from the bar. I look across to the DJ booth and see Adrienne handing her headphones to a skinny guy in a blue T-shirt. She winks at me and starts walking across.

'Everyone, this is Bryan,' the team leader tells us, 'Bryan, this is my team.'

Adrienne steps up from the dancefloor and rests herself on the back of Bryan's chair.

'Hello Alice,' she says. The team leader smiles weakly. She's always been a little intimidated by Adrienne, and I can tell she feels threatened now we're out of the call-centre. Adrienne appears to enjoy the tension, holding her hand out to Bryan and waiting for an introduction.

'Bryan, this is Adrienne. She DJs here.'

'Any requests?' she asks.

'I'm not really into dance music,' he laughs. 'I don't suppose you've got any Oasis.'

'No, sorry. Alice, anything you'd like?'

She waves her hand dismissively. 'What you're playing now is fine.'

The team leader turns her back on Adrienne, excluding her from the conversation. Adrienne winks at us and returns to her booth. Gordon starts talking to Bryan, who responds enthusiastically, clearly pleased to be included. Teri asks me, 'Why do you keep looking at your watch?'

I pull down my sleeve. 'I didn't realise I was.'

'You've done it four times in the last fifteen minutes. Am I boring you?'

'No, it's not that. There's something I wanted to watch on television tonight.'

'What?'

'Just this silly programme on Cable.'

'I've got Cable.'

'Yeah? It's OK, I don't mind missing it.'

'What time's it on?'

'Twelve thirty.'

She looks at her watch. 'We can get back by then. My flatmates might be watching sport, but I can get rid of them.'

'I don't want to cause trouble.'

'It's no trouble. I never get to watch anything. They can't complain about me having my turn for once.'

She takes her coat and stands up, waiting for me. I say goodbye to Bryan and the team leader, registering the flicker of terror when she realises I'm leaving her with Gordon. I tell him I'll see him on Monday and blow a kiss to Adrienne. She mimes catching it, in homage to some obscure video she once lent me. I follow Teri through the club and out into the street.

'It's not really important,' I tell her, 'I don't know why I want to see it.'

'What is it?'

'*Exotica Erotica.*'

She stops walking and looks up at me, her mouth cautious. 'The sex thing?'

I look at my feet. 'Yeah, I suppose so. Yeah.'

'Do you watch it every night?'

'No,' I say, too sharply, 'it's just that they sometimes have famous people in the films, and . . .'

'So who's in this one?'

'Nigel Havers and Andrew McCarthy.'

'Andrew McCarthy?'

'Yeah,' I grin, 'I'm not a pervert. Honest.'

She laughs. 'I'll be the judge of that.'

I was born in Bristol. Even at eleven thirty on a Friday night, it still seems the safest place in the world. I've watched at least three street

41

fights, witnessed countless confrontations in late-night take-aways, and cowered in the back of a bus while a man bled to death from a screwdriver blow to the side of the head, and I still feel completely at ease on these streets. Maybe everyone feels like that about their birthplace, but I still maintain that violence in Bristol occurs between people who want to fight, with none of the general intimidation you get in other cities.

It's the Centre of the city that I know best. I could write the biography of every pigeon, tell you exactly how much money each blanket person makes from begging every day. As soon as I head away from here, the streets become less familiar, especially in the direction Teri's taking me. Although I've been in Bristol all my life, I've only spent nine months of that time living in the Centre, and there's lots of the city that remains closed to me. I feel excited as Teri leads me along Gloucester Road towards the rows of run-down Victorian houses that once counted as cheap accommodation, but now cost more to rent than almost anywhere else.

'I need a wee,' Teri tells me, 'wait here.'

I don't know whether she wants me to wait because she's worried I'll walk off on my own or because she's scared I'll spy on her. No one's ever thought of me as a pervert before. I find the idea faintly arousing.

She walks down into one of the long dark alleyways they have between every house here. I don't know if it's safe to trust that this darkness is unoccupied, but I can hardly go in to protect her. I wait as instructed, trying to avoid the eyes of a dishevelled old man in dungarees and a purple baseball cap.

'Got a cigarette?' he asks.

'I don't smoke.'

'On your own, are you?'

'I'm waiting for someone.'

'Aren't we all?' he chuckles, and shuffles off. She emerges from the alleyway and we resume our walk.

*   *   *

Teri leads me so far into unknown territory that I lose all sense of how to get back to the Centre. The streets in this stretch all look identical, and it'd be easy to get trapped into following the same circuit until morning. Her front door has three different locks, and she jokes about their security worries as she undoes them.

The sound of laughter and television coming from the front room is so jubilant that it's hard to believe it hasn't been exaggerated for effect. Teri tells me to wait in the kitchen while she gets permission to change channels. I feel nervous about her flatmates' reaction and want to tell her not to bother, but then she might worry about why I've come home with her.

I check my watch. Twelve twenty. I know it's ridiculous, but I really do want to watch the second part of this film. I'm a sucker for narratives, the more ramshackle the better. In order to satisfy me, stories must fulfil two criteria: it must be impossible to divine the intelligence of the storyteller, and at any stage, it must be impossible to guess what's going to happen next. It's rare that books and films satisfy me in that way, and I usually have to adapt them to meet my requirements. I read books as quickly as possible, ignoring all authorial flourishes and pulping them for plot. But even if a story dissatisfies me, I have to follow it to the end. The few stories I haven't finished eat away at my imagination like tailless tapeworms, providing no point of purchase to pull them from my mind. The last thing I want to do is let Andrew McCarthy and Nigel Havers loose in there.

My throat feels dry after the night's drinking, so I pour myself a glass of water. The washing-up bowl is full of empty mugs, most with chips missing from their rims or broken handles. I check a couple of logos, searching for clues to what Teri's flatmates are like. Each cup is painted with the shield of a different football team. At first I think they're evidence of a divided household, a display of allegiance like the City and Rovers tops Gordon and Paul wear beneath their work shirts. But there's so many mugs supporting so many different teams that I decide the whole lot must be one person's individual collection. I didn't know you could like football in that generalised way. I thought all support had to be partisan.

Teri returns and tells me she's persuaded them. Her face is bright pink and she looks flustered. It's clear now that I was put on earth to make life difficult for this woman. I want to tell her how thanks to me she's going to lose her job. In my drunken state I think she'll understand, maybe tell me how she'd have done the same if the situation was reversed. But I don't risk it, telling myself that on Monday morning I'll go to the team leader and confess everything, convince her that if she's going to get rid of anyone it ought to be me.

I follow her to the lounge. The walls are decorated with James Bond memorabilia, the space above the fireplace given over to a blown-up still of George Lazenby ski-ing his way out of danger. The room looks enviably comfortable, with a large, sagging sofa and an expensive flat-screen TV. I've always wanted to live like this, sharing my space with people the same age as me. But after what I did to my former girlfriend, none of my old acquaintances wanted to move in with me. I think of the flatmate I've yet to meet, wondering what terrible things he's doing to my room.

Teri sits on the sofa.

'Nice TV,' I tell her.

'It's rented.' She picks up the remote. 'Which channel's it on?'

'Eighteen.'

She finds the station. It's the end of *The Sex Show*, with Helen Gibson introducing tonight's three-minute thrill. A woman is grappling with her string leotard, treating her body like a bag of oranges. I sit next to Teri, avoiding her eyes. I feel I should make a joke, but I've never been much good at dispersing tension, and I worry that I'll say something that'll make the situation even more embarrassing.

Teri changes channel. 'I'm sorry, I can't watch this. I'll turn it back for the film.'

'OK.'

'It's not the stripping, it's just the way it's done. I don't mind it with a story, but this is too blatant.'

'It's OK. You don't have to explain. It's your TV.'

She flips through a few more channels. It's mostly chat shows, smart Americans in suits wittily interviewing celebrities. Neither of us say anything. She flips back. It's the adverts: *Lonely? Or just bored?*

Teri laughs. 'Have you ever called one of those lines?'

'No.'

'I did once. It was a mistake. I was phoning for one of those give-aways in *The Sun* and misdialled the number. I ended up talking to this Scottish supply teacher for two hours.'

'On a sex line?'

She frowns at me. 'It wasn't a sex line. It was one of those "make friends on the phone" things.'

Exotica Erotica comes on. The grindhouse theme tune strikes up and the red and gold lettering begins to flash. Last night's action is quickly summarised and part two begins. Tonight's instalment starts innocuously and I can feel Teri relaxing beside me. Even in his teen comedy roles, McCarthy's always been prone to fits of petulant anger, and his frustration brings a galvanising energy to this film. Havers is still carrying on like Hugh Grant's seedier older brother, but I'm beginning to consider this film as something more than titillating trash. The best scene has McCarthy having aggressive sex with a prostitute in a shower, one of the few erotic bits in this segment. I can't tell whether Teri likes the film, but I don't think she's offended. The programme ends with a quick preview of tomorrow's episode. As soon as it's finished, Teri turns it off.

'Do you have a number for a taxi?'

She looks at me. 'You can stay here.'

Ordinarily, I would turn down this offer. Tonight, however, I feel compelled to consider it more carefully. Closing my eyes, I see my computer screen at work, flashing up good reasons not to go home:

1. With free drinks all night, so far this evening hasn't cost me anything, and the part of me that cares about money doesn't want to spoil this run by paying for a taxi.
2. I still haven't met my room-mate. He'll *probably* be asleep by now, but if he isn't, I'm in no state for introductions.
3. As far as I can tell, Teri isn't interested in me. Earlier I suspected she wanted me to make a pass at her, but now I'm certain I'll be able to survive the night unmolested.

I thank her, and we return to the kitchen to drink more water and finish half a pack of biscuits. She fetches me a pillow and a heavy pink blanket from one of her flatmates, and offers me a space on her floor. I lie down while she goes to the bathroom to take out her contacts, and fall asleep before she returns.

5

I should've drunk more water. I thought that with the biscuits
as well, I'd escape a hangover this morning. How much are you
supposed to drink anyway? Three times your own bodyweight?
I'm cautious about water to begin with, ever since I saw something
on TV about an American doctor warning students that a too-swift
process of rehydration could have dangerous consequences. In my
mental filing-cabinet, I've stored this with scare stories about
Ecstasy and brain-swelling, and now every time I go near a sink
I'm scared I'll overdouse.

As long as my head remains steady, the spiked ball inside it doesn't
damage its carriage. To check on Teri I have to turn my whole body
while keeping my neck rigid. She's still asleep. Her nightdress is a
black T-shirt with fancy stitching and a long placket. Teri really
does have an elegant face. My face looks like it was drawn by an
overenthusiastic child with thick wax crayons. Teri's is a masterpiece
of minuscule pencil lines, each eyebrow hair filigreed precision.

'You awake yet, you slag?' a male voice shouts, the tone
boisterous but jovial. The door opens and bangs into my feet. A
shaggy blond head appears around it, sniggering. 'Oh, I'm sorry,'
he sneers, 'I didn't realise you had company.'

The head retreats. Teri's eyes open.

'Damn,' she says, 'breakfast.'

'You have to make them breakfast?'

'It's our arrangement,' she tells me, defiantly. 'They do things for me in return. I'm not Snow White.' She looks at me. 'You can have some if you want. I make a big batch of sausages and stuff.'

'Thanks, but I'm not sure I'm up to it.'

'Yeah, I'd forgotten about last night.' She sits up, and winces. 'But my head hasn't.'

'I'll come with you anyway. Maybe I'll feel like food when you've cooked it.'

'You'll be surprised. Keep it down and it'll cut your recovery time by hours.'

There are four shaggy heads around the breakfast table. Teri's housemates look like attempts one to four in an experiment to synthesise the perfect late-nineties student male. Dressed in four outfits randomly distributed, each of them wears two odd socks that nevertheless match those of their neighbour. Unless you knew them well, I'd imagine it'd be impossible to tell them apart, especially as their names (John, Mark, John and Stephen) are equally interchangeable.

Teri cooks the breakfast in her black T-shirt. I watch the others to see if they're interested in the way her shirt rides up as she oils the pan, but they ignore her completely, banging their cutlery against the kitchen table. They move up to let me sit down, and one of them (John, I think) fetches me a placemat.

I manage to get down half an egg and a sliver of bacon before needing the bathroom. When I come back, my portion's been divided between the rest of them. I say goodbye to Teri and thank her for being so kind to me. The warmth of her smile suggests she is genuinely touched by my words.

I think she enjoys being a good samaritan.

I soon give up on finding my way back to the Centre and stop in a phonebox to call a taxi. He drives me as far as the hospital, where I go up to Ward Seven to check on Dad. It seems the most substantial side-effect of the operation has taken a week to kick in. Some diabolical drug has transformed him into a little old lady. Before I have chance to examine this phenomenon, the woman in the next bed tells me Dad's been transferred to Ward Eleven.

He already has a visitor, a large blonde woman wearing a man's V-necked mustard sweater. Her face is heavily made-up, and her skin is a tanned brown. She's wearing gold slippers.

'Valerie,' Dad says, 'this is my son, Daniel.'

She smiles at me, then quickly returns her attention to Dad. I don't know what drugs he's on but he looks distant, staring at me as if he's not sure what I'm doing here.

'I was just showing Valerie my ocean.'

'Your what?'

'I've got an ocean inside me. Look at my leg.' He pulls back the blanket. There are several spidery lines drawn across his skin. He points at the one closest to his discoloured foot. 'That's the high-water mark. Since then, it's fallen back a bit.'

He reaches for a glass of water. Valerie picks it up and hands it to him.

'Actually, Dad, could I have a glass too? I'm a bit dehydrated.'

'Of course,' he says, staring off into the distance, 'Valerie . . .'

She glares at me, then reaches across to Dad's bedside table for a plastic cup.

'It's all willpower,' he says, rolling the glass across his forehead, 'they told me that if the infection didn't go down they'd have to do the operation all over again, so now,' he laughs, 'the infection's going down.'

Valerie gives me my water. Her fingernails are painted orange. Dad takes her hand between his.

'Would you mind waiting while he takes me to the toilet?'

She shakes her head.

'Good. Come on, son, help me up.' He motions towards his

walking frame. I put it next to his bed, watching him as he clumsily manoeuvres his liquid-logged leg down from the elevated metal rest and over the bed onto the floor. He's wearing a black T-shirt with dribbled food down the front and a pair of red underpants. I help him up and follow behind as he makes his slow passage out into the corridor. As soon as we're out of Valerie's earshot, he whispers to me: 'The nurses have been treating me abominably. Somehow they've got hold of the idea that I'm *dating* all my visitors. They think I'm some kind of ageing Lothario.'

I remember calling the hospital, and the nurse's disapproving noises when I told her Dad might receive a number of female callers.

'Who are they then, Dad?'

'The women?' He shakes his head. 'Just friends. Members of a club I belong to.'

'What sort of club?'

'A social club.'

'You never mentioned it.'

'I didn't want you to get jealous.'

'Jealous?' my voice quavers.

'You're always saying you never get to meet anyone. I thought you might be cross.'

'I wouldn't have worried.'

'OK, it's not important. It was only somewhere to go while you were at The Pentangle. I get lonely on my own.'

Dad reaches the toilet. I pull back the door. He leaves his walking frame and holds my arm as he stumbles towards the bowl.

'It's horrible, Dan. The nurse was too rough with the catheter and gave me an infection. I haven't been able to go in two days.'

I wait.

'Turn on the taps, could you?' he asks. 'I need some inspiration.'

During the bus ride home, I have chance to think over Dad's story. I still can't believe he was worried about making me jealous, especially as I'd always assumed he envied my nights out with Ian. He was always home when I got back, and even joked about how he'd been waiting up for me. I never really thought about what he did while I was out, although he often commented that it must be nice to have a mate to go drinking with. Now I realised this was his way of sniggering at me while he ran around with seven women.

This club certainly sounded suspicious. I wondered if there were any other male members. I'd hoped to speak to Valerie alone, but she was already getting up when we returned and I thought that as I hadn't seen him for two days, I ought to stay with Dad for a while. I also felt responsible for his injured urethra, and wanted to make up for misjudging him.

The bus swings into my stop. After sleeping in my clothes, I'm looking forward to a long bath. The ginger tom is waiting for me at the bottom of the staircase.

'Miss me, did you?'

Unlike most cats, the ginger tom has fur that makes me disinclined to pick him up. The fine hairs on his head and body look as sharp as splinters, and his fat belly seems too heavy to be lifted into the air. It must be hard being a cat who's too ugly to be cuddled. He trails behind me as I trot up the steps, miaowing constantly. He's never been this desperate for affection before. My room-mate must have attached a firework to his tail or some other nefarious act of cat torture.

I check the bathroom, the kitchen, then hold my breath as I open the door. But my room-mate is out. He doesn't appear to have drilled any unnecessary holes in the wall or erected any Satanic monuments. So far, so good. Even his bed looks tidy. The only sign of his presence is a plastic powder-blue suitcase beside his bed. Looking through his suitcase seems a perfect way of preparing myself for meeting him, but I'm sure the moment I start snooping he'll appear. I go to the door and put the bolt on, thinking I could always pretend it was just a habit if he asked me why I'd locked him out. Then I return to his bed and open his case. I don't want to disturb anything inside, so I just look at the clothes as they're arranged. It seems a small wardrobe for any man, and he has less to wear than even I do. Two pairs of black leather shoes, with expensive soles and Mr Minit replacement heels, four shirts (white, with assorted designs), boxer shorts, socks, two pairs of smart trousers and one pair of blue jeans. In the inside flap there's a black leather belt and five ties, two of which are decorated with cartoon characters (Winnie the Pooh and Roger Ramjet). There's also a lined exercise book resting on top of the clothes and, hating myself, I quickly flip through it. The pages are blank. I close the suitcase and return it alongside his bed. Still in a surveillance mood, I go back to my bed and find Dad's notebooks. Before now they held little interest for me, but now I know that they're records of the secret meetings he's been attending I'm eager to decipher them.

I pull back the bolt-lock and take the diaries to the bathroom, along with a towel and shampoo. Dad and I have always kept our toiletries in the bedroom. Such precaution probably sounds peculiar, but shortly after we moved in, Dad noticed that the toilet rolls and toothpaste were disappearing far more rapidly than either of us could be using them. Shortly afterwards, Dad had a day off work and discovered that not only did our landlord come up to use our bathroom at least three times that morning, but that in the afternoon he allowed a succession of builders free access to our bath. Since then we've managed to send him back to using his own facilities by steadily making ours as unwelcoming as possible. Worried that my room-mate might take this personally, I nip back into our bedroom and fetch a toilet roll.

As soon as the bath's full, I undress and place the diaries on the nearby window-shelf. So that I don't blur the ink-written accounts, I cover my hands with the transparent plastic gloves Dad uses when he's dyeing his hair. Then I climb into the tub and read the first volume, looking for any information that might relate to the woman I met in hospital. The initials seem an obvious place to start. I try to remember some of the names from Dad's list. I forgot the numbers the moment I dialled them, but surely the names shouldn't be that difficult. *Marilyn*. Must be MS. *Brittany?* I flick forward. BC. *Valerie?* Page 1, VD.

Minutes, Week One
(Taken from tapes 1a and 1b)
Transcript: IJ
Those present:
ST, DT, MS, VD, BC, LC, CG, IJ.

Meeting begins 20:00 hrs. Session starts with a recap of events leading up to decision to begin splinter group.

VD follows general intro by stating her disillusionment with similar groups she has belonged to previously. Subsequent discussion reveals that this feeling is shared by all members of the group, with LC and CG delivering anecdotes about particularly bad experiences where they have suffered from a lack of support following personal revelations. It is suggested (by BC) that as the group-appointed chairman, ST should begin this meeting by setting out rules that will govern discussion over the weeks to come. ST responds by confessing his difficulties with being given this position of leadership.

BC suggests that it is precisely this reluctance that will ensure ST oversees proceedings in a fair and just manner. She respectfully reminds ST that he has been chosen in order to give these meetings a focus, and any querulousness on his part could prove the kind of stumbling-block that'd prevent the success of this venture. She points out that he has been appointed not because of his gender, but because of his previous experience of gestalt, TA and 'motivational' therapies. She adds that most of the women present specifically requested a male leader due to their negative experience of feminist support-groups, where the psychological focus was compromised by the imagined need to remain true to the 'sisterhood'.

ST replies that he is grateful for BC's frankness, and if her opinions are representative of all the women present, he will be happy to accept the role of chairman. He qualifies this, however, by reiterating that he nevertheless feels reluctant to dictate the confines of group conversation. He suggests that it would perhaps be more appropriate to offer a personal introduction, explaining why he needs a group such as this and what he hopes to get out of it. He begins by telling everyone that it has been almost three years since he has belonged to any sort of group.

ST: The ironic thing is that the last three years have been among the most active I've experienced, and it's only because I've recently settled down again that I've been able to approach all of you. I feel scared because it's the first time I've been in a group and had stuff I'm anxious about sharing. Even though I've heard people talk about far worse things than my relatively minor sins, I'm still nervous. Belonging to groups has always been much more a social than a psychological thing and now I feel an acute need to unburden myself, I have to admit that previously I've always been a kind of emotional voyeur.

VD: I completely understand your reluctance to reveal yourself, and I don't think you should feel guilty about using previous groups to fulfil 'social' urges. A support-group should provide all forms of support, and I believe Brittany is right when she suggests that we shouldn't be limited by fears of transgressing social or political correctness. If you look at any form of psychological assistance – from the analyst's couch to the priest's confession-booth – it is immediately apparent that all these processes are undeniably titillating. There is a passage in the Marquis de Sade's *Juliette* where the narrator accompanies her friend Clairwil to make confessions to a young friar simply for the process of arousing him. While I'm not suggesting that we should adopt this as the precedent for our meetings, there are some stories better received by a prurient ear than a sympathetic one.

When I hear someone fiddling with the slipped lock, I immediately assume it's Dad, and hide his notebook in the base of the broken shower unit. Laughing at my stupidity, I decide it's time to meet my room-mate. I quickly remove the transparent gloves and wash my matted hair in the lukewarm water.

I dry myself in the bathroom and dress again, not wanting to lose my towel when we shake hands. I return to my room and put Dad's books by my bed. The room-mate's sitting at our small hardboard table, unwrapping fish and chips.

'Hungry?' he asks. 'They've given me far too many chips.'

'OK,' I tell him, 'I'll fetch a plate.'

'No need. I've got two here.'

'Ketchup then?'

'Mmm, yeah, if you've got some.'

I nip out into the kitchen and bring back the sauce. He's already tipped most of the chips onto my plate, and now starts attacking his fish. He takes the ketchup from me, splattering it over his lunch. I watch him cut up large strips of cod and push them into his mouth. He's almost disappointingly ordinary, with bland, even features, closely cropped blond hair and a thin-lipped smile. His only distinguishing feature is his dry, wrinkled skin, which makes it hard to tell whether he's a poorly preserved twenty-year-old or a youthful thirtysomething.

He offers his hand. 'I'm Kevin.'

'Daniel.'

He grins. 'Dirty stop-out.'

'What?'

'Last night,' he says, 'did you meet someone?'

'No, it was just a work do. I stayed at a friend's.'

He nods. 'Where d'you work?'

'Quick Kall Ltd. In the Centre.'

'Sales?'

'Incoming. How d'you know Mr Farnell?'

'He's a friend of my dad's.' He looks up. 'Well, not really a friend. He knows him from the pub.'

'Which pub?'

'The Griffin. Up by the church.'

'I've never been there.'

'It's a real old man's pub. My dad's been going there since the beginning of time.'

'I don't really know Mr Farnell. I tend to keep out of his way.'

Kevin smiles. 'They're all like that. Bunch of old bastards. But I needed a place, so . . .'

'You know it's not permanent, don't you?'

'Just for a month, Dad said. That'll be long enough. You know what it's like when you live with your parents. Things get really tense, then you move out and they're desperate to have you back.'

'Yeah, I get fed up with Dad sometimes.'

'Mr Farnell says he's in the hospital.'

'Yeah.'

Kevin wipes the ketchup from his mouth. 'Would you like a beer?'

'Please. Thanks.' He gets up from the table and walks to the kitchen. I follow him as far as the hallway. 'By the way, that fridge doesn't work. Neither does the shower, or the washing-machine.'

'Really? Shit. Mavis won't be happy.'

'Mavis?'

'My mate. John Marvin, really, but everyone calls him Mavis. I told him he could wash his team's football kit this afternoon.'

'Sorry.'

'It's not your fault.' He returns with the beer. 'You don't mind me having people over, do you?'

'No, of course not. You're paying rent.'

He opens his beer and walks back to his bed. 'Now, I didn't unpack because I didn't know if there's anywhere to put my clothes.'

'You can use the wardrobe.'

'What about your dad's stuff?'

'It's in a box. He's not really one for hanging things up.'

Kevin lifts the suitcase onto the bed. 'So where's your mum then?'

'Florida.'

'Really?'

'Last I heard.'

'How come?'

'Long story.'

'I don't mean to pry.'

'No, I'll tell you. But you won't believe it.'

'Why not?' He looks quizically at me. It's a long time since I told anyone about Mum. When she first left I had to tell everyone, just to stay sane. Strange events demand their own story, and at the time I was the only one left around to tell it. As it lost its power, the anecdote became a good party piece. A conversation-starter. Now I like to pretend it's got nothing to do with me, that I went from living with my parents to living with Sonia (the GBH girl) and back to Dad with no weird dramas in between. But I could see Kevin wanted a revelation, and I thought I'd enjoy telling him something that no longer held any power over me.

'My mum won the lottery.'

'And moved to Florida?'

'No, it's weirder than that. My parents were professional gamblers. Well, not professionals in the strictest sense. They worked as teachers during the day, but purely for stake money. The bulk of our living expenses came from horse racing and nights in the Casino.'

Kevin opens the wardrobe and starts hanging up his shirts. He seems concerned about his clothes, tutting at the creases in his trousers.

'They worked as a team for seventeen years. Then around the time of my adolescence things started going wrong between them. One day, for no reason, Mum ran out of luck. All gamblers are superstitious, but my parents were at opposite ends of the spectrum. My father believed in minimising the odds, waiting till the croupiers were nearing the ends of their shift and not properly spinning the ball so you could see where it'd end up, reading all the racing magazines and coming up with accumulators. Mum relied entirely on chance, and when she stopped winning, she had no idea how to sort things out. So she went to see this psychic who told her the only way she'd start winning again was if she bet larger sums of money. She followed his advice but nothing changed, and dad had to subsidise her ever increasing losses as well as keeping the family alive. It was inevitable that she'd soon have to stop, and after one final spectacular loss, Dad told her she couldn't gamble any more. She handled it well, channelling her urge into harmless scratchcards and ten pounds a week on the lottery. The weekend she won she was visiting her mother in Portugal, and by the time she got back Dad had fled the country.'

Kevin looks shocked. 'No way.'

I laugh. 'That isn't the weird part. They'd always had a weak marriage and there'd been infidelities on both sides. What happened next was what threw me. Mum was so angry at Dad that she hired a private detective to track him down and do him damage.'

'That's not weird. I'd do the same.'

'Sure, but would you fall in love with the detective, decide you don't care about the money and move with him to his parents' house in Florida?'

'Is that what happened?'

I nod. 'And then nine months after she'd gone, Dad turns up, penniless, and asks me if I want to move in with him. I still live in fear of a hitman turning up here, and I'm not certain the road accident didn't have something to do with her.'

'What makes you say that?'

I pick up the driver's address. 'What's short for Edward?'

'Ed, Ted . . . why?'

'That's what I thought. The man who knocked down my dad was called Ted Davis. Davis was my mother's maiden name.'

'Perhaps he's a relative of hers.'

'If he is, I haven't met him. But I don't think it's a relative. I think it's an alias. You know how sometimes when you're reading a book the names don't ring true. That's how Ted Davis sounds to me.'

'Have you told the police?'

'I don't want to get involved. It's not a serious accident and he definitely deserved it.'

'Why don't you challenge her? Maybe ask for some money to keep quiet.'

'I haven't heard from Mum since she left. I don't even have her address.'

I start gathering the plates. Kevin looks at me.

'I'm sorry, do you want me to wash up?'

'No, that's OK. I'll handle it.'

Mavis arrives just after two. He's dragging a large white drawstring bag and has the ginger tom beneath his arm.

'I found this outside,' he tells Kevin. 'I thought we could get it stoned or something.'

Kevin looks nervous. 'Mavis, I'd like you to meet Daniel. This is his room.'

'Where's yours then?'

'No, we're sharing. But Dan was here first.'

Mavis looks confused.

'What I'm saying, Mavis, is that he might not want a stray cat in here.'

Mavis looks at me. He's twice the size of Kevin, with a number 1 crop and a large, almost square head. His clothes are all black clubwear, with a Diesel T-shirt and a padded *Universe* jacket. His red-lensed glasses make him look like a hitman from a Japanese comic. He's at least thirty-five and even his nose intimidates me.

'It's all right,' I hear myself saying, 'it'll be a laugh.'

The tom squints at me and jumps free of Mavis's arms. He pulls his laundry bag round in front of him and looks at Kevin.

'Bad news there, Mavis. The washing-machine's broken.'

He doesn't reply.

'There's a laundry in the rank behind the Texaco,' I tell him. 'I've got some twenties if you need change.'

'Maybe later,' he says. 'Any beer, Kev?'

Kevin goes out into the kitchen. The ginger tom is slowly

striding around the room, curious but clearly in no hurry. I can't see how getting him stoned's going to make much difference. Mavis sits on Kevin's bed. His glasses are pointed in my direction but I don't know if he's looking at me. His face remains impassive. Kevin returns.

'How's your tattoo?'

'Still bleeding,' Mavis replies, hoisting up his right trouser leg. He's stained his skin with a red robin, almost three inches long.

'You a City fan?' I ask, suddenly grateful for the conversations I've overheard between Gordon and Ian. Gordon's always drawing robins on folders in work, usually accompanied with the words BRISTOL CITY F.C.

'No. Rovers,' Mavis says, looking straight at me, 'but I was getting so much grief when people saw this . . .' He pulls up his left leg, revealing a tattoo of the Rovers pirate. '. . . that I thought I ought to get a City one. This way if anyone challenges me on the bus I can get out of it.'

Kevin hands him his beer. He turns to me.

'You got anything I can skin up on?'

Kevin and Mavis spend the rest of the afternoon getting stoned. I've already described the sacrifices I've made to remain friends with the smokers at work, and I'm not keen on letting them fill my room with the stink of tobacco. Mavis sticks to his word and feeds the tom a small lump of hash that makes him piss all over my carpet. After emptying his bladder, the cat lies comatose on his side until Kevin picks him up and says he can see his third eyelid, which, he solemnly informs me, is *not* a good sign. Mavis tells him not to be so wet and tips his beer all over the cat's back, which wakes him up but sends him scuttling under my bed. Then they head off to Mavis's house, leaving me to cope with the traumatised animal. Feeling guilty, I go up to the garage and buy him a can of sardines. But when I get back he's not interested, remaining just out of reach. He doesn't come out until half past twelve, joining me on the bed for *Exotica Erotica*. Tonight's episode is the most downbeat yet, with Havers and McCarthy lamenting their wasted lives. I watch the trailer for tomorrow's conclusion, then put the cat outside, hoping the drugs haven't destroyed his feline instincts, and that he'll live long enough to come down.

6

It's stupid to rely on Sunday buses. There's never anyone else waiting at the stops, and keeping the service running for one person is hardly economical. But the buses are there on the timetable, and even after two hours have gone by and none has appeared, the trusting fool inside me refuses to abandon hope.

I don't start until two but I head out to the stop around eleven, knowing from experience that the lunchtime buses are the most reliable. I wait alone until the bus appears, twenty minutes behind schedule. The Sunday buses are half the size of the weekday ones, with the number and destination written on a cardboard square propped up in the front window.

The ticket machine's broken so the driver gives me a piece of orange card with RETURN stamped in black ink. I sit at the back and take my book from my bag. I'm up to Chapter Six of *The Rise of the Meritocracy* and I hope to finish it today. I told the team leader I'd work on Sunday because Ian said it's the nicest shift of the week. There's no clients in the call-centre on Sunday so it's casual dress and we're allowed to read. There are also few calls between two and ten on a Sunday and Ian told me he usually uses this shift to catch up on his sleep.

Part Two of Dad's copy of *Rise* is much more heavily annotated than Part One. This seems unsurprising, given that the first part projects the rise of the elite and the second imagines the decline of the lower classes. I've already recognised many of Dad's greatest hits from the chapter on *The Status of the Worker* and I'm sure the passages about the decline of parliament will explain Dad's political position. It feels odd to have finally read this book after seeing it lying around for so long. I still can't imagine Dad paying three and six for it, probably because I've only ever seen these old Pelicans at car-boot sales and second-hand shops. They seem like Bibles. Books to be given or stolen, not bought.

I go for lunch at the World of Food in the Galleries. I like the World of Food better than Burger King or McDonald's because you can get a proper Sunday lunch instead of just hamburgers. I'm always surprised by how busy it is on Sundays, with whole families filling up the plastic tables. Six years ago I'd have put this down to Single Parent Sunday, but nowadays there are two parents at every table, their haggard faces revealing their struggle to be normal. There are not enough tables for me to have one to myself so I sit with two adolescent girls eating noodles. It's hard to be certain because I'm avoiding their eyes, but it feels like they spend the whole meal staring at me. I leave all my potatoes and half my drink and quickly look round the shops before walking to Quick Kall.

Ian's already installed behind his work-station, his eyes closed and feet up on the table. He's wearing the grey sweatshirt he usually goes clubbing in, and the bags under his eyes have turned purple. I try to sit down without waking him up, but he senses me and smiles.

'I waited for you last night,' he tells me.

'I'm sorry, I didn't feel up to it. I'd had a tough day with the room-mate.'

'You met him then?'

I nod.

'And he's a prick?'

'No, he's OK. But he's got this mate Mavis.'

'Mavis?'

'It's not his real name. He's a real meathead. Anyway, how was your night?'

'Stupid. I went really mental when you didn't show up. Adrienne had all these friends down from London and one of them dealt me a bad pill.'

'What was it?' I ask, laughing.

'An Old MacDonald. I've never heard of them before. Brown speckledy thing. It was probably a one-off though, 'cause Adrienne had one and she was OK.'

'Any unwelcome visitors?'

'No, I think Adrienne had a word with Alice after Friday and told her not to come again. You seen the latest Gordon's Log?' He passes me the book. 'You'll like it.'

Gordon's Log 6/3/9—

My Fears that the other Members of my Team do not like me were proved unfounded today when they invited me to accompany them to popular local Night-spot, The Pentangle. I have often overheard the others talking about this Place before, but its name has always led me to believe that it's the kind of Satanic Meeting-house that mother has expressly forbidden me from attending. When we arrived at The Pentangle, however, I discovered that it was, in fact, little different from the Moustache Clubs I attended as a Youth (except for the much higher number of Women on the Dancefloor). The Disco Music was a little less anthem-based than I'm used to, but I instantly recognised this Club as a place filled with Kindred Spirits. I'm still intimidated by Adrienne, but as she spent most of the Evening Djing, I felt free to relax and converse with the Team Leader and her boyfriend Bryan.

(Ah, Dear Diary, I do not need to explain that no matter how hard I try to keep this Diary a record of Emotion recollected in Tranquillity, I wrote the above with a trembling Hand. I have already filled many of these pages with Diagrams of what I would like to do to the Divine

Alice, and remaining calm in the Company of the Man who has full Rights to her Body was an impossible Torment. Little did I realise that my Enemy and Rival would turn out to be a Man of Uncommon Generosity, fully prepared to Share the Treasures of which he was sole Master. But I am getting ahead of Myself.)

I spent the early part of the Evening directing my Attentions entirely towards Bryan, hoping to hoodwink him into believing that he had Nothing to Fear from me as far as Alice was concerned. My Original Design was to convince Bryan that we were so similar in Mind that on future occasions he would insist on my Presence, thus giving me Free Passage into Heaven without even realising that he was doing so. During our Conversation, however, I soon realised that Bryan was too shrewd to be taken in by such flimflammery. He saw through my Intentions immediately, but before I had a chance to beg his Pardon for my Impertinence, he made a Confession which changed things entirely. He told me that he and Alice felt a Special Allegiance to the Men and Women of the Sixties and Seventies who went under the Collective Title of SWINGERS. He said that since getting together he and Alice had been searching for a similarly broad-minded Citizen who could help them fulfil their long-cherished Fantasies. He recounted that they'd spent the previous evening in an Easy-Listening Club, hoping that alongside the Fondue Fetishists and the Bacharach wannabes, they might find some like-minded souls who'd be prepared to aid them in their pursuit of Sexual Nirvana. Then he patted my hand and asked me if I liked the films of Robin Askwith. I replied 'Of course,' and the deal was made.

Ian tapped my shoulder. 'You better hook up. You're being watched.'

I look up and see the line manager staring at me. There are no headsets on the table so I check the drawers. I find one with not too much yellow residue, and plug in. The line manager's already walking across. He stops by our table.

'Any particular reason you're not signed on?'

'No, sir. Sorry.'

He nods. 'Sort it out then.'

For the rest of the Evening there was a palpable tension between the Three of Us. I could tell Alice was checking me out, trying to Estimate the Width of my Chest and the Size of my Package. No Doubt Bryan was also feeling Nervous now he had made the Deal, worrying that I might prove more Manly than he had imagined. If he knew how long I'd been holding a Hard-on for Alice, I doubt Bryan would have risked inviting me into their Bedroom.

The other Members of the Team clearly felt Excluded, and before long, they all went home. (I feel I should mention here, Dear Diary, that Teri and Daniel left together, just in case it should become important later on.) After a Decent Interval, the Three of Us walked out to Bryan's car.

Bryan drove us to his House. On the Way he explained that he still lived with his Parents and asked me to excuse their Mundane Choice of Furnishings. After our Conversation in The Pentangle, he confessed that I had every right to expect a fully equipped Dungeon, but his Mum and Dad had resisted his attempt to Decorate the Room with Sex Toys and Erotic Sculptures.

'Should've tied them up and beaten some sense into them,' I joked, and they both laughed.

Before long, we arrived at Bryan's House and he led us through the Hallway into the large, spacious Lounge. There was the brief Moment of Tension common to Situations such as these, when we all remembered our Daytime Lives and wondered how the Night's Activities would change our Working Relationships on Monday Morning, and then Bryan started to undress. I have spent so many hours at Home and in Work wondering what Alice's Body looks like, and I couldn't believe I was about to receive Answers to all my Questions. Few Women have excited my Imagination the way Alice has, probably because the clothes she wears do so much to Desexualise her Body that it becomes Impossible to stop thinking about it. The other Women in the Call-Centre are just as Sexually Attractive (if not more so), but they do not interest me because it is so easy to guess what they look like when they are Naked. I know, for example, that Teri has small, apple-shaped breasts, and from the tight T-shirts she wears in Summer, I have observed that her Nipples are round, regular and usually Erect. I also know that Adrienne rarely wears underwear, because I've often noticed the outline of her pubic hair bulging against her skirt.

I turn to Ian. 'I can't believe she wrote this about her pubic hair.'

'I know,' he grins. 'Pretending to be Gordon seems to be some kind of therapy for her.'

'Does she have a bulge?'

He looks shocked. 'Why are you asking me?'

'No reason.'

'I don't usually spend much time staring at women's crotches.' He sounds awkward. 'Not when they're hidden beneath the desk.'

I laugh. 'Nothing happened between me and Teri.'

'What?'

'In the diary, Gordon . . . Adrienne . . . writes about me going home with Teri.'

'So that's not true?'

'Yes, it's true, but nothing happened. I just went back to watch TV.'

He nods. 'I watched Adrienne writing that. She was really getting into it. I had to keep warning her every time the line manager came across.'

'It doesn't seem as realistic as the other entries. I can't imagine Gordon using a word like "desexualise."'

'I know. It's not as funny either. I think she was taking out her anger after the appraisal. All those details about Alice's house are true.'

'It's so self-destructive. She must know she'll lose her job if Alice reads it.'

'I think she wants to get sacked. Then she can DJ full time.'

I nod, and return to the diary.

Bryan approached me, stark naked, and asked why I had

yet to undress. I told him I thought it was a Waste of Pleasures for us all to Strip Off at the same time, and I wanted to Savour Alice's Undressing before beginning my own. He laughed, and told me, 'Nice idea, Gordon, but Alice is one of those women who prefer to watch rather than participate. Maybe on another occasion she will strip for you, but tonight she merely wishes to watch us in Action.'

Before I had chance to Complain, Bryan was unbuckling my belt and pushing my slender frame up against the Mantelpiece. I tried to look at Alice, but Bryan held my Neck, forcing my Head forward. I felt a familiar Agony as he bore into me, hoping my Pain was providing Alice with some small Pleasure.

I close the book and hand it to Ian. 'We should write Adrienne's Log. She'd love the attention.'

'I've got no talent for that sort of thing. It's hard enough thinking up anti-city jokes for Gordon.'

I tell Ian about Mavis's tattoos, and he says he deserves to get beaten up by both sides. I can see he doesn't want to talk, and leave him to his silence. Another seven and a half hours and only sixty-four pages of Dad's book. Sundays may be less hectic than weekdays, but somehow feeling bored in work is worse than being busy. It wouldn't be so bad if the call-centre didn't feel so unhealthy. The recycled air dries my throat and eyelids, and I have a permanent queasy headache. Then there's the radiation and dust, plus the backstrain and the constant fear of my lips brushing against the saliva-splattered mouthpiece.

The book's spine is already broken at Chapter Six and it folds easily onto my desk. I find my place and start reading, hoping Dr Young's rhetoric will prove strong enough to pull me through this empty afternoon.

I finish the book at half four. At seven o'clock the line manager goes home and we're left to complete our shift unsupervised. Ian loads Pontoon into our work-stations. Outside the office this game would occupy me for ten minutes tops. Here it holds an endless attraction, and even choosing the pattern for the back of the cards becomes a major operation. I plump for yellow robots on a blue background, mainly because I'm impressed by the way their eyes move every time you twist.

I feel bad about letting Ian down. Before Dad's accident, I would never have stood him up. I want to tell Ian how confused I've felt lately, but I know that once I start I'll have to explain about telling on Teri, and I can picture his disappointed face even before I've started speaking. He's often told me how protective he feels towards Teri, but I'm sure he never imagined the danger would come from his best friend.

Ian plays Pontoon much quicker than me, no doubt as a result of all these unobserved evenings. There's never anyone supervising after seven, except for the Security Guard six floors down in reception, and everyone in the call-centre has a story about these sessions. Temps are the most excitable, bragging about fucking their partners on the line manager's desk or buzzing in their friends for unauthorised office parties. Call me unimaginative, but I think most nights probably pass like this: quiet, sedately illicit, as old-fashioned as an afterhours lock-in.

I take advantage of the line manager's absence to wander down the length of the call-centre. Permission to leave your desk is one of the last privileges granted to personnel. And with good reason, as this freedom can transform your working life. Without this right, you are completely reliant on your neighbour to get you through the day. Get paired with the right person and every day offers eight hours of invigorating conversation or, better yet, unabashed flirting. (I think it's the excess energy of all those unchallenged brains that makes an office such a sexual environment. I spend most days hiding my erection beneath the desk, hoping for a release that never comes. I'm sure it's this same excitement which prompts Adrienne to write Gordon's Log, channelling her call-centre frustration into homophobic comedy. I'm also certain that the best time for any seduction is in the middle of an office Wednesday.) But sit next to someone boring and you'll be begging your bosses to terminate your employment. And it's not just time-perception that's position-dependent. The women on the Banks and Building Societies team look far more attractive than Teri and Adrienne, simply because they're stationed on the other side of the room. Of course, you can always plan your toilet trips to coincide with theirs, or better still, sneak up on them during the company karaoke evening, but nothing beats sitting next to someone nice forty hours a week. I used to believe office life was merely a simulacrum of genuine existence, but now I think the only hours that count are the ones you get paid for. The Protestant work ethic must be Western man's greatest con-trick. How did we convince ourselves that this is a virtuous way of life? There are husbands and wives who'd give anything to have their partner's undivided attention eight hours a day and yet here it's a gift with no value. These are the facts: We are paid to give our time to the company. The company pays for our friendships.

At eight thirty we stop working and walk down to the tea room. When there are only two people on you're supposed to take your breaks separately, but no one's going to phone tonight, and even if they do, there are never any emergencies on a Sunday. Outside the tea room, we have a momentary panic when neither of us can remember the code. The last two codes were logical and easy to recall: 0712 (days of the week, months of the year); 1999 (self-explanatory), but after a spate of break-ins, they've chosen a code that's harder to guess (7109). The Coke and snacks machines are still empty following the most recent burglary, and we have to content ourselves with two cups of watery minestrone.

Ian lights a cigarette. 'Any news on your dad?'

'Only about the women.'

'Which women?'

'His seven strangers. Seems they were all in a support group together.'

He nods. I sip my foul drink and look round the smoking

room, searching for something to read. Most people only buy the newspaper for the sports, and there are supplements from the *Mail* and *Express* on nearby tables. Car headlights keep challenging the room's weak illumination, making it feel like an empty tube train.

'You ever belonged to a group?' I ask Ian.

'A support group?' he says, frowning.

'Any sort of group.'

'I was a Scout, if that counts.'

'It counts.' My voice rises. 'I was chucked out of Boys' Brigade.'

'What for?'

'Pushing another boy into an electric fire. He had a two-foot blister down the back of his leg. When it popped he went into shock. Did you like being in the Scouts?'

'Sometimes. I liked camps and being a Sixer. My best friend was my Second Sixer and we used to hide in the woods and get pissed. Why d'you ask?'

'I found these books among Dad's stuff. In one of 'em he says he's been secretly attending groups for years. He keeps saying how much it means to him. I can't really imagine how that feels.'

Ian smiles. He's more perceptive than the others give him credit for. I like the conversations we have when no one's around. They seem a part of my life that can't be corrupted. I watch his eyes, knowing he's building up to something. He looks at me, and says, 'I've felt that in pubs sometimes.'

'Belonging?'

'More than that. I don't know how to describe it. The world seemed a lot friendlier when I got drunk every night. I used to have a friend who'd go to places without having anywhere to sleep, and he'd always find someone to put him up. I don't think I'd risk that, but I used to wander around Bristol OK. Snatch a quick kip beneath a hedge.'

'Maybe that's why Dad went to groups, to make the world less scary.' I pause, checking his eyes. 'It's just a shame he couldn't find one on road safety.'

The main perk of working the late shift is that you always get a ride home. The only other time you can get a company cab is if you start before six, and I can't imagine ever taking advantage of that facility. I ask Ian if he wants the first taxi. He looks at me sheepishly.

'I don't usually take a cab.'

'Why not?'

'Well, I usually do the early shift on Monday so it hardly seems worth going home. I usually just sleep through.'

'In the office?'

'No, that's too risky. But I can lock myself into the cloakroom and there's a cleaner who gets in early and wakes me up.'

'Isn't it uncomfortable?'

'Not really. I've got a sleeping bag and a pillow in my locker so it's not that hard to make a bed. Don't tell anyone.'

'Of course not. I'm impressed.'

He laughs. 'It's no big deal.'

I imagine Ian settling down for the night as the taxi takes me home, wondering how he manages to sleep without worrying about being discovered. The taxi gets me home much quicker than the bus, taking all the short cuts because the company pays a flat fee and he wants to get the journey done quickly.

I get the driver to drop me by the fish and chip shop two streets down from my room. I haven't eaten since the World of Food at lunchtime, and I'm feeling a little light-headed. The chip-shop owner is a short Cantonese man with a white pork-pie hat and a gold front tooth. His wife's the same height but twice the size, and likes to dress up in 'English' clothes. Tonight she's wearing a padded green bodywarmer over a long black dress with a red rose print. As soon as I've ordered my cod lot, she grips my wrist and says, 'We haven't seen your father.'

'No,' the man agrees, 'long time, no see.'

Their faces look anxious. Looking into the Cantonese lady's concerned eyes, I remember Teri's advice about breaking the news gently.

'He's had an accident,' I tell them. 'It's not serious, but he'll be in the hospital for a while.'

'Hospital?'

'Yeah, but it's OK.'

Her grip tightens. 'Your father,' she says, 'is a very good man.'

I nod, unsurprised. People are always saying this sort of thing about my father, particularly if they don't know him that well. He has a kind, honest face, and looks humble in his catalogue clothes. But as the woman clings on to me, I realise she really believes what she's saying. I wonder what my father's done to secure her loyalty, and try to keep my expression earnest.

The owner hovers behind his wife, as if wanting me to know he shares her feelings. I wish they'd stop this and get my chips. I try to move things on by asking for a Coke with my meal. After a final squeeze of my hand, the woman returns to the fryer. They serve up my food and I leave the shop, the couple's worried faces still hovering in my mind.

I stop at the bottom of the lane, resting my food on the third step of the metal staircase while I break off some fish for the cat. I haven't seen him since last night and I'm eager to find out if he's still alive. I walk down to his usual spot on top of the rotten mattresses, but the only evidence that he's been here is a small ball of black catshit. I don't know enough about animal faeces to tell if this is a good sign but it seems unlikely. I leave the mattresses and walk down to Mr Farnell's garages. I find a torch in the second one along, and check the space for his fat ginger face. Finding nothing, I leave the garage and walk back to the staircase.

The ginger tom isn't dead. He's sitting on the staircase eating my fish. I look at the small greasy cod chunk in my left hand

and decide I'll have his portion. I'm glad he's alive, but I wish he wasn't eating my dinner. I suppose he deserves it for putting up with Mavis. I shine Farnell's torch at the cat, checking his eyelids. They seem fine, so I leave him to his meal and jump over his head to get to my room.

Kevin's already asleep. I'm glad I've got Farnell's torch as it allows me to get to my bed without waking him. I check my watch. Ten fifty. Just over an hour until *Exotica Erotica*. I know, I know, but it's the last episode and if I can just stay awake long enough, I can forget about this film for ever. Kevin's snoring is just about bearable, and not that different from my dad's. I go to the bathroom and clean my teeth, then come back and climb into bed.

I decide the best way to stay awake is to watch *Fame and Fortune* and *The Sex Show* with the sound down. Helen Gibson presents both programmes, going from tarot readings to vital statistics in the space of thirty minutes. I spend most of *Fame and Fortune* wondering if it's shot on the same set as *The Sex Show*. Just as *The Sex Show*'s about to end, I hear Kevin say in the darkness, 'You don't have to watch this.'

'What?' I ask, unnerved.

'You don't have to put up with this soft shit. Mavis did you a favour. Turn to thirty-six.'

I do. It's the *Ten Minute Teaser*, a compressed preview of the programming for the night ahead. I start flicking back. Kevin snaps, 'Leave it on.'

'Why?'

'Mavis has a friend at the Cable Company. He's got you *Television X* and *The Adult Channel* for free. Now you don't have to make do with all this unrestricted shit.'

'That's very kind,' I protest, 'but I'd just like to watch something on *L!VE TV* first. It's only half an hour.'

Kevin doesn't answer. I take this as consent and change back. I've missed the recap, but a loose sense of the plot is enough for me.

'What's this then?' he asks.

'*Exotica Erotica*. It's just that I've been following it since Thursday and it's the last part tonight.'

I wait for his protests but he remains silent. I feel more awkward watching this with Kevin than I did with Teri. It seems OK to see sex films with a woman, but two men ogling tits together is simply seedy. I'm also scared Kevin might start masturbating. (Although given the elegiac nature of this final episode, derision seems more likely.)

It's a genuine relief when we get to the closing credits. I've been carrying this story in my head for four nights now, and I'm glad to get rid of it. Kevin waits until the adverts and then asks for the remote. I throw it to him. It crashes against the wall but he assures me it's not broken. I close my eyes and leave him to his naked ladies, praying sleep comes before he does.

7

I awake myself early, wanting to replace Farnell's torch before he discovers it's missing. Kevin fell asleep with the television on, so I get dressed watching breakfast time on the Asian station. I intend to visit Dad after work so I choose a tie from my own selection, knowing if I wear one of his he'll worry about what I've done with the rest of his wardrobe. After checking myself in the full-length mirror (a luxury I haven't had time for in ages), I head out to the garages.

It's freezing outside. I knew it was a mistake to leave my room before eight. I run across the backyard and am about to drop the torch onto a pile of oily rags when I notice my landlord rummaging through his tool box.

'Good morning,' he says in his usual languorous tone. 'You're up early.'

'Yes.'

'Is that my torch you're holding?'

I look at it. 'Ah, yeah, we had an intruder last night.'

'An intruder,' he repeats, enjoying the sound of the word. 'And you thought he was after my torch?'

'No, of course not. I was using it to look for him.'

'So where was he intruding? In my backyard?'

'I couldn't tell. I thought he might come back and break into your house.'

Mr Farnell laughs. 'I'm not scared of intruders. Not with the dog and my gun.'

I put the torch down, hoping that now he's got his property back, he'll let me go. But instead he says, 'Daniel?'

'Yes?'

'How's it working out with the room-mate?'

'Great.'

'You're getting along then?'

'Just about.'

He nods. 'His dad says he's a good lad underneath. You're just the kind of influence he needs.'

He goes back to his box. I seize the opportunity and slip away.

I've decided to read *Hypnosis: Fact and Fiction* next. Finding the minutes from Dad's secret meetings have given me a new hunger to deconstruct his philosophy, and I'm sure mesmerism must be an important weapon in his bag of tricks. After all, why else would seven women choose my dad for their father-confessor?

It's not until I'm halfway through the first chapter that I realise the other passengers are sniggering at me. I understand their amusement. They know nothing about my dad and probably think I'm reading the book to help myself get a girlfriend. But I can also tell that most of them are intrigued by the title and I'm sure if I left the book on my seat it wouldn't be long before someone stole it. Self-help guides are irresistible, as long as no one sees you buying one. Maybe I'll buy the *Kama Sutra* to read on the journey tomorrow.

My attention drifts during the second half of the journey, and I remember the Cantonese couple in the chip shop. The woman's warmth towards my father still troubles me, and I have a suspicion her emotion is connected to his secret club. I can't quite believe she's one of his seven ladies, but maybe Dad's some kind of Dr Love and the club's only part of his hidden activity.

Ian winks at me as I enter the office. I remember all the previous Monday mornings and wonder why I never guessed he sleeps in the cloakroom before. Looking at him now it seems obvious, what with his limp shirt and tousled hair. I always thought it was simply the strain of starting at six.

It's been a long time since I was the second team member into the office, but once Kevin woke up, I lost all desire to stay at home.

'Good night?' I ask Ian, grinning.

'Not bad,' he grins back.

I sit at my desk and log on. I use the extra minutes to change the set-up of my screen. We're supposed to stick with a black background and green lettering, but I like to change mine to yellow on purple, using the vertical hold adjuster to stretch the display into widescreen.

'There's a call waiting,' Ian tells me. 'You'd better take it.'

I hit *Ready*. 'Hello, Angel Cruises, how can I help you?'

'What's the weirdest cruise you do?'

'Exotic, you mean?'

'Could be exotic. Might just be weird. For example, I called another cruise company and they have a troll cruise.'

'Troll?'

'Yeah, round Denmark or somewhere. You go down fjords looking for trolls. Do you have anything like that?'

'Not really. We only do the Caribbean Cruise and the Round the World trip. Would you like a brochure?'

'OK.'

'Can I take your name?'

'Only I'm a writer, you see.'

'Pardon?'

'I'm a writer and I need a weird cruise for the end of my book.'

'Why does it have to be weird?'

'Maybe weird's the wrong word. Something elaborate. I need a big romantic set-piece for the climax.'

'Trolls don't sound very romantic.'

'That's the problem. If it was fairies or something . . .'

'Change it to fairies then. Have the couple,' I pause, 'there is a couple, right?'

'Of course.'

'OK, have the couple discussing fairies earlier in the novel . . . I don't know, perhaps the man doesn't believe in them . . . and then right at the end they could kiss and one could appear.'

The line goes silent, then the caller starts laughing. 'That's a bit OTT, isn't it? I don't want to lose my readers' WSOD.'

'WSOD?'

'Willing suspension of disbelief.'

'You're the writer. Shall I send you the catalogues?'

'OK.' He gives me his name and address. I close the call and hit *Ready*. The problem with working for an agency is that you have to keep six or seven sets of information in your head at all times. And there's always going to be one line you don't know at all. Like, oh shit, the Car Insurance care line.

'Sorry,' I tell the caller, 'all our operators are busy at the minute. You are being placed in a queuing system and your call will be answered as soon as possible.'

I put him on hold and turn to Ian. 'I've got a Car Insurance call. Can you handle it?'

He shrugs. 'I always pass them to Gordon. Leave him on hold and see if he hangs up.'

I watch the counter on my *Aspect* as it records how long the caller's been waiting. After you've been at Quick Kall a while, you learn how to cheat the system. Everyone in the call-centre is terrified about their stats (especially if they're trying for employee of the month), but if you're careful you can still fool around and escape the computer's record. The mainframe, for example, registers your call-response time, but not how long callers are left on hold. This will, of course, increase your average call-handling time, but you can always balance that out by getting another team member to call you a couple of times and hang up as soon as you answer.

'He's not going,' I tell Ian, watching as the counter reaches two minutes.

'You'd better take it. Get the Car Insurance file from the cupboard and bluff your way through.'

I scowl at him and run across to the team cupboard. All the folders are unlabelled and covered in identical black graffiti, so the only way of locating the right one is by pulling them all out. I flick through seven before finding the Car Insurance file, leaving the rest in a messy pile in front of Adrienne's work-station.

'OK,' I ask the caller, 'which policy are you interested in?'

He laughs. 'I don't know yet.'

'Right, bear with me. I'm just going to find someone who . . .'

'Excuse me,' he interrupts, 'who's paying for this call?'

'You are, sir. I'm afraid it's not a free line.'

'Then can you please stop putting me on hold.'

I lose the call. Ian looks at me.

'What did you just do?'

'I hung up. He was being abusive.' I flip through the screens, looking for the register of terminated calls. I log it as a number 6, abusive male caller. Number 5 is an abusive female caller, number 7 – abusive child. I like number 7s the best, although it's a long time since I've had one.

'What if he calls back? You know what they're like about losing calls.'

'I'll say it was an accident. Besides, he didn't get my name.'

Ian shakes his head. He takes his job seriously, and hates it when I lark around. Now that I've completed the call, Gordon comes in, two minutes too late. He looks surprised, and a little anxious, to see me in so early.

'Hi Gordon. Good weekend?'

I only ask him questions like this to start off his spasmodic nod, which always accompanies any affirmative statement.

'Y-yes,' he says, 'but Friday was the high-point.'

I remember Gordon's Log and stifle a laugh. He sits at his desk, immediately taking a call. He lifts his mouthpiece and looks at us.

'Did either of you two lose a Car Insurance call?'

'Dan did,' Ian says, disloyally.

'I've got him here. Do you want me to transfer him back?'

'No, you take it,' I tell him, 'I'd only just started.'

He sits down.

Adrienne's next into the office, dressed as always in head-to-toe black. She comes round to our side of the desk and squats so her head's level with ours.

'Excellent episode of the Log,' I tell her, 'I almost felt I was there.'

She grins. 'Glad you liked it.'

'I tried to persuade Ian to do an Adrienne's Log, but he said he couldn't think of anything filthy enough.'

'I have no private life,' she says. 'I spend all my spare time DJing and mending other people's pants.' She throws Ian a plastic bag, then turns to me. 'What happened to you on Saturday?'

'Prior engagement, Ade,' I lied. 'Besides, you've been playing the same old shit for weeks now.'

She looks hurt. 'I thought you liked the music.'

'I do. I'm only joking. I want you to do another compilation for me.'

'It'll cost you.'

'How much?'

'Two blanks for the tape you want done, plus half a pint and a promise you won't miss any more nights at The Pentangle.'

'I promise.'

'Good. Ian, you're our witness.'

He nods and she leaves us. I wait until she's out of earshot, then say to Ian, 'I can't believe you got Adrienne to mend your pants.'

He looks embarrassed. 'They weren't my pants.'

'Whose were they?'

'My ex-girlfriend's. I ripped them so she left 'em at my place.'

'Recently?'

'No, ages ago, when we were still together. But I wanted an excuse to write to her so I thought if Adrienne mended them I could send them back.'

'Are you going to get back together?'

'No, but I do miss her. I'd like us to be friends.'

He takes another call. I stare down at my *Aspect*, knowing the moment I hit *Ready*, there'll be someone waiting. Some old man booking a cruise he'll die before he takes, or a crying girl who's dropped her mobile phone and doesn't yet realise she's invalidated her warranty. I don't mind taking the odd call now and again – hell, I've got to do something to break up the day – but the Monday onslaught is really wearing.

Teri enters the office, her short hair freshly washed. I hold my breath as she sets up next to me, worrying that she might be angry about Friday.

'Hi, Teri.'

'Hi, Dan,' she smiles. So that's OK then. I wonder if she still thinks I'm a pervert. 'I watched the end of that film.'

'Really?' I ask, surprised. 'I thought you hated it.'

'No, I hated *The Sex Show*, but the film was interesting. I found it quite bewitching.'

I smile at her, pleased. 'Do you know we've been the subject of speculation?'

She peers at me from beneath her fringe. 'What sort of speculation?'

I hand her Gordon's Log. 'We were witnessed leaving together.'

Teri opens the notebook and balances it on her knees, allowing her to read it without being noticed. I watch her eager eyes quickly look over Adrienne's pages, wondering how she's going to react. There are three likely possibilities:

1. She could be pleased. Although I decided last Friday that she wasn't interested in me, it's not impossible that she was hiding her emotions and is still waiting for an appropriate moment to make a pass.
2. She could be offended. It seems more likely that Teri's offer to let me watch TV at her flat was merely an act of kindness, and she could be upset that her actions have been interpreted in such a gossipy way.
3. She could be nonchalant. Adrienne's aspersion is merely one line in a catalogue of fictive filth, and is much more innocent than the material that surrounds it. If she does react in this way, she's likely to be more perturbed by my bringing it to her attention than by the writing itself.

I look at my watch, wondering if it's too early to risk a trip to the toilet. The team leader hasn't come in yet and if I'm returning from the latrines when she arrives, she'll probably assume I'm late as usual, and I won't get any praise for my early start. Then I look at the number of calls waiting and decide to forgo my pat on the back.

The company toilets are much nicer than my bathroom at home and even knowing that I share these wooden seats with the other thirty-five male posteriors on this floor doesn't spoil my enjoyment. As well as wooden seats, the toilets are also blessed with thick toilet paper, which is a necessity rather than a luxury for a haemorrhoid sufferer like me. Anything less than a velvet two-ply and the sheets will be coated with mustard and blood, and my anus will ache all day.

After relating Teri's terror that I might watch her wee in the street, I'm reluctant to describe the toilet's third special feature, but I can't be the only employee who's tried to use the metal grille between the male and female toilets as a spying hole. The slanted metal plates make it hard to see anything clearly, but do at least allow sound to travel between the two end cubicles. Again, this is an embarrassing confession, but I have to admit that I've always found something exciting about the sound of women performing their bodily functions. It's not that I have any particular interest in either golden or brown showers, but merely that I enjoy the sensation of witnessing something private. On this morning, however, it's not the splash of piss against the pan that comes through the wall, but the less jubilant sound of someone sobbing. I feel more embarrassed eavesdropping on emotion than I do on evacuation, and finish defecating as quickly as possible.

I wash my hands and then hover outside in the corridor, waiting to see who comes out of the ladies. The first two women are receptionists, debating the respective merits of the ISDX and Mitel switchboard systems. Neither of them seems upset, so I continue hiding inside the doorway of Conference Room 2. Minutes later, the team leader emerges, dabbing a screwed-up tissue into the corner of her eyes.

'Hello, Alice.'

She looks startled. 'All right, Dan? How's your dad?'

'He's OK.' I stare at her. 'What about you?'

'Me?' she shrugs. 'I'm fine. Why d'you ask?'

'Your eyes look sore.'

'I'm overtired. And I've got my period. That's why I'm a bit weepy. Don't say anything to the others.'

'Of course not.'

'Thanks, Dan. I'll let you leave early tonight.'

She squeezes my hand. The team leader looks even more like Peppermint Patty than usual, making her sad expression especially heartbreaking. We walk back into the call-centre. I return to my team. Teri's finished the Log and left it in front of my workstation. I look at her mouth, wondering which of my predictions was correct.

'See,' I say to her, 'we'll have to be careful from now on.'

'Mmm,' she says.

Reaction 3, then, nonchalance.

*　　*　　*

The team leader keeps her side of the bargain and lets me leave at four o'clock. I, of course, have no such integrity and immediately betray her confidence, calling Adrienne on the internal line and telling her the team leader's having a breakdown. We spend the rest of the morning debating the probable cause of her tears, deciding it must have something to do with Bryan, the fat bastard management boyfriend.

I head straight over to Dad's hospital, hoping to make up for my previous neglect with a nice long visit. I stop in the Dillons beside the entrance and buy him a couple of computer magazines and a bottle of isotonic Lucozade. Then I go up to Ward Eleven in the second of the three hospital lifts, along with two nurses in green plastic uniforms standing with an old man on a trolley. The nurses rib each other on the way up, joking about a particularly grisly pick-up the night before.

Once again, Dad already has a visitor. It's not the large blonde from last time, but a similarly proportioned redhead with big round breasts and close, thick features. She's wearing blue jeans and a black T-shirt with a sewn-on velour patch in the shape of a sunflower. Dad pulls himself up.

'Hello, Dan. You're in early.'

'Yeah. The team leader's being nice to me.'

'This is Brittany. Brittany, this is my son.'

She stands up, offering her hand. After Valerie's coldness on my previous visit, I'm surprised by the gesture and lean across awkwardly. I try to remember what I know about Brittany. I can think of only two things. She shares an ansaphone with a man named Roger (who, presumably, is her husband) and took Dad to task about his timidity at the first meeting of their secret club. I resolve to go back to the minutes for more information when I get home.

'Where do you work, Dan?' she asks.

'Quick Kall Ltd. The big telephone agency in the town.'

She nods. 'My niece works there.'

'What's her name?'

'Alice.'

'Alice Hargreaves? She's my team leader.'

Dad laughs. 'We know.'

At half past five the nurse comes round with Dad's dinner. I can tell he feels embarrassed about having to eat his spam fritters in front of us, and I get up to leave. Brittany asks me, 'What are you having for dinner, Dan?'

Dad grins. 'He'll be having fish and chips, won't you, son?'

Brittany touches my arm. 'Would you like to have something in the hospital canteen with me?'

I look at Dad's plate. 'Is it anything like what he's having?'

'Oh no,' Dad says, 'you have to live here to qualify for food as bad as this.'

Brittany takes her jacket from around the back of her plastic chair and leans across to kiss Dad on the forehead. I take her chair and stack it on top of mine, carrying the two across to the pile in the corner. Dad thanks me for the magazines and nervously eyes his dinner, as if wondering whether he's up to the task of eating it.

'Bye, Dad.'

'Bye, Dan. Have fun with Brittany.'

She laughs. 'Don't worry. I'll let him go in one piece.'

The walls of the canteen are painted canary yellow, with a white dado rail and a wooden partition separating the eating area from the reception and accident ward. The partition is made up of small white cubes that drain the light and make the canteen look like the dingy set of some Australian soap. Most people hate hospitals, but now I've got used to Dad being here, I quite enjoy their flattened drama. I especially like the little kiosk just inside the entrance which competes with the Dillons by offering more traditional hospital reading material like *Puzzlers* and romantic novels.

Brittany hands me a tray and we push them round the curved circuit until we reach the hot food and cold drinks. I have a bacon sandwich with thick yellow chips. Brittany plumps for cottage pie.

We sit at a table in the far corner, two rows away from all the other friends and relatives. Brittany rests her handbag against the wall and stares straight at me.

'I feel at a bit of a disadvantage,' I tell her, 'you know my father and my team leader, and I don't know anything about you.'

'Really?' she asks, sounding sceptical.

'Don't you believe me?'

'I was just wondering how you knew to leave me a message.'

'Dad told me. But that was the first time he's mentioned you. Before he went into hospital, I didn't know you existed. Any of you.'

'Any of who?'

'The secret seven. The people in your club.'

She chuckles. 'He didn't mention us?'

'No. I still don't know exactly who you are.'

'We're your dad's friends.' She let the statement hang for a moment. 'What d'you think of Alice?'

'She's OK. I don't have much contact with her.'

'She likes you. She told me she had a problem with your team recently and you were very helpful.'

I blanch, wondering if this is a rebuke. I also realise that this is a chance to set the record straight. If I tell Brittany that I asked Teri to make a call to one of their seven members, she could talk to the team leader and ensure she doesn't get sacked. But if management really are dead set on bringing the team down from five members to four, they'd still have to get rid of one of us, and I'm not ready to risk my job.

Brittany releases my gaze and looks back down to her cottage pie. Her comment was definitely a test, but it's hard to tell whether I've passed or failed. It's like one of those *Choose Your Own Adventure* books, only I don't know which door I've gone through and can't flip back a few pages if I change my mind. Her silence doesn't seem particularly damning. It's more like my cowardice has made me complicit in whatever they're doing. This sense is increased when she asks, 'What are you doing on Friday?'

'I don't know yet.'

'Can you keep it free?'

'I expect so. Why?'

She opens her handbag and takes out a small piece of white card and a Waterman's fountain pen. 'Do you still have my number?'

I shake my head. She writes it down for me.

'Call me and I'll arrange for someone to pick you up.'

After the meal, Brittany drives me home. She doesn't talk much, except to ask me directions. I feel reassured that she doesn't know where I live, especially as I'd been worrying that Dad had been bringing these women home when I was out with Ian. I get her to drop me two streets away from my room. She hesitates before pulling my door closed, and I worry that she expects to be invited in. Then she toots the horn and drives away.

I walk through the streets and down the lane to the metal staircase, mentally preparing myself for whatever fresh horror I might find in my room. But Kevin's still out, and I've got the space to myself. I put a compilation tape in the stereo and go to the bathroom to fish out Dad's minutes from the base of the broken shower unit. Then I lie back on my bed while I look for my place. I re-read Valerie's suggestion that *there are some stories better received by a prurient ear than a sympathetic one* and pick up the account with Dad's reply:

ST: But isn't that a bit like saying paedophiles make the best baby-sitters?

[Group laughter.]

IJ: I think the most important difference, and it's something we haven't talked about so far, is trust.

[Murmurs of assent.]

MS: I couldn't agree more. We wouldn't have been able

89

to reach the stage we're at now if we didn't completely trust one another. [To ST] I think your concerns about being appointed chairman of this group are a result of you not quite believing how much the rest of us trust you. You're scared, quite rightly, about the power you've been given. But if this group is going to mean anything, you must get beyond that fear and learn how to lead us. What is it that scares you? I don't think you're worried about not being up to the task. I think you're worried about the social implications of taking an authoritative role.

CG: Every cult needs its Manson.

[Laughter.]

ST: Going back to what you were saying about trust: most of the groups I've belonged to before have begun with some sort of trust-exercise. The obvious one is the trust-fall, where each person takes it in turns to climb onto a wall or table and then drops backward, falling into the arms of the rest of the group.

IJ: That sort of exercise has never worked for me.

BC: The problem with trust-falls is the assumption that trusting someone physically is the same thing as trusting them mentally. Almost everybody here already has someone they trust physically. What we don't have – and this is why we need this support group, therapy session, whatever you want to call it – is someone we trust mentally. So clearly what's needed is a mental trust-fall.

IJ: Go on.

BC: Well, I think the best kind of bonding exercise would be if we all confessed a secret to the group.

CG: I'll show you mine if you show me yours?

BC: Exactly.

I drop the notebook and hunt in the bedside drawer for some paper and a pen. Whatever purpose these revelations served for the group (and I'd find that out in due course), they would provide me with a quick way of differentiating between the seven women. Once I'd noted these secrets, I wouldn't need to keep flipping back to work out the character of each speaker.

I feel glad the minute-taker has used initials instead of Christian names. Somehow they seem more evocative, the shorthand compressing secret energy. Although I knew V stands for Valerie and B for Brittany, I'd forgotten the other names on Dad's list and base my mental picture on the appearance of their initials. The high uprights of IJ suggest someone classy, and my impression of her is also coloured by her elegant quotation of De Sade and the fact that she'd taken and transcribed the minutes. Reading them without knowing most of the speakers, there seems a false uniformity in the women's recorded words, as if their speech-patterns are struggling against the regulating force of her pen. I quickly flip through the book and discover that each meeting's minutes are taken by a different member of the group. I make a mental note to check the consistency of their transcribed conversations.

DT had yet to speak, but shares the same initials as me. Although I know this is a meaningless connection, I nevertheless felt unnerved when I saw them on page one (especially coming straight after Dad's). When I was a teenager he used to call me DT, although lately he's switched back to Dan. He used to joke about it, saying with those initials I just had to become an alcoholic.

MS makes me think of manuscript, and *Marks and Spencer*. And S and M, although the reversed order suggests a preference for receiving pain rather than inflicting it. It also makes me wonder about a possible sexual explanation for this grouping.

VD and BC I've already met, and that the former shares her initials with a sexual disease seems perfectly appropriate. LC sounds like a name itself [*el-sie*], and, finally, the double curves of CG bring to mind a middle-aged woman with a particularly saggy stomach.

I lie back on the bed with my spare paper placed next to the notebook. The women's revelations are sincere enough to make me guilty about reading this record, and I hesitate before summarising them. Nevertheless:

IJ: Bisexual, so far only in theory.
MS: Prone to fits of irrational anger. Once slammed daughter's hand in car door.
CG: Victim-complex. Two failed marriages, both to violent men.
LC: Abused as child.
VD: Abused others as child.
DT: Recovering alcoholic (of course!).
BC: Promiscuous, usually with married men.

Brittany was the last woman to offer her secret, which seemed surprising given her extrovert behaviour earlier this evening. Perhaps she was waiting for the others to speak first, not wanting a quieter woman to clam up because the others were staring at her. Or perhaps she was acting in the hospital, unafraid of me because I was Dad's son. But the most appealing possibility is that belonging to Dad's group has restored her confidence. Considering this alternative, I feel an unusual sense of loyalty towards my father, and hope I'm not overestimating him.

Brittany's revelation ends at the bottom of the right-hand page, so that if I want to read Dad's secret I'll have to turn over. Instead of doing this, I sit up and look at my watch. It's eight thirty. It's stupid, but I don't want Kevin to discover me reading this book. Maybe I should put it away now. My throat feels dry so I go to the kitchen for a glass of water. I know I'm stalling, but I'm not sure why. I thought I'd stopped feeling squeamish about Dad's life a long time ago, and any residual timidity should have disappeared when I directed his penis into a plastic pot. It'll probably be something about gambling, or betraying Mum, or being betrayed by Mum. I'm only nervous because this book seems like a diary. I'm sure Dad's diary would be full of things I couldn't cope with, but everything in this account has been confessed in front of his seven strangers. In spite of Dad's unusual openness, I'm sure he'd only say things that wouldn't prevent the others from liking him, especially at this first meeting. No, I'm being stupid. It'll be fine.

I quickly down my glass of brown water and pour another to take back with me. I've decided I'll just read Dad's secret and then call it quits for the night, maybe watch some TV. I walk back to the room and pick up the minutes. This is what I read:

ST: I suppose my guiltiest secret is that I harbour homicidal feelings towards my son.

VD: How do these feelings manifest themselves?

ST: In dreams, mainly, although I sometimes have these scary moments where we're talking or arguing and I picture myself calmly snuffing the life out of him.

VD: Are these moments of anger?

ST: Not exactly. I mean, it's not like I get exasperated with Dan and then want to murder him. It's more that – this will sound stupid – it feels like my right.

VD: Your right?

ST: Like a primitive, intuitive sense of what I ought to be able to do. It's as if killing him wouldn't be murder. As if my duty as a father includes the question of whether or not he should be allowed to live.

VD: And you think he shouldn't?

ST: [Shaking his head.] No, it's not that. I think he should acknowledge that he goes on living at my discretion. I don't think we have a normal father-and-son relationship. For a start, we still live together.

IJ: In the family home?

ST: No, we share a flat.

LC: Then perhaps that's what lies behind your feelings. You want him to stop restricting your life.

ST: But I sought him out. He'd already established his independence. He only agreed to live with me out of pity.

IJ: So you don't think he respects you?

ST: [Emotional.] How could he?

I close the minutes and drop them into my bedside drawer. I feel shaken by Dad's revelation, but not as scared as I might be. Dad's always been melodramatic, and I'm less surprised that he's felt these urges than that they've troubled him. He's always bringing life down to basics, and picked up more than one volume of Freud during his Pelican-purchasing phase. The only disturbing thing about this passage was the way he described killing me. *Calmly snuffing the life out of him*. It just didn't sound like Dad, which could mean one of three things:

1. Dad's original choice of words has been changed by IJ.
2. Dad was deliberately striving to shock his listeners.
3. Dad was serious about this.

Well, at least I wasn't in any immediate danger. And if he came near me in the next six months I'd kick his hobbled leg and knock him over. That didn't rule out the possibility of poison, but I knew that if he did decide to kill me he'd want to do it with his bare hands.

The compilation tape has finished while I've been reading and I feel unnerved by the silence. I turn on the television and flip through the Cable. There's a Chevy Chase film on Sky Movies. I don't feel up to anything heavy after tonight's revelation, and although the film's not that funny, it's diverting enough to hold my attention.

The film turns out to be *Funny Farm*, the first of the three movies making up Sky's 'Chevy Chase Evening'. As soon as it finishes, I flip to the Movie Channel for *Memoirs of an Invisible Man*. The title seems familiar, and after a brief mental file-search, I remember buying the HF Saint novel the film's based on when it came out some time in the late eighties. I bought it from a supermarket, although I don't know why that memory should feel significant. I remember looking forward to reading it, expecting the kind of intelligent sci-fi I like best, and then giving up after twenty pages. I mentioned earlier how rare it is for me to leave a story unfinished, but I didn't get far enough into this one for the narrative to grip.

I've long since banished my copy to a car-boot sale so I can't check, but as far as I can recall, I stopped reading because the narrator followed a semi-graphic sex scene by stating that this would be the only such interlude in the entire novel. I remember being impressed by the author's bravado, and interpreting this section as both a dare to the reader and a boast about the remainder of the book. This story is so interesting, he seemed to suggest, that it doesn't need sex. Maybe if I was reading it now I'd take up the challenge, but as an adolescent I tended to read books for the sex scenes, and four hundred pages seemed an unnecessary slog.

There's no such meta-narrative play in the movie, and if the story of the film's anything like the book (which I somehow doubt), I think I made the right decision first time round. As the film's credits play out, the programme announcer instructs me to change to Sky Gold for *National Lampoon's European Vacation*, which rounds off tonight's bill. I've seen the film before – it's a favourite of my mother's – but it seems like a good way of sending myself to sleep.

Ten minutes into the movie, I hear Kevin fiddling with the dropped lock. There's something peculiar about his gait as he swaggers up to my bed, as if he's impersonating a drunken old man. His bland features lend themselves to ugly distortion, and as he reaches my bed he drops down in front of me and screws up the left hand side of his face into an ugly leer. He pauses, then does it again. I wonder if he's in pain.

'What's wrong?'

'Nothing. I'm giving you the wink.'

'What wink?'

'The woman wink.'

'I don't understand.'

'Let me lay it out for you. I've brought someone back with me.'

'And?'

'And I'd like some privacy, if you don't mind.'

'You want me to go out?'

'That's the general idea. I won't be long. Give me thirty minutes.'

I find my shoes and leave him to it. I see the woman on my way out, waiting in the corridor. She's more attractive than I'd anticipated, a tall, skinny teenager with an Alanis Morissette hairdo. She smiles at me and I nod back, feeling sorry for her. Kevin ushers her into our room and I head out into the night, wondering how on earth I'll manage to wake up for work tomorrow.

8

My body-clock's fucked. Ask anyone else about their best time of day and they'll have an immediate answer. Morning, say, or last thing at night. I wake up run-down and gradually get more exhausted. Someone once tried to explain to me about sleep-cycles and REM. It sounded like the biology of a superior alien race.

The girl had gone when I got back last night. Kevin was snoring, so I didn't have to suffer the post-game discussion. I lay awake until two thirty then fell asleep to dreams of being murdered by Chevy Chase. In the dream he scalps and decapitates me, before playing bongoes on my bleeding brain, like the Paul Simon video. I wake up every hour from five onwards, finally deciding I'm not going to get any more sleep when it reaches eight. I lie in bed a few minutes longer, deciding which tie to wear, then bring my feet down onto the floor.

I immediately feel something slippery beneath the sole of my left foot. Anxious, I swing it up onto my right knee and reach down to peel off a twisted yellow prophylactic, tied at the top and heavy with spunk. Only my empty stomach stops me from throwing up.

I rush to the bathroom and tear off a long strip of toilet paper, enough to wrap the condom three times over. I make a tissue glove out of it and pick up Kevin's collected seed from the floor. I feel a strong urge to creep across to his bed and toss the joey-bag into the open hole of his snoring mouth. Instead, I dart back to the toilet and flush it away, feeling even more disgusted than when Dad accidentally pissed on me. I wash my hands six times, running the soap down the inside of every digit.

I catch the bus that gets me in early, not wanting to be around when Kevin wakes up. I wonder whether he'll be angry that I threw the condom away (I don't know – maybe he collects them), then decide I don't care. It takes a lot to disgust me, but I've been thoroughly tested recently. God knows how I'll cope if I ever have a child.

I reopen *Hypnosis: Fact and Fiction* at the second stop. After the derisive looks I got yesterday, I'm more discreet with the battered blue volume, holding the open book against my legs to hide the cover. I start reading at the end of Chapter Three with *The Question of Shamming*, a section that somehow quickly segues into an impenetrable anecdote about scrotal tumours and cutting up patients. If this book really has influenced my dad's philosophy, I dread to think what'll come up in the rest of the minutes.

When I was very young, and knew nothing about mortgage repayments, losing streaks or marital strife, I used to ascribe the changes in my dad's mood to his choice of clothes. I'd wait on the landing while he changed after work, praying he'd choose the blue track-suit top or the cream lambswool sweater instead of the black V-neck. For years I've related this anecdote as an example of childish whimsy, but I don't think I was so far off the mark. He did wear lambswool when he was happy, and the V-neck when he felt too down to make an effort. Maybe I should strive to regain those lost powers of observation. Baby Dan would've known his father wanted to kill him.

*   *   *

Adrienne and Ian are already in the office when I arrive. She's talking to a Hank Marvin lookalike with red-framed glasses and grey hair. He's the mobile-phone rep, which means it's a mobile-phone morning. We have one of these a month, most of which I've managed to sleep through.

Mobile phones are Adrienne's speciality, and she knows as much about them as Gordon does about Car Insurance, or Teri does about record distribution. Ian and I don't really have a specialism, although I once made a half-hearted attempt to read up about Cruises. I'll settle for being a nondescript fifth columnist, waiting in terror for the day my team-mates discover my disloyalty.

Speaking of which, Teri looks angelic today. She's wearing a blue top with thin white stripes, the minature pattern perfectly emphasising her small, well-formed body. Her top's matched with a short blue suede skirt and dark tights. I don't know whether it's got anything to do with mobile-phone morning, but she's clearly stretching the limits of acceptable office clothing. Three tables away, the team leader no doubt adds *unsuitable dress* to her *Dismissing Teri* file. Teri's make-up is more blatant than usual, the electric-blue eyeshadow probably a kitsch joke. I smile at her, thinking how much I'll miss her when she's sacked.

Adrienne takes Teri's arm and introduces her to the phone rep. She introduces us every month, but he forgets our name as quickly as we forget his. From my desk, I can make out the usual routine. Feigned recognition, followed by relief as names are given. He shakes her hand vigorously, pumping it up and down at least five times.

They follow Teri across to our table, and Adrienne smiles at me as she asks the rep, 'You remember Dan, don't you, John?'

John. Of course. Everyone's called John. He smiles at me as he shakes my hand. On every mobile morning I have to restrain myself from asking John about the frequency myth. The frequency myth (for those of you not up-to-date on your conspiracy theories) is that there are certain combinations of digits which cannot be used for mobile-phone numbers because the army needs to keep these frequencies free so that handsets can be adapted for walkie-talkies in the event of a nuclear war. It doesn't make perfect sense, I agree, but it's still a compelling idea. Perhaps it's a deliberate piece of disinformation designed to smoke out potential traitors. If so, I'd like to state my allegiance to this country and my absolute hatred of left-wing fanatics (or right-wing fanatics, depending on who's doing the witch-hunt). I'm not sure whether it's fear of surveillance that stops me putting this question to John or simply my reluctance to surrender the story. Either way, there's no reason why he'd tell me the truth.

During the early part of the morning everyone's distracted, waiting for the moment when we're called into Conference Room 2. A mobile morning means coffee and biscuits, and every month we embarrass the team leader by eating and drinking as much as we can, cramming our mouths full of digestives and washing them away with at least three mugs of coffee. John overlooks our gluttony, perhaps unprepared to acknowledge how much our working conditions improve during the thirty minutes we spend in his company, but Alice always scowls at us, especially when Teri starts banging the biscuit plate.

Today's briefing begins with John plugging his laptop into the unused PC in the corner of the conference room. This procedure always lasts at least five minutes, long enough for us to get stuck into the biscuits and pour our first round of coffee. The woman who brings the refreshments is eyed with suspicion. She, after all, gets to come in here every day, and no doubt scoffs any leftovers. We suspect her of hiding the biscuits, and if we weren't being watched we'd hold her down and search her pockets for hidden Hobnobs.

As soon as he's loaded up, John talks us through a series of predesigned digital pages, each marked with the logo of his company. For a corporate rep, John has a surprisingly relaxed attitude towards his rivals, and once even confessed that he himself prefers a competitor's phone. He carries this handset on his belt, away from the company models he keeps in his briefcase and now arranges on the desk in front of us.

This month's topic is protecting caller privacy, a subject which excites John more than any he's addressed previously. He quickly drops into espionage mode, inventing a hypothetical character who wishes to conduct concurrent relationships with several mistresses. He begins with the innovations of *141* and *1471* (and its sexier American equivalent, *Star 69*), but soon moves on to call-screening, identity numbers and the projected progress of call-surveillance over land-lines, where no-number Nigels are exposed with the unambiguous message that '*the last person who called you withheld their number*'. He ends with a few thoughts about 'phone-cloning' and a joke about aural sex. Not a bad performance, all in all, but it's hard to see how it relates to our work in the call-centre. Perhaps he felt sorry for us and decided to enliven our day.

Adrienne waits behind as we file out of the Conference Room. The team leader's always been jealous of Adrienne's relationship with John, especially as she'd only been put in charge of mobiles because Alice didn't want to do it. I drag my feet on the way back to my desk, then decide to take my break earlier than usual and maintain my relaxed mood for a further fifteen minutes.

It doesn't usually occur to me because I like sitting with the others, but it is permissible to have two breaks consecutively, getting out of the office for a blissful thirty minutes. I start walking with this possibility in the back of my mind, telling myself I needn't feel rushed. Elation sweeps through me as I stride past the breaks room, as if I've just handed in my notice and don't have to worry about ever returning.

I've never been able to accept that I'll remain working at Quick Kall for the foreseeable future. It's not that I'm ambitious (one of the most relaxing things about my job is that there's no danger of career advancement), but there's supposed to be a fifty per cent staff turnover every year, and I've never seen myself as the kind of employee they'd want to keep on.

There's also a prevailing sense of transience about the call-centre itself. The artificial atmosphere makes me feel like I'm in an underground bunker after a nuclear war, and like any of the survivors, I could submit to radiation poisoning any day. I suppose I feel expendable, a character only introduced into a narrative as a potential death interest.

I walk towards the Centre, looking for a pet shop. I thought I knew the exact location of one, but when I get there it turns out to have been replaced by an estate agent. I go in anyway, and the woman inside gives me directions to the relocated shop.

The new premises are twice as big as the previous building, with two large glass windows displaying an array of hamster balls, doggy chews and tropical fish. Pet shops always seem slightly outdated, as if keeping animals was a seventies obsession that now only appeals to smelly old ladies. I tap the glass front of a couple of aquariums, prompting the fish to blow bubble kisses at me. I take a quick peek at the baby rabbits, and head to the counter.

'I'm looking for a cat basket,' I tell the assistant, a short grey-haired man in a burgundy jacket.

'Which sort?'

'I don't know.'

'Well, our most popular model is the Apollo 2000, but I wouldn't necessarily recommend it. Are you taking the cat far?'

'Not really.'

'Travelling by car?'

'Bus.'

'Is it a big cat?'

'Yes, a fat ginger tom.'

He nods, his mouth contemplative. 'Do you think it'll be happy to go into the basket?'

I don't answer, picturing myself chasing the cat around Farnell's backyard and wondering whether this is such a good idea. The assistant bends down behind the counter and brings two baskets up for my inspection. He points to the first one, a brown plastic hexagon which looks best suited to propelling an animal into space.

'The main problem with the Apollo,' he tells me, 'is that the only way into the basket is through this square door at the front. That means you have to pick the cat up and squash him inside, but once he's in, there's no danger of him getting out. If you think getting him in's going to be difficult, then you might want to try the Spaceglider 5, which is shaped like a trap with two sliding panels at the front and back. You slide the panels up and put the cat's favourite cushion in the box and wait for him to go after it. Then, once he's in, you snap down the panels and catch him.'

'So you'd recommend the Spaceglider?'

'Well, I would if you were going by car, but the panels are only held in place by two small metal pins that can easily be dislodged. And if you knock the cage when you're getting off the bus, he'll be out the door and never seen again. What you really want is a combination of the two, which, unfortunately, doesn't exist.'

'What's the difference in price?' I ask, desperate to find grounds for a decision.

'Very little. The Apollo's fifteen ninety-nine, the Spaceglider's seventeen.'

'I'll take the Apollo,' I tell him.

He nods. 'Good choice.'

I hide the cat basket in the employees' cloakroom. It's too big for my locker so I store it beneath a pile of abandoned coats. There always seems to be a pile of unclaimed coats in the cloakroom, parting gifts to the company from absent-minded temps. I check a torn parka for thickness, wondering whether it'll make a good pillow.

I go back to log on, then walk across to the square behind reception. Alice is staring at a sheaf of printed paper, rubbing her forehead. That's another good thing about being management: freedom from the glare of a work-station.

She jumps when she notices me. 'Yes?'

'Have you filled out the timesheets yet?'

'Most of them. Why?'

'I wanted to take on some extra hours.'

'The weekend's still free.'

'OK, I'll take that, and put me down for the next few weeks as well.'

She makes a note. 'Anything else?'

'What about evenings?'

'When?'

'The late shift.'

'Which night?'

'All of them. Until further notice.'

She puts down her pen. 'Is money really that tight?'

Her face shows genuine concern. This isn't team-leader behaviour. One of management's guiding principles is to encourage every employee to work to the limits of their ability. You can do anything to achieve this. Speed-freaks, for example, should be given shifts on Sunday morning, when they've yet to come down and see the job as fun. Single parents, meanwhile, should be handed out Pro-Plus and guilt-tripped into working double-shifts. Surprised by her sympathy, I decide to try my luck: 'I met your auntie last night.'

She nods. 'I know.'

'How?'

'She called me last night. Told me to look after you.'

I feel nervous again, worried that her concerned tone isn't proof of a change of character, but instead a prelude to sacking me. Perhaps she is acting like management, after all, only following rule number two: as soon as someone starts to slip, send them home.

'I can handle it, Alice.'

'It's a lot of hours. Even the best operators can only manage three evenings a week.'

I decide to change tack. 'Can I be honest with you?'

'Of course.'

'I don't like being alone.'

'What?'

'I told you before that I live with my dad. It isn't an ideal situation . . .'

She smiles. 'You don't need to explain. I share a house with my mother.'

'Then you'll know what I mean. You hate them when they're getting under your feet, but the moment they're gone . . .'

She nods. 'So working nights would suit you?'

'It wouldn't seem like work, to be honest. I sit at home most nights wishing I had something to do.'

'What about The Pentangle?'

'What about it?'

'I thought you spent your nights there.'

I sense an opportunity. 'Well, you know what Adrienne's like.'

Her lips hesitate, and she says, 'I'm not sure I catch your meaning.'

'You've been there. Is it the sort of place you'd miss? I only go there because of Adrienne and Ian. Working late would be a perfect excuse. Besides, it's such a waste of money.'

'OK,' she says, 'I'll pencil you in, but you must tell me the moment it gets too much.'

I nod, and we sit in silence. I know I should return to my desk, but I'm feeling confident today and decide to try one last probe: 'Alice, I know this is none of my business, but is everything OK with you?'

'Of course. Why?'

'You seemed a little upset yesterday.'

Her mouth sets firm. 'I told you what was wrong. It's stress, that's all. No big deal.'

'OK,' I retreat, 'sorry.'

I stand up. I'm about to walk away when she looks up, her eyes moist again.

'I'm not an ogre,' she says. 'I know you lot think I'm a bitch, but I'm not completely insensitive.'

I nod, too intimidated to speak.

'And Dan, one more thing . . .'

'Yes?'

'I've been monitoring your calls and you're still not doing the salutation properly. If you don't sort it out today, you'll get a formal warning.'

Ian holds my gaze as I return across the call-centre. The constant monitoring and call-testing creates an ever present paranoia in the office, and I can't help thinking that he's heard my conversation with Alice. Betraying Teri has separated me from Ian, as if I'm already preparing myself for the moment when he doesn't want to be friends any more. I haven't really thought about it before now, but I suppose there are greater dangers than mere loss of friendship. Ian's temper is evident from his past, and I know how strongly he feels about Teri. Maybe my general worries about mortality hide a more localised fear of my best friend.

'Where did you get to?' he asks me.

'I had some errands. You going tonight?'

'Of course. You?'

'Yeah, but I might be a bit late. I've got some stuff to sort out.'

'Meet you there then?'

'Fine.'

I plug back in and field a couple of calls. The callers are both old ladies, moaning about being given the runaround. I understand their anger, but feel no special urge to help them. Since I've started working here, I've tried to avoid phoning any help-lines myself. It's stupid, but knowing there's someone like me on the other end makes me even more exasperated, and I end up sounding like one of the pointlessly irate callers we put on the speaker-phone for the whole team to laugh at.

Whenever I feel particularly disenchanted with my job, I always start picturing miners. I'm not sure why. Maybe because all their ailments were caused by the strenuousness of their working lives, and ours will be the result of our lack of activity. Instead of bow legs, we'll have sprained wrists. Miners were crushed by coal. We're crushed by boredom. They had low ceilings, we have low expectations. And when we're replaced by robots, no doubt we'll prove just as reluctant to surrender our burden.

I finish at six. The first bus back goes at seven minutes past. It takes approximately ten minutes to get to the stop. You do the maths while I run. The cat basket is a new hindrance, bashing against my thighs as I leg it up the road. Usually you can allow for a couple of extra minutes after the designated departure time, but during rush hour the buses fill quickly and the drivers are impatient to get going. Fortunately, the women from the NatWest building delay the bus long enough for me to jump on. The driver has short hair and a droopy brown moustache. He points at my basket.

'Is that a gremlin in there?'

'No,' I tell him, 'it's empty.'

'Good job too. We don't want it getting out and eating the other passengers.'

I ignore his *non sequitur* and give him my ticket. He punches a hole and hands it back. I head for the upper deck, knowing that if I stay here I'll be harassed by senior citizens and tired mothers, losing my seat by, at best, the third stop.

The tom, of course, is nowhere to be seen. I suppose I could leave this until tomorrow morning, but if I'm out late tonight I won't want to wake up early. I stopped at the chip shop and bought an extra fish for the cat, asking the owners to leave his without batter. After fifteen minutes of waving the cod and making cat sounds, I decide to leave it on the plate and hope he shows up later.

I eat my dinner off the paper in the kitchen, then return to my room to pack my rucksack. I've decided to take as little as possible, not wanting Kevin to notice I've gone. Originally I'd considered leaving a note saying I'd gone on holiday, but it seems safer to let him imagine that I might return at any time. I want to make sure my rucksack doesn't look too suspicious if anyone comes across it in the cloakroom. A lot of the young men in the call-centre are sporty types, and no one would be surprised by a bag of clothes, but they might start worrying if they find out I'm bringing all my possessions to work every day.

Books seem important. I'm sure I'll have trouble sleeping in the office, especially during the first few nights, and I want something good to fill the dead time. I've already packed *Political Ideas, Man and the Vertebrates*, and the two volumes of minutes, but I still feel unprepared. I suppose I could always sneak off to the bookshop in one of my breaks.

I'm taking all my work clothes and a couple of hangers, which should see me through until I can persuade Adrienne to do a couple of loads. The stereo, I suppose, will have to stay, but it's going to be hard getting by without music. My decision what to take is made more difficult by my expectation that anything I leave behind will immediately become the property of either Kevin or Mr Farnell, but this doesn't seem a foolish assumption given the characters of the two men. Dad's going to be angry but I can hardly manage his stuff as well. Besides, the only valuable items are the TV, video and computer, and I've already tipped all of his disks into the bottom of my bag.

I grab a last few essentials from the bathroom (toothpaste, soap, razor) and zip up my bag. I've rarely had to pack for longer than a weekend, and can't believe I won't be coming back in a week or so. Maybe I'm just getting ready to forgive myself if I chicken out.

I leave my packed bag in the second of the three empty rooms. It seems ridiculous that I can't just move into here, but I'd never be able to afford the extra rent, and I'm sure if I changed rooms without paying, Mr Farnell would instruct Kevin to break my legs.

I change my shirt and count my money, even though I can remember exactly how little I've got. It's been rumoured that as well as taking on all manner of domestic duties, Adrienne also arranges personal loans. Before now I've always felt too scared about her rate of return to apply for one, but my decision to move into the office has made me feel reckless and I think I might ask her for an application form. I like the idea of getting a lump sum. It seems like a good way of measuring time. At least I no longer have to worry about the rent.

I hold my breath as I open the door, praying the tom has been drawn by the scent of his unexpected dinner. Amazingly, he's there, already about halfway through the grey fillet. I hide the basket behind me as I tiptoe down the steps. When I reach the bottom he stops eating and looks up at me. I smile back, hoping he's forgotten what happened last time he came inside my room. I pretend I'm uninterested in him, walking past the dish and continuing out into the lane. He keeps watching until he's sure I'm gone, then goes back to his fish. I seize my chance and run up behind him, grabbing both sides of his fat belly and swinging him up into the air. He remains remarkably placid, even when I tip the Apollo 2000 up on its side and squash him through the too-small square. By the time he freaks out he's already safely locked inside, allowing me to harmlessly transport him back up the stairs and into the empty room. I presume he'll be OK there until I get back from The Pentangle. I pat the top of the cage and leave him alone.

One of the many advantages of moving to the Centre is that I'll no longer have to catch the bus. I must spend at least an hour a day travelling those same five miles – even longer if I return in the evening. I may not yet know every driver's name but I know all their faces, the days they work, and even when one is covering another's shift. The roads between my room and the Centre form one long straight line, and it seems unsurprising that Dad had his accident exactly halfway along it. I'm sure it's significant that him going to hospital was the first event in the chain that's led to me leaving home, and as I ride down to the Centre for the penultimate time I feel scared, worried that the road will prove reluctant to let me go.

The bus completes its journey without incident, and I pop into the pub by the last stop for a quick drink. It's a thin, artificial-looking bar, only wide enough for one row of tables before the exterior wall.

It's still a little early for the club, and I eke out my pint for over an hour. I tell myself that I ought to get used to this, as when I move into the office I'll have lots of empty hours to fill. I've never had a problem with solitude, but I'm not very good at judging how long it takes to do things. More often than not I arrive at places early, unable to stay in when I've got a rendezvous.

I feel light-headed as I walk to The Pentangle, partly from the drink but mainly from anticipation of the adventure that awaits me tomorrow. It seems paradoxical that this feeling usually strikes people when they're escaping from work and for me it's exactly the opposite. For the first time in ages, I feel I'm fulfilling the life I imagined for myself as a child, staring at billboards and picturing the freedom that a clerical life might bring. Moving into Quick Call feels like staying up all night, or eating five hundred penny chews. An exciting idiocy, an act of immature recklessness. And definitive proof that I am my parents' son, finding a new way to satisfy the appetite for excitement that prompted their years of gambling and one-day-at-a-time philosophy.

I sit in my usual seat and wait for Ian. Adrienne's building up slowly tonight, mixing heavy guitar tracks with ambient dance. It's much more exciting than her usual set, and I'm particularly impressed with the smooth way she mixes Spaceman 3's 'Revolution' into early Aphex Twin.

She spots me staring at her, and trades places with her deputy. Freed from her decks, she smiles at me and walks across to my table. She looks unusually coy, tilting her head to one side as she asks, 'No Ian tonight?'

'Not yet,' I tell her, 'but he's definitely coming.'

She nods, and sits down. 'Any new gossip on Alice?'

'Not really. I tried challenging her today but she wriggled out of it. She definitely feels intimidated by us. Especially you.'

'Me?' Adrienne asks, her face pleased. 'Why do I intimidate her?'

'Because you've got a life outside work, and you don't give

a shit. She can't understand how she's ended up as the school swot.'

She laughs. 'Poor cow. Do you think it's got anything to do with the boyfriend?'

'Probably. It must be hard convincing him she's interested.'

'Oh stop it. You've almost got me feeling sorry for her.'

Ian arrives late, and remains distant throughout the evening. I want to tell him my secret, but still don't know how he's going to react when he finds out what I've done to Teri, and I don't want to give him any way of helping her get even with me. So our conversation is even more limited than usual and I leave soon after midnight.

I decide to indulge in a taxi, telling myself I'll make up for the cost with all my saved bus fares. I make the driver stop before the start of the lane, remembering Mr Farnell's serious face as he instructed me never to block the entrance to his house any time of the day or night.

I listen for the tom as I unlock the door, expecting to hear his pained howls. But the room is silent and when I bring my face down to his cage his furry body remains motionless. Worried, I release the metal catch and bring him out, pleased to see his heart's still beating beneath his ginger fur. Relief quickly turns into anger as I notice the light brown lumps sticking to his fur and now smearing onto my hands. I gag on the sour stench of catshit and hold the cage at arm's length. The tom jumps from my grasp and lands with a comically abrupt meow, sounding like a stepped-on squeaky toy. Sensing my annoyance, he retreats to the far corner to lick himself. I look at my watch and then back at his cage, not feeling up to cleaning it but aware time will be tight tomorrow. Sighing, I decide it has to be done and take the carrying case to the kitchen. Kevin's washing-up floats in a slimy film at the top of the plastic bowl. I feel an evil impulse to clean out the cage on top of it. But I couldn't cope with the guilt of poisoning him (even if it would solve the problem of my living arrangements). So I lift the bowl onto the draining board and run hot water into the back of the cage. The thin slots allow the brown goo to run out into the sink and I use my washing brush to break up the big lumps before burying it in the bin afterwards. When I'm certain it's clean I give it a final swill with washing-up liquid and disinfectant, knowing I'll never get the cat into work if the smell gives him away.

I put the scrubbed cage back with the cat and quickly clean his fur with a short length of toilet paper. I can't believe I'm doing this for an animal, but now I've invested in the Apollo and cleaned up his crap, I feel more committed than ever. I've never cared for cats before, but something about this tom touches me. I pat his cage and turn out the light, hearing myself tell him, 'Sleep well. It's a big day tomorrow.'

9

Before I leave my room for the final time, I force myself to stare at Kevin's sleeping face, just in case I'm tempted to return. Nothing about him changes my mind, so I pick up my bag and head to the spare room to collect the cat. He seems to have decided it's safer with me than Kevin and rubs himself against my arm as I push his head inside the cage. I swing my rucksack over my shoulder and bend down to pick him up.

I'm carrying the cat basket down the metal steps when I remember something I thought of in bed last night. I know enough about my mind to trust it sometimes, which was why I'd prepared slightly earlier than necessary, giving my brain time to double-check everything. I rest the basket on the ground and run across to Mr Farnell's garage. Then I put his torch in my rucksack and say goodbye to my home for ever.

The tom doesn't trouble me until I get on the bus, when he wakes up and starts butting the cage. The driver seems untroubled by the clanking box and I sit at the back of the lower deck, positioning the tom on the facing seat. The other passengers keep glancing at me and I know they're asking themselves why I'm taking my pet to work. A tall blonde woman smiles at me and I wonder whether the cat will work like a baby, drawing continous female interest. But it's the only attention I get all the way to the Centre, and I have to content myself with watching the tom scrabble desperately every time the bus hits a bump.

My first stop is the pet shop, where the grey-haired man anxiously eyes the cat basket.

'Something wrong with the Apollo?' he asks.

'Only the passenger.' I lift the tom onto the counter. 'He's got a day to kill and nowhere to go.'

'I see.'

The shop-owner looks suspicious. I decide to play it straight.

'I'm taking him to the vet's after work and I've got nowhere to store him. Any chance he could spend the day here. I'll pay you.'

He tuts. 'I'm sorry, I don't think that's possible. We've got very strict rules about keeping animals.'

'Surely you've got an empty cage you can stick him in? I don't have a car and this is the only way I can get him treated.'

'What's wrong with him? I can't have him infecting the whole shop.'

'Oh no, it's nothing. A small problem with his teeth. I wouldn't bring him in, only he's bleeding and it preys on my mind.'

The owner stares at my face. 'OK then, let's take a look at him.'

I release the catch. The tom pads out on to the glass-topped counter. He seems to have realised he's on display and sits in a neat curl, covering his head with his tail.

'He's got a flea collar, good. What's his name?'

John. Everyone's called John.

'John.'

He laughs. 'I've never met a cat called John before. Hello, John.'

The cat looks up at him but doesn't respond. The shop-keeper squints at me.

'And how much were you planning to pay me?'

'Would twenty-five be OK? I'd give you more, but I don't know how much the vet's going to charge.'

'Oh no, twenty will be sufficient. When d'you want to pick him up?'

'When do you close?'

'Five.'

'Oh.'

'Is that too early for you? What time's the appointment?'

'Seven.'

'Seven?' he repeats, clearly surprised.

'It's the evening surgery,' I tell him, wondering whether such a thing exists for animals.

He exhales. 'Well, I live in the flat above the shop so I suppose I could look after him until then.'

'Thanks,' I tell him, and then look down at John. 'You're a very lucky cat.'

As soon as I arrive at work, I want to tell Adrienne what I'm up to. I think out of everybody, she'd be the one most likely to approve. I know I stole the idea from Ian, but I'm sure he'd see a big difference between staying here the odd Sunday night and moving in permanently. And besides, I've never been certain that underneath it all Ian isn't as much of a company man as Gordon, albeit in a much less psychotic manner. But Adrienne feels the same way about Quick Kall as I do, and I'm sure she'd see no harm in making a home in the company cloakroom.

She beckons me across. 'Alice has called in sick. According to Big Gwen upstairs, the perfect couple have called it a day.'

'Any particular reason?'

'The usual.'

'Who cheated with who?'

'Bryan betrayed Alice, it seems, although Gwen doesn't know who with. Apparently, she overheard a big fight in his office after work last night. I can't imagine anyone wanting to lose a day's pay over Bryan.'

'She was pretty touchy about it.'

'So it would seem. She wants to be careful. I wouldn't say her job here was guaranteed.'

'Maybe we should try to push her over the edge. Get a new team leader that way instead. I trust you still hope to employ Daniel Day Lewis.'

'No, I've changed my mind about that. I think they should promote me to team leader, and get Dennis Quaid in to do my job.'

'What about me?'

'You can get a job with Alice. Become her care assistant.'

I notice the line manager staring at me and walk across to my desk to log on. Gordon smiles at me from across the table, his creepy grin making me suspicious. Then I remember that he's Alice's deputy, and can see he's clearly looking forward to his day in power.

'You're three minutes late, Dan. I hope you're going to make up for that later on.'

I smile to myself. *Sure I'll make it up, Gordon. You want me to do a little overtime? Put me down for twenty-four hours.* It's actually quite a relief that Alice isn't here today. She's a bit more observant than Gordon, and might have checked up on me. But her emotional crisis gives me a day's grace to work out how to avoid the cleaners and outwit the security guards. Now I've committed myself to my plan, I feel a little underprepared, like a criminal about to hold up a bank without a getaway car.

Teri waits until Gordon looks away and then smiles at me, the sympathy in her eyes suggesting she's already been the recipient of some advice from our temporary team leader. I smile back and hit *Ready*, hoping for some nice easy calls to gently break me into the morning.

There are several games we use to kill time at Quick Kall. These range from the classically simple (such as Connect 4 or Hangman, played on scraps of paper passed between work-stations) to the inventively complex (Chinese Whispers across *Aspects*, Strike It Lucky played along rows of work-stations). My favourite of the second variety is Dating Agency, a game that requires large amounts of idle time and can only be played on slow afternoons.

How to Play Dating Agency

1) Player 1 chooses a member of the call-centre whom they do not know and with whom they have had no previous contact. (Excluding team leaders, line managers or any visiting clients.)

2) Player 2 then selects a second member of the call-centre (of the opposite sex to the employee selected by Player 1) who they think would be a good partner for the first person chosen.

3) Player 1 then calls the person chosen by Player 2 and asks them to send them a recorded message in which they ask a question which they would expect their ideal partner to be able to answer (e.g. 'Which country has won the World Cup the most times?', 'How many films has Meg Ryan appeared in with Tom Hanks?', 'Where would you locate the G-spot?').

4) Player 2 then calls the person selected by Player 1 and tells them they have a question they have to answer. The person called should record a message with their answer, even if it only amounts to 'I don't know' or 'Who cares?' and send it back.

5) Player 1 then sends this answer to the person who set the question and asks them if they would like to know the identity of the second person. If they do, the identity is given and they are asked if they have a final message to return to their prospective datee. If they do, communication is continued either until the two chosen people are introduced, or they become bored/irritated/annoyed by your calls.

I don't know who invented Dating Agency, but it's an inspired creation. Decorating your workstation may be more personal, and Hangman is less risky, but few office activities can claim to have prompted marriages, and nothing can match the innocent delight of watching your chosen target peer round the office in search of a face to fit your voice.

Today's playing conditions are perfect. Gordon's sitting with the other team leaders in reception and I know he's enjoying the promotion too much to bother checking up on us. I coax Teri into selecting the first date. She opts for a fat black man on the Banks & Building Societies team, an office character renowned for his clashing clothes.

'Is he straight?'

'Does it matter?' she asks, smiling. 'No, he's hetero. His ex-girlfriend used to pick him up from work.'

'OK,' I say, and dial him up. I watch him wait three rings before hitting *Ready*.

'Hello?'

'Hello, I'm a representative from Quick Kall's social team. We're considering the possibility of replacing the karaoke evening with a singles night. Would you be prepared to answer a few quick questions?'

He giggles. 'OK.'

'First, are you single?'

'Yes.'

'And would you be interested in this sort of thing?'

'A singles night?' He giggles again. 'Maybe.'

'OK, and could you do one more thing for me. We're hoping to make up a tape to send to management and I wondered if you could message me with the question that you'd expect your ideal partner to be able to answer?'

'Is this a joke?'

'No, it's serious. My extension is 2310.'

I click off and Teri and I watch him, waiting to see if he'll take the bait. He looks round again, checks across to reception, then leans down as he speaks into his microphone.

Seconds later, my message light starts to flash. Teri grips my arm.

'Put it on monitor.'

I do, and we listen to the man whisper, 'What's the best club in Bristol?'

'Right, so we need a clubber,' I say, looking round the office. My gaze lingers on a short, plump girl who always puts her hair up in pigtails on Friday afternoons, before moving on to the cheerful blonde who heads the supermarket loyalty line. I point her out to Teri and she shouts across to Adrienne, 'What's the extension for the loyalty line?'

'2446,' she says, her eyes curious, 'why?'

'No reason.'

But Adrienne's not to be put off that easily, and approaches our table. 'This wouldn't have anything to do with Dating Agency, would it?'

I look up at her, deciding she's less likely to cause trouble if we let her join in. She's told me before how left out she feels sitting with Gordon and Alice, and now they're both elsewhere disposed, I can tell she's even more bored than usual. As much as I like Teri, I expect the days would pass a lot more quickly if I was next to Adrienne. In fact, I know they would, because when I first came here the two of us sat together, only to be split by Alice when she grew jealous of our conversation.

'Who you doing?'

I point out our targets, then watch Teri as she calls up the blonde. Adrienne leans across and puts it on monitor. 'Hello,' she says tentatively, 'I'm calling on behalf of the social committee and I was . . .'

'I didn't know there was a social committee,' the blonde interrupts, looking round the office, 'is it a new thing?'

'Well . . .'

'Only I've been heavily involved in selling tickets for the karaoke evenings and been named employee of the month three times in a row, so if you're looking for new members . . .'

'Oh yes, we've got your name on file, but for the moment we only need to ask you a few questions.'

'OK.'

'Are you single?'

'Ish,' she giggles, 'I mean, I don't like sleeping alone.'

'So if Quick Kall was to replace the karaoke with a singles night?'

'Is that what's going to happen? That'd be brilliant. Are there enough singles?'

'That's what we're trying to find out. We're putting together a tape for management, and it'd be a tremendous help if you could listen to the message I'm about to send you and record a reply.'

'Sure,' she says, 'thanks for thinking of me.'

'No problem.'

The three of us peer across the office, watching the woman's excited face as she listens to the black guy's message. Then she sends us her reply. Teri hits the button.

'Wow, he's got a nice voice. Is that someone from the call-centre? I think the Lakota is the best "club" club, if you know what I mean, but Club IQ is the most fun, especially on a foam-party night.'

'What about The Pentangle, you bitch?' Adrienne snaps at the *Aspect*, her mock-anger surprising us into laughter.

Teri sends the message to my machine and I add my introduction before forwarding it to the black guy.

'D'you think he'll buy it?'

'Probably not, but I expect he'll want her name. Few people will pass up the chance of a date, even if they think it's a joke.'

Sure enough, the black guy calls back and asks if we're going to fix him up. I tease him for a while then give him the blonde's extension. He thanks me and clicks off.

'Well, Cupid,' I say to Teri, 'that was a job well done.'

'Yeah,' she grins, 'maybe we should get out of here and set up professionally.'

'Make new friends on the phone,' Adrienne jokes, and Teri smiles at me.

*　　*　　*

The last hour always takes longest. Everyone's watching the clock, praying they won't get a call that'll push them into overtime. The team leaders monitor this period closely, watching for employees who go into idle time early to avoid taking late calls. The clever way to avoid this is to keep resetting your *Aspect*, so that you're always at the back of the answering queue. Unfortunately, everyone else on the team is trying to do the same, so unless you hit your *Ready* button sixty times a second, you'll be automatically selected as the next available operator.

Knowing I'm going straight into the late shift after everyone else has finished, I tell the team to all hit their *Ready* buttons only once, letting me cover any last-minute calls. Ian thanks me and leaves early, asking me to log him off when it reaches six o'clock. Everyone else starts packing away at five to six, and I have to fight my impulse to join in. I'm sure it'll be OK once they've gone and I'm only sharing the call-centre with the late-shift operators from the seven other teams, but at the moment my mind and body feel as if they've been pushed past all acceptable limits. This feeling is intensified at five past six when the teenage cleaners begin their rounds, emptying half-full dustbins and pushing vacuums across the static-crackling carpet.

Gordon waves to me as he leaves the office at ten past six, and I wonder if he's impressed that I'm still here. As much as I enjoy Gordon's Log, it's hard to separate what I've read from the man himself, and I'm sure beneath the disabilities and officiousness, there's someone worth talking to. The late shift is a lot easier than working during the day, and when there's no one on the team who wants to do it, they farm out the jobs to the same circle of middle-aged women who usually make money stuffing envelopes or delivering catalogues. It's the type of job they usually advertise in the *Bristol Journal* or *Evening Post*, separated from the main positions which are advertised in quarter-page box ads with the Quick Kall logo (a telephone receiver with the mouthpiece broadening out into the shape of a horn) in the right-hand corner. Most operators, however, are sent here by the Temptastic Employment Agency, which has an exclusive contract with Quick Kall to supply them with only the top twenty-five percent of the people on their books. To reach this echelon you must earn glowing reports after working at three lower level Temptastic gigs. Looking back now, it seems impossible that I should've passed this test, but I was a much more enthusiastic employee before earning my stripes. I'm sure part of my indifference stems from having reached the top of the tree, and I'd be much more committed if I needed a good report to leave Quick Kall and start working for a more prestigious client.

I take three calls between six and seven, two wrong numbers and an enquiry about Caribbean Cruises. Then I set my *Aspect* to divert all calls across to the Train-times line (we have to reception for each other whenever anyone takes a break – Quick Kall's funds don't extend to employing two night-shift operators per team) and walk to the lift. I go down to the ground floor and use the back entrance, knowing that this screen is furthest away in the security guard's surveillance bank. When I reach the pet shop, I press the bell six times, imagining the owner to be tucked away on the top floor, unable to hear anything above the noise of the animals. To my surprise, he appears almost immediately, carrying the cat in the Apollo 2000. I thank him and hand over the twenty pounds.

'I hope he wasn't any trouble.'

'Not at all. He's got real character, that cat. I see so many I have trouble telling them apart, but he's got a real personality. I used to have one just like him back in the sixties. Salty the sea cat. Maybe your John's a bastard son old Salty never told me about.'

He folds the notes into the birdshit-stained pocket of his brown nylon trousers. He's about to leave when I deliberately smack my hand against my forehead, melodramatically mouthing, 'Damn.'

'What's wrong?'

'I meant to pick up some cat stuff earlier.' I look up at him shyly. 'I suppose you've shut everything up now?'

'Well now, that depends,' he grins, 'what exactly are you looking for?'

*   *   *

I've decided the best point of entry is through the toilet ceiling. Although there are walls separating the toilets, corridors and conference rooms from the call-centre proper, these divisions end at the ceiling and the area above the polystyrene tiles is completely open-plan. I stand on the toilet pedestal and push back a tile, shining Farnell's torch inside to check for hidden dangers. It's surprisingly hospitable up here, and I fancy John's chances more than my own.

I take the orange plastic bowl I bought at the pet shop and fill it with Felix. The food is my way of keeping tabs on him, and I tuck the bowl just inside the lifted tile. If I need to find him when he's not hungry, I have a plastic catball and a squeaky mouse to attract his attention. I lift John in his cage and put him up on top of the ceiling. I turn the entrance of the Apollo away from the gap to prevent him from plummeting into the toliet, then open the metal door. For a moment I think he's not going to move, then he pads out on to the dusty surface. I bid him good luck and put the tile back in place.

There's a permanently placed skip at the back of Quick Kall's main building. It hasn't been emptied since I started here, yet never gets more than half full, no matter how much is thrown in. The explanation for this is an unofficial understanding that anything inside can be taken by employees. Quick Kall has a large office budget and frequently junks furniture for no apparent reason. Sometimes you can even score an easily repaired modem or a keyboard which works perfectly except for a sticking key. I'm a less frequent skip-visitor than most people here, although I have taken a couple of swivel-chairs and a cabinet for Dad's computer. At the bottom of the skip is a layer of broken bits no one wants to salvage, mainly made up of debris from the breaks room break-ins. No one digs beneath this level, and it seems the perfect place to hide the cat basket. It's too risky to keep it in the call-centre, and a waste of money to throw it away. So I store it beneath a layer of broken perspex decorated with a red Coca-Cola logo. Then I return to my desk.

As soon as I log on, I wish I'd bought something to eat. I don't get another break until the end of my shift, and although I'd planned to nip out for a burger to break up the empty hours between knocking off and tomorrow morning, I'm not sure my stomach can wait that long. Ian's headset has a much longer extension wire than mine, and if I pinch it I can move freely around the desks and still hear any incoming calls. I use the extra leeway to walk round to Adrienne's side of the table. Although we're discouraged from bringing personal possessions into the office, Adrienne has converted an unused mini filing-cabinet into a secret store for snacks and magazines. She's managed to keep it hidden from the rest of the team, but I noticed her taking her cigarettes out of it before going to the breaks room one afternoon and investigated the next time she was away. I check no one's watching me and look inside. There are two packets of ready salted Potato Puffs, a Milky Way and half a bottle of Panda Pop's green cola. Alongside the food is a folded copy of today's *NME*. This seems much more enticing than any of my reading material so I pinch it along with both packets of crisps. I save the Milky Way for later, but no matter how thirsty I get I'm not going to drink the green cola. I'm sure it tastes fine, but I've never liked the idea of foodstuffs not looking the way they're supposed to. I don't even like foods that naturally come in more than one colour. For me, apples are red and peppers are green. Green apples and red peppers might as well not exist.

I return to my desk and stare at my monitor. I'm sure the best way to get through these evenings is not to spend too long doing any one thing, so I decide to read the *NME* for half an hour before loading Patience onto my work-station. That way I've got something pleasant to do now, as well as something to look forward to. I open the packet of Potato Puffs and empty them out onto a piece of scrap paper. I eat them one at a time, savouring the taste and trying to pretend they're a proper meal. I've never really been interested in music papers, but tonight I try to read every word of every article, wanting to spin it out as long as possible.

The other operators leave at ten thirty. Only one of them waves goodbye, an old lady in brown slacks, who shouts 'take care, love' as she reaches the door. I know from Ian that the security guard gives everyone thirty minutes to clear the building, then takes a quick stroll through each floor before heading home. Ian manages to avoid him by shutting himself into the cloakroom, but I'm sure that would arouse suspicion on a weekday. A more sensible plan seems to be to nip out after he's gone and then let myself back in with my ID card. I know the card works after hours because there are several twenty-four-hour loyalty lines on the ground floor. So I log off and catch the lift down to the rear exit.

The last few buses are circling into the Centre, loading up with shiny-faced pensioners returning from watching *Summer Holiday* at the Hippodrome. Blanketmen approach the lone teenagers standing apart from the sated senior citizens, hoping youth will make them more generous. An old man shakes his rolled-up programme at a particularly scraggly specimen, and his voice from a distance sounds as if he's saying, 'I have to work for mine,' a curiously plantive complaint that carries none of the authority he presumably intended to convey. I wonder what they would make of me, working every hour God sends but still sleeping in someone else's office.

I buy a hamburger with relish and some french fries and take them across to the large grass area in the centre of the roundabout. There was a recent rumour that the council planned to break up these roads and persuade everyone to travel in boats around the waterways beneath. An impractical idea, but enchanting none the less. It amuses me that whenever this city seeks to distinguish itself, they look at a new transportation system. Before the waterways, there was a plan to build a monorail, a rival to the trams and tramlines of the North.

A thin stream of people head across the paved centre of the island, on their way to Club IQ. I idly wonder whether the pair we fixed up today are among them, then consider going along myself. It would, after all, be a good way of getting through the next few hours. But the money in my pocket is almost all I have left, and I can't remember how long it's been since I made my last GBH and building society payments. I've been spending wildly during the last few days, relying on getting a loan from Adrienne, and that's by no means certain, especially after she's found out that I've eaten all her food. Besides, I feel a self-flagellatory impulse to spend all night in the office, getting used to my cell.

I finish my food and throw the wrappers in a broken bin which bends down alondside the bench. The hamburger felt a lot more satisfying than the Potato Puffs, even if it does make me worry about CJD. My mouth feels sticky, so I pop back to the burger shop for a can of Pepsi. After my drink, I look at my watch and walk slowly back to Quick Kall, waiting outside until five past eleven.

I'm cautious as I return to my floor, knowing that anyone here this late will be wired on caffeine and unlikely to accept untrue stories from an unknown stranger. But I manage to get back upstairs unseen, and use my ID card to enter the now empty call-centre. The lights in this building stay on all night, playing their part in the skyline I can – could – see from my room. I feel like a filmstar as I stride into the office, the dramatic artificiality even stronger than usual. It's like I've been left alone in a dormitory, free to rifle through the private places of all the missing children. I realise, standing here, that I haven't really thought about this at all, even though I've been thinking about it every minute. It's the same paradoxical sensation I felt the first time I found myself alone with a naked woman.

This isn't a prison. Being here is strange and scary, but also sexy. Sexy in a weird way, combining the thrill of having sex in public places with something more adolescent, something hallucinatory, masturbatory maybe, a teenage test, like walking while wanking, trying to get to the toilet before it shoots in the air. It's a childish, primal thrill, like looking up skirts or hiding hard-ons. It cannot last long and yet I want to hold on to it for ever. I breathe deeply and realise it's hungry. It needs feeding with secrets, the self-exposure of strangers. So I fetch Dad's minutes from the cloakroom.

Maybe I'm stupid to bring it down to something so basic. Perhaps what I'm feeling is bigger than that: something so great that all these sex thoughts are merely self-defence. But what is it I'm facing? Self-discovery? Maybe. The meaning of life? I don't know. I can sit wherever I want, and yet I return to my usual chair. I open the minutes and read through the passage that seemed so disturbing two days ago but now means nothing to me. I pick it up where Dad says he doesn't think I respect him.

LC: Do you respect your father?

ST: He's dead.

LC: Did you respect your father?

ST: Well, no. I loved him, took care of him, gave him money every week. But I didn't respect him.

LC: No son respects his father. It's elementary psychology. Your only problem is that you take him seriously. God knows where we'd be if we all took our self-image from our children.

ST: But my father was an alcoholic, and he beat my mother. I've done everything I possibly can for Dan. No other father I've ever met is so dedicated to their son. That's why I wanted to move in with him in the first place.

IJ: What about you, Lucy? How do you feel towards your parents.

LC: I think I'm more scared of my mother now. I mean, I could never choose to see my father again, but if I saw him on the street or something, I'd be able to cope with his existence. A lot of the time I wish my mum was dead.

IJ: Why? Because she knew what was happening and didn't do anything?

LC: Well, that's the cliché, isn't it?

IJ: I'm sorry. I didn't mean to offend you.

LC: I'm not offended. It just makes me angry that I'm

not allowed to have an individual reaction. People have individual reactions to getting married or being divorced. Why can't I have an individual reaction to being abused?

IJ: I'm sorry.

LC [waving her hand dismissively]: No, the problem's not to do with my mother's behaviour. It's to do with her character. She keeps checking with me.

ST: Checking?

LC: Yes. She can't do anything without asking me if it's OK.

ST: And her concern upsets you?

LC: It's not how it sounds. I'm not ungrateful, or angry, or vengeful. I don't know how to describe it. It's like when you're a teenager and you attack your family because you don't think they appreciate you, and then later you look back and realise that your family are the way they are entirely because of you. It's like their personalities no longer exist, as if they're the shadows around a figure in a photograph. It's because of me that my mother's neurotic about the smallest decisions. It's because of me that every time she's enjoying herself she has to check that she's allowed to be happy. I hate that responsibility.

ST: It's strange that I can remember every fight I've had with my father, but none of the fights Dan's had with me. The only times I can remember are when Dan said the same things to me that I said to my dad.

VD: He's changed you.

ST: What do you mean?

VD: I've known you longer than anyone, and every time you're upset it's usually because of something he said.

I knew I had a good reason for disliking Valerie. It was always more than the fact that she ignored me at the hospital, or got hysterical when I told her about Dad's accident over the phone. I had a gut feeling that there was something wrong with her, and my first impressions almost always turn out to be right. What puzzles me, however, is what part she plays in Dad's life. He's never mentioned her, and yet in the minutes she claims that she'd known him longer than anyone. I know Dad had a lot of affairs, but I didn't know there was another woman who'd played an important part in his life. Maybe she's making it up. Perhaps she's angry because he doesn't care for her.

I look round the office, feeling deflated. I'd wanted something salacious and exciting, not a miserable woman dealing with the psychological aftermath of being abused. I walk over to Adrienne's drawer and take her Milky Way. The theft makes me happier, and I wonder how John's getting on. While I was reading, I imagined I could hear his pawfalls overhead, but I'm sure that's probably wishful thinking. I pick up my headset, wondering if it's still possible to use the switchboard. But even if I log on under someone else's number, the conspicuous call will attract unnecessary attention. When I was going out with Sonia (the GBH girl), I used to do the odd night on the linkline at her university, listening to suicidal callers through the early hours of the morning. I had no idea, then, that this would become my career (I'd been nursing the idea of becoming a house-husband and letting Sonia support me), but tonight I wish I had a few of those depressed voices to comfort me, or at the very least a television tuned to *L!VE TV*.

I look at my watch. Eleven thirty. I feel as if I'm halfway through a twenty-four-hour flight and have lost interest in all the books I've brought with me. I suppose I could start *Man and the Vertebrates*, but I really want something connected to my present situation. I rescue Gordon's Log from the desk and flip through it, rereading the section where Adrienne writes about her pubic hair being like a penis. Maybe I should commission her to write erotic fiction for me. I'm sure beneath the jokey tone of this pseudo-journal lies a genuine urge to write titillating fiction.

Thinking of Adrienne helps refuel my earlier horniness. I sometimes wonder whether it's cowardly of me not to consider her as a possible lover. This isn't the place to get into my fear of women (suffice to say it's all connected to my conviction and my time with Sonia), but maybe Ade would be just the person to help me get over it. She's certainly eligible (I know she has the odd fling now and again, but I don't think there's anyone serious) and probably lonely (when I asked her how she'd become so proficient in haberdashery and hardware, she told me you had to be like that when there's no one else to take care of you), and the arrangement would certainly have its fringe benefits (somewhere to sleep, for one. I know she owns her own house, and her mortgage is the sort of tie which might make her less nervous about taking on a love-commitment), as well as financial security (it's common knowledge that her vinyl habit and loan-sharking are funded by a small inheritance that she dips into when necessary). All in all, it seems downright stupid not to seek a space on her sofa.

I press my hand against my crotch, thinking of the light wisps of hair along Adrienne's neckline. Fear of security cameras lifts me from my desk and takes me to the toilet. I shut the heavy wooden door and sit down on the thick plastic seat. I push my trousers down around my ankles and rub the heel of my hand over my cotton-covered cock. My muscles relax and I spread my legs wide open, shoes pressing against the side of the cubicle. The front of my pants gets hooked beneath the downward weight of my balls. Odd that moving here should rekindle my sexuality. I picture Adrienne with her back towards me, headphones hooked around her neck, attention directed elsewhere. Suddenly, for no reason, she begins to slowly ease up her skirt, the motion all the more arousing for its lack of meaning. I imagine her knuckles tightly bunching the folds of black material above her bottom. Face faced away, my faceless fantasy arches her beautiful backside towards me, a pale pink target for all my energies. As I move my fingers, the legs of my lust-object slowly shorten, the black material changing from a hiked skirt to a too-short T-shirt rising up over the curve of a different girl's bum. I hold Teri there just as I remember her, the tiny tilt of pink and the hint of darkness, maybe just shadow but hopefully something more, certainly a sight to cherish. A gift unknowingly given, but no less valuable for the lack of intention. This bottom seems less chilly than the first, and I push one hand against the pan and tilt my hips towards it, bucking faster and faster until, unexpectedly, it changes again, this time metamorphosing into a backside hidden by a burgundy skirt, somehow even more exciting for not being exposed. It's against this bottom that I let fly, hoping to leave a permanent stain on the imaginary covering of Alice's imaginary arse.

Back at my desk, I feel even more deflated than earlier, mainly because I wasted what should've been a moment of cosmic oneness wiping my ejaculate from the wax-polished floor. At least my little onanistic adventure killed thirty minutes, taking me past midnight and leaving only nine hours before I start tomorrow. I'd been thinking that without having to catch the bus I could have a little lie-in, but I suppose I'll have to get up even earlier to dodge the cleaners.

I put the *NME* back in Adrienne's drawer and head to the cloakroom, realising as I do so that Ian probably sleeps here because it's the only room with a light you can switch off. I gather together a few forgotten coats and use my rucksack for a pillow. After removing my shoes and socks, I hang my suit jacket on the coat rail and lie down on the floor. I'm not undressing any further in case I'm woken by a cleaner. Somehow I think it'll be easier to explain if they're not staring at my nuts. I close my eyes and remember John above me, wondering what he makes of his new home.

10

Strange voices still excite me. Even now, I still hold out hope of meeting my perfect woman over the phone. When I hear a voice that interests me, I almost forget I'm in a call-centre, turning up the volume and crushing the black foam into the whorl of my ear. I listen intently for background noise, mentally slowing down her speech while I imagine a physical attribute to match every cadence. My voice softens as I answer each enquiry, and I waylay the caller with unnecessary information. I stare at my screen and read off what's printed there as if it were Shakespeare, imparting every line with all the frustrated love that festers inside me. If they notice, they rarely say anything, although I sometimes detect a sunnier tone, as if they're answering through a smile. It's a sad reality of call-centre existence that all the pleasant callers never get personal. They leave intimacies to the angry women who phone to complain, taking everyone's name and trying to insinuate that you have a human relationship with them. I've often wondered what makes them keep calling, even after days of being redirected to dead lines. Don't they understand that the more they moan the less inclined we are to assist them? Most callers seem intelligent, and are certainly good at articulating their complaints, and yet they remain incapable of comprehending a fact most of us learn pretty quick: a helpline is no help at all.

I knew my first caller was going to be good when she immediately broke all the above rules, being both pleasant and wanting to get personal.

'Hello,' she giggled, 'who's that?'

'Magicmix Records.'

'No, who are you?'

'Me?' I swallow. 'Dan.'

'Hi, Dan. Got some orders for you.'

'OK. Account number?'

'76956. Are you a fast operator?'

'Not bad. Why?'

'I want a fast operator. None of this I didn't catch the last bit, could you repeat it? OK?'

'No problem.'

She starts reeling off numbers at a barely intelligible speed. I miss a couple but don't say anything, not wanting to invite her scorn. After we've filled the first screen, she says: 'Do they monitor your calls at Magicmix, Dan?'

'Sometimes.'

'Do they monitor the whole call or just a bit of it?'

'It depends. Sometimes they monitor the whole call, but if they're doing that they usually sit beside you and plug directly into your *Aspect*. The rest of the time they just eavesdrop on the odd call to check you're doing it properly.'

'And what does doing it properly mean?'

'Saying the salutation, helping the caller, make sure they're satisfied before they hang up.'

'So you have to satisfy me?'

'With your enquiries.'

'OK,' she giggles, 'I have an enquiry. If they were monitoring this call and they heard me talking dirty, what would happen to you?'

'I'd get in trouble.'

'What for?'

'Not terminating the call. I'm supposed to hang up if you say anything obscene.'

'What counts as obscene?'

'Swear words, lewd suggestions.'

'Do you get a lot of that?'

'Not on this line. The people on the Banks & Building Societies team come in for most of the abuse.'

'What about lewd suggestions?'

'Again, not on this line. The people on the Emergency Contraception get the sex calls.'

'You're very serious, Dan.'

'Thank you.'

'Ready for some more numbers?'

'Of course.'

She rattles off another twenty orders. Again, I do my best to keep up, but one or two slip by me or go down wrong. Then she asks: 'Do you like the phone, Dan?'

'Do you?'

'I asked first.'

'Not really. I never use it outside work. But this isn't really like a phone. I don't think I could do this job if we had to use real phones.'

'Phones are like pornography really, aren't they?' she says, her voice arch.

'In what way?'

'The liberty, and the fact that it's a false freedom. They both give you good ideas, but it's never satisfying. You're prepared to do anything, but whatever you do doesn't mean anything.'

'I'm not sure I follow.'

'Well, I'm talking to you the way I am now because I can't see your face. If I had just met you for real instead of over the phone, I'd probably feel too shy to flirt with you like this . . .'

'Are you flirting with me?'

'Hadn't you noticed?'

'I thought you were just being friendly.'

She laughs. 'You're sweet. But you see the problem is, even though we have an intimate connection, I can't do anything about it.'

'Some people find that exciting.'

'I know, that's what I said. A false liberty. I don't know, forget I said anything. I've got some more numbers.'

'Fire away.'

She recites her last few numbers, thanks me for not making fun of her, and hangs up. I feel sad after she's gone, wishing I'd been more playful with her. Her tone changed so suddenly at the end of the conversation, her attack of self-consciousness destroying our game. I look up and notice Ian walking towards me.

'All right, Dan?' he asks as he sets up beside me, a copy of *The Mirror* tucked under his arm. 'You're in early.'

'Yeah.'

'Did you do the late shift last night?'

I look at him, trying not to feel paranoid. 'Yeah, I'm doing it all week. Why?'

'No reason,' he says, shrugging. He puts his elbows on the desk and rubs his fingers across the bridge of his nose.

'Headache?'

He nods. 'Breakfast disagreed with me, that's all. And I'm feeling pretty knackered.'

I pat him on the shoulder and look back at my *Aspect*. It's not until I've taken my next call that I remember what Ian has for breakfast. No wonder it disagrees with him. Two cans of Blackthorn isn't exactly milk and muesli, after all, and the only really surprising thing is that his digestive system's put up with it for so long. Not that my breakfast this morning (two bars of chocolate and a coffee from the breaks room) was much better, but at least I don't have it every day.

'Hello, Angel Cruises. How can I help you?'

'Hello Dan.'

For a moment I think it must be the previous caller, somehow twigging that we're an agency and returning for a second attack. But the breathing is different. So I ask: 'Who is it?'

'Brittany.'

'Oh.'

'I was just calling to check you're still free tomorrow night. The others are very keen to meet you.'

'Shit, I'm sorry, I forgot. I'm working tomorrow.'

'Until when?'

'Sorry?'

'What time are you working until?'

'Really late, I'm afraid. I probably won't be finished until midnight.'

'OK. Marilyn will pick you up outside Quick Kall.'

'At midnight?'

'If that's OK with you.'

'I guess so.'

'Good. I'm looking forward to it.'

The line crackles as she hangs up. Marilyn, I repeat to myself, trying to remember my list. MS? Abused as a child? No, that was LC. MS, MS . . . I remember the initials made me think of Marks and Spencer, but what was her problem? No matter, I'll check later.

I walk round to the other side of the table, sitting in the spare swivel-chair next to Adrienne.

'You OK?'

'No,' she says, eyeing me, 'some bastard stole my lunch.'

'Ah. Sorry.'

'You ate my lunch?' she asks, surprised.

'I meant to replace it.' I pull some loose change from my pocket. 'How much do I owe you?'

'Forget it. You can't afford it.'

'True, but still . . .'

'It's OK. I'm only pissed off because I thought someone was trying to get at me.' She looks at me, suspicious. 'How did you know it was there?'

'I watched you.'

'You watched me?' She pauses. 'I'm flattered, although I didn't know that was your thing. I'll have to start writing Daniel's Diary instead of Gordon's Log.'

'You should. Make it really dirty.'

'It's your diary. Is your life dirty?'

'Not really.' I pause while she laughs. 'Although I did get a sexy call this morning.'

'Heavy breather?'

'No, a sexy call. Heavy breathing's not sexy.'

'Depends who's doing it. What did she say?'

'Who?'

'The sexy caller.'

'Not much, stuff about pornography and telephones.'

'Sounds fun. Frustrated housewife?'

'Don't think so. It was the Magicmix line.'

'Some young woman alone in a stockroom?'

'Probably.'

'You want to be careful.'

'Monitoring, you mean?'

'Not just that. I saw this programme the other night where they tried to trap workmen by getting women to sexually proposition them and videoing the results.'

'You made that up.'

'It's true.'

'Surely that's illegal.'

'What?'

'Filming people without their permission.'

'They got round it somehow. Like those real-life documentaries. Besides, this wouldn't be filming, it'd be taping.'

'You think she might have been setting me up?'

'Maybe. They've got to make a programme about call-centres sooner or later. They seem such an obvious source of material. Are you on idle?'

'Yeah. Why?'

'Line manager's looking over. You'd better get back.'

'OK. Call me on internal.'

She looks intrigued. 'For something specific, or just to carry on our chat?'

'Something specific.'

I walk back to my desk and put my headset on. The wait-light is bright red. Adrienne's int-call comes through and I take myself off idle. Her voice sounds clearer than the outside calls and her audible breathing excites me.

'You got any new messages?'

'Nothing you haven't heard. The girl who doesn't work here any more belching "We Wish You a Merry Xmas", you and Ian pretending to have sex, someone impersonating Alice and the opening bit from *Pulp Fiction*. What about you?'

'You got "Frigging in the Rigging"?'

'What is it?'

'The Sex Pistols.'

'For real? Or someone else singing?'

'No, it's off the record.'

'I thought "Frigging in the Rigging" was the Dead Kennedys.'

'Nah, that's "Too Drunk to Fuck".'

'Oh yeah. OK, send it across.'

'No problem. What was it you wanted to talk about?'

'I need a loan.'

She goes silent, then says, 'How much?'

'Could you go one thousand?'

'Depends. What d'you want it for?'

'Nothing dangerous. Dad's in the hospital. I can't pay the bills.'

'You down one thousand?' she asks, sounding concerned.

'Pretty much. Any less and I'd be back two weeks later. I want to clear it in one lump.'

'And when do I get it back?'

'Slowly, but starting almost immediately. I'm working nights and weekends so money'll be sorted soon. I just don't want to end up in prison in the meantime.'

'So you'd pay me back how much?'

'Fifty a week, starting a month from now. And I'd pay back one thousand and five for my one.'

'And when d'you need it?'

'A. s. a. p.'

'Tomorrow?'

I hesitate, wondering if I should push it. 'That's fine. It's just, could I borrow a bit to see me through?'

'How much?'

'Fifty.'

'I don't have it on me. Are you going into town?'

'I could do.'

'Can I trust you with my cashcard?'

'Of course.'

She cuts off and I take a quick Cruises call. By the time it's finished, she's forwarded the message across. I switch out of *Ready* and listen to it. The song's a good one to hear through a headset, the 'Jolly Roger' opening and pirate declarations sounding like a TV theme tune. At the end of the song, Adrienne recites her cashcard number and I write it onto the back of my hand.

At breaktime, I make a more permanent note of Adrienne's PIN in the back of *Man and the Vertebrates*, and take the card across to the Centre. I can't resist checking her balance, but the millions must be stashed elsewhere because the screen flashes up only 520:0.0 CR. I take out exactly the amount I asked for, not wanting to give her a reason to refuse me the rest tomorrow. I get a statement with the notes and head across to the World of Food.

Money reassures me. I finger through the five notes as I wait for my plastic plate of red ribs and yellow noodles. It comes to almost a fiver with the large drink, but I suppose as I've got a thousand coming, it's not worth worrying. I carry my dinner to an empty table and eat it quickly, watching the clock the whole time.

I spend most of the afternoon watching Gordon. I still think he's a good man underneath, and the recent change in my fortunes has made me more inclined to break down the barrier between us. But his off-putting social habits are even more pronounced now than they used to be. His muttering has deteriorated into a low drone that sounds like his batteries are running down, and his headshakes have become so violent that once or twice I've noticed him crick his neck and have to re-align it by striking himself on the side of his skull.

'You OK, Gordon?'

He looks suspicious. 'Why?'

'No reason. Just being friendly.'

He nods, but doesn't say anything. I try again: 'Seen any good football?'

'Not since the derby. I thought you weren't interested.'

'I don't like watching it, but I've got no objection to hearing about a good game. I'm still waiting for someone to persuade me that I've got the wrong idea about the whole thing.'

He doesn't reply. His antagonistic attitude makes me worry I've done something to upset him. Last night when he smiled at me, I felt certain he wanted me to talk to him. I wonder if there's anything I've done today that's prompted this rebuff. He does seem to have a general antipathy towards me. Every time Ian and I are laughing he looks suspicious, and I don't think it's paranoid to worry that he nurses some kind of unknown resentment. I think he preferred it here before I arrived, and I know he sees me as a rival for Ian's friendship, even though he's got much more in common with him. It's a relief when six o'clock comes and he heads home, even if this hour does also leave me with no company other than the non-communicative night-shift ladies.

I feel less anxious about staying in the call-centre tonight, although I'm alert enough not to become complacent. I managed a reasonable sleep in the cloakroom and although my body ached when I woke up this morning, it was a good feeling, as if I'd just spent a night camping. I'd thought the constant exposure to air-conditioning would dry my eyes and inflame my sinuses, but it actually isn't as unpleasant as the asbestos or whatever it is in the atmosphere at Mr Farnell's.

There are never many calls on a Thursday, and I'm not anticipating a busy night. I leave the *Aspect* on *Ready* while I visit the toilet and fetch Dad's minutes from the rucksack, gambling that I won't get called while I'm gone. It turns out to be a safe bet, and when I return I take Ian's headset and push my chair as far away as the cable will stretch, opening the book on my lap. I remind myself of Marilyn's secret, then realise I needn't have bothered, as her initials are all over the next few pages, her statements giving me a good idea of who'll be meeting me tomorrow night.

MS: I think I'm more qualified than anyone else here to talk about what it feels like to be angry at your children.

ST: OK, then, you tell me. Am I right to feel the way I do?

MS: You're entitled to feel any way you want to. It always makes me angry when I read about cases of child abuse [to LC] . . . and I'm talking about physical abuse here, not sexual . . . that they never take into account the fact that a child is not an innocent animal but another human being, capable of saying things that can be incredibly hurtful. Anyone who's got a brother or a sister will agree that no matter how much they might be against violence, the one person who can prompt them to abandon this principle is their sibling.

ST[Nodding.]: When Dan was young, I used to smack him – this isn't a confession, by the way, just a statement of fact. I don't think smacking is a bad thing, and I would defend my right to do so – but the one thing that would drive me crazy, and make me much more violent than I originally intended, was that while I punished him in anger, he would remain utterly calm until he thought I had finished, and then say in this creepy adult voice, 'Thank you for showing me how easy it is to make you lose control.' The same thing, every time, even though it made me so angry I'd start all over again. 'Thank you for showing me how easy it is to make you lose control.'

I can't help smiling at this, pleased I'd left such a lasting impression on his psyche. This seems pretty admirable behaviour to me, and I'm surprised one of Dad's hags doesn't say, 'Sounds like a pretty cool kid.' Reading this account reminds me of being a child unable to understand the emotions of adults. I'd always thought that things would become clearer once I'd grown up, but now I'm an adult the actions of my parents' generation seem even more confusing, and there's such a schism between their beliefs and mine that I can't imagine how they'd behave if they were my age now.

MS: I know I shock you. I heard the gasp when I told you what I did to my daughter. I also know that to most of you I probably represent the kind of adult that fucked up your childhood. Some of you probably believe I shouldn't even be in this group, but I think my presence here is exactly what's needed to allow you to resolve the problems you've been nursing for years. I'm not going to sit here and agree with all your whining. I don't care how unpopular it makes me, but I think a lot of you, not you Lucy, but a lot of you, have brought your problems on yourself.

IJ: I don't have any problems.

MS: Lucky you.

ST: OK, it's coming up to nine o'clock and I think this might be a good point to bring this meeting to a—

VD: No, let her speak. If this meeting is going to work, we can't stop people speaking just because we disagree with them.

ST: Fair enough, but you've all agreed that I am to be chairman of this group, and I think we've done enough for tonight. Everyone here has been very brave, and if you want to pursue Marilyn's point further, I think it'd be better to take it up next week.

MS: It doesn't matter. I've said my piece.

ST: OK, Valerie?

VD: OK. I wasn't making an issue.

ST: Good.

ST ends the session by thanking everyone for attending, and for being so frank with one another. He warns those with less experience of group therapy that they may experience some negative aftershocks as a result of this evening. He says that it is a common psychological phenomenon that the excitement of group-revelation can prompt people to say things that they may regret having said at a later stage. It's not uncommon, he adds, to find yourself doing things to compensate for this previous openness, e.g. drinking heavily, or becoming reticent with normally trusted loved ones. Most of these patterns of behaviour are, he insists, relatively harmless, but if anyone has any suicidal thoughts, he urges them to contact either him or another member of the group.

The meeting ends with everyone swapping phone numbers, discussing whether this is a good time for future sessions, and general goodbyes.

Session concluded 21:15.

I put down the book and look round the call-centre. It's coming up to seven o'clock and I'm getting worried about John. It seemed too risky to feed him earlier (after all, if someone in the adjacent toilet saw my head poking over the top of the cubicle, they're unlikely to accept I'm trying to feed a cat), but as old ladies, for the most part, tend to stay out of men's lavatories, it seems a good time to sneak out and give him some Felix.

I leave the *Aspect* on *Ready*, and walk out to the cloakroom. Fetching John's food and toys is the most dangerous part of my mission, and I decide it's safer to take the whole rucksack into the toilet. I stand on the pedestal, push back the ceiling tile and reach inside for the bowl. My fingers rub across the dusty surface, the moulded plastic eluding me. I drop down from the pedestal and turn the bag over on the tiled floor, unzipping the side-pocket where I've stored Mr Farnell's torch. I don't know why I hadn't considered that John might move his bowl, but now he has it's going to be a lot harder to locate him. I'm not tall enough to be able to look inside the ceiling without stepping up onto the back of the toilet, so I do so, trying to rest my weight as gently as possible. I push up the tile with my head and shine the torch inside, getting a quick glimpse of the dusty ceiling structure before the porcelain top slips from the back of the toilet. My legs straddle the bowl as I fall backwards, arms reaching for the door as the top breaks into two pieces, both of which drop heavily onto my feet. The pain is bad, but not, I hope, broken-toe bad, although both sets feel too bruised to wiggle. I let myself drop onto the tiled floor, the beam of my torch aiming halfway up the cubicle wall. From in here the accident sounded incredibly loud, but there's three walls between me and the old ladies, so hopefully they didn't hear (I couldn't cope with one of them rushing in to ask, 'Are you OK, love?'). I look at the two pieces of toilet top, wondering what to do with them. I pick up the first piece and hold it against the second, checking there's no extra chips and that they'll still fit together. Then I slowly swing my legs round and kneel up, resting the broken halves on top of the overflow. The porcelain's heavy enough to rest there safely, and unless someone else tries to stand on it, the two pieces should remain stable for the moment.

When the pain in my backside dulls enough for me to stand up, I stop worrying about it and instead wonder what to do about the cat. As the ceiling space runs above the whole of this floor, I could wait until later and try a different point of entry, but the missing food bowl seems ominous, and I'm keen to check he's OK before ten thirty.

I make sure the flush hasn't been damaged, and put down the toilet seat. The rucksack can stay in the cubicle and I walk back into the call-centre. Even though I choose a chair from a corner away from the other teams, one of the old ladies still notices me wheeling it away. I stop and meet her eye.

'Bulb's gone in the toilet.'

'Oh,' she says, 'do you need a hand?'

'No, it's fine.'

She accepts this excuse and looks back at her screen. I idly wonder what she's got loaded up. Patience, most likely, although sometimes these old ladies surprise you. Most of them have whizz-kid kids or grandkids, who like to copy off stuff to keep Grandma entertained at work. It probably isn't anything that interesting (simulation games like Sim City or Civilisation tend to be too slow-paced for trigger-happy old ladies), but it might be a good shoot-'em-up (Tomb Raider 2, perhaps, or some new one).

I lift the chair up over the metal ridge separating the toilets and cloakroom from the rest of the call-centre. Then I roll it through to the cubicle with the broken toilet-lid and position it beneath the right ceiling tile. After my previous recklessness, I try to prevent another accident by filling the ridge around the castors with toilet paper, then put a whole roll in front of each of the four wheels, making certain it won't slip away when I stand up.

Then I climb onto the chair.

The bowl is about two metres from my reach. I estimate that if I want to get it back I'll have to push up a tile by the sinks in the women's toilets. I'm not going in there until the old ladies have gone, but I still want to check he's OK. So I take the plastic catball from the rucksack and rattle it through the hole. Then I wait for a response. There's a rustle in the corner, but when I aim the torch in the direction of the sound I can't see anything. I rattle the ball again. Nothing. God, I hope I haven't killed him. Another rattle. Silence. Rattle. Meow.

Yes.

'John?' I call, rattling the ball again. He doesn't reply. Despairing, I roll the ball across the ceiling. It gets about three metres before coming to a stop. I wait, but John doesn't seem inclined to go after it. I get down from the chair and take another small can of Felix from my rucksack. It seemed more sensible to get a supply of small cans and use a whole one each time rather than trying to find somewhere safe to store anything larger. I could, I suppose, leave them in the staff fridge, but unless I managed to persuade everyone I had very strange dietary requirements, it'd be a bit of a give-away.

His dish may be out of reach, but I'm sure he'll smell the food and eat it if he's hungry. I dollop out a small pile alongside the lifted tile, then climb down, put the rucksack back in the cloakroom and return to my desk.

My *Aspect* shows an accepted call that was picked up two minutes and twenty-seven seconds ago. Surprised someone would hold for that long, I pick up the headset and say, 'Hello, Magicmix Records.'

'I thought this line was open till ten thirty.'

'It is. I'm sorry, I didn't hear the call start.'

'But I've been shouting and singing.'

'Have you? There must be something wrong with this headset. Hang on, I'll replace it.' I pause. 'Is that better?'

'How would I know? The problem's not at my end.'

'Of course. Sorry.'

'It doesn't matter. Can I speak to Dan please?'

'Speaking.'

'Guess who?'

'Account number?'

'76956.'

'I thought so. You phoned this morning.'

'That's right.'

'And you're still in the stockroom. What is it, late-night closing?'

'No, I'm at home.'

'So why are you calling? Did you forget some numbers?'

'Are you alone in the office?'

'No,' I tell her, deciding a practical, down-to-earth tone is best, 'there are several other operators with me.'

'I see,' she says, sighing, 'I had this romantic idea that I might be able to catch you alone.'

'And why would you want to do that?'

'For a chat. And to apologise.'

'What for?'

'Being bitchy earlier. I thought you were one of those boring idiots they usually have on these lines, but you actually sound like a pretty nice guy.'

'Thank you.'

'Don't mention it. So, do you want to know my name?'

'OK.'

'Moyra.'

'Really?'

'Yes. Don't you believe me?'

'I'm not sure. It sounds a little . . .'

'A little what?' she asks, defensive.

'Like a made-up name.'

'It's my real name,' she says in a serious tone. 'Anything else you'd like to know?'

'Like what?'

'I don't know. My age perhaps?'

'OK.'

'Twelve.' She waits. I don't reply. 'No, I'm kidding. I'm nineteen. Is that too young for you?'

'Where are you calling from, Moyra?'

'My bedroom.'

'No, which part of the country?'

'Don't you have that on your computer?'

'I didn't input your number. I assumed you wouldn't be calling this late to order records.'

'Doncaster. Why?'

'Can you keep a secret?'

'Usually.'

'OK, if you call here at eleven o'clock, you'll find me alone.'

'Really? OK, I'll call back, Bye, Dan.'

'Bye, Moyra.'

I divert all calls to the Train-times line and take my permitted fifteen-minute break. It's just long enough to get a hamburger, although I have to bring it back to the office to eat it. I thumb through *Man and the Vertebrates* as I chew my dinner, looking for my place. I'd prefer to carry on reading the minutes, but as they're the only thing that makes my nights interesting, it's more sensible to ration them out. Besides, it's been a while since I've given any attention to the *Vertebrates* book, and I worry that if I don't start again tonight, I'll abandon my plan to read through Dad's library. This is definitely the least appealing volume in his collection, and I just want to get through it and on to *Political Ideas*. I'm not questioning the quality of *Man and the Vertebrates*: I'm sure it'd be fascinating to any anatomist, but my minor intellectual ability lies on the side of the arts rather than sciences, and I feel much more at home with Hobbes and Locke than king penguins and snapping turtles.

The middle section of *Man and the Vertebrates* is much more entertaining than the beginning, mainly because it includes sixty-four pages devoted to black and white photographs. Among the creatures depicted is the mud puppy, a large salamander that can never become an adult because it has forgotten how to grow up. The best thing about this creature is that this inability to reach maturity is a defining characteristic of all mud puppies, rather than a peculiarity of a small percentage of the species. How excellent to be an animal that was genetically incapable of becoming an adult! Maybe reading this book isn't as pointless as I thought. At least when they ask me what I want to be reincarnated as, I'll have a good answer. Dan the mud puppy. Perfect.

I manage to get to the end of Chapter Ten before the old ladies leave. The book looks a lot less daunting now I'm over two-thirds of the way through, and I leave the call-centre feeling much happier than I did yesterday. I don't feel like eating anything more after my hamburger, so I walk down to the docks to wait until I'm sure the security guard's gone home.

I always feel sentimental sitting here, watching girls hobble across the cobbles, clutching their skirts as they decide which pub to slip into. Before I joined Quick Kall and started frequenting The

Pentangle, I always used to go out clubbing on Thursdays, and it still feels like the friendliest night of the week. A woman in a grey hooded-top approaches me for change and I give her fifty pence, enjoying the brief smile she flashes me in return. Then I stare into the dark, rippling dockwaters, feeling at one with my city.

I realise I must be coming across as a right perv, but I have to admit that I feel a stirring of last night's stupid sex-excitement when I enter the ladies' toilet. Perhaps this is the sort of thing most people keep to themselves, but reading Dad's minutes has made me envious of those lucky enough to have friends who are willing to listen to their private thoughts, so let me indulge myself in this more isolated place of self-revelation. Until yesterday, I was a perfectly normal member of society. I had a few odd peccadilloes, but who doesn't? (And in our fun, fetishistic age, some personal peculiarities only add to a fully rounded character.) I'd be the first to admit that I've become a little more insular over the last year, but that was inevitable after everything that happened between Sonia (the GBH girl) and me. I may never have achieved the prerequisite clumsy blandness of being a good bloke, and I know I've always made girls uneasy, but all in all, I think I was doing a pretty good job of getting along with the rest of the world. Now, however, I've crossed the line, and although I can easily rationalise my behaviour, I can't tell anyone (except for a lonely nineteen-year-old) about my living conditions. So, seeing as I am to live in secrecy, I see no reason to deny myself the incidental pleasures of an outsider's existence. And if I feel sexually excited at the thought of being in a room where every woman nonchalantly exposes herself at least once a day, then that's my business. It's not as if I'm spying on anyone, or laying my face across toilet pans (although if I knew who used the cubicle last, I might give it a go). I'm simply looking for my cat's dish, that's all.

The faux-marble sink surround looks a lot stronger than the back of the toilet, and I can climb up onto it without worrying about another mishap. As far as I can tell, the dish is above one of these four tiles. I push up the third. It's a lot heavier than the tile above the toilet, and I'm about to give up when the left hand side tilts abruptly and John falls in front of my face, hitting the polished floor claws first. The dish drops down after him, bouncing twice as he scarpers towards the door.

'No you don't,' I tell him, jumping down and grabbing at his tail. He meows angrily, then turns to hiss at me. I watch his back arc up and then grab his body, wondering how I'm going to get him back up into the ceiling without a cat basket.

It takes three attempts. The first time I get him right up to the hole before he starts wriggling, his claws digging through my suit and tearing the skin beneath. Attempt two ends almost as soon as it starts, and I steel myself for one last go before I give in and fetch the cat basket. Bored with the game, John stays still, allowing me to put him in the roof without complaint. He even stays in the hole while I fetch another can of Felix and fill his bowl, watching me as I replace the tile.

Moyra doesn't call back. I sit by the phone until one o'clock, honing my Patience skills, but she's obviously not that interested. It's a shame, I was looking forward to talking to her. But I suppose it's safer this way. When it's clear she's not going to ring, I close down my computer and retire to the cloakroom.

11

One brown tile might've gone unnoticed. Two, however, is pushing it. It can only be a matter of time before some eager beaver brings it to the attention of management and they send maintenance up to check on the pipes. I worry for John, but what am I supposed to do? Put a litter tray up there? Any more weight and the whole lot'll come down.

I don't feel as good as I did yesterday. My face has gone blotchy from washing with the liquid soap in the toilet and I had a bad night's sleep on the floor of the cloakroom. I'd meant to wake myself up early and go for a walk, but I'd only just managed to beat the cleaners. It's at times like this that I realise I really do hate my job, just like everyone else. The thing that gets me most is only having four fifteen-minute breaks. It's nice to have the same company every day, but I'd do anything for some proper time to talk with my co-workers.

At half past ten, Ian removes his headset and picks up his cigarettes, the signal for the rest of us to log off and start walking to the breaks room. Gordon's lips always form the same shapes just before he leaves his desk, probably signing off to his imaginary audience. He doesn't tend to talk to himself as much during breaktimes, maybe because he's listening to us. As much as it unnerves me, I have to admit I'm fascinated by Gordon's condition, probably because I'm scared that's how I'll end up.

Adrienne puts her arm across my shoulders. 'Step into my office.'

She holds the cloakroom door open. I follow her, drawing suspicious glances from Ian and Teri.

'I've got your money,' she says, handing me a jiffy bag, 'if I give it to you now I don't have to worry about it getting nicked.'

'OK. Thanks.'

She pauses. 'Are you sure everything's OK?'

'Yeah, I told you. It's all legitimate debt. No one's going to break my legs.'

'I didn't mean the money.'

'Oh. Yeah, I'm fine, it's been a long week, that's all.'

She sighs. 'It's just, look, are those cuts on your wrists?'

Surprised, I look down and see the scratches John made last night. I laugh, and tell her, 'They're cat scratches. I'm trying to adopt a stray tom.'

'You want to be careful,' she tells me. 'My dad got scratched by a cat and his arm swelled up like a balloon.'

'You're always telling me to be careful,' I tease her, 'do you have maternal feelings towards me?'

'I am a mother to you lot. Without me you'd fall to pieces.'

She opens the door and we go after the others. At the top of the stairs I ask her, 'Have you ever had counselling, Adrienne?'

'Why? Are you saying I need it?'

'No, I just wondered. You seem quite open-minded.'

'What's that got to do with it?'

'You're a practical sort, that's all I mean. If something's wrong, you don't get uptight about it, you just fix it. I wondered if you're the same about your emotions.'

'What's this about, Dan? Are you looking for a counsellor?'

'No, it's not that. Do you remember when I was talking about my dad and his group?' She nods. 'Well, I've got to go and meet them tonight, and I'm worried what to say to them.'

'I don't understand.'

'It just seems so alien to me, that sort of thing. I know I'm being pathetic and repressed and British, but I couldn't bear the idea of discussing my problems, especially in a room full of strangers.'

It's colder outside than I'd anticipated, and as the wind cuts through my shirt sleeves, I wish I hadn't left my jacket on the back of my chair.

'I've phoned the Samaritans a couple of times.'

I look at her, surprised. 'Really?'

She sighs. 'It's different on the phone. Don't you find that sometimes at work you get a caller who shows a little bit of interest in you and you end up telling them your life story.'

I smile, thinking of Moyra. 'So what's it like with the Samaritans then?'

'OK. It helps if you don't let them say anything. Then you can pretend you're talking to God or something.'

'God?'

She blushes. 'You're really embarrassing me this morning. When I was little, I didn't really have the idea of God that most people do. I saw him more as an imaginary friend. I used to tell him everything. I didn't realise how different I was to other Catholic girls until I got to Convent school.'

'So you don't see him like that any more?'

'Sometimes. In my head I've got two Gods. One is like the God I spoke to when I was little. That's my God. The Nuns' God is more frightening.'

I open the door for Adrienne and she walks straight through to the smoking room. I stop for a minestrone, jumping when Ian comes up behind me.

'All right mate?' he asks.

I nod, not paying attention. He goes silent. Maybe his words were intended as something more than a friendly greeting. I look at him. He stares back at me, downtilted eyebrows emphasising his concern.

'What were you saying to Adrienne?'

I'm about to make a flippant reply when I realise he's genuinely pissed off. God knows what I've done wrong, but his body is primed, his usually friendly face twisted into a grimace of aggressive worry. I can only assume someone's been on the wind-up, but what've they been telling him?

I show him the jiffy bag. 'I needed some financial assistance.'

He looks at the money, visibly relaxing. His uncharacteristic emotion's unsettled me, and I don't like not knowing what's agitated him. I've never thought of Ian as a threat – he's my best mate, after all – but just now was definitely a tense moment. I take my drink from the machine and wait while he gets a second coffee.

'Any luck with your ex?' I ask him.

He looks at me, and I wonder whether this is such a good way of changing the subject.

'What d'you mean?' he asks.

'Those pants Adrienne mended. Did you send them back?'

'No,' he says, and his face changes, 'I knew she didn't want them back really. They were an old pair. She used to wear old pairs and let me rip them off. It was just a lonely moment.'

He takes his drink and we walk back to the smoking room. Adrienne is slowly turning over the pages of last night's *Evening Post*.

'You heard about this lap-dancing club?'

'You auditioning?' Ian asks.

She smiles. 'Is that what you want? You want me to give you a show?'

Ian doesn't reply. Adrienne looks at me, and I wonder how best to respond. As much as I feel indebted to Ade for giving me the money, it doesn't seem a good time to side against Ian. So I say, 'No thanks, Ade. I'm not sure I could cope with it.'

Adrienne waits for Ian's surprised, throaty laughter to die down, then throws the newspaper at me.

*   *   *

I fall away from the others as we return to our desks, nipping into the toilet to check my money. The king in his counting-house. I sit on the wooden seat and empty the cash into my lap, dropping the jiffy bag onto the tiled floor. I place the notes down one at a time, enjoying the knowledge that each note buys me a few more days. I love the freedom that comes with a lump sum, even though I know it'll soon diminish.

I tuck the money back into my bag and return to my work-station. The wait-light is flashing. I unwrap my headset and press *Ready*. The caller starts talking immediately, cutting off my salutation.

'I've got a problem with my mobile,' he tells me, and straight away I sense something unusual about his voice. Usually mobile callers are the hardest to deal with, especially as they all believe they have to sound like hyper-busy businessmen to get any service. They refuse to be without the phone for more than half an hour (presumably because they know that even without the handset they're still paying for line-rental) and can never decide whether they want to go into a repair centre or have the phone couriered. This caller, however, sounds distinctly unhurried.

'OK, what's wrong with it?'

'It's pretty fucked.'

'I see. Is it a problem with the aerial, the reception, the keypad, or the battery?'

'I'm not sure.'

'OK, what we normally do in these situations is if you give me the mobile's number, I'll call you and then depending on what happens we should be able to work out the nature of the problem.'

'I don't think you can do that.'

'Don't worry, it doesn't matter if you can't hear me.'

He laughs. 'I don't think you understand. There's not much left of the phone.'

'What's happened to it?'

'I've smashed it up.'

'Oh. I guess you realise you've invalidated your warranty. Who's your airtime provider?'

'What does that matter?'

'I'm just trying to gather some information so we can go about getting you a new phone.'

'I don't want a new phone.'

'We don't handle cancelling line-rental on this line. If you want to discuss that you should go into the shop where you bought the phone.'

'I don't want to cancel the line-rental.'

'So what exactly do you need help with?'

'I need someone to talk to.'

'OK sir, you sound like an interesting person and I personally would love to talk to you, but the problem is that the calls are being monitored and . . .'

'They're not all monitored though, are they?'

'Sir?'

'My girlfriend works in a call-centre. I know they don't monitor all your calls.'

'Yes, that's true, but unfortunately, they've had a couple of complaints about me, so now they're listening in all day.'

'See, now I know you're lying. If you really were being monitored, you wouldn't risk telling me all that. As I remember, you're not even allowed to tell me you work for an agency.'

'I haven't said anything about an agency.'

He ignores me. 'Just talk to me for a couple of minutes. Ask me why I smashed my phone.'

'Why did you smash your phone?'

'I smashed my phone so I wouldn't be able to call my girlfriend.'

I don't say anything. His breathing becomes heavy. Then he says, 'Ask me why I don't want to call my girlfriend.'

'Why don't you want to call your girlfriend?'

'I do, more than anything. That's why I smashed my phone.

But you can always find another phone. The only way I can stop myself calling her is to be on the phone to someone else. That's why I'm talking to you.'

'Why don't you call a chatline or something?'

'At fifty pence a minute?'

'What about your parents? Or a friend?'

'Do you think I want someone I know to hear me like this?'

I don't say anything. No one else gets calls like this. There must be some strange quirk in the switchboard that re-routes all the desperate losers to my extension. I get more disturbed callers in this job than I did when I manned the linkline at my ex-girlfriend's university. I've got nothing against talking to this caller – his problem sounds like something I can identify with – but the cumulative effect of all this stray emotion is starting to get to me.

'Never mind,' he says, 'I'm sorry for bothering you. I suppose I should stop being such a wimp and do something decisive. Cut out my tongue maybe. No, that's no good, I'd still be able to call her, just not able to say anything. Forget it. Goodbye.'

He hangs up.

At lunchtime I go across and pay my thousand into the bank. I know at least two hundred will disappear on my arrears, but it feels safer not to be carrying around that much cash in a padded envelope. There's a number of office scams that operate from the cloakroom (the most recent being borrowing chargecards from their jackets and returning them before they know they're gone) and no matter how careful I am, I'm sure it wouldn't be long before someone found out about my money.

The afternoon goes slowly, especially without the promise of an afterwork drink. I always knew Friday would be difficult. The few hours in The Friar are my favourite part of the working week, one of the few times I get to talk to anyone face-to-face without having to watch the clock. Just as everyone is getting up to go, Adrienne comes across and hands me the Suggestions Book.

'What's this?'

'Daniel's Diary, instalment one.'

'Revenge for this morning, I suppose.'

'Maybe, although I think I've been fair.'

'Have fun tonight.'

'You not coming?'

'Can't.'

'Come afterwards. They'll let you in.'

'No, that's when I'm meeting Dad's women.'

'In the middle of the night? What is it? Some kind of orgy?'

'Don't joke. That's what I'm afraid of.'

'I see. What time will it finish?'

'I don't know. How late could I get into the club?'

'As late as you like. Just mention my name.'

'Thanks, I'll try. And Adrienne, I really am grateful for the money.'

I wait until I'm sure she's gone and then flip through the book until I find the latest entry. After everything she's written about Gordon, I'm worried what she's going to describe me doing, but nevertheless I can't resist reading it. Although she's using a different-coloured pen, she hasn't made any attempt to change her style of handwriting from Gordon's Log. She has, however, made a slight break from tradition in the content of her writing, choosing to describe a day in my life instead of the night-time accounts that make up Gordon's entries.

Daniel's Diary   13/3/9—

I'm not by nature a suspicious man, but this Friday the thirteenth has been marred by a series of unpleasant experiences. The first of these was the discovery that my best buddy, Ian, has stolen a march on me and managed to seduce my dream woman, the divine lady Adrienne. I was particularly surprised to hear this news today as I had just finished stage nine of my failproof seduction system, which entailed borrowing a large sum of money from her.

In the past, I have found that being in debt to a woman is a surefire way of ensuring that they will remain in contact with you, even after the relationship has been terminated. Debt is a much more respectable connection than love. And longer lasting. A girlfriend will stop writing at the first hint of trouble. The bank can be relied upon for two letters a month from now until the end of time.

Ian told me the news at break this morning. He was discreet, as befits such a noble man, but I couldn't help wondering what their relationship might be like. After all, they are the two coolest people in the office, and both have a physical energy which makes it exciting just to look at them. The thought of Ian and Adrienne in bed together was too much for me to cope with, and as we walked back into the smoking room, I was so angry that I could barely look at Adrienne.

Being an incredibly perceptive person, Adrienne immediately noticed my frustration and tried to taunt me by talking about lap-dancing clubs. It was easy to cope with her aggressive sexuality when I thought she was flirting with me, but now I know her love is reserved for another, I don't want to hear about it. In order to put an end to her fun, I came up with a cutting retort which sounded innocuous and generalised, yet at the same time prompted a laugh of recognition from her new lover. I have to confess that I felt more than a little pleased with myself. Serves the bitch right. No one gets the better of me.

The entry ends there. No homophobic jokes, no enforced buggery. It seems strange, even for Adrienne. It's hard to know whether the stuff about her and Ian is true or made-up. Surely if they had just started going out, she'd be a bit more cautious about mocking their relationship. Although having said that, she does flatter him once or twice in the entry, and if they are now a couple, this is the sort of thing Adrienne would do to prove that she won't be sacrificing her character to their relationship. In spite of her suggestion that I'd be jealous, I hope they are together. Otherwise this seems as good a time as any to start worrying about Adrienne's mental health.

161

I wonder if she really does think Ian told me about their relationship (if it exists) this morning. It seems a natural assumption to make. After all, as she herself notes, he is my best friend. I'm not entirely sure why he didn't. Unless he's embarrassed about it. Maybe he thinks I'll disapprove.

I spend the next two hours finishing *Man and the Vertebrates*, forcing myself to read it properly instead of letting my eyes skid over the unengaging prose. After yesterday's photographs, the last section is a bit of a let-down, with no new creatures as interesting as the mud puppy. Still, it feels satisfying to have finished another of Dad's books, and now that I've only got *Political Ideas* left to go, I've good reason to feel pleased with myself.

I leave my *Aspect* on *Ready* and walk across to the old lady opposite me. She's engrossed in her computer game, the light from the screen palely reflected by her crumpled face. Even though it's a sacking offence to load unauthorised software onto the Quick Kall system, she makes no attempt to hide her activity. I walk round behind her, looking at the screen.

'What you got there?'

'Hotel Babylon.'

I don't recognise the name. The screen is split into three sections. To the right is an image of a skyscraper, with a small red dot halfway up the grey column. Along the bottom left is a row of gauges. Each gauge indicates the strength of a different emotion and most are near zero. Above this is a square which shows the inside of what looks like a hotel room. The animated image shows a skinny man with long black hair and no shirt lying on a messy bed.

'What d'you have to do?' I ask the old lady.

'All sorts,' she says. 'See that man on the bed? He's a rock star called Dave Gristle. At the moment we're waiting for a delivery.'

'What happens then?'

'We can have a party.'

'How d'you do that?'

She taps at the keyboard. Dave stands up. 'I get him out of the room.' She taps again. Dave goes into the corridor. The red dot moves to the left. 'And we knock on a few doors.' Dave does so. A blonde woman in a short pink dress opens her door and slowly shakes her head. 'See, she won't come to the party until we get some drugs.'

'What's the aim of the game?'

'It doesn't really have one. It's more like a soap opera or something. You can choose to be anyone in the building. I suppose the point is to give your character the best life possible.'

'Can they leave the hotel?'

'Yes, but that's the end of the game.'

'And is it fun?'

'It's brilliant.'

'Any chance you could make me a copy?'

'I don't know. I'll have to ask.'

'I'll give you something in return.'

'A game?' she asks brightly.

'No, not a game. I don't suppose you read at all.'

'I read,' she says, insulted. 'Are you going to give me a book?'

'In return for the game?'

'What's it called?'

'You have to agree first. Will you give me the game?'

'I don't know,' she says, looking at me suspiciously, 'what's the book about?'

'Mankind.'

'That's too general. Is it a thriller?'

'Not really, although it is exciting.'

'A romance?'

'No, it's sort of a true story.'

'A true crime book? No, I don't want it.'

'It's not a crime book.'

'No, I don't want it,' she says stubbornly. 'I've decided. I don't care what it is.'

'Are you sure? It's a good read, and it's got pictures.'

'No, I'm not interested. Besides, I don't think I'll be able to make you a copy. The game's not on the market yet. Ah, the delivery's here.'

A man in a black suit and glasses appears on screen. He's standing in the doorway carrying a black leather briefcase. The old lady taps the keyboard. Dave opens the bedside drawer. The screen fills with a close-up of five ten-dollar bills. I can't help feeling envious of the old lady and wish I could think of another way of persuading her to give me the game. I decide to try making her feel guilty.

'OK, I understand, but I'd like you to have the book anyway. I don't have any use for it.'

I leave *Man and the Vertebrates* on the table and walk back to my desk. No calls waiting. It's coming up to nine o'clock and I still haven't had my break yet. I'm getting much better at controlling the evenings. I don't feel hungry so I decide to use my fifteen minutes to check on John. I divert my calls to the Train-times line and fetch my rucksack from the cloakroom. Not wanting to repeat yesterday's slapstick routine, I wheel a chair out with me. The old lady stops playing Hotel Babylon long enough to watch me struggle with the door before looking back to her screen. I'm sure she thinks there's something wrong with me. She probably doesn't realise I do two shifts and thinks I've been moved to the evening detail because I've been disturbing the daytime operators.

I'm expecting another wasted break, but I find John almost immediately. I don't know whether he feels guilty about peeing on the ceiling or simply lonely after spending two days alone, but he starts meowing the moment I lift the tile, and as I reach out for John's bowl I can feel his rough tongue licking my fingers. I know he'll run off if I bring him down, so I place my hands on his sides and give his body a friendly shake instead. Then I refill his bowl and put it back in the ceiling. He's a good cat, really, and in spite of the trouble he's caused, I'm glad I brought him with me. I stroke his head and replace the tile.

Before I wheel the chair back, I check the top of the toilet to make sure the two pieces remain firmly wedged together. They seem OK for the moment, although maybe I should visit a DIY store in one of my breaks and get some glue to join them back properly. I could even see about getting some new ceiling tiles. In fact, a few odd jobs might be just the thing to get me through an empty weekend.

Back at my desk, I log on and load up Patience. I play a few hands but it's nowhere near as much fun now I know I could be directing Dave Gristle around Hotel Babylon. I don't feel up to beginning *Political Ideas*, and it seems a good idea to keep away from the minutes until after the big showdown, so, until the old ladies leave, I kill the time staring into space and wondering what awaits me tonight.

I still hold out hope that the old lady might take pity on me and give me the game, but she leaves without even saying goodbye. Depressed, I decide to head down to The Friar for my afterwork drink. The pub's a lot busier than it is at six, and I have to share a table with three strangers. They make no attempt to include me in the conversation, which is just how I want it. I drink three pints and leave at half eleven.

I expected a car. When a woman pulls up on a motorbike and stops to stare at me, I assume her attentions are entirely unconnected to what I'm supposed to be doing tonight. I even feel a little excited, indulging in the fantasy that this leather-clad stranger might pick me up, take me home and change my life. Instead, she kills her engine and shouts across: 'Daniel?'

'Yes?'

'I'm Marilyn. You'll need this.' She offers me a crash helmet. I stay where I am, remembering reading about Marilyn's irrational anger and wondering if it's sensible to accept her offer of a lift.

'Is it safe?'

'Of course.'

I take the helmet. 'Where do I sit?'

'Here,' she says, patting the leather seat. I walk across and climb on behind her. She starts the engine and makes an illegal U-turn. I hold on to the back of the bike, trying to keep my balance without touching her. She heads towards the Centre and then up Park Street, keeping at a steady speed until we reach Clifton Village. It's here that she parks the bike, taking off her helmet and waiting for me to give her mine. She seems different to the two other group members I've met, and it's hard to imagine them moving in the same circle. Marilyn's completely free of the aggressive suburban sexuality that oozes from Valerie and Brittany, her body looking neither plump nor aerobicised beneath the black leather and her hair naturally blonde instead of the used felt-tip colour of the other women's hair dye. I could even imagine myself being attracted to Marilyn, whereas a night spent with Valerie or Brittany would have to be my last on this earth.

Marilyn walks to the nearest doorway and presses the buzzer. There's a crackle and a voice I can't hear. She holds the door open and I follow her into the house. We walk up to the third floor. A door is open at the end of the corridor. I follow Marilyn towards the light. She tries to act naturally as we enter the room, but I can tell the others are making her feel anxious. I look for Valerie and Brittany, and see them sitting together on a brown sofa-bed. Three others sit on a low settee beneath a stuffed bookcase. The last woman is standing in front of us, asking me if I'd like a drink. I nod.

'Beer? Whisky? Orange juice?'

'Beer, thanks.'

She retreats through one of the two doorways. Marilyn puts the motorbike helmets on the table and unzips her jacket. Brittany smiles at me. The woman returns from the kitchen and hands me a cold can of Fosters.

'Now,' she says, 'introductions. I'm Lucy, that's Imogen, Diane and Claire. Brittany and Valerie you've already met. Would you like to sit down?'

Three wooden chairs have been lined along the left-hand side of the wall. I sit down. So does Marilyn. Lucy remains standing. I look round the room to see if anyone's taking minutes, wondering if this is an official meeting.

'OK, Daniel, why don't you tell us what you know about us?'

I open my can. 'You're my dad's friends.'

'Anything else?'

'Not really. I know a bit more about Brittany. Her niece is my team leader.'

'So Steve hasn't talked about us?'

'No, I didn't know you existed until his accident.'

Valerie takes a cigarette from the box on the coffee table. I watch her light it and slowly exhale. She looks at me and asks, 'Do you love your father, Dan?'

'Of course.'

'Of course,' she repeats, nodding. 'You two live together, don't you?'

'We used to.'

'So where do you live now?'

'No, I mean, *I* still live there, but he's in the hospital.'

'Right. And when you did live together, you never noticed him going out?'

'No,' I tell her, 'I'm out a lot myself. To tell you the truth, I never really thought about what Dad might be doing. I assumed he stayed home on his own. Or went to the Casino. Dad's always led a very private life.'

Imogen smiles at me. 'What about your mum, Daniel?'

'I haven't seen her in about a year.'

I don't know why, but I feel close to tears. Something about Imogen and the tone in which she asked that question. I know I should be angry – after all, she must know about my mum and no doubt was trying to get an emotional reaction – but instead I want to lie out on the carpet and tell her how lonely I've felt recently. For fuck's sake, Dan, calm down! These women are experts in psychological manipulation *and* friends of Dad's. For all you know, he might have put them up to this. Just answer the questions and let's get out of here.

'But how d'you feel towards her?' Imogen persists.

'I love her.'

'In the same way you love your dad?'

'The emotion's the same, but the relationship is different. With Mum, it's a static feeling. It won't change until I see her again. My relationship with Dad changes every day.'

'What makes it change?'

'Everything. The dynamics of living together. It's changed since the accident.'

'In what way?'

'I don't know. It's strange but I feel it's made him less dependent on me. Even though I know when he gets out he'll need my help.'

'Ah,' says Lucy, 'that's one of the things we brought you here to discuss.'

'We wondered if you'd mind if we look after your father when he gets out of hospital,' Brittany explains. 'He's going to need twenty-four-hour attention, and it'd be a lot easier for the seven of us to take care of him rather than you coping on your own. We've spoken to Steve, and he says if it's OK with you, it's OK with him.'

I smile, surprised by this unexpected solution to my problems. Maybe everything will get fixed this way from now on. I can't decide whether this proves that good luck always follows bad, or some unknown god has decided my rightful place is remaining in the call-centre, and has taken it upon himself to sort out any threats to this existence.

'Dan?' Lucy enquires.

'That's fine.'

'When was the last time you visited your dad?' Valerie asks.

'I haven't been in for a while,' I admit. 'I was hoping to get in some time over the weekend.'

'OK, that's good. You don't feel threatened by us, do you, Dan?' Imogen asks.

'No,' I mumble, 'of course not.'

'Because we want you to know we're not trying to take your dad away from you. Obviously he means a lot to us, but we recognise the importance of your relationship and want you to know that you can see him any time you want.'

'We realise this must seem intimidating,' Lucy tells me, 'and it's only natural that you should associate us with your father's accident, but it needn't upset you. Try not to think of us as a group. Treat us as seven individuals you just happened to meet at the same time. You don't have to like all of us, and if you want to talk to any of us alone, that's fine too.'

Lucy hands me a piece of paper. 'That's a list of our telephone numbers. You can call any of us at any time. Now, is there anything you want to ask us?'

'Not at the moment.'

'OK, we understand that you're probably a little overwhelmed. We just thought it might be easier for you if you got a sense of who we are as people, instead of this shadowy concept of a group. Marilyn will take you home now, if you'd like.'

'No, it's OK. I'm going to a club.'

Lucy nods. 'Right, well, it was nice to meet you.'

I stand up. 'You too.'

Imogen waves at me. 'Get in touch.'

I get to The Pentangle for one o'clock. The Italian couple let me in for free and I head to our usual table, looking for Ian. The seats are empty. I check the dancefloor. He's standing next to the DJ booth, talking to Adrienne. I buy a drink and walk across, thinking this is a good time to sort things out.

'All right, Ian?'

He looks at me, surprised. 'I didn't think you were coming down.'

'Any chance I can have a word with you?'

'Of course. What's wrong?'

He puts his hand on my shoulder and we walk through the dancefloor. He smells of beer and sweat, but definitely seems in a better mood than he was this morning.

'Are you and Adrienne . . . ?'

He laughs. 'Yeah. I think so.'

'How come you didn't tell me?'

'I didn't think Adrienne wanted me to. Listen, can I tell you something between mates?'

'Sure.'

'Adrienne's always been there, d'you know what I mean? But it's always been a secret. We've been together, on and off, since I started working for Quick Kall. This is the first time it's been official. Only I didn't know I was allowed to tell anyone.'

'Is that what was wrong this morning?'

'What d'you mean?'

'This morning. You seemed pissed off.'

'Oh. OK, I'll tell you. Promise you won't say anything to Ade.'

'Of course.'

'I felt jealous. It's stupid, but it was really good last night, and now we're a proper couple I've started feeling possessive. I know you and Ade are close and . . .'

I laugh. 'Not that close.'

'No, OK, I'm sorry. It was stupid.'

I put my arm round his shoulder. 'She likes to banter, that's all. There's never been anything romantic between Adrienne and me. Besides, I wouldn't do that to a mate.'

'I know. I'm sorry, Dan.'

'No problem.'

We look back to the dancefloor. I take a swig from my plastic pint glass. I'm feeling dehydrated so I walk back to the bar and pinch a handful of cubes from a red plastic ice bucket. I put four in my mouth and one down my back, crunching them between my teeth. Then I return to Ian and we watch Adrienne hand her headphones to her deputy and come across.

She stares at me. 'How was your meeting?'

'Scary.'

She nods. 'Did you read your diary?'

'Of course.'

'What did you think?'

'Woefully inaccurate, I'm afraid. I didn't even know you were a couple.'

She looks at Ian. 'I'm not surprised. He's hardly the most demonstrative of men, is he?'

Ian grabs Adrienne and pulls her against him. 'Is this what you want? I can embarrass you if that's what you're after.'

'Let's dance,' I suggest, worried I might have prompted another disagreement.

'OK,' says Ian, 'go tell your boy to put on some swingbeat and I'll show you demonstrative.'

Adrienne giggles. 'I don't think we've got any swingbeat. How about some Dr Dre?'

'Anything, just hurry up.'

She nips back to instruct her stand-in, then returns in time for the sudden increase in bass. The people around us smile when the record starts, and as the three of us find our own spot, I'm glad I made the effort to come here. I think about the last time the three of us danced together and how certain I'd been that Ian was annoying Adrienne. Instead of draping his arm across her shoulders, tonight he's got one leg wedged between hers, pulling her crotch down against the muscle of his thigh. Adrienne plays along, removing her hairband and flicking her head from side to side. I dance alongside them, feeling embarrassed. At the end of the song, they separate and go back to dancing normally.

I stay with Adrienne and Ian until the club closes. Adrienne loads her record boxes into the back of her car and takes us to the drive-thru McDonald's. We eat our food in the car park by Pet

City, then she drives us back to Ian's place. He finds a bottle of whisky and puts on a Jackie Chan video. I stay for the first half then make my excuses. Adrienne offers to drop me home, but I remind her she's over the limit and she agrees to let me walk.

There are more people on the streets than I expected, clumps of students returning from a party. They're much more energetic than me, jumping up on walls and charging at streetsigns. I've never envied students before, but tonight they seem to have everything I lack (a room of their own, more than three friends, postponable debt) and I'm tempted to follow them back to their hall of residence and claim I've been sent there on a scholarship.

It's almost dawn by the time I get back to Quick Kall. Sleeping in the cloakroom seems too risky tonight. I feel so tired that the only way the cleaners could wake me would be if they rode in on elephants. It seems safer to nod off at my desk. At least then I'll only get reprimanded for sleeping on the job. I flop down in my chair and close my eyes, losing consciousness within seconds.

12

Not working weekends has always been a luxury. Hardly any call-centre employees can survive on the hundred and ten basic, and most choose to make up their money on Saturday. Call-volume's the same as any weekday, if not higher, especially on the mobile lines. It's casual dress today, and all around me people are wearing jumpers and trainers, as if I'm in the phone room for some telethon.

Alice arrives at ten o'clock, dressed in grey leggings and a Sweater Shop jumper. Her hair's even more oddly angled than usual, as if she's sprayed it with gel and then slept on it. She's wearing pink moccasins with thick white nylon socks, happily building up static. It's common knowledge that the best time to approach Alice is first thing in the morning, before she's had chance to get stressed.

'Hi, Dan. What's wrong?'

'Nothing. I need to ask you a favour.'

'OK.'

'Would it be all right to take a couple of hours off this afternoon? It's just with working all week I haven't had chance to call in on Dad.'

'I warned you about taking on too much, Dan.'

'I know, and I wouldn't ask, only your aunt got very angry about me neglecting him.'

'When did you talk to my aunt?'

'Last night.'

'Weren't you working?'

'After work. I met the group for the first time.'

'I see. What did you think?'

'Do you know them?'

'Not really. Marilyn and Claire are friends of my mother's.'

'How come your mother isn't in the group?'

'She doesn't approve of it.' Alice breathes in and looks at me, as if remembering who I am and wondering if she should share this information. 'She and Brittany are very different.'

'Do you know what they do, the group?'

'They talk about their problems, don't they? Support each other.'

'Have you ever met my dad?'

She pauses. 'I think I saw him with Brittany once. Although you know what she's like.'

'So it could have been anyone?'

'What's this about, Dan?'

'Your aunt's been making me paranoid, that's all.'

'Paranoid about what?'

'She keeps dropping hints that she knows things about me. And talks about you.'

'What does she say about me?'

'Nothing really. She just implies things. She makes me feel like my life's being organised behind my back.'

'You sound stressed, Dan. Are you sure you don't want to drop a couple of shifts?'

'No, I'll let you know when it gets too much. But could I have the two hours?'

'OK, but not near lunchtime. Two till four, is that all right?'

I return to my desk. Now my only problem is staying awake

until two. Checking Alice is distracted in reception, I bend down beneath her work-station and take today's timesheets from her drawer, wondering who I'll have to keep me company. Adrienne and Ian, unsurprisingly, are taking today off, but Teri's due in at ten thirty. Good. Now that Adrienne's spoken for, Teri's my last opportunity for any romantic action, and although I don't fancy her, it's nice to have someone to flirt with.

I put my headset back on and take a few calls. They're all for Magicmix Records, Saturday staff reordering stock. I listen as they read off their lists, typing in numbers. Most of our team don't like Magicmix calls, finding the repetition boring. I quite enjoy them, preferring it when I only have to listen. After my third call, I notice Teri coming into the office. I wave but she doesn't see me, her black hair hanging over her eyes. My wait light flashes. I take another call. Teri hides her tartan bag in the file cupboard and comes round next to me. She's wearing a black T-shirt and blue jeans, her lips glossed with pale-pink lipstick.

'Did you get that last number?' my caller asks me.

'Yeah, it's coming up as deleted.'

'But it was only released two weeks ago.'

'It was probably a limited edition. Do you know the artist?'

'Bubbleboy.'

'I'll look it up for you.' I turn off my microphone and say hello to Teri.

She smiles. 'Good night?'

'I'm knackered. I didn't get any sleep at all. If I drop off, hit me, OK?'

I find Bubbleboy on my catalogue screen and turn my mike back on.

'Yeah,' I tell him, 'it was released in a bubblepack. Limited to five thousand copies. But there's a standard version of the twelve inch. Would you like that instead?'

'OK, whatever. Ready for the next number?'

'Fire away.'

He rattles off another list of numbers. My fingers move over the keyboard as I watch Teri set up. It's nice to have a day alone with her, free from Adrienne's bullying and Gordon's censorious gaze. I finish my call and quickly draw a Connect Four grid on a scrap of paper, shading in a coloured circle in the fourth line. I put it next to Teri's elbow and take another call. It's a mobile owner, complaining about poor reception. Teri finds a biro and draws in her circle. Although paper Connect Four is the most basic office game (except nought and crosses, I suppose), it's also one of the most durable, mainly because of the minimal effort it requires. There also seems something peculiarly intimate about the activity, a childish trust that the person playing with you won't make fun of you for suggesting it. I draw my circle and hand it back, enjoying the pleasure of doing two things at once.

'OK,' I ask my caller, 'do you know your airtime provider?'

He tells me and I call up a new screen, tapping in the additional information. Teri makes a show of pestering me with the piece of paper, and I gratefully acknowledge the attention. I fill in my circle and hand it back. I finish my call and ignore the wait-light, wanting a moment to myself. That's one good thing about working on the phone: it allows you to slack off without being seen. I'd hate to work as an attendant in a post office or a bank, where everyone in the queue knows you're finished and approaches you even before the electronic voice gives them permission. And although I feel like this, whenever I'm in a queue I'm as bad as everyone else, if not worse. I hate being held up, and see any hesitation as deliberate provocation.

'You on a call?' I ask Teri.

She nods. I wait for her to finish. When she clicks off, she turns her chair and looks at me.

'What's wrong?'

'Nothing. It's my break. I wondered if you wanted anything from the shops.'

'Can you get me a copy of *The Sport*?'

'The paper?'

She giggles. 'My housemates asked me to get it. They're too hungover to face the daylight.'

'There isn't any daylight,' I tell her, taking my jacket from the back of my chair and looking at the grey sky outside.

'You don't like my housemates, do you?'

'They're a bit masculine for me. I'm not very good with all that football, drinking stuff.'

'I've never noticed you having trouble with drinking.'

'I can fake it, but I'm not that good at it. I didn't drink at all until I was eighteen.'

'You're a bit of a wuss really, aren't you?' she laughs.

I smile. 'Afraid so. Although I prefer to think of myself as a man out of step with our age. I'm sure I'd have seemed perfectly masculine in the fifties.'

'And I suppose you're ideologically opposed to buying me a copy of *The Sport*?'

'No, I'll do it. Anything else?'

'A packet of blue Extra.'

'No problem.'

I had to take a break to stay awake. There's a light rain outside and the cold splashes feel good against my skin. I'd do anything for a bath. I should've asked Ian last night, but then Adrienne would've assumed I was suggesting a watery threesome. My feet and ankles feel like they're covered in a second skin and the rest of my body has a heavy, unwashed weight.

I buy three cans of Coke along with Teri's gum and paper, sitting on the bench by the newsagent while I drink the first two. I look through Teri's newspaper, wondering why that sort of stuff seems much less interesting when written down. I could happily watch Topless darts and the Weather in Scandinavian and whatever else on *L!VE TV* all night, but put it into print and the insult to my intelligence is immediately obvious.

Crushing the second can and pitching it into the nearest bin, I return to the office, dutifully keeping my break within the specified fifteen minutes. I give Teri her gum and she offers me a piece. I don't like gum, but I take one anyway, hoping the chewing will keep me alert.

'You didn't finish the game,' Teri admonishes me, handing over the piece of paper.

From the triumphant tone of her voice, I know she must be about to win, having successfully reduced the number of available possibilities so that wherever I shade my circle will allow Teri to complete her line. I shake my head and pass the paper back to her.

'Come on,' she urges, 'have your go.'

'No, it's all right. I give in.'

'That's not fair. Shade your circle.'

'Do it for me.'

'Bad loser. Another game?'

'Teri,' I ask, 'did you know about Adrienne and Ian?'

'About them going out?'

'Yeah.'

'Did they tell you?'

'No, I saw them kissing.'

'Really?' I ask, interested.

'Uh-huh.' Her voice becomes childishly conspiratorial. I draw my chair nearer. 'In the cloakroom two nights ago.'

'Just kissing?'

She grins. 'Well they weren't fucking if that's what you mean.'

'But it was passionate?'

'Listen to you. You've got a real thing for her, haven't you?'

'Adrienne?'

'No,' she says sarcastically, 'Alice.'

'You're as bad as Ian. We like bantering, that's all. Do you think I have a thing for you?'

She doesn't answer. I know this silence. Sonia (the GBH girl) used to do these silences. The problem with these silences is that they're ambiguous, and the refusal to clarify the meaning of the silence is the point of the silence in the first place. In this instance, the silence could mean one of three things:

You've upset me, but I don't want to discuss it.
You've upset me, and I want to punish you.
You haven't upset me, but you've stepped over the line.

The great strength of the silence as a psychological weapon is that the only way to overcome it is to keep talking, and any man who finds himself carrying on a one-sided conversation with a silent woman soon notices his voice taking on the self-righteous wheedle of a wife-beater, especially if, like me, you have a conviction for exactly that.

'I'm always the last to know about these things,' I bluster. 'Ian's supposed to be my best friend and he wasn't even going to tell me. I only found out because Adrienne put it in Daniel's Diary. Did you read it? Adrienne did an entry for me, like Gordon's Log.' I pass her the book. 'Read it. It's funny.'

Alice appears at our desk, teacher-faced. 'If *I* had asked *my* team leader for the afternoon off,' she says, 'I'd make damn sure I worked hard during the rest of the day.'

'I'm sorry, Alice. I only just got back from my break.'

'I know. I waited fifteen minutes before coming across. Then I waited another five. Now I want an explanation.'

'It's all my fault,' I admit, hoping candour will distract her. 'We were just gossiping about Adrienne and Ian.'

She sucks her lip. I wait, knowing she won't be able to resist. Finally, she says, 'What about them?'

After successfully fending off Alice, I log on and take a few calls. Teri seems to have forgiven me, drawing a new Connect Four grid on a fresh piece of paper. I work steadily through the rest of the morning, not taking a lunchbreak and getting Teri to bring me back a sandwich when she returns from hers. At five past two, Alice nods to me from reception, signalling that I'm allowed to leave.

I never had any intention of visiting Dad. I don't care what his harem think; I just can't go in at the moment. It doesn't matter how good a liar I am, I know I won't be able to get through a visit without revealing that I've lost our home. I realise this gives his seven women the power to say anything they want about his current beliefs and desires, but I'll just have to trust my own sense of what Dad would or wouldn't do. I'm sure I'll be able to explain away this neglect later, putting it down to a suddenly developed fear of hospitals or a delayed reaction to discovering I have seven substitute mothers.

Maybe I'll write him a letter.

I go to Dixons and buy a personal stereo that plays CDs. It costs two hundred pounds. Then I go to Virgin and buy six CDs (Madonna, Blondie, The Fall, KRS-One, Asian Dub Foundation and New Order). The non-spending period on my thousand pounds has clearly elapsed, and I know from experience that there's no way of halting the cashflow. It's simple. A grand is worth holding on to. Anything less and it's simply a question of slowing the spending. With eight hundred in the bank, you take out fifty every time you visit the cashpoint, feeling that little bit of financial freedom that lets you buy the odd round, maybe get a few CDs or some new books. Under five hundred and you ask for twenties, although this attempt at self-deception doesn't stop you spending, so that all that happens is you go to the cashpoint twice as often. Below three hundred and you stop checking your balance before withdrawing the money, using your own bank's cashpoints to cut down on charges and walking to a different machine if yours won't let you have tens. From then on, taking cash out becomes like Russian Roulette and you get extravagant again, knowing that each transaction could be your last. When you withdraw fifty pounds you live off it for twice as long as you did before, buying only essentials. You remember how rash you were in the above-five hundred days and take back your CDs, accepting half their original value and using the money for food. You remind your colleagues of the rounds you bought them and when you've had all the owed drinks you stop going out. Somehow when you had money you forgot to buy all the things you really need and now find yourself without razors, toothpaste and soap. Finally you realise you can't live like this any more and find a friend to give you another loan. And then it starts all over again.

I walk through the city Centre to College Green and lie out on the grass. It doesn't matter that the ground's wet and the nearby streets are busy with Saturday shoppers, I'm so tired that I fall asleep the moment I stretch out, my body thanking me for this long-awaited escape from work.

My life's been so full of oneiric moments recently that my dreams this afternoon are merely rerun highlights of the previous week. I hear callers' voices in my ears and see flashes of John's eyes in the dark. I see Teri standing by the cooker, then a glimpse of Adrienne. I feel Ian's arms around my shoulders and watch Gordon's lips mouthing something secret. I find myself back with Dad's women, only this time I can watch them saying the statements I read in the minutes. I listen to Alice telling me off, but instead of scowling she's smiling at me, as if the reprimand is just an excuse for a conversation.

It's dark when I wake up. I look at my watch but can't make sense of it. I stand up and check the nearest clock. Ten past six. Just over two hours later than the time I was supposed to be back at the call-centre. I pick up my personal stereo and CDs and start running back, trying to think of a good excuse. Perhaps I can pretend Dad's dead. No, that's ridiculous, she'd never believe that. And it'd be even worse if she did, and I had to spend the next six months pretending to be in mourning.

By the time I reach the bridge I remember that Alice leaves at five on Saturdays. So does the rest of the day shift. I don't know whether this makes things better or worse. On the plus side, she won't know exactly how late I was until she checks the stats (and even then she'll have to be looking specifically to locate this day on the monthly print-out). On the minus, she could've already sacked me, and maybe I'll get back to my desk only to find that my *Aspect* number doesn't work and my log-on code's been wiped from the files.

I use my ID card to let myself in and take the lift to the seventh floor. The old ladies have already installed themselves and I go to the cloakroom to fetch Dad's minutes from my rucksack. Saturday night is even quieter than Sundays and it seems safe to leave my personal stereo on and keep an eye out for the wait-light. I start with Asian Dub Foundation, knowing it's a favourite of Adrienne's and being less familiar with it than the rest of my purchases, which were bought out of nostalgia.

There are no notice papers on my desk and the numbers work so I assume I'm still a Quick Kall employee. Neither are there any messages on my *Aspect*, so if I'm going to get a bollocking, it'll be later and face-to-face. But I think I've got away with it. Alice cares as little about her job as the rest of us, and doesn't bear grudges. No doubt it'll have gone down in my file, but I can cope with that.

I open the minutes and flick through to the start of the second entry:

Minutes, Week Two
(Taken from tapes 2a and 2b)
Transcript: CG
Those present:
ST, IJ, MS, VD, BC, DT, LC, CG.

Meeting begins: 20:15 hrs.

ST begins by asking everyone about their week. He reminds them of his warning at the end of the previous session about possible emotional fall-out and comments that he didn't receive any phone-calls. He then asks if he should take this as evidence that no one suffered any psychological problems as a result of their honesty.

MS: Actually, Steve, I found the opposite was true. After talking last week, it was much easier to cope with my family.

IJ: Is that because you didn't feel guilty?

MS: No, precisely the opposite. I really shocked myself when I laid into you lot last week ... I'm particularly sorry to you, Lucy, I hope you didn't think I was being disrespectful. But something good did come of it. I've always believed that you know there's something wrong when you start being horrible to all your friends, and last week made me realise I couldn't carry on the way I was going.

IJ: So what did you do?

MS: I realised the problem was that no one acknowledged what I was doing. I managed to release my anger in such a sneaky way that even my husband didn't really know I was feeling it. Like with the car-door thing. My husband still thinks that was an accident. What I'm trying to say is, having confessed to you all that I suffer from these fits of anger made it much easier to stop myself. I still feel the same emotion ... it's just that I've admitted it to myself and found a way of dealing with it.

IJ: Which is?

MS: Have you read *The Mill on the Floss*? We did it for A levels. I didn't read it all, but I was really shocked by the bit where she punishes the doll. It reminded me of all those Virginia Andrews books because it seemed really sexy in a dirty sort of way. And it was something I did, in real life. My sister had this dolls' house and the dolls inside looked more lifelike than dolls usually do ... more like miniature people, and they were made of this really hard plastic ... you couldn't make them bend or anything. So, anyway, I had this knife I'd found in the loft. It looked like a really stupid little boy's knife. It was supposed to be an Indian's knife, with this beige leather pouch and blue and red thread woven into a pattern around the hilt, but the blade was ridiculous. It was huge and dangerous and really sharp ... big enough to kill an animal or something. And the moment my sister got this dolls' house I started thinking about the knife. What you need to know about my sister is that she's got this really short attention span. My parents never had to buy anything for me because I was happy with what my sister didn't want. Everyone thought she was really generous and a kind sister because she'd give me all her toys, but the truth was that she's one of those types, y'know, who want something until they've got it and then when they've got it they don't want it any more. So I knew I was going to get this dolls' house and every night I went to bed holding my knife and thinking about the dolls ... I think it was about three weeks before she gave it to me ... she had to get all the accessories and make my dad cut these little pieces of carpet for each room first. And the first night I just played with it like a normal girl, trying to forget about the knife. Then on the second, I got into a row with my family. I say 'got into', but it was deliberate, I provoked it, saying hurtful things until they responded, and then storming up to my room and locking the door. I got out the knife and the Dad doll – it wasn't significant that it was the Dad, I don't even think my dad was there that night – but I remember the doll had an orange top and blue trousers and they were made out of material, but the shoes were just painted onto the plastic feet. I took the doll and pressed the knife against his arm. I pressed it as hard as I could, but it wasn't doing anything, so I started sawing back and forth until I finally managed to cut through the arm. The plastic was so hard that I didn't think I'd be able to get through it and when it did the blade sliced into my thumb. I remember feeling really scared because I knew I couldn't go to my parents and I'd have to look after myself. I'd done this shameful thing, and been punished for it, but in the process I'd passed over into a different world, a world that my parents weren't part of, and now I was on my own. I didn't feel ready to accept this responsibility, but it was too late, I'd made the choice, without even really knowing exactly what I'd done. So I washed my thumb, and squashed pink toilet paper around it, until I'd made this sort of protective mould that I let dry and taped onto my hand. After that, I felt scared of the dolls' house and didn't go near it for a fortnight. Then one afternoon I had this really horrible fight with my best friend and I was so upset that I came home from school, took the Dad doll, and cut off another arm. Only this time I deliberately let the blade go through the plastic and into the flesh of my thumb, reopening the wound. It felt much more painful than before, but comforting too, letting out all of the anger. I knew I'd discovered something, and understood the conflicting feelings I'd experienced the first time I cut the doll. I didn't feel scared any more, in fact this seemed a reward for the fear. And over the next few months I worked my way through the entire plastic family. To begin with I felt lucky to have this release, but after I'd finished with the parents and moved on to the children, I worried what would happen when they were all chopped up. I tried to prolong things by cutting them up again, reducing each limb to tiny slivers, but I knew I was fooling myself. So eventually I gave in and did what I'd been leading up to, cutting directly into my skin. And that was the start of something it took many years, and lots of sessions like these, to conquer. Throughout that time, everyone took great pains to explain to me that it was OK to feel anger, that anger was much more acceptable than what I was doing. And because they made me feel so ashamed, I took what they were saying at face value, believing that the only important thing was to stop cutting myself. That was the way I felt until last week, when speaking to you lot seemed to unlock something. I went straight to bed after I got back from the session, and that night I had a dream where I was cutting the dolls again, and I realised that although I'd muddled them up in my mind, the excitement I felt when I was thinking about cutting the dolls was different to the way I felt after I cut my thumb. And although there was something shameful about it when I was a child, now it didn't seem so terrible. So I bought myself a new dolls' house. My husband thinks it's cute.

[DT laughs.]

DT: I'm sorry, Marilyn, I'm not laughing at you. It's just that your story reminded me of something funny.

ST: Come on then, share it with the group.

DT: I can't, it's too disgusting.

ST: We're all adults here.

DT: Oh, it's not disgusting in that way. Well, I suppose it is, a bit, but really, it's just gross. You don't want to hear it.

ST: Stop teasing. Share the joke.

DT: OK, but you asked for it. I hope this doesn't offend you, Marilyn, it's not meant to trivialise your confession. My mind's so perverse . . . there's no real connection at all. It's just that there was a boy in our school who claimed he had two penises. Is that right? Penises? Not peni, or something? Anyway, no one believed him, but because they thought it was just an excuse to get girls to look at his bits, no one could prove it one way or the other. So they decided I should be the one to check. I'd never seen a normal penis, let alone a double one, and I wasn't even sure I'd be able to tell, but I went to his house one lunchtime and he took me up to his room. I sat on the bed and he got it out. And in a sense, he was telling the truth. He did have two penises. Sort of. What he'd done was get a knife and cut across the centre of his helmet, waiting until it'd half healed before cutting into it again. He must have been doing it for a while because it was all scared and sceptic and swollen. To tell you the truth, I'm surprised he could still walk.

Mmm. Lovely. They're a funny bunch, Dad's friends. They seem to be just like him, even sharing the ability to move from the most sensitive declarations to crass recollections in the space of a few minutes. If I hadn't met these seven women, I'd be tempted to believe that they were figments of his imagination. I try to remember what I know about DT. So far she's been the most reticent of the group, and I can't remember her saying anything last night either. She had black hair, I remember that. And her name's Diane.

I take the list of their phone numbers from my pocket, remembering Lucy handing it to me and wondering whether I'd be prepared to call any of them. Valerie and Brittany I definitely wouldn't, but I'm not sure about the others. It'd be a mistake to do it from the call-centre – an outbound call when I'm the only one here is unlikely to pass unnoticed – but I could always use the payphone in the breaks room.

My wait-light is flashing. It takes me a minute to remember my earphones are connected to my personal stereo rather than my *Aspect*, and then another thirty seconds to find a headset.

'Hello, Magicmix Records.'

'Is that Dan?'

I nod, then remember she can't see me. 'Yes.'

'It's Moyra. I didn't know whether you'd be there or not.'

'I thought you were going to call me the other night.'

'I'm sorry, a friend came over. Are you angry?'

'Of course not. So are you ordering records?'

'Not tonight.' Her voice softens. 'Is it OK to have a chat?'

'If you like.'

'Is this call being recorded?'

'No, all the line managers have gone home. You can say whatever you want.'

'Oh good. How come you work on Saturday nights, Dan?'

'I work every night.'

'Doesn't it get lonely?'

'You'd be surprised. It's quite nice in here. And I sometimes go to clubs after I've finished my shift. I went out last night.'

'What about tonight?'

'No, not tonight. You?'

'No, I stay in on Saturdays.'

'Why?'

'Have you ever been to Doncaster?'

'I've never been anywhere in the North.'

She laughs. 'Really?'

'I'm not the jetsetter you thought I was, am I? I haven't been anywhere really. I've been to London a few times, seaside towns with my parents when I was little.'

'Well, if you'd been to Doncaster you'd understand why I stay in. Especially if you knew how I dressed.'

187

'How d'you dress?' I ask, worried I'm going to have to change my mental picture of Moyra.

'I dress for myself,' she says emphatically. 'Men abuse me on the street.'

'Why?'

'Because I don't look the way I'm supposed to. I play with people's perceptions.' She pauses. 'What about you, Dan?'

'Me?' I consider the question. 'Conservative. Boring. I have to wear a suit to work.'

'What about when you're not working?'

'I don't think I challenge people's perceptions. Occasionally people think I'm older than I am.'

She laughs. 'You're sweet, Dan. I'm glad I called.'

'Are you going now?'

'Yeah, but don't worry, I'll call back.'

'That's what you said last time.'

'Oh, it won't be tonight. I'll phone the next time I feel down. You've got a real talent for cheering people up, Dan. You ought to work for the Samaritans or something.'

'I used to work on a university linkline. Talking students out of suicide.'

'Sounds fun.' She pauses. 'Take care, Dan, all right?'

'OK. Call soon.'

She hangs up. I take off my headset and go to the toilet, wondering what Moyra wears when she's playing with people's perceptions. It's hard to tell whether she's a hardcore bondage freak or a disaffected Radiohead fan. Her sexy voice made me feel generous towards her slightly pretentious declarations, but I suppose it's probably more likely that she's a self-hating town weirdo. I know it's cruel of me to think like this (after all, I'm the one with no friends and I live in my office), but I want Moyra to be a worthy object for my affections, even if I'm never likely to meet her. I suppose the safest solution is to curtail any more conversation about what we look like and stick to faceless phone-flirting.

*   *   *

I divert all calls to the Train-times line and go across to the breaks room. They've finally repaired the soft drinks machine (no doubt it'll get smashed again by next week), so I get myself a can of Coke and sit by the window, paging through a discarded TV and Radio supplement and wondering what I'd watch if I had access to a television. I considered buying a miniature one instead of the personal stereo, but decided it'd be harder to live without music than electronic images. Besides, I haven't watched terrestrial television in ages, apart from the odd late-night film.

It might not have been the most sensible use of Adrienne's loan, but I'm glad I bought the stereo. Already it's made work seem much less oppressive, and I'm sure listening to music will help me fall asleep when I retire to the cloakroom tonight. An office is an excellent environment in which to hear CDs, the sound making the space much less utilitarian than it seems in silence. Sitting at my desk listening to my stereo, I can almost fool myself into believing I'm a pioneer, my enforced conditions really the latest in modern living.

My problem is that I don't get access to the right people. I'm sure if I met the head of Quick Kall Ltd (whomever he is), I'd be able to talk him into giving me a great job. People at the top have a natural affinity with misfits and loners, the only difference being the degree of application. It's all the nonentities in the middle who are the problem. I'm sure the top execs don't take their jobs as seriously as the promotion-seeking line managers. I thought I'd be able to take a position here without worrying about the chain of command. I'd hoped to achieve the bliss of being a cheerful peasant, enjoying working my land and not caring about the lord who'd loaned it to me. But the frustration of the other peasants distracts me, making it difficult to accept my lot.

I take a sip from my can and think about my last appraisal with Alice. The most difficult part of those sessions is not letting on that you know she cares as little as you do. You have to appear to be taking her words seriously, otherwise *bad attitude* will be added to your file. So let's do so. Alice told me the guiding principle behind the company's success is that they're prepared to treat all their workers as individuals. Now, leaving aside the obvious contradictions (if we're individuals, how come we're all doing the same job?) and pretending, for the sake of argument, that this isn't a piece of motivational guff thought up by some bored consultant, I wonder what QC's MD would think if I explained to him that I'd taken this job because I wanted the mental freedom afforded by a numbing routine and no responsibility. The truth is, he probably wouldn't care, but it'd be nice to believe that the man I make money for would be intelligent enough to recognise that calm resignation, not bitter ambition, is the mark of the perfect employee.

Pleased with my meditations, I return to the call-centre and take up *Political Ideas*, hoping to bolster my philosophy with a few quotations, and expand it to address the running of society instead of merely a call-centre. This volume is the most heavily annotated of Dad's books, although all the underlining is done in the same blue biro that has written *Harriet Onions* on the fly-leaf, so I think that all the intellectual energy expended over this book probably came from its previous owner. I don't know enough about Dad's past to be able to tell whether this woman was a friend of his or simply someone who offloaded her books in a second-hand shop, but she's also left an index card before the chapter on 'Rousseau and the General Will'. Again in blue biro, she's written *p. 158*. I turn to this page and find a frowny face doodled next to a section applying the principle of utilitarianism to the question of smoking. No doubt Ms Onions would fit in fine at Quick Kall Ltd.

I get so engrossed reading about Machiavelli and Luther that I hardly notice the old ladies leaving. I felt a bit sceptical about *Political Ideas* before I started it, finding the title ludicrously generic (no one would buy a Maths primer called *Some Sums*) but it's definitely the most interesting of Dad's books. It's also the first time I've felt like checking out the primary sources. I wonder if Waterstone's will have a copy of *The Christian in Society*.

I replace the index card at page fifty-three and fetch another small can of cat food from my rucksack. Then I go to the toilets and lift up the tile. Like last night, he's waiting for me, and, worried that being hidden in the roof might be harming him, I decide to allow John a few minutes of freedom. He makes surprisingly little fuss as I lift him out, purring as he settles down in my arms. Maybe I should start a cat obedience school, training people's pets by shutting them up in darkness.

I carry John back to my desk and put the bowl on the floor by my feet.

'Be careful with this,' I warn him as I spoon out the meat, 'don't get any on the floor.'

He slowly starts eating, his little tongue dabbing up small chunks of gravy-covered meat. Worried about his kidneys, I go out to the sink in the cloakroom and fill a foil tray with cold water. He's even more appreciative of this, lapping up the liquid as if he only has ten seconds before I take it away from him. I rub his head and he looks up at me, before returning his attention to his food.

I log off and wrap up my headset, putting it with the others in the desk drawer. In spite of my nap this afternoon, I still feel knackered and don't think I'll have any trouble getting to sleep. I pick up my book and the minutes and take them out to the cloakroom, giving John a moment to finish his food.

When I return he's sitting by the dish, looking up at me. Feeling guilty about making him so nervous, I pick John up and carry him across to the centre of the office, setting him down on the rough carpet and telling him, 'Go on then. Have a little run around or something.'

He makes a half-hearted approach towards the nearest desk. Once he realises I'm not going to grab him, he becomes a little more adventurous, sneaking beneath his desk and jumping up on a swivel-chair. Before I can stop him, he's scaled the back of the chair and bounded across to reception. Looking directly at me, he settles his furry posterior down on the carpet.

'Don't you dare.' I rush across and pick him up, finding half a turd messily spread across the floor and the other half stuck to his tail. Disgusted, I let him drop into his own mess and go out to the toilets for some paper. I suppose I should feel grateful that he chose another team's desk for his toilet. Or kid myself that I made him do it as a practical joke and enjoy a sneaky giggle. But instead I get down on my hands and knees and wrap the tissue around the solid part of the mess, hoping I'll be able to reduce the stain so it looks like something walked in on the bottom of a shoe.

'Do you want them to find you?' I demand. He hunches down, nervous again. I pick him up and carry him back to the toilet. He remains still in my arms, heart beating quickly. I stand on the swivel-chair and put him back, watching his tail bob as he trots off into the darkness. I go back into the call-centre and pick up the wrapped excrement, vigorously rubbing my foot over the wet remains. There's not much I can do about the smell, but hopefully the air conditioning will filter it out by morning.

I leave my shoes outside the cloakroom, then turn out the light and crawl beneath a few thick coats. Putting my earphones back in, I close my eyes and feel the sound filling the darkness. My shoulders relax and for the first time since Dad's accident, I feel free to imagine life beyond my immediate circumstance, looking forward to a time when this last week is nothing more than an anecdote about my crazy youth.

13

Anyone who's been paying attention could tell me why staying in the office on Sundays might be a problem. I'd completely forgotten that there was someone else who calls the cloakroom home one night a week, and it isn't until Ian arrives at lunchtime that I consider how to get round it. As far as I can see, there are three possibilities:

1. Let him in on my secret.
2. Persuade him not to stay here tonight.
3. Pretend I've decided to join him for the evening.

Solution 1 seems too drastic. I'm sure Ian won't tell on me, but no doubt he'll feel obliged to offer me a place on his sofa, and I couldn't cope with that. Spending all my waking hours with him would be hard enough, not to mention the jealousy I'd feel whenever Adrienne came over. No, that's out. Solution 2 seems more viable, although given Ian's suspicious nature, it may result in the same outcome as 1. That leaves solution 3, under any other circumstances the craziest option, but today clearly my best choice of action. The important thing is to be subtle, not saying anything until bedtime and then acting as if it's a spur-of-the-moment decision.

'Been busy?'

'Dead.'

'Good.' He drops his rolled-up copy of *The News of the World* on the table and hangs his jacket over the back of the chair.

'Hard night?'

'Hard morning. Adrienne was really on one. It's one of the few times I've been glad to come here.'

'What was she angry about?'

'Lifestyle differences,' he drawls sardonically. 'Ade doesn't think I should work Sundays.'

'But I thought she did Saturdays sometimes.'

'She does.' He exhales. I can't tell whether the sigh is an invitation to continue the conversation or a signal that it's over. Then he adds, 'It's not as if we have normal weekends anyway. We're both too knackered to do anything.'

'And what does Adrienne think?'

'She thinks lying in bed watching *EastEnders* is an essential part of a relationship. It's weird the things she wants a man for.'

I nod, trying not to feel envious. I hate being single. It's the coupley things I miss most, and it was the conversations about sleep and work and what to watch on TV that kept me together with Sonia (the GBH girl) through the nine months of physical abuse. She was much more adept at killing time than me, and while we were together I took up all her distractions, from *Company* to *Coronation Street*. Amazed that I was allowed (even expected) to have opinions on all manner of female concerns, I thought I'd achieved a blessed state that'd guarantee women would always seek out my company, only to find that my GBH conviction expelled me from that arena for ever.

Ian takes a headset from the desk and hooks up, unfolding his paper and resting it on top of his keyboard. I turn back to my screen, wondering whether to fetch Dad's minutes or *Political Ideas*.

'Dan,' Ian begins, sounding anxious, 'were you surprised when you found out about me and Adrienne?'

'I guess so.'

'Why?'

'Because you're my two best friends.'

'And you don't think we're right for each other?'

'It's not that. I'm just surprised I hadn't guessed, that's all.'

He nods. I can tell he wants to talk but don't know how to prompt him. I'm not surprised Adrienne's got him worried. I don't know much about his previous relationship (apart from the knicker-ripping) but I doubt his last lover was as self-sufficient as Adrienne. His face looks troubled as he reads the paper, and I decide to try again, 'So is she staying at yours?'

'Yeah, for the moment. I keep dropping hints about going over to her house but she ignores them.'

'Is her house nice?'

'It's brilliant. You know what Adrienne's like. She's taken this tatty terrace and turned it into a show home.'

'Why doesn't she want you to go there?'

'I don't know. She's got all these superstitions.'

'It's because she's lived on her own for so long. She doesn't want you to see her bad habits.'

He considers this. 'See, you understand Adrienne. I'm like a kid when it comes to her.'

'Don't worry, she makes everyone feel like that. I understand her, but she still makes me feel stupid every time we talk.'

Ian looks at me. He seems suspicious, as if he's not sure whether I'm faking. When we first became friends, he was visibly surprised every time I said something he agreed with, amazed we had so much in common. Since then, he's gradually stopped responding, aware that I want him to like me. Deep down, he knows I'm not really a good bloke, and although he's prepared to be my friend, he no longer believes we're kindred spirits.

'Do you think I should buy her something?' he asks.

'Maybe, but I wouldn't go for flowers or anything like that. Get her a magazine or a CD.'

He nods. 'Do you know what she'd like?'

'Pretty much anything as long as she hasn't got it. Perhaps a video would be a better bet.'

'Yeah, that's a good idea. Thanks, Dan.'

'No problem. Can you do me a favour?'

'Sure.'

'I want to go across to the World of Food for my dinner, but it'll probably take forty-five minutes. Could you . . .'

'Log you off at half past?'

'Thanks. Do you want me to bring you back something?'

'No, it's OK. See you later.'

I remove my headset and put on my jacket, pleased to be getting out of the office. I take the lift down to reception, checking my reflection in the mirrored tiles. I'm sure the architect of this building was a former employee of a similar corporation, putting in details like this to help late-comers who didn't have time to groom themselves before coming to work. All it lacks is an automatic tie-tying machine just inside the double doors.

It's warmer outside than it's been for a while. Maybe this year's about to pick up. I'm sure it wasn't this wet last March. I turn on my stereo and walk towards the Centre, contemplating which country in the World of Food will get a visit from this hungry traveller today.

I wonder if there was ever a time when Adrienne would've considered going out with me. Obviously this thing with Ian started before I came to Quick Kall, but maybe if I'd made a pass at her when I'd first arrived, she might've persuaded Ian to stay with his girlfriend and turned her attentions to me. I'm not sure why I didn't. I commented earlier that I didn't fancy her, but there's no reason why that should've stopped me. I didn't fancy Sonia when she first came after me, letting the excitement of being her prey carry me through our first few weeks together. I also told myself that she intimidated me, but that hasn't stopped Ian, and intimidation is probably as good a basis for a relationship as any. I suppose if I'm honest, what stopped me was the knowledge that Ade and I aren't right for each other. Alone, Adrienne is aspirational, and I'm just happy to get by. Together, she'd lose the desperation that gives her what little drive she has, and I'd gain just enough happiness to become dissatisfied.

That still leaves Teri. Yesterday she was more open with me than she's ever been before, her timidity giving way to what I sense is a fairly combative nature. I know so little about her, even less than I know about Adrienne. It's strange how you can sit next to someone for nine hours a day and still not know their middle name, their parents' occupations, or their favourite food. I'd learn more about Teri if I got talking to her on the bus. Working together seems to make people wary of saying anything important. Maybe if I initiated a serious conversation we'd get beyond the play-fighting that's characterised our relationship ever since I stayed at her house. She definitely seems closer to the women I've fancied before (although no one, thank God, could be quite like Sonia), and we might even do each other good. But I'm scared off by the men she lives with, and the knowledge that all the things about my character I believe are virtues, she'd consider weaknesses. Perhaps I should stop all this silly protesting and tell her about the violence in my past. I know it'd put off most women, but I've a feeling it'd excite Teri, if I told it right. Although, to be honest, I think that's what I'm afraid of.

I enter the Galleries on the top floor, walking past the Postman Pat photo-booth and the novelty T-shirt shop. Bolted to the ceiling is a white television showing speeded-up footage of customers coming into the building, a steady blur of faceless figures. I watch the screen for a moment, then carry on round to the World of Food. This area is guarded by a lifesize mannequin dressed in an American Football uniform. I don't know whether he's been put there as an ironic comment on cultural imperialism or for some other more obscure purpose. He certainly isn't the most welcoming of ambassadors, glaring from beneath his plastic helmet. I walk past him and decide to plump for my own country's kitchen, mainly because it's the only one which does a Sunday lunch. I order roast chicken and three veg, and a large Coke. Then I carry it across to the seating area, pleasantly surprised that there's space for me to sit alone. The dinner tastes a lot better than it looks, reminding me of the microwave Roast Chicken platters that my mum used to like. I eat quickly, checking my watch the whole time.

After lunch, I head back to Quick Kall. I want to look round the shops but I know I don't have enough time. I'm still itching to spend Adrienne's money, even though I know that once it's gone I'll really be stuck. Before, I'd counted on hitting Ian for a much smaller loan (a hundred or so to see me through until the end of the month), but now he's going out with my main financial backer, he'll know I've just pissed away a grand. I could try Teri, but I doubt she's got much saved up, and even if she did have, I wouldn't feel as comfortable taking money from her as I do with Adrienne. Borrowing cash from Ade seems like an erotic game, and one of my favourite fantasies is that she'll make me repay my debt through sexual favours. With Teri, it'd feel like pinching pennies from a piggy bank.

I use my ID card to get through the back entrance and take the lift with three top-floor boys. One has short blond hair and silver glasses. The other has a neat brown moustache. They hold the door open until I'm inside, then turn away.

'So what d'you think?' Glasses asks Moustache. 'Is it only a matter of time before call-centres are abolished?'

'I doubt it,' he answers wearily. 'Mertz wanted to make an impression, that's all.'

'Maybe, but he sounded convincing.'

'Cause he's a zealot, that's why. And what better way of thumbing his nose at management? Telling them their world's about to become obsolete guarantees him a future.'

'I dunno. He must be pretty sure of himself.'

'Wouldn't you be? Half the world's just converted to his cause, and the other half's terrified of it.'

'So he's right?'

'No, he's not right. It's not like TV and telephones. Doing business over the computer completely removes the human element. Most people still need a voice.'

'But they don't get a voice,' I interject, before reciting, 'all our operators are busy at the moment . . . please hold and we'll answer your call as soon as possible.'

'So why do they keep calling?'

'Because they're all crazy old ladies,' I tell him, pleased to be giving my theories an airing. 'Look, it's obvious. Call-centres are really doing three separate jobs. Giving people information, selling insurance, and listening to old people complain. Sure, the first two probably *could* be managed without operators. But computers can't cope with complaints, not satisfactorily. They'll keep us around as a public service.'

The lift stops at my floor. Both men look surprised, staring at me until the door closes. I feel vaguely insulted by their incredulity, wondering why they're looking at me as if I'm a pot plant that's decided to speak.

Back at our table Ian's asleep, his chair angled so that he's hidden behind his work-station. Line managers tend to be more lenient on Sundays, but do demand that their employees at least stay awake. The man on duty today has a reputation for monitoring everything, and the sparsity of Sunday calls prompts him to seize on anything that comes through the switchboard.

I sit down quietly, being careful not to wake Ian up. He deserves his sleep after a night and a morning with Adrienne, and I can always give him a shake if the line manager comes across. I quite like the idea of call-centres being a temporary thing, a strange shanty-town stage in the history of telecommunication. I'd also have liked to have been in that meeting with the top-floor boys, certain I would've had much more interesting theories to add into the conversation. Being an ideas man would suit me fine, throwing out suggestions for my staff to follow up.

I turn my chair away from Ian and pick up the minutes, thumbing through until I find my place.

ST: So, did anyone else experience any after-effects from last week's meeting, good or bad?

IJ: I watched a dirty movie.

[Laughter.]

ST: As a result of last week?

IJ: I don't know. It seemed the next stage after telling you lot about feeling bisexual. I wasn't ready for an affair, but I wanted to do something.

ST: Which film was it?

IJ: Why? Are you an expert?

ST: No, I just . . .

IJ: I don't know the title. It wasn't like a real film, it didn't have credits. I think it had a sort of brand-name title. Suburban Slappers 2. Horny Housewives 8. Something like that.

ST: And did you enjoy it?

MS [to ST]: You sound like a sleazy sex therapist.

ST: I knew this would happen. You asked me to chair these meetings and now you're calling me a pervert. Someone else ask the questions.

MS: I'm kidding.

ST: I'm not. You're making me feel uncomfortable. Someone take over.

BC: What was it like?

IJ Pretty sexy, to be honest. I'd expected it to be a real turn-off, but I found it exciting.

BC: Why?

IJ: I think because although there weren't any men in it, there was never any suggestion that these women were lesbians or even bisexuals. Even when they were going down on each other, somehow their actions were unconnected to any larger questions of sexual orientation.

LC: And you found that erotic?

IJ: Yeah. That probably makes me sound really weird, doesn't it?

ST: We're not here to judge one another.

IJ: I just hate classifying sexual feeling. The women in

the film reminded me of girls I was afraid of in school. It felt like going back in time and being given a glimpse of a world that's always been closed to me. I know it was probably all set up by someone off-camera, but the women were sexy in a way that really reached the core of me. Their boredom was part of it. I think as a viewer I want different things to what a man might be looking for.

ST: What do you think a man wants?

IJ: I think a lot of men still have trouble believing women are into sex. Maybe it's just me, but a lot of men I've been with, including my husband, have acted as if sex is some sort of trick.

LC: What do you mean by trick?

IJ: My husband never asks me if I'd like to make love. He seems to think that if he puts what he wants into words, I'll immediately start screaming and jump out of bed. And because he's so sneaky about it, I find myself feeling coerced, even though he's asking me to do something I like doing. Then, when we're actually having sex, he always rushes through everything, as if he's frightened I'm going to stop him. I don't know why he feels like that. It's certainly not an impression I set out to give.

ST: And how does that relate to pornography?

IJ: Well, porn's a man's game, isn't it? There's that same sneakiness. And I think what a man wants from pornography is to see a woman obeying the rules.

BC: Pornography's been an important element of most of my affairs.

CG: How does that work?

BC: I use it as part of my forbidden-fruit appeal. Men usually come to me because they can tell I like sex, and think I'll be into things their wives don't like. I stop them feeling guilty about their desires. And if a man's ready to have an affair, chances are he'll have tried pornography first.

VD: My husband likes me to look at his magazines with him.

LC: How does that make you feel?

VD: I don't have a problem with it. I only said something

because Brittany claimed it was a threat to marriage and I don't think that's necessarily the case.

BC: I didn't say it was a threat. I just think it's something most wives have trouble with. Women tend to idealise their husbands.

VD [Laughing.]:   I think you have a very naive view of marriage. Probably because you spend so much time breaking them.

BC: Sounds like you're not so sure about your husband after all. Maybe he and I should have a little get-together.

DT: Leave her alone.

ST: I don't think worrying Val is very productive, Brittany.

VD: I'm not worried.

[Silence.]

IJ: Are they just ordinary magazines?

VD: They're soft, if that's what you mean. *Penthouse*. *Mayfair*. Stuff like that.

IJ: So it's mostly pictures of women.

VD: It's all women.

IJ: And does he connect the pictures to you?

VD: In what sense?

IJ: Does he make remarks about your body while he's looking at other women?

VD: Not really.

IJ: Does he want you to be turned on by the pictures?

VD: It's not like that. It's sort of childish and dulled, and I'm not supposed to be sexual – except in a maternal way, maybe – I have to ask him if he's getting turned on, admire the size of his erection, stuff like that.

[Silence.]

ST: Shall we move on, or has anyone got anything they want to add about porn?

[Silence.]

ST: OK . . .

CG [Interrupting]:   Both my husbands liked pornography, but I wasn't as open as you, Valerie. I wish I had been, because I definitely think stuff like that was connected to their anger at me.

IJ: Did you try to talk to them about it?

CG: I couldn't talk to them about the shopping, let alone something like that.

VD: Why not?

CG: I don't know. It's something I've spent a lot of time thinking about. People say all sorts of rubbish about women who end up with violent men, but it'd be stupid of me not to at least think about that stuff. My first husband was violent before he met me, so I suppose my only mistake was being stupid enough to fall in love with him. But my second husband said he'd never hit anyone before, and whether that was true or not . . .

LC   [Interrupting.]: I doubt it.

CG: Whether it was true or not, I think being with Scott had made me sort of remove myself – I can't really explain what I mean – set up a barrier or something, as if I was so scared of him hitting me that it became inevitable. I know this sounds like I'm blaming myself.

LC: You are.

CG: But it's not like that. I'm not saying I'm a natural victim or anything like that. I know that's bullshit. But it's a fact that Jay envied my relationship with Scott. And because I talked so much about my past – I needed to, but I wish I hadn't – it became important to him, really important. A crass way of explaining what happened between us would be to compare it to telling a man about something sexual you've done with an ex-lover that you wouldn't want to do with him. In the end letting him hit me almost seemed proof that I loved him.

LC: Those aren't healthy thoughts, Claire.

CG: I don't care. It's how I feel. And it's important to me, and it's why I'm in this group. I want to talk and talk until it's all neatly boxed up. Maybe then I can make a fresh start.

Ian stirs. I close the minutes and slip them beneath the table. He blinks at me.

'How long have I been sleeping?'

'I don't know. An hour maybe. You were asleep when I got back from town.'

'Did you have a nice lunch?'

'Not bad.'

'What did you have?'

'Sunday roast.'

His eyes light up. 'Do they do that? I thought it was all spare ribs and noodles. That's one thing I really miss about living at my mum's. Is it a proper roast, with gravy and stuffing?'

'Pretty much. Do you want me to cover for you?'

'They won't still be doing it, will they? It's half past two.'

'They do it all day.'

He looks at his watch. 'No, it's OK, I ought to eat my sandwiches. Besides, it's Ade's birthday coming up and I'm trying to save money.'

'Yeah, I don't suppose you can get a loan from her to buy her own present.'

'Tell me about it. I can't get her to do any of the things she used to do for me. Before I could give her my washing and it'd only cost a couple of pints. Now there's all this emotional stuff involved.'

I smile. 'But it's still OK for me to get her to do my laundry, right?'

'Feel free, mate. There's no reason why you should suffer.'

He goes back to his paper. I decide not to risk carrying on with the minutes and pick up *Political Ideas* instead. Locke and Montesquieu. Ian probably has no interest in what I'm reading, but I'm grateful for the excuse to take a break from Lucy and her violent husbands. Her story brings back uncomfortable memories, and I'm not sure which side I most identify with. After the court case Sonia (the GBH girl) made a number of attempts to get in contact with me. I think her logic was a lot like Lucy's, although Sonia was probably more susceptible to romantic delusions, seeing me being arrested as merely the latest incident in our grand romance. The fact that I'd been legally instructed to stay away from her seemed to mean nothing, maybe because she believed love was blind to the law. I'd like to see Sonia try to find me now, just to hear how she'd re-imagine my present situation. No doubt she'd be certain it had something to do with her, feeling pleased by the new drama on offer.

Sonia always said I had low expectations. I suppose the fact that I'm happy being homeless proves her right. She also said I was a gutless fool. The fact that I'm living in an office instead of on the streets confirms her second verdict. But the reason I'm getting on OK isn't because I don't expect anything from life. It's because I'm not afflicted by nostalgia. Or false hope. I have no interest in the past, and care little about the future. I'm living entirely in the present. Isn't that supposed to be a sign of mental strength?

I read steadily throughout the afternoon, excited by the prospect of finishing the last of Dad's books. Rousseau, Paine, Burke and Hegel set out their stalls, stay for a while and then disappear, which seems a much healthier way of experiencing philosophy than getting snared by any one thinker. It's hard enough to maintain autonomous thought as it is, without letting some dead madman take over your brain. It's almost nine when I complete the last chapter, and my head and eyes feel funny from reading so long without a break. Ian seems unconcerned that I've stayed silent all afternoon, and alternates between drawing on his paper and staring out of the window. Ian's relationship with time seems much more sensible than mine. He lets minutes go in great bundles, registering the change of hours but little else. I need to know about each second, frequently checking the clock on my *Aspect* and often stopping to observe one minute go by, reminding myself of what it means to give time away. I once failed an exam because I became so fixated by the idea of only having three hours to make my brain behave that I spent the whole time watching the clock.

His wait-light glows. I tap his arm. 'Look, someone knows we're still here.'

He hits *Ready*. I hear him say, 'Sorry, love, I can't understand what you're saying. What? Who? Hang on, I'll check.' He puts the caller on hold and turns to me. 'You been breaking hearts again? Girl here in tears wants to talk to you.'

It's Sonia. Must be. I don't know how she got this number, but thinking about her must've summoned her up. I'd prefer to refuse the call, but know Ian will think it's strange if I make him ring off, and I don't want this to get back to Adrienne.

'OK, send it across.'

He tells the caller to hang on and taps in my extension. 'All yours,' he says into the mouthpiece, before his voice gives way to static crackle. I focus in on the sound and hear a girl's sobs.

'Hello?' I try.

'I'm sorry for calling,' the voice apologises, almost blubbering the words. It's not Sonia. 'It's Moyra. I'm sorry . . . I don't know why I called.'

'It's OK. What's wrong?'

'Don't cut me off, Dan.'

'I'm not going to. Tell me what's wrong.'

'It's nothing. Just a lonely moment. I get like this sometimes. I just need to talk it out. It'll only take a few minutes. I know there's no reason why I should say this to you, but your voice . . .' She breaks off, crying again. I listen to her struggling to breathe. 'I said I'd do this, didn't I? You can't say I didn't give you a warning.'

'About what?'

'About calling. I said I'd phone the next time I felt down. I just didn't expect it to be so dramatic. It didn't really come over me until I started dialling.' She exhales. 'You must think I'm crazy.'

'I don't.'

'What do you think, Dan?'

'I'm glad you called.'

'Do you remember the last time I rang?'

'Of course.'

'After you hung up, I kept talking to you. I told you all about my past and what I was feeling.'

'How did I respond?'

'You were nice. A sympathetic listener. How come you're not alone tonight?'

'They always have two people on Sundays.'

'Why?'

'I don't know, but this is Ian's shift really. I'm probably not even supposed to be here.'

'Is Ian like you?'

I chuckle, looking at my friend. 'Not really. Do you want to speak to him?'

She sounds worried. 'Can he hear what I'm saying?'

'Not at the moment, but if he plugs into my *Aspect* we can have a threeway.'

'Sounds fun.'

Ian looks at me. I unhook his headset and bring it across. He rolls his chair sideways. 'Hello?'

'Hi, Ian, Dan's told me a lot about you.'

Ian doesn't say anything.

'Ian, this is Moyra. She's sorry for worrying you.'

'That's OK,' he jokes, 'I'm used to it. Crying women are always calling here for Dan. He's such a stud.'

'Is that true, Dan?' Moyra asks. 'And you were trying to convince me how sweet you are.'

'He does that act with everyone. Don't believe a word of it. The whole office knows he's a tiger.'

'I thought so,' she giggles. 'He's got that sort of voice.'

'Well,' I say slowly, 'seeing as you two are getting along so happily, I think I might take a toilet trip.'

'Thanks for sharing,' says Moyra, 'hurry back.'

I unhook my headset and leave it on the table, then walk out to the cloakroom. I'd thought John would have to go hungry tonight, but now Ian's tied up I've got a chance to sneak my pet a tin of Felix. I fetch a chair from Conference Room 2 and use it to get up and load his bowl, not bothering to locate him. If he's hungry, he'll eat, and he deserves some solitary confinement after yesterday's incident in the call-centre.

The bowl full, I replace the tile and climb down. I sense a presence as I return the chair, but when I whirl round there's no one there. I realise this mind-lapse occurred because my brain's afraid of being caught, but as unease succeeds the jolt, I sense (for the first time) how the office could be a scary place. Odd that I should feel this on the first night I'm not here alone, but maybe it's Ian's presence that's made me self-conscious. I suppose the office doesn't seem scary to most people because they only go there during the day, although the night ops I've met haven't seemed that nervous either. The breaks room's been broken into at least nine times since I started working here, but as far as I know, no one's ever tried the main building. I wonder why. After all, the pickings are richer, and you can bag a computer instead of a few bags of crisps. Is it because burglars are put off by the security guards and electronic cameras? That's never stopped bank robbers. Buy a balaclava and a baseball bat. Is it because of the security system? Steal an ID card. Drive through the front doors. No, I think people don't rob offices because they fear them, suffering from some primitive superstition I share but cannot explain.

Ian's finished the call when I get back, standing behind his work-station and wrapping up his headset. He has a guilty smile and avoids my eye.

'Moyra gone then?'

'Yeah. I don't think she liked me as much as you.'

'What did you say to her?'

'Not much. I quizzed her about how she knew you.'

'And?'

'She was very cagey. I think she thought she'd be getting you in trouble.'

I nod, knowing he wants an explanation but feeling reluctant to give one.

'Did she sound OK when she left?'

'Yeah. A bit embarrassed, but not sad.'

'That's good.'

He puts the headset in a pile with the others and drops the newspaper into the bin.

'What time's your taxi?'

'I haven't booked one.'

He looks at me. 'Why not?'

'I thought I'd follow your example.'

'You want to stay with me?'

'No, I thought, the cloakroom.'

'Oh.' He laughs. 'Ade was cross enough about me coming to work. She'd be furious if I stayed here.'

I nod, feeling stupid. Now he knows my secret. I should've realised that dating Adrienne would change his behaviour. Why would he want to sleep in the office when he's got a woman to get back to.

'Be careful,' he tells me. 'The cleaners arrive earlier than you might expect.'

'You sound like Adrienne. She's always telling me to be careful.'

He doesn't reply.

It takes me a little longer than usual to fall asleep. I keep thinking about my anxious moment in the corridor and wondering if it was a premonition. Last night I woke up with earache, so I go without my personal stereo tonight. There always seems to be a low mains hum in the call-centre, even in the early hours. The quiet buzzing reassures me, and it doesn't take long for my brain to submit to my body's demands.

14

Waking at work does a lot to take the sting out of Monday morning. When I lived in the room with my father, I believed that my life would either carry on in the exact same way for another forty years, or change beyond recognition as a result of a single occurrence. I don't mean anything banal like winning the lottery (after all, my mum had already done that), but something predestined, yet seemingly random. I imagined a stranger offering me a lucrative job in another country, or a rich heiress falling in love with me after a chance meeting on the street. I don't suppose such fantasies are particularly original. The idle imaginings of a routine-craving under-achiever. It's strange, though, that the reality should turn out to be a dark parody of what I'd wished for. A chance occurrence (Dad's accident) leading not to freedom from my life, but freedom (of a sort) *through* this life. My fate reminds me of the way people here seem to cope with their frustration through increasing their workload, as if the only way to stop themselves worrying about work is to work until there's no time left for worrying.

Ade and Ian arrive together. She starts grinning the moment she sees me, coming over and perching on the edge of our table.

'Ian told me you tried to keep him from my bed last night.'

'That's true. I thought he deserved a break.'

'You little shit. Aren't you supposed to be being nice to me?'

'Why's that then?'

'Oh, I don't know. Maybe because you owe me a thousand pounds.'

'That reminds me. I've been meaning to come to you for a top-up loan.' I check her face, ready to try my luck. Her expression warns me not to bother. 'Relax, I'm kidding. Your money got me out of a tight spot, and for that I'm very grateful, but I see no reason why we should cease to trade insults. Unless you want me to respect you.'

'Respect. That sounds nice. Besides, you want to get in practice for when I'm your boss.'

'Why? What's happened to Alice?'

'Nothing yet, but her days are numbered. I have it on good authority that her affair with Fat Bastard didn't go unnoticed. That's the first rule of business. Don't fuck your superiors. One more management affair and she's history. It can't be long. She's a nympho and she doesn't know anyone outside the office. As soon as the itch hits, she'll be upstairs with no knickers. And there's guys upstairs who'd fuck her just for the fun of seeing her face when they sack her. It's sad really.'

'How d'you know she doesn't know anyone outside the office?'

'What?'

I repeat my question.

'Oh come on. You saw her that night at The Pentangle. Even Gordon felt sorry for her.'

'I know someone she knows.'

'Who?'

'Brittany Cuthbert.'

'Who the fuck is Brittany Cuthbert?'

'Her auntie.'

'Relatives don't count, Dan. Besides, why are you sticking up for her?'

'I feel sorry for her. Maybe I'd have enjoyed all this at school, but it seems a bit sad that we're still doing it.'

'You don't understand. Alice has never been treated badly. At school the situation would've been reversed, and she wouldn't have hesitated about being horrible to us. You said so yourself, before your attack of conscience. And anyway, I'm not doing anything to her. I'm just finding it fun to watch.'

'Whatever.'

I can tell Ade's getting angry, but her reply's cut off by a blonde woman who places herself between us. Ade glares at her. I feel pleased to have such a sour friend, particularly as it saves me the trouble of being rude.

'Can I interrupt for a minute?' she asks, hesitantly.

'Yes?' Ade snaps.

'I'm selling tickets for the karaoke evening. I just wondered if I could put you down for a couple.'

'Have you ever seen me at a karaoke evening?' Ade asks her.

'No,' she says, her voice rising.

'So why would I start now?'

'Right,' she says. Ade stalks off. The woman turns to me. She looks so convinced she's about to receive another attack that I take pity on her and smile. I know there's a connection between us, but I can't remember if it's something genuine or just that I've spent an afternoon day-dreaming about her. I get like that sometimes, especially since I've lost the outside world as a source of fantasy material. Watching the women on the bus has been replaced by wandering to the water-cooler, waiting for someone to meet my eye.

'When is it?' I ask.

'Tuesday week.'

'And you need the money now?'

'No, I can put your name down and you can catch up with me later.'

'That sounds best.'

She sits on the edge of our table and takes a pen from Gordon's

213

pot. He looks shocked, jaw operating on automatic. The blonde glances at me and I tell her my name. As I stare at her gold necklace, I remember why she's so familiar.

'Have you heard they're going to replace karaoke with a singles night?'

She frowns. 'That's just a wind-up. I got a call from someone pretending to be from Quick Kall Social Committee, but when I asked my line manager about it, he said someone was taking the piss.'

'Who were they trying to fix you up with?'

'That's a bit embarrassing,' she laughs.

'Why?'

'Well, they succeeded. Dennis and I have been together for a week now.'

'Who's Dennis?'

'Black guy. Banks and Building Societies. Weird clothes.'

'Oh, yeah, I know. Perhaps he was behind it.'

'No, I don't think so. He said he was surprised as I was when he got the call. He thought I was trying to trick him.'

'His mates then.'

'Maybe, but I think they'd have said something by now. No, I'd like to think it was someone doing a good deed.'

She smiles, and I'm ready to confess, wanting her warmth to be directed at me. She seems so good-natured, and although I know I won't go, I'm glad I bought a karaoke ticket from her. I try to imagine how she'd react if I admitted that I set her up. It'd be nice if she showered me with kisses, but I know it's more likely that all her good humour would disappear, and she'd either urge me to explain why or just be angry that her imagined Cupid should turn out to be so pathetic.

She gives Gordon his pen. His lips stop wobbling and he manages to mouth thanks. I excuse myself and take my seat. Internal call. I answer it.

'You bought one, didn't you?'

'What's wrong with that?'

'Are you going to go?'

'I don't know. Maybe.'

'You're not. You'll be working here.'

'Only till ten. I could go down afterwards.'

'What for? To screw some drunk temp?'

'Why do you care?'

'Because it's my money you're wasting.'

'I'm paying you back. Besides, I bet Ian goes.'

'What's that?' Ian asks.

I look at him. 'Ade's giving me a hard time about buying a karaoke ticket. You'll be going, won't you?'

'Yeah, probably, if you are.'

'See,' I speak into my mouthpiece. 'Ian's going, and he's getting you a ticket.'

Ian giggles. 'Don't start her off. She'll crucify me.'

'OK, Ade, I've got to go. Your boyfriend needs comforting.'

I cut her off. My wait-light's flashing so I take the call, deciding it's the safest way to avoid getting drawn into any more arguments.

Teri's late. Over an hour late. Alice has been across three times and called her at home twice. Now she's watching the doorway, waiting to let loose. No doubt Alice is secretly pleased by Teri's misdemeanour, glad to have another reason not to feel guilty when she finally gives her the sack. It's odd that Teri should start slipping now, after her card's been marked. It'd make sense if she knew she was going, but as far as I'm aware it's still a secret. Now Alice can get in and lay the groundwork for her eventual dismissal, giving her a formal warning for something the rest of us would probably get away with.

Alice ought to feel grateful to Teri. Not only is she making her job easier, but she's also giving a focus to her morning. First she gets an hour of waiting, being able to avoid more tasking jobs by claiming that she wants to know the exact time Teri turns up. Then she gets to take her to Conference Room 2 for a talk, type it all into her file, and then pass on the information to management, which, of course, will necessitate a trip upstairs. So maybe Adrienne's prediction will come true as well.

I wish Teri would arrive. I want to tell her about our successful match-making, maybe even initiate another round of Dating Agency. And I don't like the idea of her getting in trouble, especially as I'm the one who put her name on the danger list. Now I've had chance to reflect, I'm beginning to wish I told on Ian instead of Teri. Maybe if he was the one to go, I'd have another chance with Adrienne, and I'm sure he'd be much more belligerent about losing his job and I wouldn't feel so guilty. It's the fact that Teri will simply accept her dismissal with a shrug that upsets me, knowing that if I was in her position I'd react in exactly the same way.

I take a call. 'Hello, Magicmix Records.'

'Yeah, mate, I called on Saturday to order some Bubbleboy twelve inches but they haven't come in yet.'

'Well, it is only ten o'clock. Sometimes deliveries don't come in until twelve.'

'Nah, we've had the delivery. Just not the Bubbleboys.'

'OK,' I say, lowering my mouthpiece so he can hear me tapping the keys (a sound which always seems to reassure people), 'last time you called did you cancel the balance?'

'What does that mean?'

'When you make an order, the operator usually asks if you want to cancel the balance. What this means is if the record you ordered isn't in stock, it remains on order and as soon as it gets restocked, we send it out.'

'I don't know. Can you check?'

'I'm sorry, I can't call up previous screens.'

'I don't remember him saying anything about the balance.'

'OK, well, what would you like me to do?' I pause, waiting to see how he responds. Some dealers, particularly if they own the shop rather than only order stock for it, go crazy at this point. By the way, I know the operator didn't say anything about the balance because I took the previous call, and ignoring this procedure is a central part of my self-defence programme.

'If I didn't cancel the balance, and the record's out of stock, it'll get sent to the shop when it comes back in, right?'

'Yeah.'

'OK, I can sell more Bubbleboys than I ordered, so if I order it again, I'm bound to at least get some copies.'

'So you'd like more Bubbleboys?'

'Yeah, but could you check first? See if it is still in stock?'

'No problem, bear with me.' I tap the keys again, calling up the right screen. 'I'm afraid it's been deleted.'

'Is that the bubblepack?'

'Um, yes, there's an x at the end of the code, so that would suggest it is some kind of special edition.'

'I know the special edition's deleted, but last time I called the guy said there was another version.'

'Did he? Hang on.' I tap the keyboard. 'No, that's deleted as well.'

'But it only came out two weeks ago,' he protests, sounding exasperated.

'It's probably a mistake. If you like I can call the information desk. They'll be able to explain what's going on.'

'Whatever.'

'OK, I'm going to have to put you on hold.' I wait for his sigh, then leave him with muzak. I press *Line 2* on my *Aspect* and call up the info desk. It rings three times before they pick up. 'Hello, information line, how may I help you?'

'Hi, can you give me some information on Bubbleboy?'

'What do you want to know?'

'I've got a customer on the other line who wants to order the standard version of the twelve inch, but it's coming up as deleted.'

I look across to information, wondering who I'm talking to. It's one of the three women with their backs to me, but I'm not sure which.

'Where are you calling from?' she asks.

'Behind you,' I tell her, and wait to see who looks round. It's the one in the middle, a redhead wearing a cream jumper. She smiles in my direction. I wave.

'OK,' she says, 'Bubbleboy. The most recent single?'

'Are there more than one?'

'No,' she laughs, 'you're right. The twelve inch is deleted.'

'The bubblepack?'

'Both versions. There must be some problem because they're being withdrawn and reissued.'

'Oh. So when is it due out again?'

'Doesn't say.'

'Right.' Teri comes into the call-centre. She skulks down along the cupboards that line the nearest wall, pushing her tartan bag up onto her back. 'Thanks, I'll tell him.'

I end the call and check the hold time on the first line. Two minutes fifteen seconds. Keeping callers on hold is a fun game, if a hard one to judge. The temptation is to hang on as long as possible, but then if they hang up you lose all your points, and as we've got an open-ended competition running between our team, it's sometimes safer to settle for a run of small scores. Ade has the record for longest single hold (43 minutes 18 seconds), but in the overall competition I'm leading with an accumulative score of nearly two hours. Most callers will wait longer than you might expect, and a little known secret among serious players is that the more temperamental diallers tend to hang on longest, unwilling to give up before they've had chance to abuse you. The hardest people to keep waiting are the ones who aren't really bothered, as they tend to think they can always call back. Sometimes, if I'm especially bored, I like to challenge myself, trying to tie up someone who'd never usually bother waiting. My current caller is hard to gauge, sounding like a normally placid person driven to desperation by the urge to stock this record. I think he'll wait a little longer.

Alice has noticed Teri and is walking across, brushing her hands over her skirt in her usual preparatory gesture. Teri's pretending she's not the one in trouble, continuing to set up like it's only five to nine. I fiddle with my mouthpiece, awaiting the inevitable confrontation. Alice stops by our table.

'Can I have a quick word, Teri?'

Teri looks up, and without replying, follows her in the direction of Conference Room 2. I wait until they've left, then check my *Aspect*. Line one's now been waiting for ... shit, he's gone. Annoyed that I've lost my points, I take solace in the fact that this does at least give me opportunity for another time-waste. If a caller hangs up while holding, company policy permits the operator to ring back. All part of meeting customer needs. As the calls come through reception lines before being divided off to individual operators, there is no 1471 function on an *Aspect*. This means I have to visit reception and get a print-out from the logging machine, a process which entails a walk to the far corner of the office and at least three minutes of fiddling. Oh, the manifold pleasures of office existence.

Alice returns before Teri. This surprises me. Usually team leaders send the reprimanded employee before them, following some long-standing rule of office discipline. Maybe there's no Teri to send first. Perhaps she freaked out and gave Alice the excuse she was looking for. I remember Teri talking on the morning we were named worst team in the office, and the venom in her voice when she branded her a slut. Teri has always lacked Ade's detachment, unable to see any humour in Alice's dizzy haplessness. I can easily imagine Teri voicing her opinion, and know Alice wouldn't hesitate over getting rid of her. Besides, Alice only said she had until the end of the month to *decide* who should go, not that she'd wait till then to do it. Quick Kall keeps everyone on a temporary basis, and sacking someone isn't exactly difficult. I look at Teri's tartan bag, wondering if she's so cross she's forgotten it.

Then she walks in. Her cheeks look flushed but she's not

crying. She's wearing the pale-pink lipstick I like, the one that makes her look like an actress from an eighties movie. My idea of what's erotic definitely stopped in that era, and God knows how I'd respond if I ever saw a woman in a puffball skirt.

'So, did she sack you?' I ask.

'No, but I wish she had. I hate it when you've just been disciplined. They make you feel like from now on you have to be a perfect employee. I'd much rather she just said "sod it, piss off."'

'I thought she might do.'

'Why? Everybody's late every now and again.'

'Yeah, I suppose so. Did you call in?'

'No, I couldn't.'

'Why not?'

'I don't want to tell you.'

'Why?'

'Because you're so judgemental. If I tell you why I was late, you'll just make fun of me.'

'I promise I won't.'

'My housemates locked me in my bedroom.'

'What? Why?'

'For a joke, OK? None of them have got jobs and they think it'd be funny if I lost mine.' I don't say anything. She stares at me. 'Come on, aren't you going to lecture me?'

'No, if you think that's a reasonable way for your friends to behave, I'm not going to argue with you.'

'I don't want to get into it. I'm pissed off with them, but I'll get them back. It's not as if I care about this job.'

She leans down to connect her headphones to her *Aspect*. I look at her small, delicate ears, admiring the way they poke through her black hair.

'I don't want you to think I'm judgemental, Teri. I just want us to be friends.'

'We are friends, but I don't have to answer to you.'

'I know. I'm sorry I made you feel like that.'

She sits back and tucks her bag under the table. 'It's OK, Dan, I'm not really angry with you. It's just that when I was stuck in my room, all I could think of was how I'd explain it to you. I didn't care about getting into trouble with Alice.'

I'm touched by her admission, wondering what it means. Sonia used to get upset about me judging her. It's not a trait I'm proud of, but it's always been part of my character, ever since I was a kid. I suppose that's the main reason I find it hard to make friends, and explains why other men don't think of me as a good bloke.

I can't work out whether my motives towards Teri are honourable. I feel attracted to her, but not sexually. I feel protective, but I'm scared of committing to a genuine friendship. Part of this stems from the knowledge that sooner or later she's going to get sacked because of me, but it's also something to do with my history, and my sense of myself. It's going to take a long time for me to convince myself that it's a good thing for a woman to be involved with me. Sometimes I wonder if I'd still feel like this if I'd got out of my relationship with Sonia earlier, when I was still the victim. Reading about Claire's violent husbands in Dad's minutes struck a chord with me, and I wish I wasn't so scared of seeming self-pitying. Perhaps I've been too judgemental about Dad's group, and what I really need is a session of my own.

I take the list of phone numbers from my pocket and unfold it. Alice is back at reception now, catching up with the tasks she let wait while she watched for Teri. I could probably get away with an external call, but knowing that Alice noticed the last ones makes me reluctant to try it, and I walk to the callbox in the cloakroom. There are two numbers for Claire. I try the work one.

'Claire Granger.'

'Hi, this is Dan Thomas, Steve's son.'

'Dan, how are you?'

'OK.' I hesitate, then it all comes out in a rush. 'You know what Lucy said about how I shouldn't think of you as a group but just as seven friends I happened to make at the same time?'

'Yes. Why, Dan, is there something wrong?'

I wrap the phone cord around my hand, wondering if I should confess about reading the minutes. I know it's stupid to imagine that something could remain a secret between the two of us, and if I tell Claire, I'm telling all of them, but maybe that's the best next step for me. At least then I'll be guaranteed some sort of reaction, rather than the hesitant fencing that's so far passed between us.

'No, it's just that . . . look, I'm going to tell you something now and I'll understand if you think it's a betrayal but it'll be a lot easier if you don't get upset.'

'OK.'

'Right. You know the minutes you took at the meetings you had with my Dad?'

'You've read them.'

'How did you know?'

'When you visited us you said Steve didn't talk about us, but you didn't seem surprised. It didn't take us long to fig-ure it out.'

'I haven't read the whole thing,' I tell her, 'just the first couple of meetings.'

'And you were intrigued by something I said.'

I nod, then remember she can't see me. 'Yeah.'

'Do you want to meet up with just me or the whole group?'

'Just you to start with. I need to ease into this.'

'That's fine. When are you free?'

'Ah, that's a bit of a problem. I work a double shift. Days and nights.'

'We can get round that. What time would suit you?'

'Could you meet me at midnight?'

'Yes, but not for a few days, I'm afraid. How about Thursday?'

'Fine. Should I come to you?'

'Probably not a good idea. Do you know The Frog and Toad?'

'Yeah.'

'That's got a late licence. I'll meet you outside the front entrance at quarter past twelve.'

'OK. Thanks, Claire.'

'Forget about it. I'm glad you called. And honoured that you chose me. I'll see you Thursday. Bye.'

'Bye.'

I replace the handset and stare at the wall, wondering if I've done the right thing.

I tell Teri about the blonde girl with the karaoke tickets and our Dating Agency success. I want to play another round, but Teri's still getting over being disciplined and doesn't want to give Alice any more excuses to have a go at her. So we play Hangman instead, being extra-cautious when we pass the computer paper back and forth. At lunchtime I go out alone, taking half an hour instead of fifteen minutes and walking through to McDonald's. It's supposed to be an attempt at economising, but I end up going large on a Big Mac meal and spending almost as much as I would at the World of Food. I worry the whole time about my phonecall, knowing that I've taken another step along a path I probably shouldn't have started on. I wonder how old Dad was when he went to his first group. I used to see him as a fuckup, but lately I've realised he handles everything so much better than me, maybe because he's just upfront about what he wants.

I feel more confused about Dad now than I have for ages. I know I wouldn't have contacted Claire if I hadn't stopped visiting him, and part of this whole thing is a fantasy that I can replace Dad in these women's lives, the same way I pretty much managed with Mum. Claire seemed the best place to start because of the ambiguities that could be explored in any relationship with her. To wit:

1. The whole victim thing. As she had been previously attracted to violent men, I could use my situation in a double-pronged attack. I could start (as I have in this account) by portraying myself as a guilty abuser, then slowly reveal the fact that the cycle of abuse in my case was much shorter than usual i.e. not abused child becomes violent man, but instead abused lover becomes abusive lover.

2. Was she to be a prospective lover or a prospective mother? Several years before I began my assault on Dad's library, I was a frequent visitor to the side of my mother's bed, dipping into the creased paperbacks that languished there. Among the countless Erica Jongs and Marilyn Frenchs, one volume in particular had stayed with me: Lisa Alther's *Kinflicks*. I'd been drawn to it by all the sexy-sounding words on the cover (ribald, zany, raunchy, riotous), and although I never had the courage to steal it and read the whole thing, I spent hours lying on my parents' bed going over certain passages again and again. My favourite extract was about 'yummy mummies', a phrase Alther used to describe middle-aged women who slept with younger men. I'd always imagined 'yummy mummies' looking more like Valerie and Brittany, but I felt a scary, sexy uncertainty about the nature of my prospective friendship with Claire. I'd feel a lot more certain about my feelings towards these women if I knew who (if any) of them had slept with Dad, but this is also a question I don't really want answered.

3. My uncertainties about Claire's whole identity, which (although she'd been forthright throughout the minutes) seemed somehow more flexible than that of, say, Marilyn and Brittany. I also thought that of all the women (except perhaps Imogen – Dad's never been a big fan of bisexuality) she'd be the one who'd had the least contact with Dad.

Thinking about Claire reminds me of stupid teenage things like having a crush on your teacher. One of my biggest worries about sharing a flat with my father was that it might pervert my sexuality, and I'm not sure if recent events prove or disprove that I was right to worry. I know if I was Dad I'd be ecstatic about the adventure which awaits me, and wonder why I can't share the same excitement in letting my life be bent by the twin forces of psychological development and sexual opportunity. I suppose I'm scared by the knowledge that Dad arranged this, making me feel like a boy taken to a brothel for his sixteenth birthday. Except it's not just that. If it was just a father/son thing, it'd only be a matter of overcoming my squeamishness, which would be easy. Whether or not Dad's women would have attempted to contact me if he hadn't been knocked over, I'm not so naive that I don't realise there's a reason for their interest in me. I represent an end to their story, but I'm also part of the beginning. I know Dad only started attending this group when he moved in with me, but there were other groups before that (for almost all of the eight members) and I'm sure the impulse for seeking out this kind of support is connected to marriage, and families, and the desire to open opportunities beyond these conventions, and preserve in their life a self-created space. When Dad started going to groups I was a child, a son, and therefore a threat to that space. Now I'm an adult, and if they can persuade me to join their group, it will complete the circle.

I walk back to the call-centre and wait there alone while the others take their break. I think of them all sitting there smoking together and realise I've made myself into the outsider again. I used to pride myself on being a good team-member and now I've managed to annoy all of them. I wonder if things would be resolved if I made a pass at Teri. At least then we'd be symmetrical – apart from Gordon, who's never been destined to be part of the ordered universe.

They all traipse back in together and return to their seats. Conversation is limited throughout the afternoon, as if we've all been on a long car journey together and have run out of things to say. I try pushing a piece of paper towards Teri but she ignores the grid I've drawn there, concentrating on her calls. My frustration effects my phone manner and several old ladies ask for my name. I tell them I'm called John.

At five to six, I tell the others to log off and let me take any late calls. The cleaners move in with their vacuums, tidying around the departing operators and pocketing any screwed-up balls of paper in case they turn out to be love letters or dirty rhymes. The best of these discoveries turn up in *A Quick Read*, the company magazine. Most of them seem like they've been dropped deliberately, an informal form of submission that ensures that each issue is filled with the secret thoughts of the company. Once or twice I've dropped a few pages of this account, although they've never turned up in the weekly issue. Maybe I should try my hand at something more concise.

The old lady from opposite is standing behind my work-station. I look up at her.

'Thanks for the book,' she says, 'it was interesting.'

'You liked all the animals then?'

'Yeah, especially the pictures.' She hands me a disk. 'My nephew said I could make you a copy.'

'Is this . . . ?'

'Hotel Babylon,' she says. 'You have to shut down some of the Quick Kall applications and then you can load it in like a regular disk.'

I nod, staring at the small square of plastic and feeling excited. I look around for something to offer her in return. Dad's copy of *Political Ideas* is hidden beneath the table. I give it to her.

'Would you like this?'

'*Political Ideas*? It sounds a bit heavy.'

'It's not as difficult as it looks. The prose is actually pretty straightforward.'

She looks at me. 'OK, I'll give it a go. Have fun with the game.'

She walks back to her table. I remove the Magicmix and Car Insurance applications and load up Hotel Babylon. The graphics are incredible, especially as I'm not used to playing anything more complex than Patience or Minesweeper. I decide to take the game slowly, following through every possibility before moving on to the next. I've always had this denial-and-reward attitude to entertainment, a trait that working here has only exacerbated. If I buy a magazine, I force myself to read it from cover to cover, even if there's only one or two articles which interest me. The first screen that comes up after the initial sequence offers a choice of eight characters whose identity you can assume. I start with the top left corner, a woman with long red hair and strange hooded eyes. I use the keyboard to make my selection, clicking on the flashing square.

I'm still playing my first game when the old ladies go home, and if I wasn't scared of being caught by the security guard I'd stay here all night. Unfortunately, there's no save function and I have to abort the game before getting to the end. It's much more enjoyable than anything else I've played, combining the prurient appeal of something like Leisure-Suit Larry with the weight of Sim City or Civilisation. There's also something satisfyingly literary about the game, a neat formal elegance which will no doubt become more impressive when I've inhabited a few other characters and understand how the whole thing links up.

I straighten my workspace and take my nightly stroll into the Centre. I've passed the point of real hunger so I content myself with a bag of chips, eating half and then tipping the rest on the floor for the pigeons. It's cold outside and I keep looking at my watch, wondering what's the earliest I can go back. I consider buying something for John, but I can't be bothered with walking to the chippy and I'm not sure what else he'd like. Do cats eat

Matt Thorne

chicken burgers? I know he wouldn't want the bun and lettuce, but maybe he could chew on the meat. Who cares anyway? He'll just have to settle for Felix.

I give it another five minutes and then walk back. I let myself in through the back exit and take the lift to the seventh floor. Feeding John takes about fifteen minutes and then I wash my face, the liquid soap stinging my eyes. I spend longer than usual cleaning my teeth, worrying about the discolouring at the bottom of one of my canines. I hate looking in the toilet mirrors. Every time I do so the harsh light reveals another new defect.

I hang my suit jacket on the coat rack and gather up the abandoned coats I use for my bedding. I can't stand sleeping in my trousers, and always wake up with a hot, itchy crotch. But I don't want to risk being found naked by the cleaners and suppose a little discomfort is just something I'll have to suffer. I unbuckle my belt, scratch my balls and switch off the light, then bury my head into a soft quilted jacket.

Since I've started sleeping in the office, I've had several nightmares about being discovered. In the dreams it's always been Ade or Teri who finds me and when I hear Alice's voice I simply assume it's the next instalment in the series. But as her questions become more insistent, I realise pretending to be asleep is futile.

'I asked you what you're doing here,' she repeats.

I look up at her. She's wearing casual clothes, the same grey leggings and stretched white T-shirt she wore to The Pentangle two weeks ago. She's also wearing an oversized burgundy jacket with wooden toggles that comes down to her thighs. I don't know what she's doing here this late, but I have the presence of mind to realise that if I've got any chance of getting out of this without losing my job, I have to exploit the strangeness of this situation. As long as I don't say anything, I'm safe. But I've got to find a way of extending this silence. I stand up. My trousers fall down around my ankles. Alice stares at me. I hold her gaze, knowing that if she checks me out, I'm home free. I wait. Her eyes flicker downward. I seize my moment, hopping across and shoving her up against the wall. Her breath slips from her lips. I kiss her hard, waiting to see how she reacts before going further.

She stares. It's been a long time since I've seen anyone's eyes so close to mine. Although she hasn't struggled, it's hard to tell whether she's just waiting until our clinch breaks off before screaming. I decide to keep kissing her until her eyes close. But what if she's only keeping them open because mine are open too? I want to close mine, but then I won't be able to see if she's closed hers. I decide to do so anyway, at least long enough for her to copy me. I move my lips, then open my eyes again. Yes. They're closed. What next? It's been so long since I've done anything like this. I try to remember all the office sex scenes I've seen in films, but the only one I can think of is from *Jungle Fever*, and I can't recall anything about the mechanics, only that it didn't seem very realistic. Perhaps this is the wrong way to approach things. It'd be nice if we could pause for a second and I could ask Alice what she'd like me to do next, but somehow I don't think she'd respond very well. I wonder how Fat Bastard did it. Alice must be used to this by now. Maybe being in the office is a turn-on in itself, and it doesn't matter who she's with, or what I do.

I slow my kisses, tentatively pushing the tip of my tongue against her lips. She opens her mouth and my tongue slips inside. This is clearly a cue for my next move, so I try putting my hand between her legs, stroking the seamed crotch of her leggings. I realise this probably sounds a bit Neanderthal, but after everything Adrienne said about Alice this morning, I figure a direct approach is best. My trust in Ade proves well-founded when I realise from the prickle of Alice's pubes through her leggings that she was right about her not wearing knickers. Her hand goes to my crotch and I have to restrain myself from jumping backwards, allowing her fingers to slip inside my underwear.

We stay like that for a moment, kissing and touching. Two things distract me:

1. I don't want to have sex in the cloakroom. I'm not sure why – it just doesn't seem right.
2. Given Alice's reputation, I'm reluctant to have sex without a condom. (Oh. I know all that stuff about how it's almost impossible for a man to catch AIDS from a woman, but I still don't want to take that risk tonight, especially when I'm not going to enjoy the coupling that much. Really good sex would be worth dying for, sure, but not a quick fuck designed to distract your team leader from realising you've started sleeping in the office.)

I decide it's time to say something. But before that, I turn Alice around and push her face up against the wall. 'Not here,' I tell her, before reaching down and whipping her leggings down around her bum. 'Run.'

She plays along, opening the door and waddling out onto the floor of the call-centre. Alice looks back at me and I spring up at her, knocking her onto the carpet. I give her a second to start crawling before grabbing hold of the leggings' material and pulling her backwards. She struggles to get free, twisting and twisting until her feet are out. I let her get away again, before catching up with her and pushing her down onto one of the two reception tables.

'Do you have anything?' I ask her. She looks at me, offended. 'I mean, that we can use.'

She looks up at me. 'Check my drawer.'

I nip across the office and do as she says. There's an open packet of blue Mates beneath a lever-arch file. I try not to think about who she was with the last time she used them. I pull my underwear down and roll the condom onto my erection, making a mental note to tidy up later on. After all, this could all be in vain if I leave my pants behind. Alice is still positioned on the desk, and I drop down to my knees behind her. My tongue licks up and over her vagina, although I have to move almost beneath the table to get to her clit. She reaches round and pulls my face into her.

I lick quickly, worrying about how long it's been and wondering if I still remember how to do it properly. Hiding beneath a table reminds me of school. This is just one of the pervy associations that makes the call-centre such a sexy place and keeps me erect as I struggle to keep sucking Alice. She's really pulling at my neck now, and I'm anxious about dislocating something. I gently lift her hands away and come out from beneath the table, checking the ridge at the bottom of the rolled-down condom and standing up behind her. She looks over her shoulder at me and then rolls onto her back, shuffling her buttocks down along the smooth surface of the reception table. I'm surprised she's changed position, but also pleased, as if this absolves me from some unknown responsibility. Looking at her half naked in front of me I'm surprised by how aroused I am, and remember how when I last masturbated it was Alice's arse that brought about the desired result. I reach up under her white T-shirt and touch her breasts, feeling excited by the plain, stiff material of her ordinary bra. I move forward. My rubber-wrapped cock presses against her soft, wet cunt. I flex myself against her, feeling calm now I know I can go through with this.

Alice is unimpressed by my delaying. Her fingers rub over my helmet as she pushes me inside and I can feel the tickly throb that my thoughtful penis provides as an early warning system before premature ejaculation. (It has been a while, after all.) I push myself deep inside Alice and then pull back slowly, deliberately allowing my cock to slip out. As Alice frustratedly looks up at me, I give myself a quick, hard squeeze and hold my fingers there until the tickle disappears. That's better. I push myself back in and reach under Alice to undo her bra. As soon as her breasts are freed, I pull up her T-shirt to look at them.

All this pushing and pulling. But that's what it's like in those first few minutes before Alice and I find our rhythm. I wonder if Alice goes through this every time. I just can't imagine the physical differences between making love to Fat Bastard and making love to me. It's not just ego. I'm well aware that there's just as many things wrong with me as there are with him. It's simply the mechanics. More office sex scenes slip through my mind. Soaps, mostly. *Melrose Place* and *Models Inc.* Sex in those programmes always seems so *corporate*. Maybe we should be wearing suits.

I'm not very good at judging breasts. The main reason why I preferred watching *Dish of the Day* to *The Sex Show* was that the focus was on one exposed vagina rather than fifty exposed breasts. You can see breasts anywhere: they're an integral part of British culture. Barbara Windsor's breasts. Melinda Messenger's breasts. I realise all this is obvious, but sometimes I feel that not being obsessed with breasts is an act of philistinism as limiting as hating literature or modern art. Breasts, I realise now, are very much a Dad thing. Vaginas are trendier, and maybe our legacy for the next generation should be to make them as omnipresent as breasts are today. After all, people have already started on the penis. Actually, I think the penis will become part of pop culture long before people come round to the vagina. It's strange because the vagina is the only one of the three (or four, if you count breasts as two, or five, if you count the bum, which I think is unnecessary) that has a legitimate reason for turning up on TV. Think about it. Any home can have a home video of a vagina, so long as it appears in a recorded document of someone giving birth. We need a baby's head to hide the hole.

Anyway, Alice's breasts. And yes, an appraisal is necessary. If I expect my team to forgive me, I'd better return with full details. I try to look at Alice as Adrienne might, knowing she's much better at appreciating women. Nipples: normal, almost celluloid worthy. (I've never understood why all film stars have perfect nipples. I realise a lot of girls get into the business through pornography or acting as escorts, so maybe there's a mandatory check there, but surely some women get through to their first celluloid sex scene without their breasts being on show. Do women with anything other than the standard circles decide to give up on acting and join the circus instead? If so, this seems an awful act of sexual discrimination, especially as you can tell just from looking at their faces that most Hollywood actors probably have horrible dicks.) As for the remainder of Alice's breasts . . . I don't know, Adrienne brought Teri's breasts to mind when she described them as apple-shaped, so maybe what's needed is an appropriate fruit. Grapefruits, I suppose, although this seems a pretty puerile comparision.

I come. No need to tell you how that feels. Alice hangs on to me, and I flop down on top of her. I slowly pull out, and let my softening cock hang against her. I kiss her. We lie like that. Remembering my original motive, I ask, 'So what now?'

'You're living here?'

'Yes.'

'Money problems bigger than you claimed?'

'Exactly.'

'This can't go on.'

'So I'm sacked.'

'Not necessarily. Why did you make love to me?'

'Because I wanted you.'

'And now?'

'What d'you mean?'

'Will you want me again?'

'Yes.'

'Do you have any objection to coming home with me?'

'On what basis?'

'As my new boyfriend.'

'And I can carry on working here?'

She looks at me. I worry I've been too blunt. But she says, 'Of course. Where's your stuff?'

'In the cloakroom.'

'Go get it. I'll meet you downstairs.'

She pulls her legs up and turns away. I stagger back and stare at the filled teat of the condom, wondering where best to dispose of it. I feel an adolescent urge to leave the seed-sac where it might be discovered, but I'm certain that somewhere in the basement of Quick Kall Ltd they have a machine that can take my DNA and spit forth my ID. I like the idea of our sex becoming the object of speculation. My only previous experience of this sort of situation has come second-hand through office gossip. I've never been that interested in making love in the call-centre: it's just that it's so obviously something I'd never do. It's like the way that the only people who get invited to orgies are those who don't find them fascinating. *Coming to the orgy?* Sure. *Only don't tell Dan because he'll be too interested. Wait till afterwards and we'll tell him all about it.* Great. Good idea.

Bastards.

The other thing about hearing that sort of gossip is that you can't help feeling you missed out. Even if the people involved are utterly repellent. It's like watching couples kiss. Instead of coming to the logical conclusion (i.e. you are watching two people in love sharing a romantic moment), you think that the fact that this woman is kissing her partner means she's prepared to kiss anyone, and all you need do is catch up with her when he's not around. This may sound like a strange conclusion to reach, but isn't it the principle behind most mainstream pornography? Here's a woman who's prepared to fuck an ugly, brutal man with gelled hair and a hip rhythm that'd put most women in hospital. If that's her idea of a hot date, just wait till she meets me.

Alice rescues her leggings from the call-centre floor. I watch her buttocks muscles contract as she pulls them back up, then snap the condom from my cock. I don't want to be seen fiddling, so I pat her backside and walk to the toilet. Choosing a different cubicle from usual, I find my fingers are trembling too much to tie a satisfactory knot in the condom. Without a knot, the damn thing will never flush, and I don't want people to discover this evidence tomorrow morning. So I turn round and climb up onto the toilet, lifting a tile and giggling at the fun of hiding my semen in the ceiling. The top holds and I drop down onto the floor, fishing my cock from my underwear and firing a stream of piss into the bowl.

'Got everything?' Alice asks as I come out through the back entrance.

'Yeah, don't worry, I haven't left any evidence.'

Alice reaches into the pocket of her burgundy jacket and pulls out her car keys. The fob is a strawberry with a hole in it.

'Can I have a look at your keyring?'

She hands it to me. I squeeze it. A small plastic penis with a garishly red helmet pops from the hole.

'I haven't seen one of these in ages. Where did you get it?'

'On holiday in Spain. Three years ago.'

'Did they have any other fruit?'

'Yeah, bananas and watermelons. And monkeys as well.'

I follow her across to the car. She asks for her keys back and unlocks the door. Then she climbs inside and starts wrestling with the crook-lock. I wait till she's finished and she lets me in. I put my stuff on the back seat, then watch her checking the rear-view as she reverses.

'Fasten your seatbelt,' she admonishes.

I do so. As soon as we get out onto the road, she leans across and whispers, 'Get your cock out.'

'What?'

'I want to hold it while I'm driving.'

'Isn't that dangerous?'

She ignores me. I wait a second and then unzip my trousers. I push down the waistband of my pants and let the material support my cock as I get it out. It looks a little the worse for wear, my foreskin crinkled into alternate lines of pink and red. Alice leans across and takes hold of it. It stiffens immediately.

'That feels nice.'

'I use a lot of handcream.'

I nod and sit back, wondering what she's going to do to me. It feels as if her fingers are moving slightly, but it's hard to tell whether it's deliberate or merely the motion of the car. She moves her hand to the gear stick and then back again. This feels disconcerting and I worry she might get muddled up and put me into reverse.

'So how long have you been living there?' she asks.

'Not long. A week or so.'

She nods, moving her hand again. This time when she brings it back she starts masturbating me properly, her motion quick and soft.

'Can you get the tissues from the glove compartment?'

I do so. She looks at me and says, 'Warn me when you're going to come.'

'I'll do it,' I tell her, plucking three tissues from the box.

She's moving her hand steadily now, only occasionally going back across to the gear stick. I feel a familiar tremble in my legs and then press the tissues against the head of my cock.

'Nice?' she asks.

I nod.

I'd assumed Alice lived in a part of Bristol unknown to me, some suburb near the Centre. But we drive through all those areas, continuing along the road that starts where my father got run over and eventually runs parallel to my room. I look back as we pass it, expecting to see Farnell's kingdom reduced to a burnt-out shell. I've been thinking about the room a lot recently, wondering whether a return visit might solve my financial difficulties. I realise Kevin will have sold the computer by now, but he'll probably have held on to the TV and video. And as Farnell would sooner move house than go to the trouble of changing locks, it shouldn't be hard to sneak back in.

Alice continues driving out towards Bath. None of the suburbs here seems a likely home for her, except perhaps Kingswood. I watch her profile, worrying that she's a sex-crazed serial killer, and is really searching for a patch of wasteland where she can dig my grave. If she is a psycho, she's one of the creepily calm kind, her hands remaining steady on the steering-wheel.

She stops in Keynsham. Now this is a surprise. I wouldn't have imagined Alice lived out here. I remember her telling me that she still lives with her mother and conclude this woman must be more elderly than I imagined. Not that Keynsham is full of old people: it's just that you don't end up here by accident. You have to desire a certain kind of calm, rural life. Although I suppose there are plenty of buses to the more frenetic parts of the city.

Alice has parked outside a large bungalow. The garden looks neat and well-tended, even in the dim illumination of the streetlight. It's the sort of house that might appear in a building society ad, all straight lines and bright paintwork. We both get out and Alice locks the car. I walk round to her side and she whispers, 'We have to be quiet. My little brother's a light sleeper.'

'What about your mum?'

'Oh, it'd take a herd of elephants to wake her up. I hope you can cope with loud snoring.'

I look at her, smiling. 'I don't have to sleep with her, do I?'

'No,' she giggles, 'but her room's next to ours.'

I follow her up the footpath and wait while she carefully unlocks the front door. Alice holds it open and I slip in behind her, reaching out to touch her hip. She turns and smiles at me. Along the hallway are photographs of a small boy with a big mop of blond hair. There are no pictures of Alice. I'm about to ask her why when she says, 'Would you like something to eat?'

'No, I'm fine, but ... if I was careful not to be too noisy, would it be possible for me to have a bath?'

'Of course. You can use the en suite.'

I follow her through the hallway and into a large square bedroom. She opens the door to the en suite and says, 'I'll just get you a towel.'

I walk across and look inside. There is a large corner-bath, a bidet, sink and toilet. The whole suite is in the same beige as the thick carpet. I sit on the edge of the bath and unlace my shoes. Alice returns with a Flintstones towel.

'This is the only clean one, I'm afraid.'

'That's OK.' I take the towel. 'Are all the rooms like this?'

She laughs. 'No, this is much better than the others. Before Dad left he fucked his mistress on that bed. Mum wanted a fresh start so we did a straight swap.'

I turn on the taps, wondering if Alice is going to stay with me while I wash. I'm embarrassed by how long it's been since I last cleaned properly, and pour lots of bubble bath beneath the running water to obscure her vision of my body. But she walks back into the bedroom, shutting the door behind her.

I unzip my trousers and drop them onto the floor. Then I remove my underwear and examine the stains, scared now I've entered this world of family washing-machines. It's clear that I have to get rid of these pants. Nothing can excuse the state they're in. I step on the pedal of the flip-top bin, wondering if I can hide them beneath the tampon wrappers and empty razor boxes. But somebody has to empty the bin, and I know from experience that this sort of thing doesn't go unnoticed.

There's a Lady Protector in its purple plastic tray on the edge of the bath. I examine the blade. It's already clogged with hair so I don't think she'll notice if I blunt it. Besides, there are three spares next to the plastic tray. I take my pants and use the blade to make a ragged cut through the waistband. Once I've sliced the elastic the rest of the material is relatively easy to tear through, and I rip the pants into small strips. Then I wrap each piece with toilet paper, run cold water over the parcels, and flush the first two down the toilet. The bath is nearly full now, and I decide to wait until after my wash before getting rid of the rest, not wanting Alice to wonder what I'm doing behind the bathroom door. I put her razor back in its tray and climb into the hot water.

I cannot describe how fantastic it feels. I've always enjoyed baths, but this immersion has got to rank as one of the most sensual experiences of my entire life. For the first few minutes the feeling around my buttocks and feet is so overwhelming that I daren't risk lowering the rest of my body into the soapy water. I reach down and pull back my foreskin, the tiny tingles of water rushing in there sending me into new shudders. I close my eyes and slide along the bottom of the bath, wondering if Alice will mind if I sleep here.

Once my body has adjusted to being in water, I take the soap and start rubbing at my body, amazed at the thickness of the white pellets that form in the hollows behind my toes and up my arms. I explore between my toes and push a finger deep into my anus, rotating it gently before replacing it with the edge of the soap. Then I shampoo my hair, using Alice's conditioner and repeating as necessary (which is about four times). After my wash is over, I just lie and luxuriate in the water, forgetting that I can now do this as often as I want.

I pull out the plug and flush away the rest of my pants, dropping the parcels into the bowl two at a time. Then I wrap myself in the stiff, scratchy Flintstones towel and walk back into Alice's bedroom. She's lying on the bed, wearing a burgundy nightdress.

'How come there are only pictures of your brother in the hall?'

She laughs. 'I was a bit of a tomboy. I didn't get many pictures taken.'

'You must have a few school snaps. They have to take them for the files.'

'Yeah, but your parents don't have to pay for them.'

'So you don't have any pictures?'

'I have one. But I'm not sure I want you to see it.'

'Go on. I promise not to laugh.'

'Oh, you won't laugh.' She rolls over and walks to the wardrobe at the other end of the room. I look at her legs as she stretches to reach a shoebox on the top shelf above the rail of clothes. She brings the whole box down and goes through it on the edge of the bed.

'Here you are.'

The photograph shows a boy with spiky red hair and a missing front tooth holding Alice in a headlock.

'I thought you said your brother was younger than you?'

'He is.'

'He doesn't look it in the photo.'

'He isn't in the photo.'

'Who's that then? The school bully?'

'Yeah. Me. I'm the one with the missing tooth.'

'That's you?'

'Yeah, at thirteen. I was going through a difficult period.'

I sit on the bed. Alice takes the photo from me and pushes me backwards. She unwraps my towel.

'Mmm,' she sniffs, 'freshly washed man. That's got to be my favourite smell.'

Alice runs her fingers across my damp thighs and I feel myself stiffening again.

'You tired yet?' she asks.

'Not really.'

'Good.'

She lifts up her nightdress and lowers herself against my legs. As she takes my cock and starts rubbing the head against her cunt, I have another panic.

'I left your condoms at work.'

'God, you're a worrier,' she chides me. 'I have some here.'

She leans over me and opens her bedroom drawer. This time she rolls the condom onto me herself, holding the teat as she straightens it down. I close my eyes when she mounts me, hoping that after she's finished I'll finally get some rest.

Part Two

Rip Her to Shreds

15

I awake in a panic, kicking Alice and yanking the duvet from her. It's not just disorientation, but also fear that I've forgotten something. Alice embraces me, the gesture surprisingly tender.

'What's wrong?'

'I don't know. Have we overslept?'

She laughs. 'Just a little bit. It's half past eleven. Do you know anything about toilets?'

'Half eleven. Why didn't you wake me?'

'That would've spoilt it. I wanted to give you a treat.'

'I don't understand.'

'I'm still your team leader, and I've decided you've been working too hard. So consider this a day off.'

'Oh. Thanks. Why did you ask me about toilets?'

'The one in the en suite seems to be broken. I had a shit this morning and it won't go down.'

Visions of Dyno-rod extracting my underwear from Alice's toilet prompt me to tell her, 'Yeah, I can fix it. The landlord in my old place was pretty hopeless, so I've become a bit of an odd-job expert.'

'Excellent. Do you need anything?'

'An old coat hanger, if you've got one.'

'Probably,' she says, walking over to her wardrobe. I wait while she looks inside. 'Will this do?'

She hands me a hanger. I sit up and start untwisting it, straightening the metal into a long spike. Alice smiles at me.

'You don't have to do it this minute.'

'It's OK, I don't mind. But I think I will get dressed first.'

She smiles again. 'Mum's washed some clothes for you.'

I climb out of bed and Alice hands me a shirt and a pair of trousers on a wooden hanger. I lay the clothes on her bed.

'If you're looking for your pants and socks, I've emptied out a drawer for you.'

She fetches my underwear and a balled pair of black socks. I try not to worry about what Alice's mum must've thought when she did my laundry. Alice leaves me to get dressed and says, 'Come and meet my mum when you've finished with the toilet. She's looking forward to talking to you.'

I crouch by the toilet, looking at the wadded pink paper and the small, fat turd that's slipped out and sneaked to the surface. The water level's risen almost to the top of the bowl, and it's obvious that another flush will spill the contents onto the carpet. I use the coat hanger to stick the paper against the ceramic, carefully avoiding the shit spinning in the whirlpool I've just created. I can see the pants package blocking the bend. Hooking the hanger into the toilet paper, I give it three hard tugs and it comes free, floating up with Alice's excrement. The toilet gurgles, but the water level lowers only slightly. I now face a difficult decision. If this is the only package that hasn't gone through, another flush should return the water to its normal level. But if there's more of them hiding out of sight, I could end up with a hideous mess to clear up.

I pull the flush.

Alice is standing in the lounge doorway, talking to someone out of sight. I walk up behind my new girlfriend and tickle her side, catching her as she jumps back.

'Mum's engrossed in this book someone gave her at work. You won't get a sensible word out of her.'

Alice's mum sits in a green armchair. Her feet are covered by thick woollen socks and elevated by the footrest. A battered copy of *Political Ideas* is perched in the sag of her crotch. She grins at me.

'Enjoying *Hotel Babylon*?'

Alice looks confused. I decide to play along. 'I haven't got very far. Although I suppose it's not that sort of game.'

She nods, and holds up her book. 'I want to talk to you about this when I'm finished.'

'OK,' I say, before adding, 'I'm not sure I remember that much.'

My admission provokes a disappointed scowl, and I decide to bring Alice back into the conversation. 'You didn't tell me your mum works at Quick Kall.'

'I didn't think you'd know her. I can see I underestimated what happens when I'm not in the office.'

'It's one big orgy, isn't it, Dan?' she says, holding my eye. I don't know which unnerves me most; her question, or the casual use of my name. Seeing Alice's mum makes me worry about John. I hadn't intended to leave him this long. I know he'll probably be fine, but I'm worried I haven't left him enough food.

Alice's mum looks different outside the office. Younger, and more malevolent. She also seems less like a generic old lady, although maybe that's only because I can see traces of Alice in her wrinkled face. I mentioned earlier that Alice looks like a Peanuts character, and her mum shares these cartoon features, looking like Charlie Brown in a witch-hair wig.

'Alice, can I have a word?'

'Sure. What's wrong?'

'It's about the toilet.'

*   *   *

When the water continued to rise and floated Alice's shit over the rim of the bowl, my first reaction was *get rid of it!* Unfortunately, there's not all that much you can do with excrement apart from flushing it, and now that was no longer an option, I realised a rash decision could get me kicked out of my new home before I'd even had chance to settle in. Running through the alternatives (throwing it out of the window, squashing it down a plughole, breaking it into pieces and feeding it through the overflow), it became clear that the most sensible course of action was to leave it on the floor and take advantage of the now-shitless bowl to remove another pants parcel. I pushed my hand deep into the dirty water and grasped inside the U-bend. Locating two of last night's droppings, I withdrew my hand and discovered (to my great relief) that this unblocking was enough to stop the water pouring onto the carpet, even if the bowl stubbornly refused to drain more than a couple of inches. Now that the water was below danger level, I wrapped my fingers in tissue and, turning my face away, picked up the turd and returned it to its rightful home.

Although this might sound like a successful operation, it still left me with a waterlogged (and shit-specked) carpet, a blocked bowl, and (most distressingly) three soggy packages. After what had happened to the toilet, I now knew that disposing of them anywhere inside the house was clearly a bad idea and decided to hide the parcels in my rucksack until I had chance to get outside and drop them down the drain. I put them inside a dirty sock and zipped them into the front pocket of my bag, then went out into the lounge to meet Alice's mother.

Alice follows me back into her bedroom and through to the en suite. She ignores the damp carpet and peers into the bowl, saying, 'So you couldn't do anything then?'

'No, sorry, it seems to be blocked further down.'

'It's probably a tampon or something. Don't worry, we'll tell Mum.'

We go back into the lounge and Alice explains the problem.

Her mum looks at her and says, 'I'll give Arthur a ring. You two go and get ready.'

Alice drives us to the supermarket. I get the impression that they're making the trip especially for me, and can't decide how I feel about that. I'm not used to this sort of special treatment, and worry that somewhere down the line they'll turn against me (probably when Arthur arrives to fix the toilet and they discover what I've been doing with my pants). I want to behave like a decent guest, but I'm only too aware of all the things about me that will prove difficult for them to understand.

I'm trying to avoid saying anything to Alice's mum. When we were in her bathroom, Alice told me to call her mother Cathy, but I've always been uncomfortable about addressing authority figures by their Christian names.

'What sort of thing do you like to eat, Dan?' Cathy asks, looking at me in the rear-view.

Even the most laid-back of mothers would be horrified if I answered this question truthfully. *Fish and chips.* Anything else? *No. Except for Chinese take-away and the occasional hamburger.* What about vegetables? *What about them?* Fruit? *Never heard of it.* OK, how about this? What if I do you some cod in the deep-fat frier? *Well, sure, you can try that if you want, but if it doesn't taste exactly the same as the stuff from the shops I'm not going to eat it.*

'I'll eat anything,' I tell her.

'No special dietary requirements?'

'I don't eat dairy products.'

'Right. But you're not a vegetarian?'

'No.'

We walk round the supermarket together. Cathy pushes the trolley while we trail behind. Most of her purchases are automatic, hand going to the shelves while she stares down the aisle. I read somewhere that the wobbly wheels on shopping trolleys are a deliberate part of their design, slowing you down and dragging your attention to products you'd normally sail past. Every couple of aisles, Cathy asks me a direct question. I respond by only saying I don't like things when it's something I really hate, rather than turning down everything I haven't tried before. Cathy's choices seem less scary than I'd anticipated, consisting mainly of vaguely infantile 'family foods' like Alphabites and fish fingers. I know I can cope with these meals from childhood visits to friends' homes and years of school dinners. Maybe they'll make a normal man of me yet.

Once we've packed the shopping, Cathy asks us if we'd like to eat in the restaurant. Needless to say, I'm enthusiastic about this idea, especially as the meals here are similar to the World of Food and it puts off the problem of her cooking for me. Sometimes eating seems like the biggest burden of existence, a constant question that can never be satisfactorily answered. Part of the reason I've stuck to the same diet for so long is that this way I know I'm doing myself harm and don't have to weigh up the respective merits of everything I put in my body.

Alice leaves the trolley by a table and the three of us queue up for food. I have chicken and chips and a large Cola. Alice and Cathy have all-day breakfasts. We take the required sauces and cutlery from the plastic trays and then sit down.

'So Dan,' says Cathy, 'I understand you're friends with my sister?'

'Not really friends, as such. I've only met her once.'

'You remember, Mum,' Alice prompts, 'Dan's dad runs Brittany's support group.'

Cathy stares at me. 'And that's where you met her?'

'No, I met her in hospital. She was with Dad when I went in.'

'That reminds me,' says Alice, scraping her chair backwards, 'when I let you visit him last Saturday you didn't come back.'

'I did come back. Just a bit later than I said I would.'

'I see.'

'Am I in trouble?'

'Leave the boy alone,' Cathy tells her. 'What's wrong with your father?'

'He got hit by a car.'

'Oh, I'm sorry. Is it serious?'

'He broke his leg and his elbow,' Alice answers for me. 'That's right, isn't it?'

I nod.

'I'm sorry to hear that,' says Cathy, smiling sympathetically. 'That's really unfortunate.'

After our meal we drive home and carry the shopping in. Cathy and Alice put the stuff away while I sit in the lounge, watching lunchtime TV. A few minutes later Alice joins me, stroking her hand down along my thigh. A car horn toots outside.

'That'll be Arthur,' she says, going to the window. I start thinking through explanations, wondering whether the packages that remain in the toilet can be easily identified as underwear. The best excuse I've come up with so far is that I ran out of toilet paper and had to use my handkerchief to wipe myself. The only problem with this lie is that I'm sure there's half a roll left in Alice's bathroom. But maybe if I win Arthur's confidence he'll swallow my story and I'll be able to persuade him not to say anything to the women.

Alice lets him in. He's a short man with curly brown hair and a wide, shiny face. He seems ill-dressed for fixing a toilet, wearing a brown suit jacket and cream chinos. He also has no visible bowl-unblocking equipment. Alice notices Arthur looking at me and tells him, 'That's Dan.'

He nods. 'Hi, Dan.'

'Would you like a cup of tea, Arthur?'

'That'd be lovely.'

'Dan?'

'No thanks.'

'Something else? Coffee perhaps?'

'A Coke would be nice.'

'Coke, OK.'

She leaves the lounge and walks through the hallway to the kitchen. Alice comes over and sits next to me.

'You watching this?' Arthur asks.

'No.'

He picks up the remote and lowers the volume.

'So you're Alice's boyfriend?'

'Yes.'

'Have you been together long?'

I giggle. 'One night.'

He pushes his shoulder into the green settee. 'Do you know who I am?'

'Arthur.'

'Yeah, but do you know my relationship to Alice?'

'No.'

'I'm her uncle. But I can't stand that word so they just call me by my Christian name.'

'Right.'

'I just want you to understand who I am.'

'OK.'

'So how was it?'

'What?'

He winks. 'Last night.'

'Nice,' I reply. He looks expectant. I wonder how I can satisfy him without going into details. 'Unexpected.'

'Why was it unexpected?'

I look at him. 'I didn't know I was going to kiss her until it happened. I was completely lost in the moment.'

Arthur frowns. 'So you didn't have a crush on her?'

'No, it wasn't like that.'

'But you're sticking around?'

'Of course. I really like Alice.'

He nods. 'Good. I'm glad to hear it.'

Alice returns carrying a plastic tray. She gives Arthur his tea and hands me my Coke. Cathy comes in behind her, sitting in the chair with the footrest.

'Thanks for coming over, Arthur.'

'Not a problem. It's good to get out.'

Alice sits next to me. I open my can. Cathy smiles at us. 'Arthur, did Dan tell you he knows Brittany?'

'Is that right?'

I nod. 'My dad runs this group she's in.'

'Really? What's his name?'

'Steve.'

'Yeah, I think I've met him. Big chap.'

'Pretty big, yeah. Dark hair.'

'Yeah, Brittany had him over to dinner when I went round once. He seemed friendly.'

Alice glances at me. I drink from my can, wondering why she looks concerned. Maybe she thinks I'm upset by his accident and don't want to talk about it. I'm about to reassure her with a joke when Cathy says, 'Do you want Alice to get your tools?'

'Yeah, and I could do with some gloves if you've got any.'

'Will Marigolds be OK?'

'Anything, as long as they cover my hands.'

Cathy looks at Alice. 'The gloves are beneath the sink.'

Alice gets up and walks to the kitchen. I watch the muted TV, waiting for further interrogation. Arthur leans forward, rubbing his hands on his trousers.

'I haven't done a toilet in a while. My one at home is pretty reliable.'

I decide not to tell them about the toilet in my old place, worried they'll realise I can't be trusted around bathrooms. Alice comes back with the tools and gloves.

'Do you need any help?' I ask Arthur, eager to have a moment alone with him to explain.

'No, that's OK. It's only a one-man job.'

*   *   *

The next twenty minutes are torturous. Cathy keeps up the conversation, occasionally smiling proudly at the pair of us. I reply whenever she asks me a question, but keep my answers short so I can hear any noise from Arthur. I feel tense in family situations anyway, and the added suspense makes it even harder to come up with appropriate responses. I realise as I'm speaking that my lies don't fit together, and worry Alice is waiting until we're alone before challenging me.

Arthur returns, snapping off his pink Marigolds. 'OK, it should be fine now.'

I can't resist. 'What was wrong with it?'

'Just some stuff that hadn't flushed properly. I dragged it all out and now it's fine. Although you should probably throw away the black bag I used.'

'Thanks Arthur. How much do I owe you?'

'Don't be silly. You know I only charge for parts.'

'Well, at least take a bottle of wine or something. Have a look in the kitchen and see what you want.'

Arthur smiles. 'OK, that's fair. But I'll only take a cheap bottle.'

After Arthur leaves, Alice laces her fingers through mine and nods towards her bedroom. I look at Cathy.

She laughs. 'Don't worry about me. I don't care what you get up to.'

Cathy's candour embarrasses me, and I avoid her eye as I follow Alice to her bedroom.

'So,' she says, 'what do you think of my family?'

'They're nice.'

'My brother will be home from school soon. I think you'll enjoy talking to him.'

'How big an age gap is there between you?'

'Eighteen years.'

'Wow.'

She sits on the bed. 'Do you have any siblings?'

'No. I think my parents looked at me and decided not to risk it again.'

She laughs, then looks seriously at me. 'Are you nervous?'

'A bit.'

'You weren't last night.'

'I know, but I feel funny about your mum.'

'Why? She doesn't mind. And she's really impressed with you. Especially after Bryan.'

Hearing this name makes me think about Alice in a way I haven't done since entering this house. I recall the night in The Pentangle after she'd disciplined us, remembering Teri and Adrienne's scorn when she showed up with Fat Bastard in tow. I've been so concerned about the toilet and befriending Alice's mother that I haven't thought about what'll happen when I return to work. I can probably con Adrienne into believing I'm screwing Alice as a perverse joke, and no doubt Ian will hide his disappointment in me, but there's no way I'll be able to sustain a friendship with Teri and I'm sure if I told her the full story of the last few weeks she'd see this as a bigger betrayal than getting her sacked.

Alice notices my discomfort and says, 'I'm sorry, I shouldn't have said that. I don't want you to feel you're on a conveyor-belt.'

She puts her hand on my chest. I look into her eyes and see the concern is genuine. She enunciated the word 'conveyor-belt' as if it had a personal emotional resonance and I realise she must be repeating a criticism made by a previous lover. I find her worry touching, although I'm not sure how to reassure her without confirming her reputation. So I kiss her instead. She responds enthusiastically, drawing me down onto her bed.

I lie backwards, letting Alice unbuckle my belt. I watch her unzip my trousers and pull my pants down around my ankles, opening my legs so she can position herself between them. There's something reassuring about submitting to a blowjob at this moment, even with her mother sitting in the next room. It feels like an important stage in balancing out our sexual relationship, a process Alice began last night when she masturbated me in her car. I know it's too early to tell, but I think Alice's lust might be just the factor that will stop this relationship following the pattern of my previous one. Even now, I still don't know how much Sonia liked sex, although she was always an eager, willing partner. It's just that for her fucking was always part of a much larger, more destructive cycle.

Alice nuzzles my balls, giving them careful kisses before moving to the root of my penis. I'm glad she's doing this after I've had chance to shower. She grabs my thighs and takes me in her mouth, resting her lips around my helmet. I draw breath. Her sucking is quick and satisfying, her tongue dotting against me while the sensation rises. I think about Cathy next door, trying to find her sanction erotic. When that doesn't work I think about Teri, wondering how she might fellate me. No doubt she'd be less adept than Alice, her little teeth nipping my foreskin as the head of my cock bashes against the roof of her mouth. I also can't picture her swallowing my sperm, and imagine her letting it drip over her lips and run back over my cock. I picture her dark hair and wonder how it might part with her head moving in my lap.

I come. Alice swallows, then sucks me again softly before drying my cock with her fingers. It's the most pleasant sexual experience we've shared so far, and I feel peaceful as Alice lies down beside me.

'You lied to me.'

'What?'

'You didn't visit your dad on Saturday.'

'Who told you?'

'Brittany. She said your dad hasn't seen you for weeks and he's really worried.'

'OK, I didn't see him. I fell asleep on College Green. I'd been up all night and I was really tired. That's also why I was late back to the office.'

She turns on her side. 'I forgive you. But why haven't you visited your dad?'

'I don't want to talk about it.'

'Why not?'

'It's family stuff. Nothing that interesting, but it upsets me to bring it up.'

'Is it to do with your mum?'

I look at Alice, wondering what Brittany's said about me, and how much of this is going to get back to her.

'Why d'you ask that?'

'I'm interested. You haven't told me anything about your mother.'

'Can I talk frankly to you?'

Alice looks excited. 'Of course.'

'No, I'm serious. I need to know if I can trust you. I don't want to come across as a paranoid lunatic, but I'm in a really risky situation here. Not only are you my team leader, but your aunt's shared her innermost secrets with my father and no doubt wants to know everything about me.'

'I wouldn't tell her anything.'

'I don't have anyone I can trust, Alice.'

'You can trust me.'

'When my dad went into hospital I found the minutes from the meetings he's been chairing. I read some stuff in there which made me feel strange about seeing him.'

She nods. 'So you're never going to see him again?'

'No, I'll see him. I just don't know when.'

'Would it make any difference if I went with you?'

'I don't know. Maybe. I'm supposed to be meeting one of the women from his group on Thursday. I think I might feel better about getting in contact after I've spoken to her.'

'OK, just let me know.'

We cuddle for a while and then go back into the lounge to watch TV with Cathy. At four o'clock Alice's brother Tim returns from school. He's older than in the pictures, his hair cut back into a normal style. He too shares the Peanuts features, as well as a head that comes closest in the Hargreaves household to matching the Schulz-patented shape. Alice introduces us and he sits next to me.

'How was school?'

'OK. We watched a film in the afternoon.'

'What film?'

'*Shoah.*'

'I don't know it.'

'We didn't watch all of it. Only about three hours.'

'Three hours. Sounds like a long film.'

'It's nine hours altogether. We're watching it over three days.'

'Are you sure it's not a TV series?'

'No, it's a film.'

'What's it about?'

'The Holocaust.'

'Nine hours on the Holocaust. Isn't that a bit depressing?'

'No, I'm enjoying it. The rest of the class just make sick jokes, but I'm really getting into it.'

'What sort of jokes do they make?'

'Oh ... oh, I don't remember, but before we watched *Shoah* we watched this documentary about how Alfred Hitchcock filmed some of the footage of the bodies in the camps, and you know how Alfred Hitchcock makes an appearance in all of his films, well, some of the kids were joking about looking out for his cameo.'

'That's pretty sick, I agree. Did you see *Schindler's List?*'

'No, I haven't seen that, but I like Spielberg films.'

'Well, if you're interested in the Holocaust you should definitely see that. It's not quite nine hours, but it's pretty long. Alice, is *Schindler's List* out on video?'

'I think so. It's been on TV.'

'Are you members of a video library?'

'Yeah,' says Tim.

'Then I'll phone up and reserve it for you. We'll watch it together.'

Alice looks at me. 'Not tonight, though.'

'No, I wasn't thinking tonight. He's already sat through three hours today. Some time next week.'

Cathy comes through from the kitchen with two trays. She places one in Tim's lap, the other in mine. On the tray is a glass of orange squash and three Penguin biscuits placed evenly on a china plate. While I'm wondering whether this is an evening meal or an afternoon snack, Cathy returns with another tray for Alice and one for herself. She settles back in her armchair and turns up the volume on the TV. I sip my squash. It's so strong that I have to swallow immediately to stop myself spluttering.

'Are you going out tonight?' Cathy asks Alice.

'Yeah, I thought I'd take Dan to the Speckled Hen.'

'That's nice,' she says. 'Tim?'

'Darren's coming over. We're gonna play Fifa 98.'

'Right. Well, I want to do a bit of shopping before I go into work, so we'll have to have dinner about five, OK?'

'Great.'

Sitting here watching TV seems stranger than anything I've done during the previous fortnight. I know I sit in front of a screen all day at work, but that's something I do for money, and after my enforced break from this type of entertainment, it's hard to remember why watching children's programmes is supposed to be fun. The interest seems esoteric, and I keep wanting to talk or go for a walk. I'm sure I'll get back into the habit after a few days, but at the moment the ornaments on top of the mantelpiece seem more interesting than the flickering screen.

I notice the black box on top of the video and my heart lifts.

'Do you have Cable?'

'Yeah,' says Alice, 'but . . .'

'Mum doesn't like it,' Tim explains. 'We're only allowed to watch it when she's not here.'

I look at Alice and wonder what she watches. A few instalments of *Exotica Erotica* might be just the thing to make television appealing again. (Actually, if I'm honest, part of the reason these programmes seem so peculiar is that no one's undressing. The dialogue doesn't seem that different, the direction's identical, and yet there's no nipple-count to keep you interested. TV's perfect for pornography. Anything else just seems like a missed opportunity.)

Cathy goes into the kitchen to start dinner. Tim grins at me, picking up the remote and flipping through to *The Box*. I find the music videos much more diverting than the shows we were watching, and from the way Tim keeps up a constant commentary, I sense he might be a good source of stuff to discuss with Adrienne. Every time his mum comes in Tim flips back, making Alice and me laugh so loudly that Cathy twigs what's going on and tricks him by only pretending to go out before ducking back. Then she takes the remote from him and switches to BBC 1, leaving the lounge before he has chance to protest.

We eat dinner on the table in the kitchen. This arrangement surprises me, and I wonder whether it's Cathy who insists on the formality. Tonight's special is cottage pie and chips, something I can just about stomach (although I leave the pie's potato topping and only eat the meat). Cathy seems pleased to see me eating, and as odd as it feels to admit this, I do (for a moment) feel like part of their family.

After dinner, I volunteer to wash up and my offer is accepted, leaving me at something of a loss. Before now, clearing up after a meal has consisted of throwing away the fish and chip papers, and although I do – in theory – know how to clean plates, I'm worried my efforts will be too pathetic to meet with Cathy's approval. Luckily, she sends Alice to supervise me, and she explains that they have a dishwasher and all I really have to do is scrape the food off the plates, stack them in the machine and turn it on. Relieved, I quickly complete my task and then give Alice a long embrace.

Alice changes before we go to the pub. It's the first time I've seen her dress up, and I don't understand why she feels the need to impress me. She's the one who's taken me in: I should be trying to convince her I'm not a hobo. She wears a blue blouse with a lacy collar and a black knee-length skirt. Although her clothes still aren't that flattering, I can tell she feels attractive in them, and she shyly grasps her fringe when I tell her she looks beautiful.

The Speckled Hen is only a short walk from Alice's house. She tells me it's her favourite pub because she knows she can always stumble back safely.

'Although I did fall asleep there once,' she says, pointing to a bench.

'All night?'

'Yeah, I woke up really stiff. It was so stupid because I had a broken arm at the time. I was in agony.'

'You didn't notice you'd broken your arm?'

'No, I'd broken it already. It was in a plastercast. It just hurt because I'd been banging it around.'

I remember the pictures she showed me last night. 'Was this during your difficult period?'

'Yeah,' she admits, covering her mouth with her hand, 'I think I was about fourteen.'

We arrive at the *Hen*. It's an old man's pub, with a separate bar and lounge. The latter is empty apart from a middle-aged woman sitting in the corner with a half pint of Guinness. Alice sits at a table opposite the open fire and I go to the bar. The woman serving is out of orange juice so Alice has to have Britvic 55 with her vodka.

'What were you like when you were little?' Alice asks me as I sit down.

'The sort of kid you'd probably beat up.'

She laughs. 'I doubt it.'

'I'm serious. When I was about seven these girls from down the road said I wasn't a boy, and the only way I could prove it was to show them my willy.'

'What did you do?'

'I ran away. That's my point. Most boys would've turned it round, made it into an "I'll show you mine if you show me yours" sort of thing. I'm sure that's what they had in mind anyway. But I got scared.'

Alice frowns. I can tell from her mouth that she's offended by my story, but I don't know which part of what I said upset her. It seemed perfectly in keeping with the vaguely bawdy conversation she engages in all the time. Maybe she just doesn't expect that sort of talk from her boyfriends.

'Alice,' I began, 'you know you said you wanted me to trust you?'

'I do.'

I laugh. She looks worried.

'Sorry,' I apologise, 'it's hard to put this into words.'

'What?'

'How I'm feeling.'

She takes my hands. 'You can talk to me.'

'I'm not sure I can.'

'Why not?'

'I feel too scared to say anything. I'm so grateful to you for giving me somewhere to live, and I don't want to make you regret that decision.'

'Did my family overwhelm you?' she asks, concerned. 'I know they're a bit much.'

'No, your family are lovely. It's just that it's a long time since I've been in a relationship.'

'And you think we're moving too fast?'

'No.' I stop, smile, and take her hand. 'It isn't any of those things. Shit. I want to talk about this, but I'm terrified of offending you.'

'Dan,' she says, her face pained, 'just tell me what's wrong.'

'OK, don't get cross, but this seems too good to be true. Everyone else you've gone out with has been higher up in the company than you, and I can't understand why you'd go from them to me. I have nothing, Alice. Literally nothing. All that I own is in the bag in your room.'

I sit back and drink my lager, waiting to see how she responds. This is a delicate business, and I still don't know enough about Alice to be certain of making my desired impact. I took a risk mentioning her upward sexual mobility, but she doesn't seem that angry, and I need to test how safe I am here.

'You don't know, do you?'

'What?'

'Mum said you didn't know. Brittany too. Apparently your dad's the same.'

'The same as what?'

'It must be something he's passed down to you. A gene or something.'

'I'm not following.'

'How would you describe yourself, Dan?'

'Quiet, friendly . . .'

'No, your appearance.'

'I don't know. Average, I guess. Having dark features helps, but then again a lot of women only go for blond guys.'

Alice laughs. 'Do you realise how sexy it is?'

'What?'

'OK, let me try to explain. Do you remember Bryan?'

'Fat B . . .'

'What?'

I swallow. 'That's what Adrienne calls him. Fat Bastard.'

She laughs. 'Exactly. He was pretty ugly, right?'

'Right.'

'But he didn't think he was ugly, Dan. He thought he was God's fucking gift. And then there's someone like you, walking round with your head down and acting like you've never had any female attention in your life. You could have any woman on your team, Dan.'

'That's not true. Adrienne's with Ian, and Teri's not interested.'

'Of course she's interested. She's just like you, thinks she's hideous. It's hilarious, watching the two of you shuffle round each other like a couple of lepers. It amazes me how many people are scared of making a pass at someone who's clearly interested.'

'But I was the one who made a pass at you. You'd never have tried anything.'

'I didn't say I don't have my own insecurities. I thought you thought I was stupid. Every time I come over to your desk you all start giggling, and that night after I had to discipline the team, even though I made a real effort, even though I came to The Pentangle, and not only that but dragged Bryan along as well ... and it took a huge argument before he agreed to go ... you all just sneered at me.'

'I don't think it was you as such. Just that people were shocked to see Bryan.'

'What was I supposed to do? I couldn't come on my own.'

'But you know what they're like, Alice. It's like a little army or something. Ian has all these ideas about loyalty, and Teri and Adrienne are even worse.'

'I can't stand those two, Dan. Ian's a good bloke ... I don't mind being snubbed by him if he genuinely feels I've done something wrong, but Teri and Adrienne are vicious for the sake of it. I know it sounds terrible, Dan, but I'm really looking forward to getting rid of Teri.'

Ah. It would've been easier if she hadn't put it like that. I've been waiting for this conversation, hoping I'll be brave enough to confess my lie. After all, relationships are supposed to be strengthened by the swapping of intimacies, and at least it's not a lie connected to our becoming a couple. But if I deny Alice her justification for sacking an enemy, it's not going to stop her getting rid of her: she just won't feel so self-righteous about doing it. So there's no reason to say anything. Far more sensible to keep quiet.

Alice has finished her vodka. I offer to get her another, and she nods eagerly. I return to the bar for her drink and a second pint for myself. I look at my watch. Only eight. It's going to be hell getting up for work tomorrow.

We stagger back after last orders, Alice clinging to my side. I lie down on her bench and she climbs on top of me, kissing my neck. I move sideways and she slides down next to me, trying not to fall off.

'Any romantic moments on this bench?'

Alice giggles. 'One or two.'

I smile at her. 'Really?'

'It's a pretty quiet road,' she says, stroking my chest through my shirt. I shiver. 'Finger me, Dan.'

She takes my hand and guides it beneath her skirt. I realise what I thought were tights are stockings and slip my fingers underneath the soft material of her knickers. Alice shifts on the bench, looking uncomfortable.

'Do you want to swap places?' I ask.

'No, hang on, let's arrange ourselves properly.'

I pull my hand out of her underwear and sit up. She swings her legs down beside me and says, 'Put your coat over my lap.'

I do as she instructs. She reaches up under the coat and pulls down her knickers, stepping out of each leg hole before handing them to me. I'm about to continue touching her when she reaches up again and unzips her skirt. She tugs it down over her hips and hands it to me. I nervously check for anyone walking near by.

'Isn't this a bit risky?'

'I told you. No one comes down here. Besides, I want you to eat me and you can't do that if I keep my skirt on.'

She smiles at me and I get down on my knees, allowing Alice to put the coat over my head. I kiss along her thighs, being careful not to bruise my Adam's apple on the bench as I strain my face towards her vagina. I know that staying in this position for any length of time is going to be agonising, but the sado-masochist inside me says we can cope (in fact, it's pleasantly nostalgic. Sonia loved having me kneel before her when I gave her head – so much so that I still get the occasional twinge from housemaid's knee). I know from experience that in a strained situation the best response is to lock on to the spot. Any attempt at a more subtle approach is likely to aggravate the recipient, particularly if the rhythm is interrrupted by any twisting or changed movement. It also helps if you hang on to her legs, creating the illusion of mounting drama.

It's not until Alice's taste fills my mouth that I realise cunnilingus is the sexual act I've missed the most. When it comes to women, taste is the hardest sense to satisfy. Think about it. If you need to see a naked woman, turn on *Television X*. Wanna hear a female orgasm? Any number of sexline girls will give you a fair imitation. Smelling women is second nature: you do it all the time, every day. Even touching can be done surreptitiously. Go to the right place (a gig, say, or a fetish club), and you're bound to find a fellow frottage freak. But if you want to *taste* a woman, you're out of luck. The closest you're gonna get is chewing on someone else's dirty underwear, and even then there's not that many places where women are happy to air their soiled knickers.

Alice tastes of Alice. I realise this sounds stupid, but it's still something I struggle to understand. Sperm seems easier. While I don't deny that some women could probably identify their partner's produce in a blind taste test, I'm sure most think of sperm as something separate from the penis that pumps it out. I don't like sperm, they might say. Not I don't like John's sperm. Or Fred's sperm. Or Bob's sperm. Sperm in general. But with a woman's fluids, everything becomes more difficult. For a start, there's the question of what to call it. Lovejuice sounds too, I don't know, seventies porn mag . . . a word to be banished to the back of the closet along with climax and pussy. *She climaxed so hard that lovejuice poured from her pussy.* Sure she did. When I was in school, the girls used to call it gunk. As in, I saw so-and-so's knickers and they were all gunked up. It's fine for adolescents, but I'm not sure I can get away with it as a grown adult. Mmm . . . have I ever told you how much I love the taste of your gunk? No, that won't work. What about *secretions*? I suppose that'll have to do for the moment, although I don't think I'd risk saying it in bed. Anyway, the point of my argument is that a woman's secretions always, inextricably, taste of the woman who produced them. I don't think the word *essence* is out of place here. Maybe it's just a mark of my inexperience, but I can't imagine making any generalisations about the flavour of vaginas. Sure, there are consistent elements – urine, for example – but on the whole, eating out a lover is a surprise every time.

Still, I suppose I should try to be more specific about what Alice tastes like. She's sweeter than other women I've sucked, her flavour dulled a little by soap but still pleasant. It's citrus-y, but not lemon. Maybe grapefruit. Actually, the closest taste is probably one of those tropical fruit drinks. Five Alive, or, I know, Um Bongo.

A man sits on the bench. I'm scared, dropping down onto my bottom and trying to hide myself beneath Alice. (I keep my head in front of her cunt as a protective measure.) This is exactly why I don't like *al fresco* sex. It's not the fear of being spotted, but rather that the person who sees us will go through the thought-process I go through when I see a couple kissing and assume that the fact that my partner is fucking me means she's prepared to fuck anyone, and all they have to do is push me to one side.

It's hard to hear under my coat, but I don't think Alice is talking to our new friend. There's no indication (from this vantage) that she's disturbed by this person's presence, but I don't want to carry on eating her in case I'm tempting fate. So I remain there on the floor, staring at Alice's nether lips as if they can give me some indication of what her upper ones are doing.

The man leaves. I wait long enough for him to have reached the end of the street, then pop up between Alice's legs.

'Who was that?' I demand.

'John.'

'And who the fuck is John?'

'Some old loony. A care in the community case.'

'And what did he want?'

'Nothing.'

'Did he notice me?'

'I don't think so. Why did you stop?'

'Because I thought *John* might've been some rapist,' I tell her, my voice rising. 'I was getting ready to defend your honour.'

She smiles. 'That's sweet. But it really wasn't anything.'

'OK,' I say, calming, 'so what do you want to do?'

She looks at me as if the answer is obvious.

'But what if he comes back?'

'He won't notice. Besides, who cares? He's fucked in the head. Please, Dan, I'm so close.'

I look at her again and reluctantly return beneath my coat. Alice edges forward on the bench and I move into my previous position, leaning in closer so my hands are holding her buttocks instead of her thighs. This seems to please Alice and she angles herself upward, letting me take a firmer grasp of her flesh. I lick quickly, straining my tongue into a thin point. Her thighs are trembling. My index finger slides between her buttocks and pushes against her pulsing anus. Her hand moves down to mine and I think she's going to take my finger away, but instead she pushes it harder inside her. I dot my tongue, then get into a faster rhythm as I feel her vagina doing a dummy contraction. She freezes, bucks twice, then comes, forcing my face into her wet pubes. I slowly withdraw my finger from her bottom, then lift the coat to look up.

'Thanks, Dan,' she grins, 'that was lovely.'

I give Alice her skirt and underwear and we walk home. Cathy and Tim have gone to bed. We creep through to her bedroom and I leave her to undress while I clean my teeth and wash my face. When I return she's in her nightdress, setting the alarm clock.

'What time do you want to get up?'

'I don't.'

'OK,' she laughs, putting the clock back on the bedside table.

I get into bed. Alice kisses me and walks to the en suite. I turn out the light and watch Alice washing through the illuminated doorway, worrying once again about how I'll explain all this at work tomorrow.

16

Cathy wakes me at midday. I stare at her, not really remembering who she is and worrying for a second that she's my new girlfriend. She laughs at my concern and says, 'I can see why Alice didn't want to wake you. You act like you haven't slept in weeks.'

'Where is she?' I ask, still confused.

'Alice? She's at work. It's lunchtime.'

'Why didn't I go?'

She laughs again. 'Alice said to tell you she's given you another day at home, but make the most of it. She says it's the last one you'll get.'

I sit up. 'I'll go in for the afternoon.'

'Don't be stupid. She's made arrangements. There's no point going in now. Besides, it'll be nice for us to have some time together. You can tell me all about your life without worrying that you're repeating yourself in front of Alice. And, who knows, maybe there's some stuff you can't share with her that you'll be able to tell me. I'm a very broadminded mother.'

I must look nervous because she sits up and says quickly, 'Of course, I don't want to rush you. First things first. I'll leave you to get up and then we'll see about making you some lunch.'

She retreats from the room and shuts the door. I get out of bed and walk through to the en suite, wondering whether to have a bath. It seems a good way of hiding from Cathy for a while, and after the sensual excitement of my last soak, I'm eager to see if it'll be as good again. I put in the plug and turn on the taps, then swing round to urinate. My cock still feels sore after all the unexpected attention, and I shake it gingerly. Then I clean my teeth and climb into the tub. As I do so, a familiar furry face floats in front of my eyes. *John!* I'm so sorry, my friend, I forgot all about you. Two days without food: is that too much for a cat to cope with? Every time I've filled his dish before now, there's always been a few dried chunks he's overlooked. I know felines are fastidious, but do they forget about their fads when it comes to starvation? I'm sure I remember spilling some food up there that didn't get eaten, so maybe he'll be OK. I'm sure Mother Nature must've fitted cats with an upscale survival system. Why else would people talk about them having nine lives? John's probably found a whole family of rats to feed on, and has forgotten all about his occasional tins of Felix.

The water's just beginning to cover my body now, and although it feels reasonably invigorating, it's not a patch on my last wash. It'd almost be worth abstaining from washing for another fortnight just to recreate that experience, although I've no doubt Alice would soon complain. Oh well, I suppose there's enough sensory compensations in my new existence, and if I have to live a normal life I might as well enjoy it.

Cathy looks up from her chair as I come into the lounge, laying *Political Ideas* on the coffee table.

'Have you really forgotten about this book?'

'Pretty much. Why?'

'I just wanted to ask you what you thought about some of the people it mentions. I remember a few of them, although it was years and years ago, from school, but some of the others I've either forgotten about or never heard of.'

'Which ones?'

'Well, I remember Luther from history, and I think I remember Machiavelli, but I'm not sure.'

'Machiavelli's a bad guy.'

'That's what I thought. But what about Rousseau?'

'What about him?'

'Good or bad?'

'Good guy.'

'Right.' She picks up the book. 'Paine?'

'Good guy.'

'Burke and Hegel?'

'I'm not sure. I think of them as bad guys, but only because when you say their names together it sounds like Burke and Hare. But I suppose there's no reason to link them so that's a silly reaction. I think some people might consider Hegel a bad guy.'

'Locke?'

'Good guy.'

'Montesquieu?'

'Don't know.'

'Harriet Onions?'

'Who?'

'The name on the fly-leaf. Harriet Onions. Is she good or bad?'

'I don't know. This is my dad's book. She must be an old friend of his. Unless he bought the book at a car-boot sale.'

'Did your father recommend this book to you?'

'No. You know I was living with my father before his accident?' I look at her. She nods. 'Well, when he went into hospital I started really missing him and reading his books seemed the best way of keeping in contact with him.'

'Better than visiting him?' she smiles.

We exchange glances. 'I see Alice has been talking to you.'

'It's OK, Dan. I told you earlier. You can talk to me. I can tell you're a very mature man and there are probably lots of things you can't discuss with Alice. I'm her mother and I love her, but she's a very silly girl in lots of ways.'

I don't say anything. She stands up and holds on to the back of the chair as she walks round to me.

'Anyway,' she says, 'what would you like for lunch?'

'I don't mind.'

'I usually have ham sandwiches. Is that OK for you?'

'Lovely.'

'Come out into the kitchen while I make them. Now, you can't have butter, is that right?'

I nod.

'What about marge?'

'No, I don't eat that either.'

'Right. I suppose the texture reminds you of butter. What would you like instead?'

'Nothing.'

'Just plain bread?'

'That's fine.'

She shakes her head and unwraps the Mighty White, laying out two slices on each plate and covering hers with butter. She takes a packet of American thin-sliced ham from the fridge and places two slivers on each piece of bread. Then she reaches back into the Mighty White bag and completes the sandwiches, handing the plate back to me.

'Crisps?'

'Yes please.'

'Any particular flavour?'

'Salt and vinegar.'

'Oh dear, that's Alice's favourite too. I'll have to eat all the Cheese and Onions. What would you like to drink?'

'Is there any more Coke?'

'I think we've probably got a few tins.' She opens the bottom cupboard and leans down to pull a can from the cardboard box. 'There you go.'

I take my drink and return to the lounge. Cathy follows me through, sitting back in her usual chair.

'So do you think you'll be able to put up with us?'

'Definitely. You've made me feel very welcome.'

Cathy smiles, releasing the legrest on her chair and letting her feet swing out in front of her. She turns on the TV, but mutes the volume, still looking at me.

'So has Alice said anything to you about living with me?'

'In what sense?'

'Does she think I'm an old nuisance? Did she warn you about my funny habits?'

'No, she hardly said anything about you.'

'You're a very discreet man, aren't you, Dan? I like that, but you don't have to be so nervous. I won't mind if she said something bad.'

'She didn't. The only time she mentioned that she lived with you was when I was talking to her about my living situation and I was embarrassed because I lived with my dad.'

'Why were you embarrassed?'

'Living with your parents is a fairly standard thing to be embarrassed about, isn't it?'

She looks at me. 'I'm surprised you'd worry about something like that.'

Her dry comment makes me feel childish, and I feel compelled to defend myself.

'You don't understand. It wasn't like here where there's a whole house and it's easy for you and Alice to live separate lives. My father and I were sharing the same room.'

'And you hated it?'

'What?'

'You hated living with your dad?'

Cathy stops eating and stares at me, obviously eager to hear my answer. I feel I've been tricked into a dangerous admission. Her question follows naturally from everything I've been saying, and yet answering it affirmatively seems like shutting the door on my family. Cathy senses my discomfort and asks, 'So what happened to the family home? I assume there was one?'

I nod. 'It got sold.'

'Did that upset you?'

'Not really. I was living with my ex-girlfriend at the time so I didn't think about it. I suppose I was pleased to lose my safety net.'

'Why?'

'Stupid reasons. Things I'm embarrassed to talk about.'

Cathy grins appreciatively and shuffles her buttocks further towards the edge of the chair. Her slippered feet now poke well over the footrest, making her look like a hospital patient with her limbs raised by pulleys and weights. It's hard to tell who's tricking who. I know what she wants to hear and can't help getting off at her ridiculous excitement every time I hint at anything personal. I also know I have a great story, and Cathy is the perfect audience. Almost every time we've talked since I moved into this house she's pleaded with me to tell her my dark secrets, and I've no doubt that the story of my time with Sonia would more than satisfy her. But maybe her interest is only faked, the result of a lifetime of thinking up ways of getting people to reveal all. I've never trusted good listeners, rarely encountering anyone who didn't have an ulterior motive for eliciting personal revelations. Still, I can't deny this is fun, and like a child fabricating falsehoods to entertain Grandma, I'm reluctant to stop showing off.

'It's not that I'm trying to hide anything. Just that I used to be a very different person to the one I am now.'

'What kind of person were you?'

'A romantic.'

She smiles. 'And what's wrong with that?'

'Depends on your definition of romantic. I don't mean that I liked love poetry and watched Meg Ryan movies. I thought love had to be all or nothing, and thinking like that made me do some stupid things.'

'What did you do?'

'I fell in love with the wrong woman. And because I knew she was wrong, I tried to make it so I couldn't get away from her.'

'Which is why you were pleased that your parents sold your house.'

'Exactly.'

She frowns. 'Are you planning to make yourself dependent on Alice?'

'Of course not,' I say, worried that I've overplayed my hand. 'Like I said, I'm not that kind of man any more.'

'Only I think I should warn you that Alice hasn't got a very good track record,' says Cathy, still frowning. 'You do know that she's promiscuous?'

I have no idea how to reply.

'I think she's usually faithful to her partners while the relationship's going on, but they don't tend to last long. You're a much better calibre of man than her usual choice, and if I had my way you'd be married tomorrow, but Alice can be quite unpredictable, and the fact that I like you might not necessarily count in your favour.'

'Right.'

She bites her lip. 'Can I give you some advice?'

'Of course.'

'Whatever she does, don't argue with her. That way I can let you sleep on the sofa without her feeling betrayed.'

Cathy turns up the TV. I obviously overestimated the appeal of my revelations. She finishes her lunch and picks up *Political Ideas*. I can tell she's using the television as both background noise and an indication that our conversation is over. So much for Cathy wanting to hear my history. I feel foolishly pleased that I didn't tell her too much, and resolve to remain on my guard during any further exchanges. When I'm certain she's not about to start speaking again, I take the trays out to the kitchen and go to Alice's bedroom for Dad's minutes.

Cathy smiles at me as I sit back down. I worry she's going

to ask me what I'm reading, but she doesn't say anything, fully engaged in her philosophy. I find my place and reread Claire's account of living with violent men. Last night I'd been tempted to cancel my meeting with her, but now that Cathy has turned out to be such a crap confidant, I find myself craving a proper conversation. Before now, I've always defined myself through what I won't do. It's seemed so much easier to create my character using a process of exclusion. And, on the whole, the things I don't like have tended to be anything anyone else is fanatical about: football, fashion, fast cars. I'm so used to not liking things that it's hard for me to list anything I do like. And over the years this attitude has evolved into a general disdain of almost everyone, and, more than that, the belief that any kind of personal involvement is a sign of weakness. A lot of this was due to my fractured emotional state after the business with Sonia, but it was also because I believed that if I gave myself nothing – and could sustain my life in such an extreme state of privation – I'd learn something which would allow me to re-enter everyone else's world with a specialist knowledge that'd elevate me from their existence and give me the freedom to participate in their mundanity without the fear that all my support systems would one day slip away and leave me facing something I couldn't cope with. Living with Dad (although it wasn't an arrangement I'd have necessarily chosen for myself if circumstances had been different) proved the perfect environment for this sort of experiment. Apart from the lack of privacy, I also had to fit in with Dad's strange pseudo-utilitarian lifestyle. Any indication that I was indulging myself (alcohol, too much TV, expensive soap) would provoke criticism and, worse still, disappointment. And although I felt betrayed when I found out that throughout his time Dad had been rewarding himself with the pyschological indulgence afforded by his group, at the time it seemed like the perfect test of my character. Dad and I got by on nothing, living hand-to-mouth and enjoying every night's fish and chips as if it was our first. I should've told her that even though it was like entering a second adolescence, during the year or so I spent living in that room, I came closer to my true self than any other time before or since.

I open the minutes.

ST: Thanks, Claire. This isn't something I feel comfortable talking about, but I know if I don't say something now I'll regret it when I leave tonight, so, anyway, you remember how last session I was talking about harbouring homicidal feelings towards my son? Well, although these thoughts have flickered in and out of my head since he was born, they only became serious when Dan was about thirteen. And it was an incident involving pornography that really created the divide between us.

IJ: Go on.

ST: OK. I don't want to talk about my wife too much in this session – most of you have known me long enough to know my feelings about her – but it had always annoyed me that whenever I argued with her, Dan automatically took her side. I realise it was probably an Oedipal thing, but even though I could intellectualise it, I couldn't help feeling hurt, especially as most of the time I really didn't think that I was the one in the wrong.

IJ: Did your son understand what you were arguing about?

ST: I think so. Not necessarily the specific events. Most of the arguments started after infidelities – hers and mine – or gambling stuff, but it was the principles underlying the conflict that I wanted him to understand. Look, we had an unorthodox marriage. Not many couples spend their nights staying up to the small hours in seedy casinos, but I had a philosophy that I thought she shared. I wanted to make things better – the gambling was simply a means to an end. And it didn't stop me doing a good job of raising a son.

IJ: What about the adulteries?

ST: They were necessary.

[Laughter.]

ST: I know it sounds funny, but I'm serious. I only ever slept with other women to retaliate for something my wife had done. She was unfaithful loads of times before I strayed. And when I did it was only because I wanted to keep the marriage alive. The point is, I was the one who was committed to keeping the family together. If it wasn't for me our marriage wouldn't have lasted seven minutes, let alone seventeen years. I don't know. What was I talking about?

IJ: Pornography.

ST: Oh yeah. I think this made me angry because it was the first time I'd seen Dan exhibiting any morality. I'm not going to make a big deal out of this, especially after what's already been said tonight, but I've always been interested in pornography, ever since I first saw a magazine. I never said anything to my wife about it, although she knew I kept a pile of *Fiesta*s beneath my bed. Anyway, when he was about thirteen, Dan discovered them. A typical rite-of-passage, nothing particularly interesting or unique about it. Except that Dan saw it as some kind of betrayal. He kept making comments about how I'd let down his mum, let down the family. At first I thought he must've found out about an adultery or something, but as his comments became less cryptic, I finally realised what he was upset about. So I asked him if he and I could have a man-to-man chat to sort everything out, but he refused to say anything unless his mum was there. So we had to have the whole conversation as a family, with him crying and holding his mum's hand the whole time. And when I'd finished explaining, she said that my son was twice the man I was. I guess it was about then that I decided I wanted to kill him.

I stop reading, feeling scared again. I suppose this *was* an important moment in our relationship, although I'm surprised Dad's still troubled by it. I also have to admit that once again I feel proud of little Daniel (however much I've slipped as an adult) and can't believe that Dad would say all this stuff in front of his seven women. He's certainly more open than I'd ever be. I never say anything that doesn't make me look good, and would never admit to feeling jealous of my son. I can picture Mum's proud smile as

I told her why I'd become so difficult and remember how funny I found Dad's reluctance to talk about his magazines. I know it probably sounds as if I was being a little vindictive, but at the time it really did feel like a tremendous betrayal. Sure most boys would've just stolen the magazines and taken them into school, but there's a legitimate explanation for my delicacy.

No matter what Dad told the group, I didn't understand what my parents were arguing about. Not at thirteen. They lied to me so often that I still don't like thinking about my childhood, worried that an adult perspective will reveal yet another hidden motivation behind what heretofore seemed like normal family memories. Married couples have to take their opportunities where they can find them, and I remember countless friends of the family who were around for a while and then disappeared, their sudden departures prompting a fresh round of arguments. As a child, I thought my parents were blaming each other for driving the friend away (which, in a way, I suppose they were) and thought of my parents as these socially inept people who were incapable of making lasting connections. I got angry at my father for reading porn because it was the first time I'd found a reason why my family might be unwelcome in polite society.

I look across at Cathy, watching her reading Dad's book and wondering what she and Alice fought about when Alice was growing up. Going by the photos of the spiky-haired psychopath Alice showed me last night, I expect there was no shortage of confrontations. Perhaps I'm wrong to feel intimidated by the Hargreaves family set-up. There could be just as many hidden problems here as there were in my past homes. After all, no one's mentioned Mr Hargreaves, and there must be a reason why Alice chose to spend her childhood disguised as Johnny Rotten.

Cathy looks up. 'You OK, Dan?'

'Yeah, I'm just feeling a bit restless. Is it OK if I give Alice a ring?'

'Of course. The phone's in the hallway.'

I get up from the armchair and walk to the phone. As I pick

up the receiver, I realise that I don't actually know the number for Quick Kall. I'm too embarrassed to ask Cathy so I dial the operator. Then I phone reception and ask to be put through to Alice.

'I'm sorry, she's busy at the moment. Can I get her to call you back?'

Typical. I'm nervous about leaving my name so I ask him if she's likely to be long. He says no and offers to put me on hold. I accept and sit there listening to 'Greensleeves', waiting two minutes before Alice picks up and says,

'Hello.'

'Hi, it's Dan.'

'Hi Dan. Everything OK?'

'Yeah. Would it be OK if I came in to meet you from work?'

'Oh,' she says, 'I'm not sure that's such a good idea.'

'Why not?' I ask, worried Cathy's prophecy has come true quicker than I imagined.

'Well, I wasn't sure how long you were going to want off, so I had to tell everyone you were really sick.'

'I didn't even want a day off. Why didn't you wake me?'

'You told me not to. I asked you what time you wanted to be woken up and you said you didn't.'

'I was joking.'

She breathes into the mouthpiece. 'Don't let's fight. Why do you want to meet me? Are you getting fed up of Mum?'

'It's not that. I've just been stuck in the house all day. How about if I meet you in a pub or something?'

'OK, but not The Friar. We're bound to run into someone if we go there.'

'What about The Old Fish Market?'

'All right. Why don't you wait and get Mum to drop you in?'

'No, it's OK. I'm gonna come in now and have a walk round town. I just want a bit of space to think.'

She cuts off the call and I replace the receiver. I walk back into the lounge. Cathy pulls herself up in her chair.

'I'm just going into town for a bit,' I tell her, 'if that's OK.'

'Of course. Do you want me to drive you?'

'No, I'll be all right.'

'Do you know where to catch the bus?'

'I think so.'

'OK then. Have fun.'

It's a relief just to be outside. There's even a bit of sun today, although I can still feel the cold through my shirt. The bus stop is just along from the bench where Alice made me eat her out. (I love that expression. It's the *out* bit at the end that makes it work for me; it seems redundant and yet it does so much, changing the claim into a childish boast. It's not like *wanked him off*, which should be ridiculous but isn't, mainly because the extra word suggests a conclusion. *Eating her out* wants to sound exhaustive but fails because it relies on the optimistic assumption that there's a finite amount of stuff inside a woman.) There's no timetable at the bus stop, but today I don't mind waiting. It's good to have a few moments alone.

The bus arrives ten minutes later. It's a single-decker and I sit towards the back, above the wheel-arch. I check my watch. Two thirty. I take my discman and cue up New Order, watching through the window as the bus pulls away from the stop

I get off the bus round the back of the Marriott and cut through to the shops. I feel an urgent need to spend some money. I don't particularly want anything; I just crave that transaction. I enter a newsagent and purchase two cans of Coke. I put one in my pocket while I open the other and check how much cash I've got left. Eight pounds. Time to visit the bank.

Town seems surprisingly busy this afternoon. I suppose I should be enjoying my day off, but I feel like a studious kid too guilty about playing truant to appreciate the freedom. The music in my discman fits well with the daytime shoppers, the repetitive sound structuring their movements. I join the queue at the cashpoint, feigning disinterest in the actions of the people waiting before me.

When it gets to my turn, I put in my card and tap in my PIN number, holding my breath as I wait to read the balance. Two hundred. Right. I'm gonna lose two days' pay this week so I'll only earn about sixty quid. Twelve pounds to Sonia, twenty-five to the bank, and ten to the building society. That leaves me thirteen quid to get through next week. I think I'd better take the two hundered out now.

I fold up my wad of twenty-pound notes and hide it inside my jacket pocket. Dealing with money always leaves me a little dazed, and as I stumble away I bump into a tall woman with dark hair. She scowls at my apologies, and I reach inside my pocket for a twenty.

'What's this?' she asks as I hand it to her.

'For bumping into you.'

She looks at me as if I'm crazy and walks on without taking the money. As she goes I feel relieved she didn't accept and don't know why I offered it to her. I put the note back inside my pocket and continue walking, wondering what's wrong with me today.

It seems important to process the information in my head. I could do that while shopping, but I tend to mutter to myself when I'm thinking and I don't want people to imagine I'm a lunatic. I suppose I could go into a pub, but I'll probably feel self-conscious sitting on my own, and besides, I don't want to get drunk before I've met Alice. When I was a kid I used to go to the park whenever I felt like this, running through my thoughts while I swung along a climbing frame. There's a nice wooden animal park not too far from here and I suppose I could go across, but I expect I'd attract too much attention to get much thinking done.

I stop when I reach the Odeon, wondering whether to watch a film. I usually reflect when I sit in a cinema, and I'm sure I could turn my thoughts away from death and examine my present situation. I walk across and check out the programme times, but everything's already started. I decide to go to Mad Harry's. A few games of pinball should serve the same purpose as dangling from metal bars, occupying my hands while my brain works out what to do next.

There used to be an arcade next to Mad Harry's – I think it was called Cascade – that was only open to people over twenty-one. The management seemed determined to offer a significantly different arcade experience to Mad Harry's, and it looked more like the lobby of a large corporation. Most of the people playing there were businessmen in suits, and I frequently observed large sums of cash being exchanged after frames of pool. I'm sure the only reason for placing an age restriction was to stop the kids spilling in from next door, but whenever I went there with friends we always speculated about other possible explanations. Perhaps the arcade was really a pick-up point for gay men (a discreet predecessor to *Friends of Dorothy*, the internet café that now stands in Old Market) and the guys who pretended to be fascinated in the spinning wheels were really waiting for us to signal that we wanted them to take us home. But this wouldn't really explain the sense of excitement we all felt whenever we went there. None of us were gay (as far as I know – these things aren't always decided by age fifteen, and as I'm no longer in contact with any of my friends, I don't know how they all turned out) and I was the one who kept leading us back for the early part of every Friday evening. Personally, I don't believe it was a pick-up place, and think the thrill we felt came from the knowledge that this space had been designed wholly for the wasting of time and money. What made our arcade unique was the fact that there was no sense of tension between the gamblers and the management. This is definitely not the case in Mad Harry's, where the average age is about seven, and it's impossible not to notice the exploitation inherent in this early initiation into bad habits. In Cascade no one cared about the money they lost, and it was more like we were all taking advantage of a benevolently offered service. The only other time I've sensed energy like that is in the Quick Kall coffee room, another place where every moment

lingered is a guilty pleasure. Now, of course, it's been bought out by its neighbour and renamed Mad Harry's II. You just can't compete with the kids.

I go into Mad Harry's and change up a twenty. Then I find a pinball machine and feed it three pounds. I exhale, then pull the plunger. Now, if I'm not mistaken, it seems I've been offered the opportunity to solve all my problems. In spite of Cathy's warning not to rely on Alice, I believe I can inspire her to stick with me. Last night's admission that I make her feel stupid is the key. Sonia used to say that every new partner should be an improvement on the previous one, and although I doubt Alice shares that ambition, the fact that I'm much more attractive and intelligent than anyone else she's ever been with must surely count in my favour. I think Cathy was trying to warn me not to criticise Alice – not to make her feel bad about her past or set any standards she can't reach. That, I feel, is the only danger. I can already hear her apologies: *I'm sorry, it's just that I feel so worthless next to you and needed to shag someone else to boost my confidence.* Nah, Alice, I'm on to you. I'm not going to give you any excuse.

OK, so let's assume (for the sake of argument) that Alice sticks with me. Her mother likes me, I can cope with her brother, and although there might be some dark secret with her father that I don't yet know, there doesn't appear to be any familial tension. So that means free food and board for the foreseeable future, which gives me a bit more flexibility about my finances. I'm never going to earn enough to save anything, but I should be able to be a little more relaxed about pocket cash. My only real money problem (and this is what I need the pinball game to think through) is that thousand pounds Adrienne lent me. When Alice told me she can't stand Adrienne, a plan popped into my mind: why not make Alice jealous about the fact that her rival has given me money, and persuade her to take over the loan. Maybe I can even talk her into some whole new refinancing deal, and get a little extra cash out of her to tide me over.

*   *   *

I leave the arcade at four thirty and head across to The Old Fish Market. A couple of pints before Alice arrives won't do much damage. The pub is empty so I sit by the door in the front bar, wondering what time Alice will show up. I should've brought Dad's minutes with me. What I really need is a good book. I fancy tackling a novel after all those social science volumes, but it's so long since I've read anything new that I wouldn't really know where to start. Perhaps Cathy might have something. I didn't see any books in Alice's bedroom, but I can't believe her mum hasn't read anything. Even if it's only Jilly Cooper.

Alice arrives just after six. I've been staring out of the window for almost an hour when I see her on the other side of the road and immediately sit up. I still haven't quite adjusted to the fact that she's my girlfriend now as well as my team leader and I don't have to feel scared every time I see her. She doesn't notice me until she's come through the door and I've shouted across, 'Alice!'

'All right,' she says, approaching my table. She's wearing her usual burgundy work suit, and I enter that hyper-real world I often find myself in during sexualised scenarios. I've already explained how I think this particular outfit is ridiculously erotic, and can't quite believe that later I might just be allowed – hell, who am I trying to kid, you know Alice, *expected* – to take it off. It's partly because the suit is so hideous. This is the first time Alice has worn the suit since we've got together, and as I stare at the place where the jacket ends and her neck begins, I realise that although I've never imagined myself as the sort of person who'd have a uniform fetish, that's exactly what this is. I wish I was better versed in sexual psychology. I think I must be a bit repressed about fantasising. I'm kind of a puritan when it comes to erotic imaginings. Again, I haven't really analysed these thoughts, but I think I feel the same way about sex as I do about everything else. (I realise this sounds a little basic, but bear with me.) If I restrict myself to thinking about the vanilla variety, then all the other stuff will still retain its power when I eventually get round to it. Sure, sodomy and bondage are nice things to think about, but if I can survive without them then so much the better. It's only recently, after all, that I've started having sex again. (Actually, all this is a lie. Bondage and sodomy are Sonia-related subjects: that's why I don't think about them.) But getting back to the uniform thing . . . this is genuinely new for me. I might have had a few fleeting thoughts one night in front of *Erotica Exotica*, but it's not until now – as I allow myself to picture my cock spurting semen onto the stiff black fabric of a policewoman's jacket – that I realise just how much masturbation material these fantasies could provide. Perhaps I should invest in some women-in-uniform pornography.

'So how was your day?'

'Terrible.'

'Did anyone ask after me?'

'No.'

'Do you think they know about us?'

'I haven't said anything. I thought I'd leave that to you.'

She looks at me and I feel awkward, not wanting her to notice how little I'm looking forward to telling my workmates about my new love. I change the subject by asking her what she wants to drink.

'Vodka and orange, you know that.'

'So that's what you always have?' I ask, embarrassed by her reproach.

'Not always,' she says, 'but it's my usual.'

I go to the bar. The pub's filling up now. Baldwin Street seems to be popular with people seeking an afterwork drink. All the pubs along this street are full in the evenings. It must be nice to have a real job: something so stressful you need a few pints after, before heading home. I order my drinks and carry them back to the table.

'Cheers,' says Alice, taking a sip from her glass.'

'No problem. Do you fancy going for a meal after this?'

'Why?'

'Oh, OK, it doesn't matter . . .'

'No, I don't mind going. I just wondered if there was a special reason. Do you hate Mum's cooking?'

'Why do you think I don't like living with you? I love your mum and the food she cooks is fantastic. I'm a very fussy eater and I've never met anyone who's been able to cope with my foibles before. I just thought it might be romantic to go to a restaurant.'

'Romantic?'

'Yeah. Is that OK?'

'Of course,' she says, taking my hand. 'Dan, I'm sorry. Where do you want to eat?'

'I don't know. Do you know anywhere?'

'What about Chinese? Is that OK?'

'Yeah, Chinese is great. I only really have a problem with French or Italian.'

'OK then, well, China Palace is just along the road. But it's pretty expensive.'

'That's no problem,' I tell her, pulling the roll of twenties from my pocket.

'Wow. What have you been up to this afternoon?'

'Oh, it's not as impressive as it looks. I just needed to get the money out of my account so it wouldn't disappear on repayments.'

'What repayments?'

'Just boring bank stuff. You don't want to hear about it.'

The meal costs fifty pounds. Alice offers to split the bill, but I make a big show of paying for her, saying it helps me feel less guilty about her hospitality. I haven't mentioned money over dinner, wanting to pick the right moment. In my experience, most people will lend you money, as long as you time it right. The only potential problem I can foresee is Alice's own financial situation. We haven't really discussed how she's off for money, but her startled reaction when I mentioned having to make repayments left me a little nervous. I don't know how much more a team leader earns than a regular grunt, but she must've saved a bit living at home with her mum (although you never know with these women: she might still be repaying the mortgage on some semi bought somewhere with a previous boyfriend).

We walk back to Alice's car (an Audi 80) and she drives us home. I'm waiting for her to unzip my flies, but tonight her hands stay on the wheel.

Tim is sitting in the lounge, watching someone on TV talk about gas chambers.

'What's this?'

'*Shoah*. The rest of the class didn't want to watch it again today so the teacher gave me the tape.'

'Do you have to watch it now?'

'That depends,' he grins. 'Am I allowed to take the video into my bedroom?'

'If you don't tell Mum I let you.'

'Deal.'

Tim disconnects the video and takes it to his room. Alice sits on the settee and gestures for me to join her.

'Thank you for my dinner, Dan. That was really kind of you.'

'No problem. When's your mum due back?'

'What time is it now?'

'Eight thirty.'

'She doesn't usually get back until eleven. Why?' She smiles. 'What did you have in mind?'

We move a table in front of the door to stop Tim barging in and Alice does what I've just told her to do, lying across the settee and staring at a muted screen. She seemed a little scared when I answered her question with such a detailed description, but now she's relaxing into it. I came clean to her about how I felt about her burgundy work suit and she admitted she feels sexy whenever she wears it, the fabric reminding her of all the nice times she's had wearing uniforms before. Then I told Alice I wanted her to lie down and pretend I wasn't there. At first she looked at me as if I was crazy, but when I explained that tonight I wanted to watch, she settled back and asked me what I'd like to see.

'I want you to pretend you're at home on your own watching TV. It's a boring afternoon and you're getting turned on – not really by anything in particular, it's just a lazy, horny mood that's overtaking you – and I want you to touch yourself. It's up to you how you do it, but by the time you reach orgasm, I want your breasts and vagina to be exposed.'

I push the TV trolley away from the wall so I can stand behind it. Alice is very good at this. Her eyes remain focused on the television, and her lack of self-consciousness is so convincing that I almost believe she can't see me and am amazed at how easy it was to make myself invisible.

Sonia also used to be good at this. If you're surprised at how quickly I've gone from being told what to do to calling the shots, then I should explain that it's all Sonia's doing. Having a girlfriend like Sonia . . . well, let's just say that there are certain women who can set a man up for life. I'm not suggesting that it's easy for me to get girlfriends (you already know that's not true), but once I've got one, I know what to do with them. While I'm not suggesting that all women are like Sonia (thank God), her fractured psyche did allow me to get to the heart of the darkness, as far as sex is concerned.

Alice reaches inside her jacket and starts to unbutton her blouse. Lots of finger action around the throat: she's clearly an expert. I don't know whether to unzip my trousers or just continue staring impassively. Depends how long she's going to spin this out. I decide to await her next move.

She rearranges herself on the settee, putting a cushion behind her back and taking off her shoes. I crouch down, staring at her face. Alice shakes free the two sides of her blouse and spreads them out over the jacket. In the TV light, her tummy looks invitingly sallow. I watch her stroke the stiff cones of her supermarket bra, suddenly conscious that – however tawdry it sounds – this is my ideal sexual situation. There is no other scenario that'd give me as much pleasure as seeing Alice spread out on the settee. I could have my fingers inside a supermodel and my nose resting in a kilo of coke and I still wouldn't feel any more aroused than I do now. Even though we're in Alice's house, I still feel that sex-in-a-public-place thrill (probably because Tim could come in at any minute, and even though the table in front of the door should keep him out, he's bound to be able to hear what we're doing through the wall). I also feel the adolescent hallucinatory, masturbatory thing, doubly powerful because the few photographs in my father's pornography that I did find exciting were those of readers' wives, and spread out on the settee with the family photographs behind her, that's exactly what Alice looks like. She also resembles the women on the Adult Channel's *Dish of the Day*, and as she reaches behind her back to undo her bra, I realise what's missing.

Music.

I go across to the family stereo and flip through the CDs, looking for something suitable. They're mainly compilations (*The Greatest Love III*, etc.) and soft rock. I'm about to give up when I find a copy of *Purple Rain* towards the back. Guess that'll have to do. I skip forward to *Darling Nikki* and then angle Alice's mother's chair so I can sit down and study her closely. She seems pleased by my choice and starts moving more quickly, taking off her blouse and bra before slipping back into her work jacket. The sight of her breasts angling out between those burgundy lapels is too much for me, and I unzip my trousers and push them down. I slip my hand inside my pants and grip myself. I don't masturbate as much as I used to (I got out of the habit when I was living with Dad), but when I was younger I remember been surprised at the qualitative differences between individual wanks. And as I was so prone to self-denial, it took me ages to discover that the same things that improve sexual encounters also improve solo sessions. There was a boy at our school who'd moved to Bristol from Wigan and he told us that on their estate masturbating with a condom was called a *posh wank*. I'm sure if he was here now he'd be able to come up with the perfect description of what I'm doing. Something like *sleazy-bird wank* or *top-watch cock rub*. I've never been able to justify going the whole hog on my own (y'know: baby oil, magazines, scented candles), but now I'm with Alice I feel free to indulge myself.

I shuffle my hand quickly, then squeeze my cock as I move forward again, climbing up on the arm of the settee Alice lies on. It's a biological phenomenon I don't pretend to understand, but with both good sex and good masturbation, the quality is registered inside the penis, and I know it's good when there's a solidity to the sensation, a feeling I can only really describe as *penile anticipation*.

Alice unzips her trousers and pulls them down around her thighs. She's wearing underwear today which makes me feel secure (now she's got her catch, she can clothe her cunt again), a small pair of pale pink knickers that look perfect with her burgundy suit. I want to tell her how beautiful she looks, but I'm scared that speaking will spoil the moment.

She smiles up at me while she rubs herself, twisting the cotton so her pubes sneak out either side. I groan and she pulls her knickers tight, pausing to lick her fingers and mould the material around her shape. I instinctively reach out to touch her there myself, but she grabs my hand and we both seem to experience a weird spasm at the moment of contact. I'm trembling and can't decide whether it's better to spin this out or give in and fuck her. Sometimes it's hard to make those sort of judgement calls. It's like, anything's *OK*, but to be a really good lover you have to get it *exactly* right. You need to be the perfect combination of sadist and masochist, know precisely how long to tease someone, and understand the meaning behind every motion. Prince's moved on to *When Doves Cry* and I notice Alice's hips shuffling in the same way Sonia's used to when she read erotic novels in bed. I take this as my sign and pull down Alice's underwear, disentangling her trousers from her feet and opening her legs. I get rid of my own trousers and slowly slip the tip of my penis into her wet vagina.

'What about a condom?' she says.

'Oh, right . . .'

'I mean, *I* don't mind, but you seemed so worried before.'

'No, you're right. Where are they?'

She looks at me lopsidedly. 'In my bedroom.'

I feel my cock sliding inside and try to remind myself of everything I know about Alice. I picture Fat Bastard's penis and all the others before him, imagining a dense wall of management ejaculate lining her insides. But it's no good, the voice singing *Come on, it's impossible to catch AIDS from a woman* is far more persuasive, so I close my eyes and let myself slide into her, feeling a familiar pleasant strain spreading through my thighs.

I move the table back and go to the en suite to get toilet paper for Alice. There's a bit of mess on the settee, but it doesn't look so bad once we've rubbed some 1001 over it. I want to spray some Pledge to hide the smell, but Alice says that'll make it even more obvious.

'Besides, Mum'll know whatever we do. She's got a nose for that sort of thing.'

I nod, thinking of Dad. Not having a sense of smell probably gives him a great advantage over the other patients. Alice is still dabbing at herself, grinning at me as she wipes round the cleft of her bottom. I go back to the settee and kiss her, patting her cunt and handing across her underwear and trousers.

'OK, OK, what's the rush?'

'Tim . . .'

'It's nothing he hasn't seen before. We are brother and sister, you know.'

I try not to read anything into Alice's comment, thinking that this is just another normal family thing that an only child can't understand. Still, I'm relieved when she puts her underwear back on and pulls up her work trousers.

'What sort of stuff do you watch on Cable?'

'What?'

'What Cable shows do you watch?'

'Do you want to watch something?' she asks, handing me the remote.

'No, I just wondered if you'd ever watched ...' I smile shyly at her. 'You know ...'

'The adult channels?'

'Well, yes, but not the ones you pay for. Have you ever watched *Exotica Erotica*?'

'I watched it once or twice, but it got a bit boring. They always show the same films over and over. I quite like *The Sex Show* and *Skin Tight*.'

'What's *Skin Tight*?'

'Haven't you seen it? It's like QVC, only instead of selling necklaces and rings, you can call up and order vibrators and lingerie.'

'Have you ordered anything?'

She looks away. 'That's a bit personal, isn't it?'

'Sorry, I didn't mean anything by it. I'm just interested, that's all.'

'I've bought a couple of things,' she says, 'but I don't know if I'm ready to show you them just yet.'

'That's OK. I'll look forward to it. It'll be fun trying to earn your trust.'

She smiles. 'So what do you want to do now?'

'I don't mind. Maybe we could go to bed. I know it's early, but I want to try to get my sleep pattern back to normal.'

'OK. I'm just going to make myself some hot milk. Would you like anything?'

'No thanks.'

'How about some hot Vimto or something.'

'Yeah, OK, that sounds nice.'

She goes out into the kitchen and I check my watch. It's only nine thirty, probably the earliest I've gone to bed ever. I know it'll take me ages to get to sleep, but I'm hoping post-orgasmic lethargy will help me along. Is it eight or nine minutes that it takes your body to shut down before sleep? I'm sure this won't work now I've told you about it, but I usually manage to beat insomnia by concentrating on staying very still. I picture the process as if I'm a robot and the energy is slowly draining out of my batteries.

Alice returns with the drinks. She hands me my Vimto and we walk through to her bedroom. I wait while she goes to the en suite and then returns to undress. When she's naked she pulls on her burgundy nightdress and comes over to me.

'How come you like burgundy so much?'

'I don't know. But you like it too, right?' she asks, smiling coyly.

'I didn't until I saw it on you. Before it only made me think of theatre curtains and cinema seats. Now it seems like the sexiest colour imaginable.'

'I'm glad you think so.'

She pulls back the duvet and climbs into bed. I down my Vimto and go through to the en suite to clean my teeth. I spit the paste in the sink and then urinate, still feeling sensitive down there. Alice smiles at me as I walk back in, pulling herself up to watch me undress. There's something touching about the fact that she's still excited about seeing me naked so soon after we made love. I wonder if Alice was this interested in the bodies of her past lovers, or if she's like this simply because she can't believe she's with me. Sonia used to have a thing about cocks. You could tell from her fascinated attention that she was mentally comparing yours to all the others she'd seen. I found her enthusiasm touching, although looking back I'm surprised I wasn't more jealous. All that stuff seems so strange. I wonder if any unfaithful lover has ever turned to their partner and said, 'I'm sorry, honey, I just wanted to see a different cock/cunt.' I suppose porno obsessives must find themselves becoming attached to specific vaginas instead of faces. It's not something you often hear discussed, is it? Another imagined comment: 'Her face is ugly but you should see her vagina.' I bet gynaecologists have their favourites.

I leave my clothes on the floor and join Alice in bed.

*   *   *

'Now, I don't care how tired I look. Promise that you'll wake me up in time for work tomorrow.'

'I promise. We can go in together.'

'Great. Goodnight.'

'Goodnight.'

17

Alice keeps her promise. At seven thirty she shakes me awake and asks what I want for breakfast.

'Toast'll be fine.'

'Do you want anything on it?'

'No.'

'Just dry toast?'

'If that's OK . . .'

'Of course. Do you want to shower?'

She makes the enquiry sound like an instruction, so I get out of bed and walk through to the en suite. As I pass the open doorway I can see Cathy in the lounge. Fortunately her back is towards me.

'There are clean towels in there,' Alice tells me. 'The green ones.'

I climb into the shower and try to get the balance right before turning on the water. I've never liked showers: they seem foreign and unnecessary, like muesli. I use Alice's hair and body shampoo, then climb out and towel off. It feels strange to be getting ready for work in such a conventional way. Maybe mornings like these will transform me into the perfect employee.

A plate of toast awaits me in the kitchen. Cathy grins at me, saying, 'Now, are you sure you want to go in today? You know it's much more fun staying home with me.'

'Sorry, Cathy, I can't have any more time off.'

'Course you can. Alice will cover for you.'

I look to her for help. She smiles and says, 'No, Mum, he's right. Any longer and he'll need a doctor's note.'

'That's no problem. I'll take you up to see Dr Sugar. He'll do anything I tell him.'

I bite into my toast, hoping this will be enough to end the conversation. Alice is eating a bowl of cornflakes. Her hair's wet and curling at the ends. She's not wearing her burgundy uniform today, instead dressed in a dark-blue suit I've only seen a couple of times before. It looks smarter and more expensive than the burgundy suit, but much less sexy, mainly because the cut is flattering and seems something she could happily wear outside work.

Cathy takes my empty plate from me and runs it under the tap.

'Would you like anything else?'

'No thanks.'

Alice looks at her watch. 'We should be going.'

'OK.' I stand up. Cathy hands me a tupperware box. 'What's this?'

'Sandwiches. And a penguin biscuit and a packet of salt and vinegar crisps and a can of Coke.'

'Oh. Thanks.'

'Don't mention it, love.'

Alice has the radio on as she drives to work. I can't tell whether she's listening intently or just concentrating on her driving, but she doesn't say anything the whole journey. When we reach Quick Call she parks behind the main building and clips the crook-lock to her steering-wheel. I nervously check the seventh-floor windows, fully expecting to see Adrienne, Ian and Gordon standing there pointing at me.

Alice leans down and holds her ID card against the magnetic pad. The door clicks and we go through. I didn't realise how scary coming back to work would be. The last couple of days with Alice have made me forget how betrayed my workmates are going to feel (and if there's the slightest truth in what Adrienne writes in Gordon's Log, the fact that another member of the team has moved in with his goddess could be just the thing to tip him over the edge).

The lift door opens. I follow Alice inside. She touches my chest.

'You OK?'

'Yeah.'

'Are you scared about telling everybody?'

'A bit.'

Alice reaches out and stops the lift at floor five. 'I've got someone here I can talk to.'

'I don't understand.'

'So you can go in ahead of me. We don't have to act like a couple in work.'

'Close the doors.'

She does. I kiss her. 'Dan . . .' she exhales. 'You're so nice.'

'I'm not ashamed of us.'

We enter the office together. It's eight forty so the only person in is Gordon, who sits at his desk, dealing with an early call. I go across and check out my area. All my stuff is missing, of course (two days away and they sell your possessions) and I have to steal a headset, bungee cord and pen from Adrienne's drawer.

'All right, Gordon?' I ask as he finishes the call.

Gordon doesn't reply. I assume he hasn't understood and repeat the question. Again: nothing. Either he's angry at me or something inside is malfunctioning. I think it's safe to assume the latter.

I log on and type in my password. The light on my *Aspect* starts flashing. But it's an internal call. I hit the requisite button.

'That kiss made me feel so horny.'

I look up, but can't see her.

'Where are you?'

'Behind the screen. Look.'

A hand appears at the top of the middle of the three purple screens. I laugh.

'Are you going to be monitoring me today?'

'Maybe. So you'd better be on your best behaviour.'

'Look who's talking. I thought internal calls were supposed to be restricted to emergency use only.'

'Nah, who told you that? You can't be monitored on an internal call. Do you have my extension number?'

'Yeah.'

'Well, if you feel the urge . . . although you probably shouldn't do it that often or it'll show up on your stats.'

'Right. Is that the end of this call?'

'Yeah, I'd better go. Some of us have work to do.'

Teri's the next in. She's wearing the blue top with thin white lines and carrying her tartan bag. It's nice to see her, and I'm glad of the opportunity to check out group feeling before facing the formidable Adrienne and Ian. But before I can think of the right question, Teri tells me, 'They're not talking to you.'

'Who?'

'The rest of the team.'

Gordon takes off his headset and glares at Teri.

'Oh come on,' she says to him, 'I'll do it when Ian's here.'

He looks away. I take Teri's hand.

'Thank you.'

She hands me the Suggestions Book.

'You might want to take a look at this.'

Daniel's Diary   16/3/9—

Dear Diary, you'll recall how last time I wrote I was in a deep depression over my discovery that the Divine Lady Adrienne is now dating my former best friend. Well, my misery has turned out to be rather short-lived. In fact, I should really thank Adrienne for freeing me from my bondage. When I lusted for her, she turned my working life into a constant torture, as I wasted my days waiting for some sign that she shared my feelings. Every time she looked at me I felt trapped, longing for the emotional freedom a receptive lover would bring. Every time she spoke to me the words sounded like curses, evil spells that killed my hopes, then resurrected them, then destroyed them again, like a mad scientist cheapening the miracle of life. While there was any chance that we would end up together, I saw no reason for seeking anyone else, and found our few conversations more rewarding than any intimacy could be. If I existed as a sexual being during this period, it was only through masturbation (as with any real unrequited love, the main interaction occurred between my palm and my penis) and my occasional glimpses of the bits of her body I so hungered to see revealed. I never went as far as dropping my pencil beneath the desk, but Adrienne – knowing full well the extent of my desire – would occasionally lean forward and remain perfectly still while I unsuccessfully attempted to resist looking down her top and, on the extremely rare occasions that she wore anything shorter than her usual long black skirts, she'd roll back in her chair and look away, waiting while I sneaked a peek at her underwear. Although those were the moments that thrilled my soul the most, sometimes looking at her fully clothed would be enough, and despite the fact that she doesn't normally dress in a particularly provocative way, on many occasions I'd find watching Adrienne so arousing that I had to leave my desk in the middle of the day and run to the toilet to wank myself off.

I stop reading, shocked. OK, so I masturbate at work a little more often than I've let on so far, but I had no idea that Ade realised what I was doing. Her writing this makes me feel paranoid, and I worry that she's been tipped off by someone else. Maybe Ian was in the cubicle next to me once, or getting even more suspicious, perhaps my belief that there's some kind of human rights law preventing my employers from taping me in the toilet is wrong, and they're secretly transmitting an endless loop of me masturbating on some secret screen on the thirteenth floor. I read somewhere that in America they can take your piss from the toilet bowl and submit it to urine analysis without you even knowing. I didn't think we were that advanced in England, but maybe my belief that there's any difference between the two sides of the Atlantic is another outdated notion. Three nights ago I thought hiding a filled condom in the ceiling was an outragous wheeze, but maybe they watched me doing it on the CCTV and have already rescued my sperm and produced and raised half a dozen Dan Thomas clones. I realise Teri's watching me and don't want her to guess where I've stopped, so I start reading again.

Now that I know she's not interested – and not only that she's not interested but that she is interested in someone else, and that someone else is someone I'd never risk slighting, not just because he's my best friend but also because I know he could destroy me in a fight – I am free to allow my love to curdle into hatred (borrowing money from her helps in this department: it's much easier to despise someone when you're in their debt) and use this hatred to spur me into sleeping my way through the rest of the office. For a long time I thought I'd start with Teri – we've been flirting a lot and I once slept over at her place – but then I realised I couldn't cope with another rejection and decided to go for the safe bet.

I know my team-mates will be pissed off when they find out I've slept with Alice, but fuck 'em, especially Adrienne. I want to make them angry. After all, Adrienne and Ian didn't show much concern for my feelings when they decided to get together.

Anyway, Dear Diary, I guess you want details. Well, it happened like this. I was coming back up to the end of the night-shift when Alice arrived back at the office to pick up some papers she'd left behind. I logged off and walked across to her, starting up a conversation. The others find Alice really hard to talk to, but that's only because they refuse to see her as a human being. Once you've got past that stupid 'don't talk to teacher' mentality, you realise that most authority figures are grateful for any offers of friendship, and because of their position they value personal contact more than other people. For a while I thought it was really important to be loyal to Ian, but now I realise that he's got enough people on his side and it's far more rewarding to trade that loyalty for a connection with Alice.

Alice told me that she'd come back to pick up the timesheets and I asked her if she wanted to go for a drink. She seemed surprised but quickly agreed, telling me to wait while she went to the toilet. I packed up my stuff and walked through to the cloakroom, trying to resist the urge to go after Alice and surprise her with an erect cock while she was in the middle of shitting. I pictured myself picking her up off the toilet, turning her round and pushing her face against the pan while I penetrated her cack-covered arsehole.

Teri taps my arm and I look up. Adrienne has entered the office. She walks across to our table, avoiding my eye. Teri taps me again. It's obvious she wants me to put the Suggestions Book away, but I don't see any reason why I should stop reading. After all, Adrienne wrote this for me, so she might as well know her satire has reached its intended audience.

'Hi Adrienne,' I say, shooting her a smile before adding, 'this is good stuff. Maybe your best yet.'

She ignores me. I realise this feud is serious (hell, if Ian gets some of his more psychotic mates involved it might even prove fatal) but right now I just can't take it seriously. I don't even understand why they feel betrayed. Surely it's my business if I want to date Alice.

I go back to the book.

Alice returned and asked whether I was ready to go. I said

yes and we walked down to the back car park. She drove home quickly and we rushed inside her house, both eager to get down to business. I could tell she was excited by the way she kept looking down at the bulge in my work trousers. The minute we got inside, I picked her up and carried her through to the bedroom. I laid her out on the bed and took off her shoes. Then I undid her skirt and pulled it down. Adrienne had already warned me that Alice doesn't wear underwear when she's in heat, but I was still a bit surprised to see the shadow of her muff beneath the material of her tights.

'You'd be amazed at how accurate some of this is,' I call across to Adrienne, 'you've got a real talent for observation.'

She doesn't reply. Ian comes in behind her. I feel a little more worried about Ian ignoring me, and my stomach twists as he sits next to me and sets up without speaking. I don't want to wind him up so I keep quiet for the moment, waiting until I've thought of the right reply to the silent treatment.

I knew she was into rough stuff so I tore her tights along the front seam and started kissing her minge. Her pubic hair was so thick and scratchy that it was as if someone had stapled a piece of carpet to her genitals. I ignored the nasty taste and did my best to bring her off. Just as I thought she was getting close, she grabbed my greasy chin and pulled me up. I wanted to use a condom, but she unzipped me and had my prick wedged in her vagina before I had chance to bring it up.

She kept grabbing me while I fucked her, wrapping me in her arms like a grandmother embracing her grandchild. I tried not to be distracted by this and concentrated on keeping my rhythm steady. I've always thought of myself as a good lover, and even if Alice wasn't the sort of woman I usually go for, I saw no reason why I shouldn't at least attempt to satisfy her.

I felt her come and the contractions did something to

me. I hadn't been planning to orgasm myself, but her moans made me feel like Mr Sex and I had a sudden fiery desire to leave my seed inside her. I gripped her bottom and fucked her hard, not stopping until I'd shot my load. The poor bitch was so grateful that she started crying and cooing in my ear. I felt like such a stud. Fuck the lot in work – fucking Alice makes me feel good. I'm glad I did it and I'm going to stick with her. At least until she throws me over for some management fat cat.

'Bit of a serious ending,' I call across to Adrienne, 'what's happened to all the sodomy jokes?'

She doesn't answer. I close the Suggestions Book and take it across.

'Still, a good effort. You definitely seem to know how I think.'

I drop the book in front of her and go back to my work-station. Teri isn't saying anything, and I remember what she said to Gordon and realise she's also going to ignore me now Ian is here. But I'm grateful to Teri for tipping me off and don't challenge her, instead putting my headset on and taking the first call.

The morning passes quickly. Being ignored isn't that bad actually, and the silence is almost preferable to our usual pointless conversations. It's like being back at junior school and getting through quiet time by concentrating on my work. Of course, the repetitive tasks do little to exercise my imagination, and my thoughts soon stray beyond the enquiries of each caller. I start thinking about John, wondering when will be the best time to check on how he's doing. (There are three new brown marks on the ceiling tiles, which must be a good sign, right?) It's hard to resist the urge to go find him immediately, but I don't want to risk breaking another toilet-top, and everyone's bound to notice if I try rolling a swivel-chair out of the call-centre. No, I'll have to forget about it until tonight.

Teri waits until Ian's looking away and then surreptitiously sneaks me a folded piece of paper. I open it and read:

TAKE LUNCH 11.45–12.15. WE'LL GET OUT OF HERE.

She nods at the Breaks Book and I turn to today's page. She's written her name in the 11.45–12.00 and 12.00–12.15 slots and left two blank spaces alongside them for me to add my own signature. I do so, and then reach under the table to squeeze her hand, pleased to have a friend.

The light on my *Aspect* is glowing red. I take three calls in a row to get it back to yellow. Then the fourth caller says,

'Hi, is that Dan?'

'Yes.'

'It's Moyra.'

Moyra. I remember how upset she was last time she called and feel pleased that she's still alive, although of course I don't say this to her, not wanting her to think I'm being melodramatic.

'Hi, Moyra, how are things?'

'Good. Have you really been sick?'

'Of course. Why d'you ask?'

'I just thought you might have been getting people to cover for you.'

'Why would I want to do that?'

'Because I embarrassed you last time I phoned.'

'What makes you think that?'

'I was all upset and you passed me on to your friend. Come on, Dan, it was obvious.'

'You didn't embarrass me . . . although I was worried about you. Especially as you went before I had chance to say goodbye.'

'I had to go. I knew your friend didn't want to talk to me and I thought you wouldn't be coming back. And then when all the others kept saying you were ill, I thought you must be sitting there laughing.'

'But you still kept calling?'

'Yeah, but only because I didn't want you to get the wrong idea. It's like what I was saying before.'

'About what?'

'About why I don't like the phone. It makes you seem like someone you're not, and then paranoia about seeming like the kind of person the phone makes you seem like, actually makes you into that person you didn't think you were.'

I laugh. 'I don't follow.'

'OK, I'll make it simple. The phone is probably the place where you get the clearest indication of how other people think about you, right?'

'In what way?'

'Well, whether they take your calls, how quickly they get back to you after you've left a message, that's assuming they get back to you at all.'

'I didn't know you'd left a message,' I protest.

'Oh, I'm not getting at you. I told them not to tell you I'd called because I wanted to get hold of you personally, and I didn't want to get you in trouble. But it's funny you should say that because it leads on to my second point.'

'Which is?'

'The fact that although the phone seems to be the place where you get the clearest indication of how people think of you, it's actually deceptive because while you're deciding that so-and-so hates you because he's taken three weeks to reply to your message, chances are he never got it in the first place. But then again, you never really know what they think of you because the people who did get your message and don't want to talk to you can use the whole uncertainty that's created by using a phone to pretend that they didn't know you'd called. And because of this, even when you're talking to people who genuinely didn't get your message, you can't help feeling a little paranoid and examining your friendship in a way you might never have done if you'd only ever met face-to-face.'

'I see you've given this a lot of thought.'

'You say that like I'm being weird, but I think it's people who aren't afraid of the phone who are weird.'

'I thought you liked using the phone.'

'What made you think that?'

'I thought you said something like that the first time you called. Something about how you felt phones gave you freedom.'

'You remember stuff I've said to you?'

'Of course.'

'I didn't realise you were paying attention.'

'I like talking to you. Especially today. Today is a really good time for you to call.'

'Why?'

'I can't really talk about it.'

'Ah. Right. Are you being monitored or something?'

'I hope not. No, it's not that.'

The line goes silent for a moment, then Moyra says, 'It's the people in your office, isn't it?'

'Maybe.'

'Right, say no more. I'll call you back after office hours.'

'OK, but not too late. Between six and nine is probably the best time.'

'No problem. Talk to you later, Dan.'

She clicks off and I check my watch. Almost time for lunch with Teri. I wonder if Alice will want me to stop working nights. Actually, I've got a funny feeling she might have already said something about changing my schedule that I've forgotten. I call her on internal.

'Hi Dan.'

'How did you know it was me?'

'Don't play dumb. You know the number comes up on the *Aspect*.'

'Morning gone well?'

'Not really. Are the others getting at you?'

'A bit.'

'Really?'

'I can't talk about it.'

'OK. Tell me at lunch.'

'I can't.'

'Why not?'

'I really can't tell you.'

'Right. Conference Room 2.'

'What?'

'I'm going to Conference Room 2. Wait for a couple of minutes then follow me across.'

'OK.'

She clicks off. I watch her head appear above the purple screens of the reception area, then follow her legs as she walks out of the call-centre. I don't want to risk taking another call in case it goes on for ages and Alice gets upset that I've left her alone for so long. So I just sit there sucking on my mouthpiece, waiting until two minutes have passed.

I get up from my work-station and walk through to Conference Room 2. Alice is sitting on the table, her feet resting on a swivel-chair.

'If this was *Melrose Place*, I could get you to fuck me.'

'Is that what you want me to do?' I ask her, smiling.

'No, we'd better not risk it. Some other time.'

'OK.'

I walk over to Alice and lift up her leg while I slide underneath it, sitting on a swivel-chair and staring at her crotch.

'Are you wearing underwear today?'

She laughs. 'Why don't you check?'

'Is that what you want me to do?'

Alice straightens her upper body and I unzip the fly of her dark blue trousers. Her knickers are light pink. I gently stroke the smooth material, pushing my finger against the soft spring of her pubes. She smiles and I do her back up, holding on to her left leg.

'So what have they been saying?'

'Nothing.'

'I thought you said they were giving you a hard time.'

'They are. Ian's told everybody not to talk to me.'

'How do you know it was Ian?'

'Teri told me.'

'So Teri's talking to you?'

'Not really. She's whispering things and passing notes. That's why I can't go to lunch with you.'

'Why?'

'Because Teri's asked me to go to lunch with her.'

She looks away. 'Oh.'

'Don't be upset,' I say, stroking her leg. 'I have to go. Teri's my only ally.'

'Are you that worried what they think?'

'No, not at all. It's just boring when none of your workmates will talk to you. Surely you understand that.'

'It depends. Where are you going?'

'Nowhere exciting. Somewhere I can eat my sandwiches.'

'The breaks room?'

'No, I don't think so. Teri doesn't want Ian to know that she's talking to me.'

'Fucking babies. How long are you going for?'

'Thirty minutes.'

'So you've still got two breaks left?'

'Yeah.'

'Spend them with me, OK? This afternoon.'

'All right. What time?'

'Three thirty. I'll be free for a while then.'

'OK. Should we go back?'

'Give me a kiss first.'

She leans down to embrace me. I squeeze her thigh. Alice is a good kisser, keeping her tongue muscles tight as she gently probes the front of my mouth. I finish our kiss and we stand up together. Alice laughs as I wobble slightly and pats my bum as I go back into the call-centre.

Teri's already gone. I walk over to my desk and log off, then fetch my sandwiches from the cloakroom. She's waiting in front of the lifts, her fingers fiddling with the front buckle of her tartan bag.

'Where we gonna go?' I ask her.

'I thought maybe by The Friar, if that's OK.'

'Fine by me, but isn't it a bit close to work?'

'Nah, no one goes further than the breaks room. Besides, Ian and Gordon never have their lunch this early.'

The lift doors open and I follow her inside. Being together with Teri in so small a space is a real turn-on, especially so soon after snogging Alice. I remember what she said about *Melrose Place* and it crosses my mind that if I was in that soap, getting off with Teri would be the perfect second scene after an opening credits Conference Room conquest.

But I keep control of myself (OK, I'm sorry, I know that makes me sound like I'm feeling all studly now I've pulled Alice – the truth is I don't do anything because I've got no idea how Teri'd react to my advances) and stand just behind her, staring at her neat hairline as the lift slowly descends. I've already explained how easy Teri is to ignore, and how this is nearly always a mistake, but today she seems to be holding back even more emotion than usual, and I sense that if I did reach out to touch her, she'd whip round and punch me in the face.

We reach the ground floor and Teri walks out in front of me. I follow behind, trying not to be too obvious about how much I like looking at her backside. She leads me through the rear entrance and across the car park, remaining silent as if she's following Ian's orders until we're out of his domain. The moment we're off Quick Kall premises, she says, 'I'm sorry I didn't talk to you this morning.'

'That's OK. You were in a difficult situation.'

'Ian's very serious about this, you know.'

'I know, and I'm grateful to you for tipping me off. Especially in front of Gordon.'

'Oh, Gordon won't say anything. He knows what I'd do to him if he did.'

She smiles and darts across the busy road. I follow behind her, more cautious between the traffic. We reach The Friar and she sits down. Behind the bench is a pyramid of paving stones, pulled up by the roots of the tree that arches over Teri.

'I'm just going to get some lunch from the newsagent,' she tells me, 'would you like anything?'

'No, I'm fine.'

I show her my sandwich box, feeling vaguely fraudulent. She knows I'm really a Panda Pops and Potato Puffs person and must realise that the only reason I've got a packed lunch today is because I've moved in with Alice. I'm anticipating a sarcastic comment but she doesn't say anything, turning her back on me and walking over to the newsagent.

She comes back clutching a sandwich, Mars bar and can of 7 UP. She sits down.

'So tell me why you did it, Dan.'

'What?'

'You know what. Tell me why you did it and then maybe I'll forgive you.'

'I had to.'

'OK, that's a good start. Now tell me why.'

'She caught me.'

'Doing what?'

'Sleeping in the office.'

'So now she's forcing you to live with her?'

'No, but I don't have a home. It's either Alice's place or the streets.'

Teri unwraps her sandwich and takes a bite. I watch her chin as she chews, wondering why she's not surprised by what I'm saying.

'Did you know I was sleeping in the office?'

'Not for certain. There were rumours. Adrienne said Ian had said something.'

I keep quiet for a moment, considering this. I feel like a child discovering that everyone had known what I thought was my big secret all along. I suppose deep down I knew I probably hadn't fooled Ian on that Saturday evening when I slept in the cloakroom, but finding out that his suspicions had filtered through the office disturbs me for two reasons:

1. It makes me realise that throughout all this I haven't really considered my team-mates capable of independent thought (this is a frequently observed fault of mine, and even though I've been caught out many times before, I still find it hard to comprehend that what other people *think* might be different from what they *say*. Because, on the whole, I am usually honest with everyone – no, I am, I really am, although of course I realise the irony of making this protestation in the middle of an aside about the public reception of my lies – I always think that other people are honest with me, and if they don't catch me out about something face-to-face, I automatically assume I've got away with it. Discovering that Ian has seen through my fibs and instead of confronting me, has talked to the others, is a terrifying idea (made worse by the fact that he's usually so stoic and I can't imagine him saying anything about me to anyone, especially when I'm not around. I realise he's going out with Adrienne now and it's inevitable that she'd start shit-stirring, but still, this is *not* something I'm happy with.) What scares me more than anything is that Adrienne probably doesn't realise how seriously Ian takes things, and that what seems like a big joke to her could have dangerous consequences.

2. And this follows on from the first point, it reawakens my larger feelings of paranoia (trust me, no one could work in a call-centre and not feel paranoid) and I worry that if everyone knew I was sleeping in the cloakroom, Alice's discovery of me could've been a set-up and maybe this whole thing is just a sick joke at my expense. After all, everyone getting together, making me sleep with Alice and then ignoring me isn't that different from the scenarios depicted in Gordon's Log, and it doesn't seem that far-fetched that Alice would want to make her strange recastings of reality three-dimensional.

'So, can you forgive me?' I ask Teri.

'I suppose so, although I can't help feeling a little let down,

Dan. It's just the thought of you and her together.' She puts down her sandwich and looks at me, her face serious. 'How can you bring yourself to do it? Do you find her attractive?'

'No, of course not.'

'But you can still fuck her?'

'It's not that big a deal.'

'Oh wow. I can't believe you can think like that.'

'Think like what?' I ask, irritated by her tone.

'Doesn't it mean anything to you? You can be naked with her and not feel strange? You can have that sort of intimacy without feeling anything?'

'I didn't say I don't feel anything. I force myself, OK?'

'So what do you do? Pretend she's someone else?'

'Not when I'm fucking her.'

'When then?'

'When she's wanking me or sucking me off. When we fuck, I make her seem sexy. You can find something sexy about most people. Alice isn't that grotesque.'

'I still can't picture it.'

She opens her can and takes a long drink. I can see she's pleased about getting the final word and decide to change the subject and allow Teri her victory. Still, that doesn't mean I'm not out for revenge. So I ask, 'How are your flatmates?'

'Fine. Why?'

'They haven't tied you up or locked you in your room recently?'

'No.'

'Did you get them back?'

'What?'

'Last time we talked about this, you said you were going to get them back. Have you done anything yet?'

'I decided not to. They're at home together all day every day and if I start anything, they've got all the time in the world to plan nasty surprises. It's best to let the whole thing fizzle out.'

*   *   *

314

Teri's worried they'll be watching us through the seventh-floor window so she waits while I go back first. Alice looks up as I enter the office, waving at me. I smile and return to my seat. As soon as I've logged on, the *Aspect*-light starts flashing. I check the screen to see which line the call's come through.

'Hello, Angel Cruises. How can I help you?'

'Is that Dan Thomas?'

'Yes.'

'It's Claire Granger. Is this OK? I know no one's supposed to come through on these lines, but Brittany told me it was the only way to reach you.'

'It's OK.'

'Good. I was just calling to check you still wanted to meet tonight.'

'Yeah, I think so ... actually, I need to make a quick call to check I'm working tonight. Is it OK if I put you on hold for just two secs?'

'Of course.'

I do so, then call Alice on internal.

'Hi Alice, it's Dan.'

'Hi Dan. Are they still giving you a hard time?'

'No, but I can't really talk. Let's discuss it when we go on break this afternoon.'

'OK. Did you call for a reason, or just to exchange sweet nothings?'

'No, I'm calling for a couple of reasons actually. We haven't really talked about it, but am I going to carry on doing the late shift?'

'Do you want to?'

'I'm not sure. Maybe for the moment.'

'Yeah, it'll be good if you do it tonight and tomorrow. It's a bit short notice to find a replacement.'

'OK, and the other thing is, I'm supposed to be meeting a friend of your auntie's after work tonight.'

'In the middle of the night?'

'Yeah, I know it's weird, but she's another one of Dad's group and you know what they're like.'

'Right. Do you want me to come with you?'

'No, you'd better not. She wants to talk privately. She's going to tell me secrets about Dad.'

'How are you going to get back?'

'Hopefully she'll be driving. If not, I'll take a taxi.'

'And who is it?'

'Claire Granger.'

'Claire. I don't think I know her. OK, I suppose, although that's twice today you've gone off with other women.'

'Come on, Alice, you know it's not like that.'

'OK, but make sure you wake me up when you get back in. I want to know all about it.'

'No problem. Speak to you later.'

'Bye.'

I cut off the call and check the wait-time for line one: 3.28. Nothing special, although I suppose she's not a proper caller so it wouldn't count even if I kept her on hold for ages. I press the grey rectangle above the *Aspect* light and say,

'You still there, Claire?'

'Yeah.'

'Tonight's fine. Midnight at The Frog and Toad, is that right?'

'Quarter past.'

'Right. I'll see you then.'

I suppose I can always wait them out. No doubt Ian would be able to blank me for ever, but I bet Adrienne says something to me before the end of the week. (Actually, looking on the bright side, at least the silent treatment means she can't ask me for her thousand pounds back.) But I must admit I'm surprised at how good they are at all this, and at how bad their withdrawal makes me feel. I've always felt slightly above the companionship offered to me at Quick Kall, but now it's gone, I feel a bit silly. I've got no reason to feel superior to my team-mates, and although I think they're treating me unfairly, I can understand why they feel betrayed. Yes, it's childish and like being back at school, but work is childish and like being back at school. It's us versus them, and no matter how much I protest, I've crossed over that line.

I take a few calls. Magicmix mainly, the mid-week restock after the initial supply has sold out. After fifteen minutes, Ian gets up and goes for lunch with Adrienne. Gordon's facial expression is that of a favoured pupil after the teacher has gone out of the room, miserably aware that the usual sense of order is about to collapse.

I lean across. 'What's wrong, Gordon?'

He doesn't reply.

I'm in the middle of a call when Alice gets up from her desk in the reception area. Curious about where she's going, I peep round the corner of my work-station, worried that I'm about to witness her talking to another man. But, instead, she comes straight across to our table, her gestures instructing me to interrupt my call.

'Excuse me,' I ask the man moaning into my ear about his mobile phone, 'is it OK if I put you on hold?'

'What? Oh, all right.'

I look up at Alice. 'What's wrong?'

'It's three thirty.' She pauses. 'Remember? You said you'd go on break with me.'

'Right, sorry, I'm in the middle of a call.'

'Can't you finish up?'

'Not quickly. This guy's got a pretty serious problem with his mobile.'

Alice looks at Adrienne, who's deliberately avoiding her eye. 'Ade, can he transfer this one to you?'

Adrienne stares. 'That's not really allowed, is it, Alice?'

'I think we can make an exception.'

'Right.'

'Go on then, Dan,' she tells me.

I do as she instructs.

Alice leads the way over to the breaks room. I spend the time in the lift trying to persuade her that going into town might be a better bet, but she says it's a waste of our thirty minutes. She takes me into the smoking room and sits by the wall, elbows on table and lighting up a fag. I can't help feeling proud to be beside her, and remember the photographs of Alice as the school bully.

'I'm going to call a meeting tomorrow,' Alice tells me.

'What?'

'I'm going to have another meeting. This can't carry on.'

'You can't.'

'Why not? Do you like being ignored?'

'No, of course not, but drawing attention to it is only going to make things worse.'

'I'm not going to draw attention to it. I'll pretend it's a follow-up to that bollocking I gave the whole team. I'll just have you all in together and ask how things are going and if you think there's been any improvement since the last time I spoke to you.'

'Come on, Alice, you know how they're going to react.'

'If any of them do anything, I'll have them all in individually and threaten them with the sack. Starting with Ian.'

'Great. So instead of being ignored, I end up dead.'

'Don't be ridiculous.'

'I'm not. You don't know the connections he's got.'

'I know more about Ian than you might think. Most of his connections are people I've met at one time or another. Don't forget who I've been out with. Bristol's a pretty small city.'

'Still, I don't think it's a good idea to antagonise him.'

'Look, Dan, I appreciate that this is difficult for you, but I've still got a job to do, and I'm being monitored as well, you know. I wasn't winding you up when I said that management thinks you're the worst team in the office. And despite what I said before, as I'm your team leader they do hold me responsible.'

'OK, OK, I understand that, but I think if we wait things will soon get back to normal.'

'And if they don't?' She swallows. 'I'm taking a big risk going out with you, Dan. And it's much more of a potential disaster than when I was going out with Fat Bastard or any of the others.'

'Right.'

She looks at me. 'Don't be like that. I'm simply saying that I've got a reputation for dating management, and now that I'm going out with you, and you're much younger, and much more attractive than any of them, they're bound to be feeling pretty pissed off, and if they think that my relationship with you is making me turn a blind eye to problems with my team, then they're gonna get rid of me immediately.'

'But what are you going to say to Ian?'

'I'll threaten him with the sack. Management told me to get rid of a member of the team. Doesn't have to be Teri. Could be Ian.'

'But you know what'll happen if you threaten him. He'll never give in.'

'Then I'll sack him.'

'And he'll come after me. Alice, I know you've got responsibilities, but please think how this is going to end up.'

'Relax, Dan, you know it won't come to that.'

'I don't. What you've just described sounds like a perfectly plausible scenario.'

'Nah, it won't happen. I don't know why you're so afraid of Ian. As long as you talk to him properly, he's a pussycat. Besides, I thought he was a friend of yours.'

'He is. I mean, he used to be.'

'Listen, Dan, I bet you this is all Adrienne's idea. And no matter how much she moans or slags me off, she needs her job and knows when she's overstepped the mark. Getting everyone together is a great idea. And it'll clear the air. You'll see.'

She opens her handbag and looks inside her purse for some change.

'I didn't want a coffee when I came in but I feel really thirsty now. It's because you agitated me. Do you want anything?'

'No thanks.'

She puts her hands on top of mine. 'Relax, Dan, it'll be fine. I promise you.'

Alice gets up and walks over to the coffee machine. I want to believe Alice, but I can't help thinking her vision of how this will all work out seems unlikely. I know I've got paranoid tendencies, but Ian is definitely a proud man, and I can't see him giving in that easily. I saw how he reacted when Alice attacked the whole team, and I can't imagine what he'll be like if she singles him out.

I watch Alice unclip her filled cup and walk back to the table. She smiles at me and I do my best not to look worried. Maybe she's right. Maybe direct action is what's needed.

'So tell me about your secret assignation.'

'What?'

'This mysterious woman you're meeting in the middle of the night.'

'I told you. Her name's Claire Granger and she's one of Brittany's friends.'

'And why are you meeting her?'

'I've already told you all this. I've got stuff I need to discuss.'

'What stuff?'

'Stuff about Dad.'

'Don't you trust me, Dan?'

'You know I do.'

'Then why are you being so vague?'

'Because it's family stuff. You're the same.'

'What d'you mean?'

'You've been just as cagey about your family.'

'In what way?'

'You haven't told me about your dad.'

'I told you he fucked another woman in my bedroom.'

'Yeah, but that's not it, is it?'

'Not what?'

'Nothing. Forget it. This isn't something I want to get into. Especially not here.'

'Dan, I'm sorry to make you spell this out, but I really don't understand what you're talking about.'

'I shouldn't have said anything. Please, be angry at me later, but let's talk about something else.'

'Well, go on then.'

'What?'

'Change the subject.'

'OK, is Cathy working tonight?'

'Cathy works every night.'

'Right.'

'I'm not going to forget this, Dan. I accept that you don't want to talk about it here, although that does seem a little ridiculous given all the other things you're prepared to do at work, but I want to have a long conversation about whatever it is you can't say to me when you get back tonight.'

'OK.'

'I'm serious. I know it'll be late and I'll probably be asleep, but I want you to wake me up, and don't worry, no matter how sleepy I am I'll still remember what I want you to tell me.'

'I understand.'

'Good.'

'Alice . . .'

'Yes?'

'I realise this is going to make you even more pissed off, but I'm going to have to pop out to the shops for a minute. I'm sorry, but this is my last break today and there's something I forgot to buy.'

'What?'

'Pardon?'

'What did you forget to buy?'

'I can't tell you.'

I try a cheeky grin (not my speciality). It doesn't work, and Alice howls as she lunges at me. Luckily, her waist knocks the table and shoots her coffee into my lap. It's worth the scalding to escape unquestioned, and I ignore her apologies and tell her I'll be back in five minutes.

The pet shop owner is pleased to see me. I hadn't noticed this before, but apart from the flecks of crusted bird shit, his burgundy jacket is just like Alice's. As I approach the counter he relaxes his shoulders, asking me, 'How have you been?'

'Fine.'

'And how's John?'

'Good.'

'Did the vet sort out his teeth?'

'Yeah. Thanks.'

'Do you want me to do another spot of cat-sitting?'

'No, that won't be necessary.'

'Shame. He's got real personality, that cat.'

'Yeah, I remember you saying.'

'So, what can I do you for?'

'Food. A few cans of Felix, please.'

'Right. Any particular flavour?'

'Doesn't matter.'

'That's good. I like a cat that isn't picky.'

'That's John all right. He'll eat anything.'

He smiles. 'Salty was like that. To be perfectly honest with you . . .' He tails off and looks up at me, clearly embarrassed that although he can remember my cat's name he can't remember mine.

'Dan,' I tell him.

'Right. To be perfectly honest with you, Dan, I think a lot of that gourmet stuff is crap. Real cats don't want processed meat, they want fish tails and braising steak.'

'OK, give me a bucket of fish tails.'

He laughs, and hands me my cat food. I pay him and leave the shop.

I stop in the newsagents on the way back. They have three grey buckets of limp bouquets by the door.

'How much are the flowers?' I ask the old lady behind the till.

'Do you know, I don't know, love. How much do you think they're worth?'

I stop, fazed by the question. What is it with people around here? This old lady could be the pet shop man's imbecilic older sister.

'Two fifty?' I suggest.

'That sounds about right.'

I nervously check my watch as I get back into Quick Kall's car park, praying that Alice will stay in the breaks room until I return. I suppose it would be fairly easy to invent a fake reason why I'm scrabbling in the skip (after all, everyone here does it, and no one wants to get caught, so I'd have an excuse for looking guilty) but things would be much easier if she stays sat sipping coffee while I hide the cat food beneath the top layer of broken perspex.

I watch the breaks room door as I dig, then nip back across, holding the limp flowers in front of me. Happily, Alice is still there, staring into an empty cup.

'Hi,' I say.

'Hi.' She looks at the flowers. 'Is that what you had to buy?'

I look down. 'Well, I suppose "had" was a bit of an exaggeration, but I knew you wouldn't let me go otherwise.'

She takes the bouquet. 'Where did you get them?'

'From the mad lady in the newsagent. I know they're a bit limp, but I just wanted to get you something.'

'Thanks.'

'Alice, you do know my feelings for you are genuine.'

'What are you saying?'

'I just think things are in danger of getting distorted because of the situation.'

'You're going cryptic again.'

I sigh. 'If I tell you something, do you promise to trust me?'

'That depends.'

'Right, then I can't tell you.'

'OK,' she says, 'I promise.'

I look at her, knowing that what I'm about to do is wrong (and that it will inevitably intensify the current office drama), but nevertheless wanting to go ahead. Alice's decision to call a meeting tomorrow has pissed me off, and as I can't persuade her to abandon the idea, I feel a perverse urge to increase the chaos.

'They have a book.'

'Hang on. Who has a book?'

'Adrienne and Ian. I think it used to be the Suggestions Book, although as most of the cover's ripped off and it's covered in graffiti it's hard to tell, but anyway, in this book Adrienne writes pretend diary entries. She used to write from Gordon's perspective, but now she writes from mine.'

'Why are you telling me this?'

'Because I don't want you to discover the book by accident and either think I genuinely wrote it or worry that it's some big joke that I'm in on.'

'So what does it say?'

'Well, most of the entries are about you. The running joke in the bits about Gordon is that you're his dream woman and there's all these scenarios where he thinks he's going to have sex with you but ends up getting buggered instead.'

'What happens in your bits?'

'Adrienne imagines what's been happening between us and then writes her version of it as if she's looking at it through my eyes.'

'And what sort of things does she write?'

'Nasty stuff about you mainly.'

'What sort of nasty stuff?'

'I don't want to tell you.'

'Come on, Dan, you brought it up. If you don't tell me I'll only go and have a look for myself.'

'You can't. You promised.'

'OK, so tell me what she's written.'

'Just nasty remarks about your body.'

'My body?' Alice asks, genuinely surprised.

'Yeah.' I look at her. 'It's not, like, serious stuff. It's just nonsense. Absurd rubbish.'

'Give me an example.'

'I don't know. OK, she's got this bit about your pubes.'

Her tone rises. 'What does she say about my pubes?'

I look away. 'That's what I mean. It's just gobbledy-gook really. She says your pubic hair's like carpet.'

'Is that what she writes?' She looks at her fingernails. 'I'm having real trouble imagining this. Is it funny?'

'I don't think so, but then most of the jokes are at my expense.'

'Why does she write it?'

'Oh, you know, it's just more office rubbish. People do all kinds of things to kill time. I bet every team in the call-centre has got their equivalent, even if they're just writing "so-and-so's a queer" on a piece of paper and passing it under the table.'

'It all sounds so childish.'

'It is childish.'

Alice looks at her watch. 'God, we're really late. I'm going to get in trouble.'

'You can't get in trouble.'

'Course I can. You've got a really weird idea about what being a team leader is like. I still have to answer to people. I can't just come and go as I please.'

She stands up and we walk through the breaks room and back out into the rear car park. I look at my watch. Four twenty. We really are late. Before I reached the top level of the Temptastic Employment Agency tree, my first three trial jobs – while offering less money than conventional office work – involved several days when I was left to complete my menial tasks unobserved. As my contract lasted only until the work was completed, I of course tried to spin it out as long as possible. Like thousands before me I soon realised that the easiest way to get away with this was to appear to be thoroughly conscientious, and a little stupid. No one bothers getting angry with a drudge, and as long as I appeared to do the same amount every day I knew I could get away with it. After a few days of this slowed-down existence, I started to worry that I might never finish the job and scared myself into speeding up. But before that I remember experiencing this weird daze on the second or third day of my stretch when I found myself unable to stop watching the clock. That odd lethargy was probably closest to the way I'm feeling now, slightly overcome by the psychological immensity of having a job. It's only when I stray away from my usual daily routine that I realise the immense amount of willpower needed to keep me at my desk. People think having a job is perfectly normal, but it's not, and although this sort of low-level office work is seen as the least interesting employment imaginable, personally I think it's pretty fucking bizarre. The human element of this sort of service is so unnecessary, and it can't be long before all telephone transactions are conducted by an electronic voice. The only reason we're here is for people who still need that illusion of human agency, unaware that all we're really doing is reading from a computer screen. Sure, we serve as a good front for filtering out the flak, yet it can't be that hard to programme a machine to make pathetic protests and claim it's sorry but it can't do anything to help the caller.

'Are we going to go back in together?' I ask Alice.

'Is that a problem?'

'Not for me. I just thought you might not want people to know you were coming back late after a break with me.'

'Good point. I'll go in first cause I'm the one who's being watched. You pop to the bathroom.'

'No problem.'

The toilets are empty. I stand there staring at myself in the mirror, trying to resist the urge to check on John.

After another couple of minutes, I go back into the call-centre. I can see Alice sitting in the sectioned-off area behind reception, wearing her headset and frowning. I go back to my table.

'Hi everyone,' I say brightly, 'are you all having a good afternoon?'

No response.

It's much harder to cope with the silent treatment during the dead end of the afternoon. Usually I'm relieved when I reach this final session, feeling pleased as the calls slacken off and I have more time to gossip and flirt with Adrienne and Teri. Today, however, I'd be happy to talk to anyone, and no matter how banal the complaint, every caller would receive my complete attention. But even the mobile moaners aren't interested today, and no doubt if they did call, my sympathetic ear would disgust them. Part of the Quick Call job description should be that a good call-handler must at all times appear to be inefficient and uninterested, making sure that as many callers as possible lose their temper and maintain the necessary emotional connection with their service-providers. I bet if you did a survey of the buying habits of customers who call in to complain, no matter how often they trotted out that tired old threat of 'taking their business elsewhere', you'd find that they were the most brand loyal. The people who don't expect anything from the companies that manufacture the products they buy, who start with a Ferguson TV and when it breaks switch to Sony, or vice versa, are never going to be the bread-and-butter of a major corporation. It's the ones who put their faith in a single company and buy all their products blindly believing in some spurious notion of quality connected exclusively to that name, not realising that it's unlikely that one company are going to produce the best televisions, videos and mobile phones, and not only keep this belief themselves, but also try to instil this quality-confidence in their family and friends, sticking to their chosen company when the time comes to buy electronic equipment for their children and their children's children: these are the ones you need to exploit. And once you've won these people's support, you'll find their relationship with your corporation can be best likened to a masochistic love affair. Now that they've chosen you as their beloved, you'll find it impossible to kill off their devotion. But the thing is, they don't love you, they love the idea of you. Your name now has associations you might never understand, and as they are subservient to you (you, who has many lovers), they have put themselves in a situation where disappointment is inevitable. For their undying devotion comes with the heavy price of expectation, and no matter how hard you try, you will never satisfy them. And as they notice your weaknesses, they'll start by refusing to believe them, and then, when disillusion threatens to set in, they'll call you and beg you to tell them that they're wrong: to prove you are perfect after all. It doesn't matter that every time they ring you get someone else to answer the phone, they'll keep calling for months after their first disappointment, only stopping when self-respect returns and they realise they're never going to get an adequate explanation. Then, just when you think the whole thing's over, they'll decide to give you another chance.

My message light flashes. Grateful for the diversion, I straighten my slipping headset and play it.

'Hello, this is Alice. I'm just letting you know that there will be a meeting for the whole team tomorrow morning at nine thirty. Attendance is compulsory, and it will take place in Conference Room 2.'

I look round anxiously, watching everyone else stop to check the message. Ian sucks on his pen, then turns to me and says in a clipped, even voice, 'This better not be anything to do with you.'

I suppose I should see his speaking to me as a tiny victory, but instead it makes me more worried than ever. I want to tell Alice, but I know if I call her on internal he'll hear me, and if I suggest we go to Conference Room 2 now, he'll know what I'm up to. After all, the worst thing for me to be seen doing now is running to teacher.

I look over to the reception area, wishing my new girlfriend wasn't so belligerent. Maybe if I didn't have to work and meet Claire tonight I could make love to Alice and extract her promise to drop everything by tormenting her at precisely the right moment.

I suppose I could still try that at one or two or whatever time I get back from my late-night assignation (especially as she wants me to wake her up when I get back in and a quick fuck would be the best way of overpowering her fractious tendencies) but pillow talk at that hour is easily forgotten, and I doubt it'd make much difference.

Alice gets up from her desk and walks across the office. I worry she's going to come over to me (God, going out with your boss is like being a teenager embarrassed about being seen with your mother), but instead she starts rooting around on the table. It takes me a moment to realise what she's up to, but when it sinks in I'm horrified. *She promised!* I allow myself a moment of fake surprise before chastising myself. *Come on, Dan, what did you think she'd do? If you knew there was a book of jokes about you sitting on the table across the room you'd be straight over to have a look. Besides, now that you've told her, what difference does it make whether she takes you at your word or checks for herself? Maybe she doesn't believe you and needs to see it with her own eyes before taking further action.* Adrienne's pretending to ignore Alice, but when she sees what's she going for, it's all she can do to stop herself leaping from her chair. She must realise that if Alice chooses she could be out of a job tomorrow, and no matter how blasé she is about working at Quick Kall, I'm certain she doesn't want to get fired. She may have secret money stores, but they won't last long if she's forced to pay her mortgage without regular employment. She looks to Ian for support, but he hasn't realised what's going on, and probably doesn't even know which graffiti-covered folder Alice has picked up.

'You wanker,' Adrienne snarls at me.

'What was that?' Alice asks.

'Nothing.'

'I hope not, because there's going to be some serious consideration in the meeting tomorrow, and certain people might find themselves in very sticky situations.'

'I understand,' she says.

'Good. Now was there something you wanted to say?'

'Yes. That folder is private property.'

Alice slowly and deliberately examines the folder. 'It doesn't look like private property. It's hard to read because of the doodles, but I believe it says Suggestions Book on the label on the front.'

'Yes, that's right, it used to be the Suggestions Book, but no one was writing anything inside it so I asked one of the line managers if I could have it and he said yes.'

'Which line manager?'

'I don't remember.'

'I see. And do you remember the rule about private property?'

'You're supposed to keep it in the cloakroom.'

'So why is it on the desk?'

'Because I lent it to Ian and he returned it to me this morning and I didn't want to stop working, so I thought I'd take it out during my break but then I forgot.'

'Good try,' she says, 'but that folder's been there for weeks.'

'No it hasn't, you're getting it confused with the other files.'

Alice turns. 'Is this true, Ian?'

'Yes, I brought it in this morning.'

'And what's in it?'

'Stories,' he says.

'Stories,' Alice repeats, 'and who, pray tell, is the author of these stories?'

Ian looks at Adrienne. He can see the trap coming. I have to admit I'm impressed by the way Alice is setting him up, and I can certainly see why she's the team leader. OK, so I should really be scared, but there'll be plenty of time for that later.

'Ian?' she prompts.

'Adrienne wanted to show me a story she'd written, but I'm not sure all the ones in the book are by her.'

'Well, isn't that nice,' says Alice, turning over the folder, 'I had no idea Quick Kall was running a Creative Writing class.'

'It's stuff for the office magazine,' Adrienne tells her. 'Ideas and things.'

'I see. Well, perhaps you'd like me to pass it on to the editors?'
She waits. They don't reply. 'I didn't think so. OK, Adrienne, this
is what I'm going to do. I shall ignore your protest that it's private
property.'

'You can't.'

'I can. It looks like it says Suggestions Book on the front and
if anyone asks I shall tell them I was impressed that my team had
come up with so many ideas and thought I should take a look at
what they'd suggested.'

'I'll complain. You're invading my privacy.'

'Really?' she sneers. 'Look, Adrienne, even if they do take you
seriously, which they won't, management's gonna want to know
what you're so eager to hide. And while I still consider you my
friend and would like to see this work out in such a way that you
get to keep your job, I doubt they'll be so understanding.'

She stares at Adrienne.

Adrienne doesn't respond.

'Right, then that's settled.' She tucks the book under her arm.
'Looks like we'll have lots to discuss at our meeting tomorrow.'

Alice walks back to reception. Adrienne sits staring at me,
keeping quiet. I thought her calling me a wanker meant the
silent treatment was over, about to be followed by a new stage
in hostilities. But now she seems to have collected herself, clearly
aware that I find this subtle form of intimidation much more
unnerving.

I feel close to tears. Why am I so weak? Surely the best thing
to do would be to ape Alice's bravado, pretending that going out
with the boss has put me beyond the bounds of their criticism. I
remember talking to Adrienne about how Alice must be upset that
after all those years spent rebelling she's ended up as a combination
of teacher and school swot. Last week I was only too happy to
mock my team leader, and saw her as an incurably tragic figure. I
never imagined I'd end up as her boyfriend.

I break Adrienne's gaze and look over to reception, wanting to
see if Alice has started reading the book. But she's hiding behind

the purple screens. I feel a vague sense of betrayal, cross that she's stirred up this chaos and then returned to her bunker.

Ade's stopped staring and gone back to avoiding my eye. I can't tell for sure, but I think she's receiving telepathic instructions from Ian. Maybe Gordon's getting the signals too. Ian certainly seems to have a firm hold over the actions of the group.

It's coming up to five thirty. I get the impression that the action's over for today but then again I thought that before Alice came across, so maybe I shouldn't relax just yet. Ian usually starts getting restless about now, especially if he's done an early-morning shift, but today he seems entirely focused, unconcerned by the fact that there are no calls coming through. I think back to how I felt after that last appraisal, when I wondered whether Alice calling us the worst team in the office was a motivational exercise. Then that seemed a brilliant piece of team management, stopping us from arguing among ourselves, giving us a common enemy and yet at the same time scaring us with the news that one of us was to be sacked and consequently making everyone eager to prove their own worth. It's part of that whole paradox: what exactly are the qualities of a good team player? And if the focus is on the dynamic of the group, how do you make your employer aware of your own individual ability without seeming disruptive? Now that Alice's actions have turned me into an outsider, I'm beginning to worry that calling us the worst team in the office was only stage one, and despite Alice's assurance that she's going to sack Teri, all that's happened over the last few days has been part of a plan to turn me into the fall guy, so that when she announces that she's changed her mind and decided to get rid of me instead, there'll be no one who wants to argue my side of the case. Once again I remember Cathy's warning, increasingly convinced that she intended me to take it far more seriously than I initially imagined.

There's also the possibility that Alice might want Quick Kall to get rid of me so that I become dependent on her. It worries me that my thoughts about Alice seem incredibly inconsistent. I'm sure that's another after-effect of what happened with Sonia. I knew my ex-girlfriend so well that the only way I could carry on going out with her was to pretend I had no idea what she was thinking. 'You're such a mystery to me,' I'd tell her, watching her smile and wondering how she could believe me when I'd rumbled her lies so many times before. I don't want to understand Alice, but if I don't try I could find myself, once again, in physical danger. The most important thing when analysing relationships is to keep your own ego out of it. The men who live in ignorance of their cuckolding are the ones who can't believe their wives would do such a thing to them. I've already revealed that I think I'm the most attractive man Alice has ever gone out with, but I don't know how serious I am about this boast. At the moment I don't think Alice is that interested in me. I mean, I'm sure she feels good about the relationship and thinks that she's got a great catch, but it's yet to reach obsession-point. When Alice said she wasn't going to sack me, it was mainly because she knew that I was in financial difficulty. It'd be easy for her to get me sacked and tell me not to worry because she could support me. But why would she do this? Three possibilities:

1. Because she doesn't feel we're equals. Losing my job would emasculate me and make me totally reliant on her.

2. Because she doesn't like having her lover in her workplace. She's probably read a thousand articles on how office romances never work, and the call-centre has always been a highly eroticised place for Alice, and she must be worried that she can no longer pop upstairs for a quick fuck on the photocopier (unless it's with me).

3. Because she's jealous of my friendship with Adrienne and Teri. I admit there's little to threaten her at the moment, but you saw how she got when I went for lunch with Teri, and once we're over this difficult period, no doubt we'll go back to flirting with each other, and, given her position, it's inevitable that Alice will feel threatened.

At ten to six, I tell everyone to transfer any late calls to me.

No one says anything, but they do start packing up. Except for Gordon, who always works right up until the last minute. Gordon has a watch you can programme to tell you the time all around the world. Only instead of setting it for different continents, he's synchronised his watch with the clocks in the call-centre, breaks room and cloakroom. (I bet he feels lost when he goes for a dump, stuck in that chronometrical no-man's land.) The clock in the office is three minutes slow, ensuring that the company gets that extra bit of your time. In theory this should work to our advantage in the morning, allowing us to arrive a few minutes late, but of course it doesn't happen that way, as a good employee is supposed to be at his desk at least ten minutes before the working day begins. By the time you get to the breaks room, however, you'll find you've lost eight minutes. That's because the clock there is five minutes fast, prompting you to rush your coffee and hurry back. Of course, once you've been here a while it's easy to work out how long you've really got, but it's surprising how authoritative an inaccurate clock face can seem. And the one in the cloakroom is five minutes slow, making you feel you've finished too early, which – although unlikely to send you rushing back to your desk – ensures that you go home guilty, perhaps subconsciously pushing yourself to get in early the next morning.

The cleaners hover by the doorway, waiting to move in with their hoovers. I shall miss doing the evening shift after tomorrow. I think six to six twenty is the nicest time to be in the office, as you get to see people remembering their humanity, looking up from their work-stations in disbelief that they're allowed to leave. It's always interesting to see how different types respond to hometime. Most of the temps (especially the ones who are only here for a week or so) head straight for the door, putting their walkmans on to deter anyone from waylaying them. The older employees (the ones with families who through some unforeseen disaster or bad planning have found themselves stuck in this shanty-town twenty years too late) take a little longer to leave, mentally preparing themselves for whatever new nightmare awaits them at home.

The rest can be separated into two catagories: those who have a life outside the office and those who don't. The employees with parteners waiting at home gently remove themselves from the office existence, trying to sound sincere as they apologise to the others for having somewhere to go. Everyone else behaves like barflies at closing time, desperately trying to gather up a group to keep the conversation going. These are the ones who stake out the pubs around the Centre, their office clothes doubling as good evening outfits, suits made suitable by undoing the collar and loosening the tie. When I saw these people in pubs when I was a kid I assumed they'd got dressed up to go out, and looked forward to the day when I could traverse the town in a smart sports jacket.

Ian leaves first. I expect Adrienne to follow, but she stays behind, presumably to keep an eye on Teri. Gordon also remains seated, even after it's passed six o'clock. Teri, poor fool, can't help giving herself away, her divided loyalties obvious from the way her eyes keep flipping back and forth between us. Eventually she satisfies her obligation to me by reaching for my hand beneath the desk and giving it a squeeze. Then she stands up, slings her tartan bag over her shoulder, and heads for the cloakroom. Only then do Adrienne and Gordon give up their headsets, leaving me to continue alone.

I watch the old ladies as they slowly filter in, waiting for Cathy. There's no sign of Alice and I wonder if she's left without saying goodbye. Then I notice my light flashing.

Internal call.

'Hello?'

'Hi Dan.'

'Hello Alice.'

'Are you angry at me?'

'Why would I be angry at you? Because you broke your promise?'

'Come on, Dan, don't get all serious.'

'I don't understand, Alice. You know how difficult this is for me. This morning you were being really considerate. Did I do something to piss you off?'

'No.' She swallows. 'I'm sorry, Dan. It's just that I can't take those two seriously. The minute Ade and Ian start giving me dark looks, I feel a real urge to wind them up.'

I don't reply. There's no need. She knows how I feel.

'So don't you want to know what I think?' she asks.

I look up. Cathy comes in.

'Your mum's here,' I tell Alice, 'I'll call you back.'

'No need,' she says, 'I'll come across.'

Her head and body appear above the purple screens. Cathy smiles and comes across, hitching her bag up on her shoulder.

'How was your day, Dan?'

'Terrible. Your daughter's got me in all kinds of trouble.'

'Really?' she laughs. 'Well, you can't say I didn't warn you.'

'Yeah, I want to talk to you about that.'

She's about to say something when she realises I'm serious and goes silent. Good job too, for at that moment Alice approaches behind her.

'All right Mum?'

'Yes thanks, love.' She nods in my direction. 'Is he still doing the nightshift?'

'Until the end of the week.'

Cathy remains silent, absorbing this. I can tell she's looking forward to another intimate chat, and I wonder whether I'm still prepared to be open with her. Most mothers are peculiar in one way or another, but Cathy seems especially odd. I suppose it's not that unusual to find a mum who criticises her child, but I can't help worrying her candour is a trick. I don't know why I don't trust her, but I'm certainly going to watch what I say from now on. Although I suppose it won't hurt to ask her advice, as long as I keep things vague and don't reveal how much Alice has annoyed me.

I look up at the two of them, waiting to see what will happen next. It feels odd to see them both together in the office, and I think back to the time before I knew they were related and Cathy was just a little old lady who loaned me computer games. (Actually,

I might have a quick go on *Hotel Babylon* later on, seeing as it's one of the last chances I'll get to complete it.) Alice doesn't seem that upset by Adrienne's lampoons, although she's still holding the book tightly beneath the arm of her smart blue suit. I want her to tell me what she thinks, but I'm reluctant to bring it up in front of Cathy.

'How am I going to get in tonight?'

'Why?' asks Cathy, turning on me. 'Where are you going?'

'He's got a midnight meeting with a friend of Auntie Brittany,' Alice tells her mum, raising her eyebrows.

'I see. Well, he better have my key then.' She hands it to me and I look at Alice. 'Are you going to be up when I get back?'

'I'll have to be.'

'OK.'

'You ought to set up. It's almost five past.'

'All right, Missy, you're not my team leader.'

'Still, it wouldn't be hard for me to get you in trouble.'

'And it wouldn't be hard for me to kick you out.'

'It would while you haven't got a key,' she laughs, jingling her strawberry fob.

Cathy lets Alice have the last word and takes her place at the Train-times table. I want to kiss my girlfriend but she's already heading out the door. I content myself with staring at the soft heart of her buttocks squeezing together as she walks, amazed at how affectionate I feel towards her. Oh well, let's store up all this emotion for when I get back tonight.

I wait for Cathy to finish setting up, then call across.

'Hi,' she says, 'so what do you want to tell me?'

'Nothing yet.'

'Oh.'

'But I wonder if you could do me a favour.'

'I expect so. What is it?'

'I need to check on something but it's too early for me to go on break. Could you . . .'

'Take your calls? Sure.'

'Thanks. And we'll have a gossip when I get back.'

I go down to the skip and rescue two cans of Felix. I realise John won't be able to eat that much, but I want to make up for any previous neglect, and ensure he doesn't go hungry if I'm indisposed again. I'll do anything to atone for the way I've mistreated him, and would've bought some cat toys from the pet shop if I didn't know he already has the best adventure playground imaginable up there.

I hold a tin in each hand and push them up inside my cuffs, conscious that there are still plenty of employees on their way out. It's clearly too early to start rolling chairs into the toilet – especially with all the guys pausing for a last piss before heading home – but once I've got the tins into the call-centre, it'll be easy to sneak out later.

The lift back up is empty, thank God. Now the old ladies are safely installed, there's no one else to come in. I hold my arms stiffly as I slowly return to my desk, not wanting anything to fall out accidentally. It feels like shop-lifting, and I'm convinced one of the line managers is going to tap me on the back and invite me into their office. Sitting back behind the work-station, I pull open the nearest drawer and let the tins drop inside. Then I call Cathy.

'Who's Moyra?' she asks.

'What?'

'Some woman phoned for you. I asked her if she was the one you're meeting tonight but she just laughed and hung up.'

'Moyra.'

'So who is she? Are you cheating on Alice already?'

'No, of course not. She's some weird girl who works in a record shop and keeps calling to complain about her life.'

'How did you meet her?'

'I haven't met her. She came through on the Magicmix order line and decided she liked my voice. Since then I haven't been able to get rid of her.'

She laughs. 'Oh, I don't think she'll call again.'

'Why not?'

'I got the impression she was a tad annoyed with you.'

'I thought you said she laughed.'

'She did, but it was a bitter little chuckle, and she muttered something peculiar before that.'

'What?'

'I don't know, I couldn't hear. Does it matter? You said you wanted her to stop calling.'

I hope Moyra's OK. After our conversation this morning she must know I'm not avoiding her, but if I was as paranoid as Moyra, I wouldn't relish a conversation with Cathy.

'So what's she done?'

'Alice? Just made things difficult for me.'

'How?'

'The rest of the team aren't talking to me because I'm going out with her.'

'And you hold Alice responsible for their reaction?'

'No, I knew they'd be like that. But instead of letting me handle it my own way, she came over and had a go at everyone. And now she's set up a meeting for tomorrow morning.'

'What would you do?'

'Pardon?'

'You said you wanted to handle it in your own way. What would you do?'

I can hear Cathy breathing into the mouthpiece. I'm amazed how reluctant I am to open up to her. Before I went to the skip I was feeling a little guarded, but still prepared to be persuaded into talking properly. Now she's upset Moyra, I don't want to say anything. I had a whole evening of confessionals lined up, and was looking forward to growing more candid with every subsequent interlocutor. First Cathy, then Moyra, then Claire: a progression of people I thought would be perfect to help me work through my current neuroses. But now I've decided any real conversation will have to wait until after office hours.

'How would I handle it? In a low-key way. I don't feel any anger towards my team-mates.'

'But you must agree they're being a bit childish.'

'That's what Alice says. And OK, they are being stupid. But as long as she can see that, she must realise having a go at them isn't going to help.'

'So what do you want me to do? Make her call off the meeting?'

'No, I don't need you to interfere. I just want to know some more things about Alice and figure you're the best source. When you told me not to trust her, was that just in relation to sex stuff or did you mean more generally?'

'I didn't tell you not to trust her. I told you not to become dependent on her. Why? Has she done something else to upset you?'

'No, not particularly. But she's so *gung ho* about everything. And that makes me feel scared.'

'Why?'

'I don't know. It's not that this job's important to me, and I suppose when it comes down to it I can cope with the friction. But I've lost so much recently, and it would be a relief if I could stop feeling so scared.'

'She's your girlfriend, Dan. She won't just get rid of you overnight.'

'That's not what you said the other day.'

'I was just telling you to be careful, that's all. I didn't intend to make you feel paranoid.'

'OK, I'm sorry.'

'Forget about it. Was there anything else?'

'No. Thanks.'

'OK. Talk to you later. Bye.'

She cuts me off and I check my watch. Six thirty. Probably still a little early to begin a full-scale cat hunt, but soon, John, soon. First break, I promise. It doesn't seem as much fun being alone at my desk now Cathy is no longer an anonymous old lady.

She probably watched me just as much then as she does now, but somehow it didn't seem so restrictive before. I think again about playing *Hotel Babylon*, then remember I've left the disk in my rucksack at Alice's. Shit, I don't even have Dad's minutes to read. I click through to the secret files and load up Patience, the last refuge of the lonely operator.

I wish Moyra would call back.

At seven o'clock, I close down my card game and hide the two cans of Felix back up my sleeves. Then I go through to the toilet and leave them on the cubicle floor by the bowl, before taking a chair from Conference Room 2. I realise Cathy's seen me rolling chairs from the call-centre into the corridor before, but my guess is that so far she hasn't given it much thought and I don't want to give her a visual prompt. So I keep my back covering the door's glass section as I sneak the chair into the gents. Then I go through my usual routine of gathering toilet rolls from each of the other cubicles and wedging one against each wheel. After a quick steadiness test, I step up onto the chair.

I gently raise the first ceiling tile, reaching for his bowl and then remembering that it's long gone. My fingertips brush against small solid pellets, which could equally be dried food or dried faeces. It'd be easy to tell by giving one a squeeze and smelling my fingertips, but I'm feeling squeamish and decide to remain ignorant of the lump's substance.

Remembering my previous accidents in this cubicle, I'm not sure if it's safe to climb up onto the arms of the chair. I suppose I could just dump the food and wait to see if he's attracted by the smell, but John's always been an awkward animal and is unlikely to appear that easily. No, I need to get my head up above the tiles, and have a proper look around that hidden, dusty space.

Fuck it. I step up onto the arms, trying to keep my weight evenly balanced. I remove the tile completely, lifting it up and pushing it back inside the ceiling. But I've forgotten how dark it is up there, and without a torch I can hardly see anything. I keep looking anyway, scared in case his furry body comes thundering out of the darkness and into my face.

But . . . nothing.

I want to call him but I'm worried about the acoustics and fear my voice might carry through to the office. I suppose it is a big space. The fact that John hasn't immediately appeared doesn't mean anything. This will sound stupid, but when I brought John here I assumed I was doing him a favour. I've always had a kinship with cats, feeling envious of the way they pay no heed to human rules, escaping the house every night and heading out to write their own stories. But John seemed to have nowhere to go: he was a cat without an adventure. So it was only natural to let him share mine. Only now I realise that all I've really done is subject him to a week of deprivation. The lack of light probably isn't a problem, but failing to keep him fed and watered is a genuine act of cat cruelty.

I can't decide what to do with John when I get him down from the ceiling. This morning I considered taking him back to the metal staircase outside my old home, but now I feel he's earned the right to the same privileges I enjoy. I'm not sure I can sensibly explain to Alice how I came by the cat, but perhaps if I don't tell the truth she might let me keep him. There's no sign of any family pets in the Hargreaves household, but unless there's any unknown allergies I expect they'll be as welcoming to him as they were to me.

I close my eyes and concentrate on the sounds above the ceiling. There are lots of whirring and the faint murmur of old ladies talking, but nothing that could be identified as an animal noise. When I first put John up there, i felt terrified he might give himself away by meowing too much. Now I'd give anything to hear his plantive cry.

I get back down and pick up the two tins. I hate remaining in suspense like this, but I really don't know what else to do. I suppose the best thing is to dump the Felix up there and then wait to see if it's been eaten tomorrow. If it hasn't, I guess I've got no choice but to get up there and start searching. Will the tiles hold me?

I remember in *The Breakfast Club* there was a scene where Judd Nelson was crawling above a set of tiles much like these. Sure he fell through when he reached the library, but I'm sure that was only to serve the story, and he was back up there a few scenes later. I spend the majority of my days staring at the ceiling and yet I'm still not sure exactly how it's structured. I wonder if the plastic lattice is put in place first and then the tiles dropped in or whether the holding pieces go in around each square. I think I'll be all right as long as I keep my weight evenly distributed and move very slowly.

I empty both cans above the ceiling and drop down onto the floor. Then I replace the toilet rolls and trundle the chair back out to Conference Room 2.

It's a boring evening. Moyra doesn't call back, and I have nothing to read. The only thing that keeps me awake is thinking about my midnight meeting which, however worrying it seemed before, has now become the most important event in my life. Fucking Alice seems to have gone a long way towards banishing my sexual snobbery, and I feel like no new conquest is beneath me. Last Friday I was a timid celibate, nervous even about accepting a lift on the back of Marilyn's motorbike. Tonight I've been picturing all kinds of erotic scenarios, from a one-on-one with Claire to a much more elaborate fantasy where she takes me to a dungeon with the rest of Dad's harlots arranged in various supplicant positions and she advises me how to service them.

Cathy and the other operators leave at ten thirty. When I was sleeping in the office, I fooled myself into thinking that I was on duty until I bedded down, but the truth is after everyone else goes there's no reason for me to be here. I suppose I really ought to log off and spend the next hour or so wandering around the city streets. It just feels so much nicer in here. It's stupid, but I've really started thinking of the call-centre as my private space. I bet if some enterprising housing company took some of the disused office complexes that stand in the centre of every city and turned them into upmarket dormitories, they'd clean up. I have so many great business ideas.

I close down my computer and leave the call-centre. I take the lift to the back exit and walk through the rear car park. I haven't eaten since lunchtime and decide to get a hamburger. I won't have to worry about nutrition now Cathy's taking care of my meals, so the odd bit of fast food doesn't matter at all. The usual Thursday crowd is out in force, and there's already a queue spilling out of the burger place. It's odd how this night has such a different atmosphere to the rest of the week. It's probably easily explained by the proliferation of student/alternative nights on offer every Friday, but I prefer to look for a historical explanation. Perhaps Thursdays have always been a truce-time in the city, a mild night before the madness of the weekend. Maybe it was the day before ships docked in the port, an evening for Bristolians to enjoy their streets before the onslaught of new debauchery.

I order my hamburger and the guy behind the till gives me my ticket. Then I stand by the window and watch the cars, wondering what to do next. A car pulls up outside the shop and two women get out. They both look about my age, one with long brown hair and a cream top, the other blonde and wearing blue jeans. I feel vaguely sad watching them, distanced by their obvious light-heartedness and wishing I still had a life that would allow me to feel carefree. I should be out there with them, not on my way to visit a woman probably twice my age. I can't tell just from looking at them whether they're students or work in the city, but I bet they aren't any more socially mobile than me. I used to feel my lack of control over my life was cool. Now it just seems stupid.

'Two-oh-four,' the burger guy announces.

I turn round.

'Two-oh-four,' he repeats, 'burger and chips.'

'Right, thanks,' I say, taking the yellow plastic box.

I sit on a bench by the docks and eat my burger. It's coming up to eleven and I decide to go straight over to The Frog and Toad. The pub has two entrances, one on Frogmore Street (hence the name), the other on Park Street. The latter is less heavily guarded and it's there I head for now, not up to facing an interrogation. The one man standing outside the pub lets me slip through and I go up to the bar for a pint. There seems to be some sort of disco on tonight, although I can't see the DJ booth and there's hardly anyone dancing. That's not to say the place isn't packed, and I worry Claire won't be able to find me. But then I remember that the first time we talked about it she suggested meeting outside.

So I have a few drinks to take me up to midnight and then stand outside in Frogmore Street.

18

Claire arrives on time. I didn't have a very exact memory of her from our first meeting, and my mental picture was constructed mainly from Dad's minutes. So when she first approaches I'm not sure it's her, and have to wait until she says, 'Hi Dan. Have you been waiting long?'

'No, I got here early. There's been some changes in my lifestyle.'

'So I heard,' she says. 'I understand you're now living with Alice and Cathy.'

'How did you know that?'

She laughs. 'Come on, Danny. Don't waste breath with questions you already know the answer to.'

'I'm not. I thought Cathy didn't talk to Brittany.'

'She doesn't. Our information comes from a different source.'

'Who then? Alice?'

'Wrong again. Would it help your mental process if I told you we now have a little keepsake to remind us of you?'

'Not really. Is it something I gave to someone?'

'No, I wouldn't say that. Anyway, I'll leave you to figure it out. We have much more important business to attend to.'

'OK,' I say, puzzled, 'shall we go back into the pub?'

She wrinkles her nose. 'I didn't think there'd be a disco tonight. It's too noisy to talk properly.'

'Where then?'

'Shall we go for a walk?'

'OK.'

'Or we could go to my place.'

'Would that be OK?'

'Of course. Why?'

'You said it wasn't a good idea before.'

'When?'

'When I called you.'

'Oh, I don't remember why I said that. I was probably just being weird. You mustn't take me too seriously.'

She holds my gaze. Claire has a very pretty face, even though individually her features are quite odd. Her nose is too big and pudgy, with two completely round nostrils. Her clear blue eyes are disguised by some strange muscle that jerks the skin around them. It's almost as if she's cross-eyed, although I'm fairly sure it's only an optical illusion and not a genuine defect. Her lips are normal, except for a twist at the side and a pull at the middle which makes them seem too flat. Still, taken as a whole, her face looks quite lovely, and I wonder why I didn't pay her more attention before.

'It's this way,' she says and starts walking. We go round the back of the Hippodrome and out into the Centre. I follow just behind Claire, wondering if she's dressed up specially for meeting me. She looks at least ten years younger than Brittany and Valerie, and much closer to Marilyn in dress and looks. She's wearing cream trousers and black thin-strapped sandals with a raised heel. Her blonde hair is loose and the fringe flops over her eyes. Her top is black and she's wearing a light-blue jacket.

She heads straight out into the road. The traffic is crazy at this time of night, and I have to move quickly to stay safe behind her. We get to the other side and she carries on down Baldwin Street. She stops at a building about halfway along with an ornate entrance. It looks more like a solicitor's offices than a place where someone might live. Claire unlocks the door and we walk inside.

'Do you own all this?' I ask.

She laughs. 'Nah, I just rent a room on the fourth floor. Why, do you like it?'

'I love it. I wish I lived in somewhere like this.'

'That's very kind of you. But I know you're only being nice. It's ridiculous to be my age and living in a one-room flat.'

'I don't think I'll ever earn enough to own anything bigger than a one-room place.'

'You'll be surprised at how weird things get. Unless you're the most cautious man in the world, you'll find it fluctuates your whole life. One minute you'll have a mansion, the next you'll be back on the streets. I've only just got myself out of temporary housing.'

'Yeah, it's like my dad. He had a lot of setbacks.' I stop, look at her and laugh. 'I'm sorry. I keep forgetting you know him. We're a right pair of amnesiacs tonight.'

She smiles. 'Maybe there's a reason for that.'

'What d'you mean?'

'I don't know. Are you susceptible to those sorts of things?'

'What sort of things?'

'Coincidences, mental tricks, Freudian slips.'

'Freudian clit.'

'What?'

'There's a woman at work who says Freudian clit instead of Freudian slip. That's pretty typical of her sense of humour.'

'Who's that?'

'Adrienne.' I look at her. 'I suppose you know all about her as well.'

She doesn't reply. 'Shall we go up?'

'OK.'

I walk towards the spiral staircase. She follows. I look over my shoulder. 'You know, I really didn't know about the group. I thought Dad stayed at home when I went out.'

'Yeah, Steve's a very complex individual. But to be honest, part of the buzz about that group was the secrecy. I don't think any of us talked about it that much.'

'You make it sound like it's over. Don't you meet any more?'

'We've met a couple of times, but they've been kind of emergency meetings. It's hard to know what to do without Steve. Most of us have been into the hospital to get his advice, but we've had to go individually or in pairs. The nurses won't let us all go in together.'

'I think they started off thinking Dad's some kind of rabid womaniser. They thought he was going to bed with all of you. Is it this floor?'

'Yeah. Straight ahead.'

I stop and wait while Claire unlocks the door. She lets me into her room and I say, 'I thought you said you only had one room.'

'It *is* only one room. It just has a division down the middle. There's only a bed back there. The kitchen and bathroom are shared between everyone on this floor. To be honest, I think it probably began as student accommodation. Would you like a drink?'

'I'd love one.'

'What would you like? I've got beer.'

'Great.'

She smiles. 'Or you could help me finish off a bottle of whisky.'

'OK.'

'Good.' She goes out into the corridor. I take a moment to check out Claire's decoration. I'm finding it hard to place her, both culturally and socially. The only thing I've got so far is the psychological peg that she's a two-time violence victim and serial support-group junkie. My appraisal is made more complicated by the fact that it seems a characteristic of everyone in Bristol — myself included — that we like to avoid any of the more obvious fads that sweep through the other big cities. There's an almost European discernment about the stuff we let through, and while this might make us fascinating individuals, it doesn't help when you're trying to come up with a thumbnail sketch of someone.

Claire returns with the drinks. She hands me mine and we both sit together on a blue futon.

'So how are you getting on with Alice?'

'OK. It feels strange being in her house.'

'I bet.' She puts her glass on the coffee table and pulls her legs up underneath her. 'I hope you don't think I'm prying, but I must ask. What was it like living in Quick Kall?'

I look at her. 'OK. I didn't do it for long.'

'Sure. But wasn't it odd staying in the same place all the time?'

'Not really. It's not that different from people who work from home.'

'I suppose not. But it sounds a lot more exciting. I wish I had the guts to do something like that.'

I laugh. 'It's not really a question of guts.'

'Of course it is. Striking out on your own like that. It shows real spirit and ingenuity. I bet if Alice did tell her bosses they'd be more impressed than angry.'

'She's not going to, is she?'

'No, relax, of course not. But I am really impressed. People think these business mavericks we hear so much about are blessed with extraordinary gifts. But they're not. They're just like you. It's just that they're using their talents in an environment which rewards their recklessness, and where survival is no longer an issue. I mean, your father's resourceful, but I doubt he'd show the brilliance of intellect you've displayed.'

'Does Dad know I moved out of our room?'

She nods. 'But don't worry, he's not angry. Just a little concerned about what's happened to his stuff.'

'Tell him I've got the minutes and all the disks. I had to leave the electrical equipment but I'm going back for it.'

'Why don't you tell him?'

'What?'

'Your dad could really do with a visit from you, Dan. A lot of strange things have gone on in Steve's head since he went into hospital. He's experiencing, I don't know, a kind of spiritual rebirth.'

'Dad's found religion?'

'No,' she smiles, 'nothing like that. But he's come to terms with himself. I know it's silly of me to tell you stuff about your own family, but your dad's never really been an honest man. You must know that from the way he managed to keep so much of his life secret from you.'

'Did he say why he didn't tell me about the group?'

'You already know the answer to that. He was ashamed. Even though he's been going to them all his life, Steve's never really come to terms with the fact that he needs a support group, and he's always been embarrassed by the way you seem much stronger than him. You only have to look at what's happened over the last couple of weeks to see why he's likely to feel intimidated by you. He had an accident, which of course he blames himself for, and because of that he can't help you with the rent. But you tell him it'll be OK, and when it turns out that it's not OK, instead of telling anyone, you fix things yourself, in a really ingenious way.'

'But it wasn't like that.'

'What do you mean?'

'The money wasn't the only reason I moved into Quick Kall.'

'Why then?'

'Lots of reasons. Our landlord arranged for someone else to move in and pay Dad's share of the rent and I didn't like him. And there was also something I read in the minutes.'

'What?'

'That Dad wanted to kill me.'

She laughs. 'Oh, that. It's funny, Steve was worried about how you'd react to all sorts of stuff in the minutes, but that never concerned him. He said that you two had an intellectual freedom whenever you talked about anything serious. He said that kind of conversational ease was one of the things he valued most about your relationship.'

'We never talked about him wanting to kill me.'

'He doesn't want to kill you,' she grins, 'at least no more than any father wants to kill his son. I can't believe you took him seriously.'

I'm not sure I can trust this woman. I thought the fact that she'd been battered by her husband would make her sensitive to threats of violence, but that's clearly not the case. OK, what she says fits with Dad's character: he's never been the type to let common sense get in the way of a good argument. But I hardly think he was voicing the hidden desires of every father.

'Was that what you wanted to talk to me about?'

'It wasn't just that.'

'OK, what else is worrying you?'

'I don't know if I should say.'

She looks at me. 'I don't mean to belittle your concerns. I can see why you were scared. I would be too if I knew my parents were saying stuff like that about me. But you must've understood from the rest of the minutes that what people say in the group isn't necessarily what they think. When I had an analyst, he told me that I should think of our sessions in the same way I might think of a diary. When loved ones read what we've written in our diaries, they inevitably get upset, but that's only because they think what's recorded there is the truth. This is partly due to the power of the written word, but also because when we write diaries, we're following a formula that, whether we realise it or not, distorts our recollections. It's quite a complex process, and even the most self-aware individuals don't fully understand what they're doing. Because we believe a diary is a place where we should be honest, we write down all the thoughts we've been unable to reveal in public. As social convention forbids us from offending others, the unspoken observations tend towards the negative. As we write we feel liberated, because we're removing the mask of dishonesty we're forced to assume in our day-to-day existence. But these negative thoughts are no closer to the truth than the nice things we've said in public. The real us is a composite of the public and private sides. You know, ego and id. When your dad tells the group he wants to kill you, he's simply acting out a role, trying a different version of himself than the one he shares with the world. Being a father is a very complicated business.'

'Have you ever had sex with my dad?'

'What? No. Is that what you want to talk about?'

'No, it's not that. I just wondered how you knew him so well.'

'I wouldn't say I knew Steve. I wouldn't say any of us did.'

'What about the stuff you said in the group? Were those your true feelings, or were you just playing a role?'

'That depends. Which things are you talking about?'

'The violence. The husbands who beat you up.'

'That was true.'

'And what about now? Are you still in a violent relationship?'

'I'm not in any relationship.'

'And how do you feel about violent men?'

'That depends. In what context?'

'Do you feel you have a special insight into the way they think? Or do you just hate them all?'

'I don't hate anyone. But I sense you're testing me. Is it important how I answer this question?'

'Yeah. But only because I don't want to get into certain things if they're going to upset you. It's not that I'm worried about being judged.'

'OK, Dan, Lucy told you before that it's important that you should think of us as friends, and I want you to know that the same rules apply to this conversation as to everything that goes on in the group. Except that you're only talking to one person instead of eight, and this conversation will remain entirely confidential, and the only record of what's been said will be in our memories.'

The way she says this immediately makes me suspicious. I hadn't asked her if we were being recorded, and there's no reason why she should bring this up. Unless, of course, she's (consciously or not) giving me a clue. After all, why else would she be so keen to get me back here? I look round the room for hiding places, wondering if this conversation is being preserved on video or audiotape.

Claire notices my agitation and asks, 'What's wrong?'

'Why did you say that?'

'What?'

'About there being a record.'

'Because we were talking about the minutes.'

'But you were very specific. This is being recorded, isn't it? That's what Lucy meant when she said I shouldn't think of you as a group, just eight individuals I happened to meet at the same time. If I talk to one of you, I'm talking to all the others, right?'

'No, Dan, of course not. This is one on one.'

'I'm sorry, Claire, I wanted to trust you, but I can't cope with stuff I tell you in confidence being recorded and studied later. I'd better go. Do you have a cab number I can call?'

'Come on, Dan, there's no video, I promise.'

'I don't believe you.'

'Look, I'll prove it. Let's go to the bathroom.'

'What?'

'If you think I'm taping you, let's go to the bathroom. Or do you think I've got a camera set up there as well? Perhaps you think I like spying on my neighbours while they wash.'

'I'm not paranoid, Claire.'

'Then come with me.'

I look at her. 'OK.'

We go across the hallway to the bathroom. She bolts the door behind us and starts undressing.

'What are you doing?' I ask, panicked.

'Well, I might be wearing a wire. You want to check that, don't you?'

'I don't think you're wearing a wire.'

'Why not? Why would that be any more far-fetched than secret cameras?'

She looks at me, waiting for an answer. While she waits, she reaches behind her back and unclasps her black bra. She pulls it down over her arms and lets it drop onto the floor. I stare at her breasts, unable to speak.

'Turn on the taps, Dan.'

I do as she instructs, sitting on the side of the tub as I try to take in the situation. Claire is unbuckling the first of her sandals, her breasts squeezing softly together as she discards the shoe. I keep thinking I should do the honourable thing and tell her to stop, but I'm transfixed by her body and the fact that simply by keeping silent I can see this woman naked robs me of my voice.

She takes off the other shoe and unzips her cream trousers. She's wearing black knickers with a thin satin strip at the front. Claire holds my gaze as she pulls them down over her thighs. I want to make some kind of devotional gesture, but it seems inappropriate so I just keep staring. Her pubic hair is dark brown, getting lighter as it spreads outwards. She climbs into the tub.

'See, no wire.'

I laugh, and she grins at me. Her smile is so open and innocent that all the tension dissipates and I decide it'd be best to join her in the bath. She smirks when I start unbuttoning my shirt and says, 'Can you put a little more cold in? It's not good for girls to have very hot baths.'

I ease the cold tap round and stand up to undress. I leave my watch on the sink's soap-plate, taking a quick peek at the time and hoping Alice isn't waiting up for me. I turn round while I finish undressing and then slip in at the tap end.

'OK,' she says as I slide my legs round the outside of hers, 'so now can we talk?'

'I guess so. But I'm still scared you're not going to like what I'm going to say.'

'I understand your nervousness, Dan, but sooner or later you're gonna have to trust someone. And I think the fact that I'm sharing a bath with you ought to count for something.'

'It's not that I don't trust you.'

'What is it then?'

'I just feel so ashamed.'

She reaches for my hand. 'Dan, these feelings are perfectly normal. But as soon as you talk to me, you'll find they disappear. Honestly, it'll make you feel so much better.'

We stare at each other.

'Fuck, forget it, you're right. I'll tell you my story and if you hate me, then so be it.'

She smiles. 'Good.'

'I guess it's fairly obvious that I don't often get beautiful women offering to wash with me.'

'I don't know. I would've thought you'd have had lots of women.'

'Not really. I've had a few false starts here and there, but only one relationship that amounted to anything. Her name was Sonia and I met her when I was twenty-one. She was nineteen when we started going out and we stayed together for nine months. You'll find this hard to believe by the end of what I've got to tell you, but initially she was the one who pursued me. Did you go to university?'

'Yes.'

I nod. 'Well, I didn't, I went straight into work as soon as I was old enough, and although I've never regretted that decision, I didn't realise quite how isolated it'd make me feel. I wasn't one of these people who think that university is a waste of time and want to start earning immediately, I'm just lazy and thought that as it was inevitable that I'd end up in a low-grade profession sooner or later, I might as well face up to that reality straight away. I've seen a lot of people pass through Quick Kall, from the sort of individuals who'd clearly be better off in a mental institution to graduates with Phds, and although most people would say that working in a call-centre is only something you'd do if you were incapable of getting a job elsewhere, I think it's the perfect employment for anyone who understands that all work is a stupid, cynical transaction, and doesn't want to bother with the bullshit of pretending what you do to make money means anything.'

'Why does this make you so angry, Dan? Is it something you don't get chance to talk about?'

'I'm sorry, I know I'm going on, and this is only really a preamble to my story. I just wanted to communicate the frustration I was feeling around the time I met Sonia.'

'I understand. Feeling that no one was interested in me was the main reason I started going to support groups.'

Claire puts her arm around her left leg and pulls it up out of the water. Then she balances her chin on her knee and waits for me to continue.

'OK, I know there are lots of places for office people to go clubbing, and although I find those sort of women attractive, there were times when I saw students going out in groups and felt that I wanted to join them. So I started going to the Bierkeller on Thursday nights. I went on my own, and nothing ever happened. I'd see girls I fancied, but felt too nervous to chat them up. Occasionally I might get into a conversation by the bar or the toilets, but even though I sensed that the girls would be happy to come home with me, I didn't have the courage to make a move. Then just as I was starting to get fed up of going out on my own and considering limiting my social life to The Pentangle, Sonia came over and started chatting to me. It was obvious she was really drunk, even though it was only nine o'clock, and I thought I should make my excuses and leave. Although she looked quite old, I knew appearances can be deceptive and had no interest in going to bed with someone underage.

'She wasn't making much sense and kept mumbling about some course she was taking at university. She asked me if I knew anything about Greek tragedy and I just laughed at her, dismissing her as some boring middle-class girl too dopey to get into Oxbridge and now desperate to prove her intellect even when pissed. She asked me why I was laughing at her and I said, "Don't you realise, you silly little girl, I'm not a student. Find one of your own kind to impress with your erudition."

'It was the way Sonia responded to my spiteful outburst that made me interested in her. Most girls, particularly of the class I imagined Sonia belonged to, would've done one of two things. Either they would've simply walked off, or if they were a little bit more confident, they'd have called my bluff and asked me what sort of books I liked. But Sonia stopped swaying, looked me straight in the eye and said, "Oh good."

'I asked her what she was thinking at this moment loads of times later in the relationship, but she claimed she was too pissed to remember anything and didn't even realise she'd picked me up until we'd left the club and we were walking to her place together. Just before we set off she asked me if we could go to my house, but I made some excuse and she said if I didn't mind student accommodation there was always her place. I told her that was fine and asked if she was OK to make it home. She laughed and told me she'd been in much worse states than this. She said once we got back she'd have a quick puke and a few slices of toast and she'd be set up for the evening.

'We fucked three times that evening. Each time was more aggressive, as if we were both testing how far the other was prepared to go. It was only normal sex, no bondage or sodomy, in fact I think we stayed in the missionary position the first two times. But she did all that stuff most people don't really go for, even though it's relatively innocent. Girl stuff, scratching and spitting, making me put my fingers around her throat. It's odd how that sort of thing can make sex seem really exhilarating, much more so than all that soft-caresses and scented-candles shit. She chewed almost all the way through my bottom lip, and left deep red gashes down my back. The spitting she didn't really start until she was on top, but it wasn't just gentle froth, she was really hawking up on my face. Maybe if I'd been making love every night it wouldn't have seemed so exciting, but I hadn't been with a woman in ages, and couldn't help getting swept away.

'After the third time she fell asleep literally the second she came, dropping her head on my chest as if she'd suddenly been zapped with a stun gun. I let her lie on me and waited while my cock shrunk back and slid out of her. We hadn't used a condom and it felt lovely to have all that slippery mess dripping out on me. God, I didn't mean to be so graphic.'

'That's OK,' she smiles, 'I like hearing about other people's sex lives.'

'I'm sorry about that too,' I say, nodding down at my stiff cock, 'it's the water.'

'Not just the water, I hope,' she giggles, 'you're allowed to find me attractive.'

'Do you mind if I put a little more hot in? It's getting a bit chilly down this end.'

'Feel free. But be careful not to burn yourself.'

'No, I'll move.' I sit up on the side of the bath while I turn on the hot tap. I'm amazed at how easily Claire's managed to make me feel totally uninhibited. Feeling comfortable naked isn't the problem: I've always been at ease with my body. But being able to talk about Sonia amazes me. After the court case I thought I'd never tell anyone my story again. I stop the water and slide back into the bath.

'Anyway, I had to tell you how much I liked the sex in order for you to understand my subsequent actions. I was woken the next morning by a heavy blow to the head, followed by a series of slaps in quick succession. Too dazed to respond, I waited for her hands to stop stinging me before attempting to open my eyes. Sonia was sitting over me wearing a man's purple muscle vest. Her eyes were red and her open palm was raised as if she was about to slap me again. Then she called me a cunt and muttered something too softly for me to hear. She glared at me and when I didn't respond she screamed, "I was a fucking virgin, you cunt." I had no idea how to answer her and to be honest I did feel guilty. Part of me knew the previous night was too good to be true and I suppose I'd secretly been anticipating this. So I just told her I was sorry it was me, and although I wasn't a virgin I hadn't slept with many other people and the night we'd spent together had been really special to me.'

'You sweetie,' says Claire, smiling. 'How did she respond?'

'She calmed down, but went into a sulk and it was clear she wanted me to leave. So I got dressed and disappeared, hoping my memory of the evening was still intact.'

'What d'you mean?'

I look at her. 'The connection between sex and memory seems really weird. I guess I must've made love to Sonia about three hundred times when we were together, but I can only remember, at most, about a dozen occasions. As it turned out, that night is one of my most vivid memories. Anyway, you know from what I've told you already that that night wasn't the last time I saw Sonia, so I won't make a big mystery about how we got back together, but a few details are important. For the next couple of days I was really depressed, thinking I'd never be able to go back to the Bierkeller again. But by the time Thursday came round I'd decided it was stupid to let Sonia spoil my social life and headed back to the club. I felt a bit nervous about bumping into her, but when it happened she wasn't anything like she'd been the week before. She came up behind me while I was queuing at the bar, wrapped her arms around my middle and kissed the back of my neck.

'"I'm sorry," she told me, and offered to pay for my drink. I accepted Sonia's charity and let her drag me off into a dark corner for a quiet word. But before I'd said anything she was passionately kissing me again, using her knee to pry open my legs and rubbing at my cock and balls. Although I knew this was a stupid situation and had realised by now that she must have some sort of mental problem, I went home with Sonia once again and enjoyed the same violent love-making we'd shared the week before. This time when we finished fucking she didn't fall asleep but got all lovey-dovey, playing with my nipples and asking if spending two nights together meant we were going steady.

'I had horrible dreams all night long, my subconscious unable to free itself from the suspicion that the morning would begin with another physical attack. But when she woke me this time it was with breakfast in bed, albeit of a pretty pathetic nature. I felt funny about entering a relationship, especially as I had little to offer and my home life was in disarray, but nevertheless I was willing to give it a go.

'My biggest worry was the obvious imbalance in the relationship. Work does a lot to deaden your emotions, but I knew that once I'd got involved with Sonia, I'd find it hard to give her up. She'd told me she didn't have many friends at university, but the fact remained that as soon as she decided she didn't want to date me any more, there'd be plenty of people to help her get over our relationship. Two days before Dad disappeared, I asked him what I should do. He told me all love was a risk, and there was no shame in getting my heart broken. But he also said it was a mistake to let any woman know how you really feel, and I should make sure I could trust Sonia before I started pouring my heart out to her. This seemed pretty sensible advice, so I cautiously agreed to go out with her.

'I guess you already know all about Dad's disappearance, but from what I've read so far Dad seems fairly self-pitying in the minutes, so I doubt he had much understanding about what it was like for me when he went off with Mum's winnings. Discovering Dad's dishonesty didn't shock me, but I couldn't believe he'd put me in that situation. He knew my mum had a vicious temper and must've known how she'd react when I told her what he'd done. Only a couple of weeks after I'd been beaten up by Sonia, I had to cope with Mum screaming at me for hours on end and threatening me with a knife. She was convinced I was in on Dad's scam and any maternal feelings were destroyed by her anger at being swindled. Money had long since replaced love as the motivating force in my family, and she saw Dad's escape as the ultimate betrayal. She didn't believe I was as surprised as she was, and she ran off with Doug without even saying goodbye.'

'Doug?'

'Douglas Smart, the detective she hired to track down Dad.'

'Right.'

'And when Dad came back and made me take him in, I could hardly sleep at night for fear that Mum might come back for some sort of retribution.'

She looks at me. 'Do you think your mum had anything to do with Steve's accident?'

'I did for a while, but as awful as this sounds, I think if it was Mum she'd have finished off the job. There doesn't seem any point in just having someone run over.'

'Unless it was a warning.'

'I suppose so, but I think she'd have left more clues. Mum tends to be pretty direct. I also think something would've happened to me by now.'

'Are you scared, Dan?'

'Yeah, but mainly about what Alice is going to do to me when I come home at the crack of dawn.'

'I'm sorry, I've led you astray. Go back to telling me about Sonia.'

'OK. In spite of Dad's warning, I started confiding in Sonia almost straight away. I'd been terrified about fitting in with her friends, knowing that although the differences in our ages was negligible, I didn't really know anything about films or football or economics or whatever it is students talk about. The divide between the university and the town wasn't as big in Bristol as it was in other cities, but I knew her friends would still think it weird that she was dating a guy like me. But Sonia seemed happy to separate herself from her social circle and didn't make me go to student-union events or anything like that. The only university-related thing she did keep up was working nights on the linkline, and early on she arranged for me to take over the telephone beside her. I started off feeling envious that she was as interested in the lives of these suicidal strangers as she was in me, but it didn't take me long to become just as addicted to unknown voices. I was also worried that our relationship might become unbalanced by the way I'd confided in her much more than she had in me, but I could tell from her behaviour that she was just as disturbed as I was, if not more so, and decided if she wasn't ready to talk openly, there was no harm in waiting. I'm not the most sensitive of men, but one thing I had realised was that it'd be a mistake to force Sonia into speaking. I'd just be there for her, offering support she could take or leave.

'I also felt anxious about the sex. I knew that despite the statistics, lots of good-looking girls were virgins when they went to university, and it was perfectly plausible that I'd been her first without realising it, but nevertheless there'd been something about her anger after our first time which didn't seem real. Our sex life also stabilised really quickly, which seemed surprising if she wasn't used to fucking. This sounds crude, but what I mean is, if you've been in a relationship before, once you've got over those initial anxieties you soon relax into a pattern of love-making that's not all that different from what you had with other partners. I know the fact that she was really good at blowjobs and handjobs doesn't mean anything, in fact, her expertise in these areas backed up her claim that she was saving herself. Anyway, it was just a gut feeling.'

'But the sex was good?'

'It was OK, but nowhere near as exciting as those first two times. I knew she was holding back in bed just as much as she was about talking about herself. And although I could wait for her to reveal her secrets, I began to notice that there was something contemptuous about her attitude towards me in bed. She didn't say anything, but I felt a judgement in her silence and decided it was time to force an argument. I made up all kinds of peculiar motivations and assigned them to her, wanting to prompt Sonia into revealing her true feelings. And although she managed to keep calm for an amazing length of time, my persistence paid off. She told me that while she was happy about not seeing her friends, she desperately missed drinking.

'At first, I thought this was funny. I'd been worried about all kinds of potential problems, and hearing that everything could be resolved by a few nights in the pub came as a great relief. But then I remembered her drunken approach on that first night in the Bierkeller and started to get paranoid. What if getting drunk was really a euphemism for other desires, like casual sex or time away from me? So I asked if she wanted to get drunk alone or with other people. "No," she told me, "I want to get drunk with you." We'd been going out for about three months when she told me this and although initially I felt hurt, wondering if there was something about my company she couldn't tolerate without drink, I realised that most of the time we'd spent together had either been spent with me going on about my terrible life, or us having sex. I've never really been a big drinker, and I suppose the puritan in me was offended by her *need* for alcohol, but I also knew I was over-reacting. So the next Friday we headed down to the off-licence and loaded up on drink. I only really drink lager, but Sonia bought all kinds of things, mainly liquor in little bottles, but also a couple of litres of cheap wine. I couldn't believe she was going to drink all that in one night and wanted to ask her about it, but worried I would sound like I was criticising her.

'So we went back to her room and she got utterly wrecked. I tried to keep up, but the volume I needed to consume to match her mix of spirits was beyond me. So I gave up and just watched the change in her character. I realise this makes me sound prudish and stupid, but I was really intimidated by the way she started treating me. It wasn't that she became particularly lascivious, it was more psychosexual. She kept saying she was never going to have sex with me again, but at the same time pulling up her skirt like a little girl and staring me straight in the eye. I tried to reason with her . . . God, this sounds so pathetic . . . asking Sonia what I'd done to stop her wanting me. "I still want you," she told me, "I'm just not going to do it any more." I knew I should leave, but also that if I did it'd be over between us. Eventually, and I knew I was taking a risk, I decided to force her.

'She really fought me, biting and scratching and spitting just like she'd done the first time. There was real anger in her eyes and I realised she'd quite clearly said no and what I was doing could be construed as date rape or whatever, but something convinced me I was doing what she wanted. I tore her clothes and she screamed and slapped me and I carried on, assuming this was all the act of an adolescent girl who'd seen *Blue Velvet* at an impressionable age. I told myself if she was dry inside I'd stop, but to be honest now I'd made this gamble I knew the only way things would be all right would be if I made her come.'

I stop and stare at Claire, feeling nervous. Now I'm getting into this, her nudity worries me. I'm also embarrassed that I still have an erection, not wanting Claire to think that talking about what I did to Sonia turns me on. I stare at a small pink scar curving up over her tummy, wondering which of her husbands inflicted the wound. The light and the water make it hard to tell if the rest of her body is similarly marked, and my eyes flick down to her pubic hair, watching how it rises up in the water.

'Are you getting cold?' she asks, sweetly.

'Yeah. Can we go back to your room?'

'Aren't you worried about hidden cameras?'

'No, I trust you. I'm sorry about earlier.'

'Forget about it.'

She stands up and steps out of the tub. So do I. She hands me a clean white towel and wraps herself in one. Then we quickly nip back across the corridor. We're both hobbling, trying to carry our clothes and shoes and stop our towels from unravelling. Claire closes the door behind me and drops her towel. I stand where I am, keeping mine wrapped around my waist.

'You can get dressed,' I tell her, 'I said I trust you.'

'Do you want to get dressed?'

I quickly look round the room, feeling lost. 'I'm worried.'

'What about?'

'Talking about this stuff in a sexual situation. Especially given our histories.'

She flinches. I feel guilty. I knew bringing this up would upset her. I've met women like Claire before. They exist in an idealised, oneiric reality, where anything can happen so long as it's not acknowledged. But I'm only telling the truth, and it does feel scary to be talking about my time with Sonia in a situation that demands similar risks. Especially as Claire's supposed to be a proponent of bringing things out into the open.

'I'm sorry,' I tell her, 'this is lovely and everything, but I'm about to start talking about really shitty stuff . . . horrible things that I'm totally ashamed of . . . and I don't want to get confused.'

'Confused about what?'

My voice falters. 'I'm just like them, Claire . . . it shouldn't make any difference that I'm articulate.'

'Just like who?'

'Your husbands.'

She laughs. 'You little prick. Why do you assume my husbands weren't articulate?'

'I just thought . . .'

'Scott was a deputy head and Jay wrote for *Venue* . . . my husbands weren't stupid guys.'

'I'm sorry, you're right, I shouldn't have assumed.'

'I'm not a victim, Dan. What happened between me and my husbands was a complex, strange thing. You should know from your experiences that these things aren't always black and white. Just because I went through the things I went through doesn't mean I can't understand what happened to you.'

'But I don't want you to understand.'

'Why, Dan?' she asks, walking towards me. 'Why are you being so hard on yourself?'

'Because I hurt Sonia. I hurt her really badly.'

'Dan,' she says, putting her arms around me, 'it's OK. I'm not here to judge you. Or condone what you did. Or come on to you or whatever it is you're scared of. Let's just lie on the bed.'

Her breasts feel hot against my face. My erection's caught in the front of my towel, and as we lie down I pull back the material and let myself rest naked in her arms. All rational appraisal of what's going on between us has vanished from my mind and I cry openly, clinging tightly to my confessor. When my sobs slow down, Claire asks me, 'So, did you make her come?'

'What?'

'Sonia. You said you knew the only way things would be OK would be if you made her come.'

'Yeah, she came. And when she did it was just like the first time, with her falling asleep straight away and leaving me with all these unresolved thoughts and emotions. And once again I was terrified of how she'd react the next morning. Only this time I was right to be scared because she beat me again. She didn't do it while I was asleep, but waited until I was awake and asked me to describe everything that had happened the night before. So I did, but whenever I suggested that she'd been in any way complicit in what had happened between us she screamed "liar" and punched me in the face. I was crying the whole time, partly out of guilt, and partly out of genuine pain. I mean, she was really laying into me.'

'But you didn't hit her back?'

'No, that never occurred to me. As far as I was concerned, I'd done a terrible thing and deserved to be punished. So after she'd finished flailing I told her I was sorry and said I'd leave straight away.'

'But your mum had sold your house?'

'Yeah.'

'So you had nowhere to go?'

'Something of a recurring problem. Anyway, once I'd said this Sonia seemed to realise that if I went she'd never see me again and changed her tune. She was still angry at me, but tried to turn it round as if she was only cross because I'd taken advantage of her. She kept asking what was wrong with normal sex and I had to reassure her that I was happy and that the previous night had been a drunken mistake. But this only set her off again, with her saying that I'd done it deliberately because I didn't like her getting wasted and that I'd betrayed her trust. I could see if I carried on arguing I'd end up on the streets, so we came to one of those compromises that allows couples to stay together after a violent conflict. From now on she'd spend one day a week away from me, drinking with friends.'

Claire adjusts herself against my body. 'Shall we get under the duvet?'

'OK.'

We do so. She moves slightly away from me, lying on her side. 'So what happened?'

'Exactly what you imagine. I should've gone out myself, but I didn't know anyone and felt a self-flagellatory impulse to force myself to deal with all the shit in my head alone. I managed about an hour before the suspicious thoughts started. Then I searched through Sonia's stuff and when I didn't find anything incriminating I tortured myself with worries that what happened the previous week had been a total set-up: Sonia's mendacious way of getting her freedom back.

'So when she came back I wasn't in the best of moods. Especially as she was trying her drunk act for the third time in a row. I'm not proud of much of what happened between Sonia and me, but I do feel pleased that for one night at least I stood up to her, refusing to make love while she was out of her head. All this meant was that she attacked me then instead of waiting for the morning, but I pushed her out of bed and she soon fell asleep on the floor.

'The following morning she was full of apologies, saying how this time she remembered what she'd been like and realised I'd been telling the truth the previous week. But I'd had enough of her game-playing and told her that I wasn't sure what she was up to, but whatever it was I was getting fed up with it. So she started crying and said she'd always known I'd leave her. This time her emotion seemed genuine, making me feel more inclined to talk openly with her. I told her it was pretty obvious that there was something in her past that had given her a weird perspective on sex, and said that rather than go through these ridiculous arguments she ought to tell me about it.

'So she did. It wasn't as bad as I'd expected. There was no child abuse, or anything like that. She wasn't a virgin. That was a lie. She'd had one previous boyfriend who'd been completely fucked up. She only went out with him because he threatened to kill himself if she didn't, and throughout their relationship he'd made her do extreme things. There were lots of things he made her do that she really didn't like. These included walking through town in nothing but a fur coat and making love with razors pressed against her thighs. But there were other things she'd really got into. Sodomy, for example. And bondage. She wasn't sure exactly why she liked these things, but thought it was something to do with her very liberal parents. They'd talked to her about sex from a very early age, telling her there was nothing dirty or shameful about it. But the thing was, she wanted sex to be dirty and shameful. And Tom was great at that.

'But after a while, she began to worry that what she was doing with Tom was permanently damaging her. She felt scared that she'd never be able to have a normal relationship, and didn't want to be stuck with Tom for ever simply because she was the only one to whom she could confess her dark desires. So she broke up with him. It was a long, protracted process that only became permanent when she went to university. And Tom killed himself.

'Since then she'd been living in a permanent state of guilt. Counsellors told her she wasn't to blame, and that she shouldn't worry about finding someone who'd be prepared to share her fantasies with her. They seemed absurdly overconcerned that she shouldn't connect her desires to Tom's death. Sonia had a sense of humour about the whole thing, aware that she was a wet dream made flesh to the nervous young men who talked to her about her problems. One of them even went as far as admitting he was into S and M, expecting her to feel grateful and seduce him. But Sonia wanted a healthy relationship, and knew that was impossible with someone intent on sexual catharsis. So she started going to clubs alone, looking for someone to make her whole again.

'I was her fourth one-night stand. All three previous attempts had started with her staggering up to someone and ended with violence the next morning. The first guy had been stoic about it, the second indignant, and the third, a tall, skinny goth, had overpowered her and left bruises all down her back. But I was the only one who'd made her regret what she'd done.

'I knew if I sounded too enthusiastic about the S and M stuff she wouldn't want to stay with me, but at the same time I had to convince her that I wasn't disgusted. I could tell the latter was less important, aware that Sonia was a lot more knowing than she pretended. It seemed obvious that she was presenting me with a challenge. Come up with a way we can continue this relationship, she seemed to be saying, and I'll stay with you.

'So I asked her to trust me again. I told her to stay with me next time she got pissed and asked her if she'd ever done any role-playing with Tom. She said that although she had lots of fantasies, Tom had been pretty single-minded and the only scenario they played out more than once was a teacher–student fantasy. She was a good schoolgirl, she said, but now that Tom was dead it didn't seem right to do that any more.

'I asked her what she wanted to do and after initial embarrassment she told me the main things she thought about while masturbating were brother–sister incest and being taken advantage of by a baby-sitter. Once she said this, I knew what she expected from me.

'I shan't go through everything we did over the subsequent three months. All you need to know is that afternoon, after we talked, I made her dress up like a child and persuaded her into some mildly kinky sex. She was so grateful afterwards that she clung to me and cried, which made me feel wonderful. I still didn't know much about Sonia's background, but now both my parents had disappeared I felt more dispossessed than ever. Our relationship had become my only source of stability and I believed that everything we were sharing would guarantee she wouldn't leave me.

'At the time it felt like I was the dominant one, but looking back I realise she was always in control. Throughout our time together she'd give me little hints about what she wanted to do next, and then wait for me to lead her into it. The only time she ever seemed irritated was if I became hesitant about something, and she wanted me to pretend that I was much older and more experienced and intent on corrupting her. We did all the standard stuff, and despite her claim that Tom had a one-track mind, Sonia could get really fixated about some things, making me repeat certain scenarios over and over again. I realised pretty quickly that the only thing I was doing wrong was seeing our sex life as something that should continually develop. Sonia was much more indulgent than me. She liked to wallow.'

Claire yawns. 'So where did it go wrong?'

'It was inevitable really. I'd known from the start that Sonia would soon be worried that she'd isolated herself. If I'd been a rich, handsome potential husband that wouldn't be a problem. But I was a homeless, poorly paid office worker whose only real link with my lover was that I was prepared to indulge her sexual neuroses. To her credit, Sonia tried hard to make our relationship work, slowly introducing me into her previous social circle while ensuring I didn't feel threatened. She emphasised her connection with me by doing little sexual things like letting me surreptitiously finger her in dark corners at parties, but despite all her best efforts, as soon as we stopped hiding ourselves in Sonia's bedroom, the balance between us was destroyed.

'I could sense she was looking for someone new and began to see parallels between her relationship with Tom and her relationship with me. She'd always been proud of our sexual honesty, but now I realised that our time together was serving two purposes for her. Firstly, it was proving that she didn't have to worry about her desires and that it was possible to explore extreme sex within a loving relationship. But at the same time I could tell that the reason she wanted to do certain things over and over again was to get them out of her system, finding out what she needed and what she could live without. And just as she'd decided she didn't want to get stuck with Tom, so soon she'd realise that she didn't want to spend the rest of her life with me. She was going through her experimentation period, just like other girls flirt with bisexuality before settling down. And there were lots of eligible men in her circle. It was clear from the general flirtatious mood that Sonia could take her pick from these men, maybe even try out one or two before making her choice.

'One of the only lessons I'd learned from observing my parents was that talking gets you nowhere. It's pointless moaning or feeling jealous . . . that'll just make your partner despise you. No, to keep things equal you have to be active. Whenever Dad betrayed my mum, she spent a night with someone herself, and vice versa. So, instead of making a fuss, I looked round for someone who'd be prepared to sleep with me if Sonia proved unfaithful.

'I suppose my mistake was choosing one of her friends. But the girls at Sonia's university were much sexier than the women in work, and it seemed silly not to consider them. The one I went for was called Ellen and I suppose she was the obvious choice. Sonia hated her because of her social ease. She was blonde and healthy, and although I've no doubt her sexual imagination was just as tortured as Sonia's, she seemed determined to keep her life out of the shadows. In her first year she'd managed to combine an active sporting career with an affair with her tutor, and was now ignoring his increasing hysteria and concentrating on firming up her former friendships. As Sonia's own plan was so similar, it was inevitable that they'd start spending time together.'

Claire kicks me.

'What did I say? That wasn't offensive.'

'No,' she laughs, 'I'm sorry, my foot's gone all funny. I think it's because I've gone straight from the bath into bed.'

'Do you want me to rub it?'

'No, it's OK,' she says, shifting around on the sheet, 'I just need to give it a hard squeeze . . . there, that's better. Go on with your story.'

'OK, anyway, to begin with I made a play of hating Ellen, knowing that this would make Sonia like her more, and stop her getting jealous if we spent any time together. She kept reminding me how she hadn't liked her either at first, but had come to realise she was a really nice person. I don't think Ellen knew what I was up to . . . certainly Sonia never said anything . . . although sometimes I had to pretend to be mean to her so Sonia wouldn't get suspicious.

'While all this was going on, Sonia seemed to have settled on someone herself. He was called Will and came from the Isle of Wight. He fancied himself a poet and Sonia told me she'd been in his room one time and come across all these sonnets about her. She said this in a scornful tone, but I could tell she was flattered. No one's really upset about finding someone fancies them.

'So we carried on playing our little games. The sex stabilised a bit, but it was still exciting, especially this one time when Sonia wore a G-string and a short skirt and walked in front of me up the steps of Cabot Tower. I'd been completely accepted as part of Sonia's group, and got invited to every outing. They particularly liked hosting dinner-parties, pretending to be adults. And then, towards the end of term, it was Will's birthday.

'There was tension between us even before we got to the party. Sonia wanted to go to the pub for a few drinks beforehand and I thought this was a bad idea, especially as I knew how much she could get through on these occasions. We had a big argument and she accused me of not trusting her, which was true, I suppose. But I also knew her outrage meant I was right to be suspicious. I know that doesn't really make sense, but if you knew Sonia you'd understand.

'Sonia was furious by the time we arrived, and immediately began her attack. She sat next to Will and started in on a bottle straight away, refilling her glass three times before I'd finished one. I retaliated by steering Ellen to the other end of the table and sitting opposite Sonia. One of the reasons I liked Sonia so much was that she always responded to any sort of attention. Even though she was much in demand, she'd stay talking to someone until they moved on, never looking over their shoulder and seeming happy to stay in one conversation all evening.

'I watched Sonia get progressively drunker, worried by the way she was avoiding my eye and giggling conspiratorially with Will. I'd had a few, but was still quite sober and felt genuinely surprised when Ellen put her hand on my leg. I looked at her and then across to Sonia. It was obvious Ellen had worked out that there was something wrong between Sonia and me, but I still felt surprised she'd been so direct.'

'Did Sonia notice?'

'Not while we were at the table. But then someone had the bright idea of going on to The Triangle.'

'What happened there?'

'Ellen did it again. But by now I was so pissed off with Sonia that I reciprocated, putting my hand just under the hem of her skirt.'

'What did Sonia do?'

'She left with Will. I figured that was the end of it, thinking that the next morning she'd either break up with me or confess her infidelity and ask me to forgive her.'

'So you left with Ellen?'

'Of course. If Sonia was about to turf me out, I needed somewhere new to sleep. I took Ellen by the hand and led her out of the bar, unconcerned by the looks we were getting. To tell you the truth, I was excited about the way the night had turned out, pleased that I'd be the subject of gossip and turned on by the prospect of a night with Ellen.'

'What was she like?'

I look at Claire, surprised by her question. 'It didn't happen. We got back to her room and started making out when there were these violent hammerings against the door. To begin with we ignored it, but then Sonia started making these incredible wails. Ellen was clearly terrified and yelled at me to take care of her.'

'Did you let her in?'

'Sort of. I unlocked the door intending to open it a little bit and see what was up. But as soon as I released the catch Sonia hit the door with the full force of her body and sent me staggering back across the room. Ellen ran to her bed and Sonia marched straight over to me. Before I'd said anything she punched me in the face, as hard as she could, and shouted about how Ellen was such a slut and everyone had told her I'd been fingering her under the table throughout the dinner. Then she started flailing against me, really violent, slapping and scratching and gouging, and when I didn't respond she walked over to Ellen's desk and started hitching up her skirt, pleading with me, saying stupid shit like, "Come on, Danny, fuck me right here. Fuck me in front of her. Show Ellen it's my cunt you prefer." And then she stopped talking, just bent over the table like that with her skirt and knickers pulled down and her bum sticking in the air.'

I look at Claire. 'I know this sounds terrible, but it's how it happened. And I couldn't help feeling all these weird things at once. The strongest sensation was a surge of ridiculous excitement, knowing that what was going on in this room was melodramatic and unreal and the sort of situation most people don't get into in their entire lives, and here I was at the centre of it, me who'd hardly experienced anything before I met Sonia. But at the same time I felt disgusted by my girlfriend, a really primitive, misogynist disgust, as strong as if she'd covered herself in shit and demanded that I hold her. I couldn't believe she wanted me to fuck her in front of Ellen and yet at the same time I understood exactly why she was doing this. Sure she was drunk, but I'm not even sure if that was a factor. Sonia would've done this stone-cold sober if she thought it was the only way of reclaiming the evening. And standing there between the two of them, I realised what kind of person I was, sharing Ellen's fear but also knowing that there was a part of me just like Sonia. So when I walked towards her I still wasn't sure what I was going to do. Sonia continued to goad me, Ellen couldn't stop crying. And I put my arms around Sonia's waist, intending only to move her out of that obscene position. But she felt my erection pressing against her bottom and turned to grin at me, and I looked at that grin and felt overcome with self-revulsion and let her fall. She turned to spit at me and before I knew what I was doing I was kicking her as hard as I could, watching her try to stumble up and then kicking her again, and then somehow, I know I did it but I don't know how, I brought the desk down on top of Sonia's head and all I could hear was Ellen screaming.'

'What had you done?'

'Enough. A fractured skull was the worst of it. Ellen gave evidence and I got done. We only spoke in the courtroom and I haven't seen either of them since.'

I lie back on the bed, utterly exhausted. God knows what time it is. It feels strange for all this to be out there. At least my penis has shrunk back to normal size. That part of me is still human after all.

Claire reaches for my hand. I'm awaiting questions, but she seems settled, as if the proper response to my story is a period of silence. After five minutes I start worrying about Alice, remembering that she wants me to wake her up when I get back in.

After ten minutes I'm asleep.

19

Claire's an early riser, shaking me awake at seven thirty. She's already made breakast and hands me a white towelling robe to wear at the table.

'I've called Alice,' she tells me.

'What did she say?'

'Nothing much.'

'She must be furious.'

'No, I don't think so. She's heard Brittany talking about us. She knows how things stand.'

'That sounds unlikely.'

'Look, if there's any problem, get her to call me. I'll set her straight.'

Claire walks through to the laid table. She's already dressed and I feel vulnerable as I pad behind her.

'Now, you don't eat dairy, right?'

I'm past being impressed by tricks like this, aware by now that Dad's group must have all my details on secret file.

I sit down. Claire goes out into the hallway and returns with two plates. All my life avoiding breakfast and now in the space of two days I've got two women cooking for me. I still don't know how to respond to this sort of generosity and feel guilty as she puts the food down in front of me. Claire's wearing a light-blue sweater and the same cream trousers as last night. She smiles at me and I'm suddenly aware how little I know about this woman. OK, I've read about her personal history, but what about her daily life? What does she do for a job? Will she have to leave soon or does she have to get in for nine like me? I could clear everything up with a couple of questions, but there's something nice about leaving things vague. I'm sure I'll find out the full story soon enough.

'How do you feel?' Claire asks.

'What do you mean?'

'Does it feel good to have told me your story? Or do you still feel vulnerable?'

'It feels strange. It's like I've died and it's turned out not to be as bad as everyone thinks.'

'That's a common reaction.'

'Oh.'

She laughs. 'I'm sorry, that sounded patronising. All I'm trying to say is that even though what happened last night was only between you and me, as an experience it wasn't that different from what goes on in group therapy, and with group therapy it's quite common to experience, I don't know, a sort of negative aftershock. It's usual to feel regret about what you've said, a bit like the self-loathing you feel after a drunken night at a party. But if you can cope with the fact that you've psychologically exposed yourself, then you're on the road to recovery. The only problems come when you try and compensate for sharing your secrets, drinking too much or shutting out the people to whom you feel closest. Anyway, I don't want to tell you how you should be feeling. What do you think?'

'I guess that makes sense.'

'How do you feel towards me?'

'I don't know. I suppose I feel like we've had a one-night stand or something.'

'Good, that's normal too. So do you feel that you want to get away from me?'

I blush. 'Yeah.'

Claire giggles and stretches her fingers out towards me. 'Oh, you're so sweet. It's OK, you know. Don't hide your feelings. I'm not offended. But the point of this breakfast is to help you get over that stuff and understand that you're safe with me. I'm your friend, Dan. I know it feels weird because in your mind I'm connected with your dad, but as I told you last night I've never slept with him and I'm not his girlfriend. The fact that you've worked on a linkline shows you're hip to the healing power of conversation, and as long as we can keep the lines of communication open, I can help you get your life back on track.'

I shrug. 'OK.'

'Did you dream last night?'

I look at her, struck by the conviction that she already knows what passed through my mind while I slept. I suppose she must've felt me shifting about, but her question seems more insinuating than that. I check my temples for the left-over stickiness of attached electrodes.

'Yeah,' I tell her, 'I have this recurring nightmare and I got a version of it last night.'

'What happens?'

'Well, I don't know if Dad talked about this in your meetings, but the worst family arguments always took place on holiday. My mum used to get angry with me because I hated going away, but the reason I disliked it so much was because that was the time I realised how little my parents cared for each other and got the strongest sense of the sadness at the heart of my family. The things that happened when we were away together always seemed more significant than anything that went on at home, and to this day I still find myself disturbed by memories of little exchanges that have only become clear years after they happened. And in the dream I'm talking to my mum and she's explaining that the reason why she never really loved my dad was because of his terrible temper, and I tell her that I don't remember him being that bad. So she goes into their bedroom and brings down a shoebox full of photographs. And in all the pictures he's wearing the same red tracksuit and his face is screwed up in this grimace of terrifying anger.'

Claire nods. 'Why are you so scared by your dad?'

'I don't know.'

'Has he ever been violent towards you?'

I swallow a mouthful of beans. 'Not really. He smacked me when I was a kid, but that's all. I think Dad talked about that in one of your early meetings.'

'Right.'

'You don't remember?'

'Those meetings were a long time ago, Dan. It seems fresh to you because you've recently read the minutes, but I can hardly remember what I said in the last meeting, let alone the first one.'

I continue eating, feeling chastised. Claire is becoming an oddly maternal presence, and I'm surprised she thinks this is the best way of getting me to open up. But the food is good, and if I have trouble swallowing the psychobabble, I can't complain about the bacon and eggs.

'I think it's really important that you see Steve soon,' she tells me.

'So you said.'

'Will you go in this weekend?'

'I'll do my best.'

I leave Claire's at eight thirty, after another hour of working through our 'renegotiated relationship'. I've got that strange mind-trick thing where you know something bad has happened, but you can't remember what. It's like that sensation after incest dreams when you wake up thinking you've ruined yourself and then gradually remember that nothing's happened. I can totally empathise with the suicide urge, but also believe Claire's assertion that once I've come to terms with this I'll feel much stronger.

There's a light drizzle and the drops feel good against my face. I wonder why I'm so scared of exercising any control over my existence. It's like I decided at an early age to surrender any responsibility and now can't work out how to get it back. I always suspected it'd take a woman to bring me round, but never that it'd happen like this.

It's only a short walk to work and I get there almost twenty minutes early. I go to the breaks room but can't remember the code and have to wait for an overweight woman in a black cardigan to let me in. It's nice to have a moment to myself before starting work, and I take my cup of watery minestrone and sit in the corner, watching the cars through the window. Each passing tyre shoots up a spray of dirty water and I'm glad to be inside.

After a short reverie, I turn my chair round and watch the door, worried about what'll happen when Alice arrives. I don't believe she's as unconcerned about last night as Claire suggested, and worry that she might attack me from behind. I'm also nervous about Adrienne and Ian, especially facing the prospect of this morning's meeting.

At five to nine, I decide no one's going to show and head across to the main building. Adrienne, Ian and Gordon are standing by the back exit, smoking. They look like a bunch of schoolkids and I can't help smirking as I catch up with them, wondering if they're going to stick a 'kick me' sign on my back.

'I didn't expect to see you hanging around here, Gordon. Aren't you usually at your desk by now?'

Gordon looks away. I can tell he wants to ignore me, but he can't resist the urge to look at his watch.

'See,' I say to him, 'you wouldn't want to be late, especially not just before an appraisal.'

His head jerks.

'Come on, Gordon, I know you're not like this. You've just got in with a bad crowd, that's all. Why don't you come upstairs with me?'

Adrienne glares at me. Gordon stays where he is.

'OK, but don't say I didn't warn you when Alice gives you a ticking off in the meeting. This is very surprising behaviour from someone who's always been such a model employee.'

I use my ID card to open the door, then walk past them. I get in the lift and go up to the seventh floor. My reflection looks a little ruffled, but nowhere as bad as before Alice took me in. The lift slows to a stop and the doors open. I walk through to the call-centre, immediately scanning the floor for Alice.

She's in reception. I go straight across, knowing she'll probably be angered by this direct approach, but wanting to get the awkwardness out of the way early.

'Can I have a quick word?'

She gives me a long slow look and then says, 'Sure. Do you want to go to the Conference Room?'

'Yeah.'

'OK.'

She turns and mutters something to the other woman in reception, then walks round in front of me. She's wearing her dark-blue suit and has fixed her hair even more forcefully than usual. I follow her to the Conference Room. She sits on the table.

'Claire said she called you.'

'Yeah.'

'And that you were OK about last night.'

'Why shouldn't I be?'

'I don't know. You wanted us to talk about something.'

'Did I?'

'Yeah. You said you wanted to have a long conversation when I got back.'

She looks away. 'We can do that tonight.'

'You are angry.'

'No, Dan, I'm not angry. Let's not keep going over this.'

'Can I kiss you?'

She runs her fingers through her fringe. 'If you want.'

I kiss her. She's not very responsive so I put my arms around her, squeezing her sides.

'I missed you.'

She looks at her watch. 'We ought to go back out. It's after nine.'

*   *   *

The meeting takes place at nine thirty. From twenty past we're all looking over to reception, waiting for Alice to come across. When she does so, she's holding the Suggestions Book. Adrienne glares at me.

'OK,' says Alice, 'make sure you've logged off properly.'

Ian's the first to get up, taking the headset from around his neck and dropping it on the table. Adrienne copies him, and the rest of us follow, Teri walking beside me. The campaign of silence has continued into a second day, with no one talking to me this morning. Alice stands at the front of the room, her hand going for one of the pens by the whiteboard. Ian moves slowly, pulling out his chair in a very deliberate manner.

'Where are the biscuits?' Adrienne asks.

Alice ignores her. 'OK. Now, I think everyone here knows they've been a bit silly, and I want you to tell me how you think we can sort this out.'

Adrienne wraps her arms around her body and rocks forward.

'I resent that implication.'

'Pardon?'

'I don't think this is a group thing.'

Alice stares at her. 'So you're denying that you're responsible for any of the stuff in this book?'

'No, I'm just saying that there are lots of different concerns here, and I don't think it's sensible to treat us as if we're a bunch of naughty schoolchildren.'

'Reductive,' adds Gordon.

'What was that?'

'It's reductive,' Gordon repeats, 'and unfair.'

'I see. OK, Adrienne, what are the different concerns?'

'Well, as you said, there's the Suggestions Book, which I take total responsibilty for . . .'

'So you've changed your tune since yesterday?'

'No, I always admitted it was my book. I just pointed out that it was private property.'

'OK. So let's deal with that first. How do you think I should feel about you writing that sort of stuff about me?'

I look at Alice's eyes, wondering how she can deal with this so calmly. I feel the same admiration towards her as I might to an unpopular teacher, amazed that she can take her ego out of this and talk about Adrienne's insults so frankly, especially as she must've spent last night sitting alone reading that rubbish while she waited for me.

Adrienne shifts in her chair. 'It's not just about you.'

'No, that's right, it's about Gordon as well. Has he read what you've written about him?'

Alice raises her eyebrows. Adrienne looks quickly at Gordon, who frowns, his jaw wobbling. Perhaps Alice isn't handling this as well as I thought. I always assumed this'd be the moment that Gordon would be tipped over the edge, but, once again, it turns out to be another anti-climax.

We're all watching Gordon. He swallows, then says bravely, 'What has she said?'

Alice opens the book and seems as if she's about to read an extract from Gordon's Log, but instead looks at Adrienne and says, 'Why don't you tell him, Adrienne?'

Ian looks at Gordon. 'It's only a joke, Gord. Nothing serious.'

Gordon nods, clearly calmed by Ian's intervention. But there's obvious emotion in the room, and I'm curious to see what'll happen next. Thankfully, Alice seems to realise the riskiness of sticking with this subject and says instead, 'Right. Let's assume Gordon and I are prepared to forgive you. What else should we be talking about today?'

'You ought to give us an update on how we've done since the last appraisal.'

Alice laughs. 'What do you think?'

'I think you should look at our print-outs. I'm sure I've cut down my call-response time.'

'Maybe, but if you remember our previous meeting, Adrienne,

bad stats were only part of the problem. The main concern is the group's dynamic.'

'We're getting along fine,' Adrienne protests.

'You're not even talking to each other.'

'That's not true. There's a problem with one specific member of the group.'

'And who's that?'

'Dan.'

'Right. What's the problem with Dan?'

Adrienne looks at me.

'He's a suck-arse,' Ian says quietly.

'Literally,' Adrienne adds.

Everyone giggles. Alice doesn't blink, keeping her eyes trained on Adrienne and Ian.

'So you've got a problem with my relationship with Dan?'

No one says anything. Alice waits.

'Well, I don't think that's any of your business. And if that's what's causing such a consternation amongst the group then you're being very silly, because we're going to have to resolve this situation and if you can't cope with our relationship, then you're going to find yourselves without a job, because this group is going to get along, and stop all this stupid silent treatment nonsense, and if that doesn't happen straight away, I'm going to take direct action.'

'I don't think that's fair,' Adrienne tells her.

'Why?'

'It's stupid to punish the group when the problem is with one person. Why don't you move Dan to another team?'

'Because Dan isn't the one acting like a child. I want you to know that I'm very serious about this. You're all still on temporary contract, and if I have to get rid of all four of you then that's what I'll do. And before you start running to my superiors, you should be aware that I have absolute authority over the management of this team and won't hesitate to exercise it.'

She waits.

'Is that understood?'

Gordon nods.

'Good. Now I want you all to start talking to Dan again. Starting with you, Adrienne. Apologise to Dan.'

'What for?'

'Not talking to him.'

I turn round. She looks at me and then says sulkily, in barely a whisper, 'I'm sorry.'

'Good. Now tell Gordon you won't write any more rubbish about him.'

She does so. Gordon smiles. Alice stares at him.

'OK, Gordon, apologise to Dan.'

His jaw starts wobbling and he turns to Ian. Ian stares out the window. Gordon looks to Adrienne instead. She nods her consent and Gordon says sorry.

'Ian, Teri . . .'

'Sorry, Dan,' Teri says quickly.

'Yeah,' adds Ian, shrugging.

'Right,' says Alice, bringing her hands together, 'is there anything else we need to discuss?'

No one says anything.

'Good. Then let's get back to work.'

I stay behind while everyone else files out, wanting to talk to Alice alone. She smiles at me.

'See. There's nothing to worry about.'

'What are you going to do with the book?'

'Keep it as evidence.'

'You don't think you should sack Adrienne instead of Teri?'

She looks at me, surprised. 'I thought you were scared of them.'

'Who?'

'Adrienne and Ian. If I sack her now, they're bound to think it's got something to do with you.'

'Yeah, I suppose you're right.'

'Why don't you want me to sack Teri?'

'No reason.'

She waits. 'Hmmm. Anyway, can I get my request in early today?'

'What request?'

'Lunch. Let's take an hour off and go into town.'

'An hour? I don't know if I can cope with no other breaks all day.'

'OK,' she says, turning away.

'No, wait, I'll manage. What time should I put in the Breaks Book?'

'Twelve.'

'OK. Fine.'

I walk back to our table and put my headset on. I know Alice thinks she's had a great success, but whatever they said in the Conference Room, Adrienne and Ian aren't going to end their campaign that easily. But at least Teri's talking to me, saying, 'I got revenge today.'

'What?'

'My flatmates. You were right. I did deserve to get them back for locking me in my room. I was scared about starting a war, but then I realised all I had to do was be subtle about it.'

'So what did you do?'

'Ex-lax in their breakfast. I realised later that it was pretty stupid because I'll have to clean up after them, but at least it felt good while I was doing it.'

'Good for you.'

She smiles and starts picking at a small white stain on her black skirt. Teri's face is so attractive in profile, especially her elegant eyebrows. She's got the kind of beauty you really need a camera to see. She may be small but she'd make a perfect model.

I ask Gordon to pass me the Breaks Book and he does so without speaking. I'd like to know whether he's curious about what Adrienne's written, but don't want them to think I'm shit-stirring. Still, there must be all kinds of explosions going on inside that juddering cranium.

*   *   *

Lunchtime comes quickly. Teri and I play a few games of Connect Four and there's a fair number of calls for a Friday. I log off at eleven fifty-seven and walk over to the reception area, wanting to keep Alice away from the team. She smiles and stands up, holding my hand as she walks round from behind the purple screens. It's hard to accept that disaster is no longer imminent, but I expect Alice is probably right and after this morning it won't take long for things to return to normal. I doubt I'll ever be friends with Ian and Adrienne again, but I can learn to live with that.

The most sensible thing to do now is consolidate my friendship with Teri. That way when Alice gives her the sack I can get her to stay in contact. She probably won't be able to see me as separate from Alice for a while, but once she's got over that she'll make a good confidante.

'Where do you want to go?' I ask Alice.

'Don't mind.'

'World of Food?'

'Why not?'

Alice walks slowly and it takes us ten minutes to reach the Galleries. We enter on the top floor and walk round to where the plastic quarterback waits for us.

'What do you fancy?'

'Ribs.'

I laugh. 'Right. Won't your mum mind that we haven't eaten our sandwiches?'

'Not if we don't tell her.'

I wait with Alice while she gets her ribs. I was planning to get a hamburger but the thin red strips of bone look so enticing I have a plate myself. Alice smiles and I pluck out a thick wedge of serviettes.

'I don't get the craving very often,' she says, 'but sometimes spare ribs are just what you need to fill the gap.'

'I know what you mean. Ribs seem too nice to be food. It's like they only exist for special treats.'

We carry our plastic trays over to the raised seating area. It's not that crowded for a Friday lunchtime and we have room to spread out. I have a large gulp of Coke before starting on my food.

'I think we should go to The Pentangle tonight.'

'Really?' I say, surprised. 'I thought you hated it there.'

'I hated it last time. But that was only because I was with Bryan. It'll be fine going with you.'

'But I'm working late.'

'I know. We can go afterwards.'

'That late?'

'Why not? I'll let you go there first and sort things out with Adrienne, then I'll come along later.'

I nod and pick up the first of my bones, deciding not to antagonise her. I was intending to check on John after the old ladies go home tonight, but I suppose I'll still have time to do that before going to The Pentangle.

'Right,' she says, 'so I'll meet you there at eleven.'

'Better make it twelve. Leave me long enough to properly smooth things over.'

'OK. Will I still be able to get in?'

'Yeah, I've gone that late before. Just mention Adrienne if there's a problem.'

'So, are they talking to you?'

'Yeah,' I lie, 'you were right.'

'I knew it. You're far too cautious.'

She strips the meat from another bone and uses her finger to wipe the red sauce from her cheek.

'Nah, leave it. You look really sexy with that stuff all over your face.'

'Don't be disgusting. How's your food?'

'Good.'

'Did Adrienne say anything about this morning?'

'Not really. Why?'

'I just thought if anyone was likely to ignore me, it'd be her.'

'No, she was fine. Alice . . .'

'Yes?'

'I know I'm always starting conversations like this, but can I talk properly with you?'

'Is this about the same thing as this morning or something else?'

'Something else.'

'OK.' She puts her elbows on the table and stops chewing.

'It's to do with money.'

'Look, I've already told you that I want you to stay with me. I know you can't really afford to pay rent at the moment and that's fine. Don't bother feeling guilty. Just let me know when things get easier for you.'

'No, it's not that. I do feel guilty, but my financial problems are a bit more serious.'

'Go on.'

'Well, you remember the other day I told you about how I have to make repayments?'

'Yeah.'

'The thing is, money has always been a struggle, and the debts have been stacked so that I'm always a bit behind, which meant that when Dad went into hospital, I not only had to pay the rent, but all this other stuff that'd been mounting up as well.'

'But he's only been in the hospital three weeks.'

'I know, but this was debt going back over a year.'

'Right, so you need to borrow some money?'

'Sort of. What happened was that when things got really tight I went to Adrienne for a loan.'

'How much?'

'A thousand.'

She breathes in. 'Right. And when does she want it back?'

'She's being very lenient, but that's sort of the problem. Without my rent, my outgoings are forty-seven pounds a week. I've used the thousand to clear some of the backlog on other things, but there's none of it left now, and Adrienne wants me to pay her fifty quid a week, which means . . .'

'Which means you're only going to have about twenty quid a week to live on.'

'Less, now I'm stopping doing nights. But it's more the psychological thing of being in debt to *Adrienne*. I know you've made things OK now, but yesterday I realised how scary it is owing money to someone who might turn against you.'

'So what do you want me to do?'

'I wondered if you could take out a loan for me. Or let me take out a loan using your house as insurance. I don't really know how all that works, but I'd be much happier owing money to you or a building society.'

I bite a small pocket of red meat from the identation at the top of my last rib. When I hand her a serviette, she wipes her lips.

'I don't want Adrienne to know I've given you the money.'

'Why would she?'

'She's bound to wonder where you got it from.'

'I'll say I got it from my dad.'

'Won't she want to know why you didn't go to him before?'

'I'll tell her I felt too proud. She'll understand.'

'I won't be able to give it to you straight away. I'll have to get it from my savings account and that'll take a while.'

'That's OK. Thanks, Alice.'

'When will you pay me back?'

'I can manage about twenty-five a week, maybe a little more.'

'No, twenty-five will be fine. But you'll have to pay it straight into my account. Otherwise I'll just end up spending it.'

'Right.'

She holds my gaze for a moment, then pushes away her plate. I feel like I've just inserted a dodgy disk into my computer and I'm waiting to see whether it'll be accepted. Alice blinks. Everything seems to be running OK.

Of course, it'll be a while before I know whether I've really got away with it. First I've got to keep Alice in a good mood until she's given me the money, then I have to be sufficiently grateful, and even after that I'll have to watch out for changes in the relationship resulting from this transaction. Maybe later we'll look back and point to this moment as the beginning of the end. Or perhaps it'll work the other way and the financial obligation will allow us to move on to greater emotional commitment.

I really should get a handle on how I feel about Alice. Last night still confused me, and I'm surprised she hasn't brought it up. Claire was much closer to my type than Alice, but although my body responded to being in bed with her, I don't think I ever seriously considered betraying my girlfriend. I'm not saying I'm in love with Alice . . . that would be going too far. But I can imagine a future with her, once we've got through the next few weeks.

'We should be getting back,' she says.

'Already?'

'Afraid so. If we want to get back on time.'

'Right.'

We leave our trays on the table and walk back to Quick Kall. Alice was right about the time and we're only a few minutes early. We go up in the lift together and Alice holds me from behind, her palm spread across my stomach. We pause for a kiss outside the double doors, then go our separate ways.

I walk back to my team. Ian remains silent, refusing to forgive me. Clearly spooked by this morning's meeting, Gordon makes a few lame attempts to start a conversation, but only for appearance's sake. Teri is now chatting freely, which would be enough to keep me happy if she made more than three remarks an hour. Adrienne pretends that none of us are here, ignoring everyone accept Ian.

The few calls that make it through on a Friday are usually fun, especially on the Magicmix line. Everyone ends by asking me what I'm doing that evening, or over the weekend, and after I've replied 'nothing much', go on to detail their own plans. People in record shops tend to be pretty clued up, and since I started working at

Quick Kall, I've developed a thorough knowledge of the best clubs in Manchester, Leeds and Glasgow. Should I ever leave Bristol, I'm certain this information will come in useful.

At ten to six, I tell the team I'll take their late calls. Everyone's eager to vacate the office, hardly surprising given what's happened this week. I really ought to stop Adrienne and warn her that Alice and I are planning to drop in to The Pentangle, but I know she won't respond so it'll just have to remain a surprise. After they've all gone home, my wait-light flashes.

It's Alice, confirming our plans for this evening. I tell her everything's sorted and say I'll meet her at midnight. She clicks off and I watch her head emerge above the purple screens.

Cathy mouths hello as she enters the office, popping over to reception for a quick chat with her daughter before starting work. I watch Alice leave, then turn my chair so I can follow her path as she exits the building and walks across the rear car park.

Once my lover has gone, there's not all that much to do. I'm reluctant to start another conversation with Cathy (even though she's smiling and waving from her side of the office) and as I haven't been home I didn't manage to pick up dad's minutes or the disk containing *Hotel Babylon*. I could nip to the toilets for a quick check on John, but if I found him I'd have to call off tonight's search, and I'm quite looking forward to getting above the ceiling tiles.

I sit there for the best part of an hour, staring into space. An ordinary shift at Quick Kall is just short enough not to represent a real threat to your sanity, but I've been at my desk now for six hours straight. If I didn't have an anti-glare screen, I'd probably be blind by now.

My wait-light flashes.

'Hello, Magicmix.'

'Hi, Dan.'

'Hello Moyra. I'm sorry about last night.'

'What about it?'

'That I wasn't here when you called. Especially after everything you said about feeling paranoid. But it was true. I genuinely wasn't there. Did Cathy say anything terrible?'

'Who?'

'The old woman who answered.'

'Not really, although she did seem pretty nosey. Who was she?'

'My new girlfriend's mum. She said you were angry at me and wouldn't call again.'

Moyra laughs. 'I wasn't angry. Maybe a little frustrated, but only because I was looking forward to having a chat with you. So you've got a new girlfriend?'

'Yeah.'

'When did that happen?'

'Earlier this week.'

'And her mum works at your office?'

'Not just her mum.'

'Oh, Dan. Is she your boss?'

I don't reply. Moyra starts laughing.

'That's terrible,' she tells me. 'Is she older than you?'

'A little bit. Not a disgusting amount.'

'Right. So, is she rich?'

'No. But she is helping me out.'

'How?'

'By letting me live with her and lending me a thousand quid.'

'Nice one. Are you going to stop doing nights?'

'Yeah. This is my last one.'

'She wants you to stay home watching TV with her, right?'

'Not really. We're going to a club tonight.'

'I'm not doing anything tonight. I'm just going to stay in and plot.'

'What are you plotting?'

'Terrible things, Dan. Things a nice man like yourself wouldn't believe. Did I tell you I'm writing a book?'

'No.'

'It's my revenge on the world. Every guy who's ever been near me is in for a big fucking surprise.'

'Am I in it?'

'No.'

'Oh.'

'Don't be disappointed. You don't want to be in it. It's full of all the shitheads that have taken advantage of me.'

'I see. Anyway, listen, I'm not going to have much chance to talk to you any more. You can call me during the days but there's always the risk that I might be being monitored so I won't be able to say much.'

'That's OK. I've decided it's time for me to stop calling you.'

'Why?'

'Because you don't really want to listen to all my rubbish. It's very kind of you to be nice to me, but I need to find someone real I can talk to.'

'I'm real.'

She laughs. 'I mean someone who's not just a voice. But thanks for everything, Dan. You've been very kind to me.'

She clicks off before I have chance to protest.

Losing contact with my midnight caller depresses me. It'd be hard to talk to her during the day, but it seems sad now I know she'll never call again. I ended up feeling rather fond of that strange, isolated girl, and my conversations with her brought back fond memories of my nights on the linkline, talking intimately to people I'd probably never see. Sometimes I think we'd all be better off if we were just voices, liberated from our bodies and all the stuff that goes along with that and gets in the way.

At half past ten the old ladies go home and I'm left alone in the office. Cathy asks me what time we'll be back and I tell her about Alice wanting to go to The Pentangle. She nods and says she hopes we have a good time.

Right. So this is it: the moment of truth. I log off and walk to the gents. I know John's up there, somewhere or other, and I'm not going to leave the call-centre until he's back in my arms. I place the squashed bog-rolls under each wheel and step up onto the swivel-chair.

I push up the usual ceiling-tile, forlornly hoping this might be easy. All I want to see is his furry face and those sad eyes staring back at me. But of course there's no sign of him. The solid pellets I'm still not sure about lie a short distance in front of me. I pull my suit sleeve over the top of my fist and sweep them out. They plop into the toilet bowl, splashing my trouser leg. Still, not a bad shot. I pull the flush.

There's no getting round it. If I want to find him I'm going to have to climb up there and start crawling. My biggest fear is that I won't be able to see him in the dark and he'll tear holes in my face. It was hard enough to explain why I had scratches on my arm. God knows what people will think if I show up with a bleeding face.

I step lightly on the back of the chair, worried my weight will make it tip up and leave me spread-eagled on the tiled floor. But aided by the impressive wheel-wedges, the chair stays in place and I decide to try getting up. I know I have to move quickly, although I'm not sure what to do with my legs once the top half of my body is above the tiles. No amount of thought is going to help me, though, so I'll just have to take a risk.

Ready? Here goes.

I bring down both feet on the back of the chair and use this motion to propel myself upwards, reaching for something to hang on to. My fingers find some kind of metal supports and I use them to bring myself forward, simultaneously pushing back my feet in a ridiculous attempt at air-swimming. I'm up! More than half my body is now supported by the ceiling, and it's clear that all I need to do is keep moving forwards very, very slowly. I inch myself along, waiting for that inevitable movie-moment when the tiles give way.

But no! John Hughes is a liar. Turns out it's perfectly possible for a man to get above the ceiling. (Maybe Judd Nelson is heavier than me.) I always thought that was probably the case, but like believing in God, it took a leap of faith to confirm my suspicions.

And now I'm filled with the fervour of a new believer. Workers unite! You have nothing to lose but your terminals. There's a whole new world waiting above your desks, a dusty heaven hidden above the hell of the office. I take it all back: I feel no guilt about putting John up there. He's certainly been enjoying a much better existence than I have.

Back to the matter in hand. I'm listening out for any indication of feline occupation, wondering which distant corner is hiding the ginger tom. Hearing nothing, I lose my enthusiasm. OK, so it's exciting to be defying gravity (sort of), but there's a large surface to be covered here, and I'm not yet settled enough in my new belief to risk moving quickly (I'm a recent convert). So I keep moving slowly, making progress by gently pushing my hands and feet against the tiles like some kind of insect.

Actually, now I come to think of it, I really don't know the cat's a tom. To be honest, the only reason I've assumed he's a guy is because he's ginger, and therefore has to be a *ginger tom*. And also because I've called him John (although that doubles-back as I only called him John because I thought he was a tom). I try to remember what the pet-shop owner said. Surely he'd know the difference between a boy-cat and a girl? But I can't remember him saying anything and think he just took my word about it's gender. So maybe John is a Jane, and if so, maybe she's pregnant. I don't know why this possibility should suddenly leap to mind, but once I've thought about it this explanation makes a lot of sense. After all, that cat was pretty fucking fat, and it's probably gone off into the darkness to body forth new life.

It'd be nice if this fantasy turned out to be true, but I think it's probably unlikely. Finding a pregnant pet is a standard renewal dream, not something that happens in real life. No, John's a tom and I should stop all this procrastination and just find him.

I wonder where I am now. I can tell from the positioning of the metal supports that I'm past the toilets, but I wonder whether I'm above the corridor or the call-centre proper. I could always lift up the nearest tile and have a peek, but I'm so paranoid about falling that I don't want to do anything to alter the ceiling structure.

I tell you what I really need now. Farnell's torch. It was silly to get up here without any form of light, and unless I have an amazing stroke of luck I'll be crawling around all night. I'm particularly worried about going halfway across the ceiling and then getting stranded. It's a fair distance between the ceiling and the floor, and if I dropped down in the wrong place I could end up with a broken neck.

It also doesn't help that I can't look behind me. Then I could see how far I've come from the light of the lifted tile. My movements are incredibly restricted, and all I can do is keeping pressing onwards, hoping John will make himself known before I get stuck. I suppose I should rely on a systematic plan of action, dividing the space into sections and trying them all in turn. Wherever John's hiding, he's either too far away for his movements to be heard or keeping very still.

I'm feeling quite anxious about cutting my hands. There's all kinds of rubbish lying in the dust up here; screws, bolts, broken strip-lights, cat-crap. God knows what state my suit's in. I'm planning to dump my jacket in the locker before going to The Pentangle, but I hope my trousers can be cleaned. People don't really notice your clothes when you're clubbing, do they?

I think I'd be able to see John if he was in the middle of the ceiling. So what I'm going to do is slowly move round the edges, following a vaguely rectangular path. I push my wrists down to turn round, then aim for the wall. Once I get there I feel more secure, although I'm not sure why. Maybe it's just because I'm freaked by the flexibility of the ceiling and it's reassuring to have something solid beside me.

I keep one palm against the wall and get up onto my knees. Then I slowly start shuffling, pleased that I'm doing my job properly. I'm aiming for the far wall, aware that it'll take me a while to get there, but happy to have a plan. Dad used to say I was useless around the house because I got too inventive, unable to accept that the best way to sweep the floor is the way it's always been done. Searching for John in this straightforward manner suggests I've finally learned how to be sensible.

I'm entering uncharted territory now, and it's like dreaming or deep-sea diving, a secret darkness experienced alone. I continue shuffling for what feels like twenty minutes, but it's hard to measure time passing up here. I'm about to enter the scary mid-point of my mission, and soon it'll take as long to get back as it will to complete the task. It's a little worrying that my movements don't seem to be reducing the distance in front of me, and it all seems so onerous that I begin to fear that maybe I am dreaming and will never recover the cat.

These anxieties don't last long. Three more shuffles and my knees come down onto what feels like a firm, but giving, pillow. It's not wet so I know it's not catshit and as the pressure of my weight doesn't prompt any sound it seems obvious what's happened. I instinctively jump back and wait until I feel up to further exploration. When I've recovered from my initial revulsion, I sniff the air, wondering if he's already begun to rot. The cat's corpse felt solid enough when I knelt on him, but maybe he's stiff in some patches with soggy maggot holes in his more vulnerable areas. I suppose I could just leave him here, wait until the heat from the air conditioning has caused him to melt and drip down through the holes in the ceiling. Maybe flies will hatch from his fur and escape into the office, giving management an excuse to send their maintenance men on a search. But unfortunately my sense of duty gets the better of me and I decide that as I put him up here, it's my responsibility to take him out.

I breathe in and slide my fingers under his body. He's as heavy as he's always been, which makes me hopeful that he didn't die of starvation. I return my palm against the wall to turn round, then start shinning back the way I came. John's weight helps me concentrate, and I pretend I'm saving a baby from a blazing building. I close my eyes and move faster, seeing no reason to prolong this now I've found him. The illuminated square is still a long way off, but I can reduce the distance by taking a diagonal. Just keep shuffling, Dan. Let's get this over with.

I guess about fifteen minutes pass before I reach the square and have to work out how to get down. I lie John's corpse beside the lifted tile and swing my legs through the hole. I hold on to a metal support and drop onto the chair. My weight makes it slide forward slightly, but fortunately the toilet roll wedges stop it moving too far. Then I strain upwards to lift the cat down. I do this with my eyes closed, still too anxious to look at the body. Now he's no longer breathing he feels like a cuddly toy, his fur like stiff synthetic hair.

I open my eyes and look at John's face. His eyes are open and there's a strange translucent ridge sticking out of his mouth. At first I think it's probably just a crust of dried spit, but when I gingerly test it with my finger it seems too solid. So I put my fingers under his black gums and lever his jaw open. The ridge slips inside his mouth and I realise it's part of the rolled circle of a tied condom. The rest of the prophylactic is pulled inside his throat and I feel queasy as I tug at the spermy knot and fish the Mates out of his mouth.

So it is my fault. I hold the scumbag in one hand and the cat in the other, wondering if I'm going to cry. But I feel too strange to get emotional, overwhelmed by the fact that John died trying to eat my sperm. I remember how mischievous I felt when I first hid the condom in the ceiling and can't understand why I didn't consider this possibility before. The cat's death confirms that there's something wrong with my relationship with Alice, and even though she was nothing to do with my stupidity, John's death seems an omen of worse to come.

Cradling the cat's body, I no longer care about keeping him at arm's length and pull him against my chest. It seems obvious now that this is a warning against motiveless behaviour, proof that doing something just because it's funny isn't always a good idea. Still, there's no point standing here all night and I should really get to The Pentangle. So I carry the cat and the condom out to the lift and use my elbow to jab at the down button. I've left the tile up, but then I need to go back to put my jacket in the locker so it should be fine for the minute. I have my usual panic about security cameras, but then again if they are filming in the lifts, they would have seen me bringing John up in the first place and I would have lost my job already.

I go through the back entrance and stop by the skip, leaving John on the tarmac while I lean inside it and push up all the discarded computer bits and shards of broken glass to clear space down to the bottom. I don't want some unsuspecting skip-ransacker to push his fingers into rotten cat-corpse and they don't tend to go beyond the first couple of levels. Everyone knows that most raiders visit the skip at least once a day, clearing the good stuff from the top and leaving only junk underneath. No, John should be able to remain there undiscovered until there's little left of him.

I chuck John inside and pull the junk back down over his body, arranging it so there's no way you can see even a glimpse of him. Then I allow myself a short, silent prayer, drop the condom down the drain and go back inside the call-centre to clear up the scene of my crime.

It's not as late as I thought. I still have to get to The Pentangle and smooth things over with Adrienne, but I should just about be able to manage it before Alice arrives. There's not enough time to get anything to eat, but I can always buy a packet of crisps at the club. I think they might even do chips after midnight, following some city council legislation about having to serve food with drinks. Besides, the club used to be a restaurant.

There's a small queue outside the front entrance and I join it at the back, watching as the bouncers stop and search everyone coming in. For a long time the Italian couple tried to run The Pentangle without bouncers, but then a bunch of local psychos got wind of the relaxed door policy and targeted the club. Still, even with the bouncers The Pentangle is probably the most laid-back club in Bristol, and I always feel at home when I spend an evening here.

I let the bouncers run their hands across my body and then pay my way in. It's a lot more expensive without one of Adrienne's fliers and I worry how I'm going to pay for my drinks. Maybe I can get Alice to buy a couple of rounds.

Adrienne's standing behind the decks, her lips pressed tight in her usual DJ-ing expression. She's playing an old acid track, an unusual choice for her. It's not until she mixes it into Cola Boy that I realise she's on a nostalgia trip. The club's not as full as it usually is on a Friday and I quickly look round for anyone from work. Dealing with the cat has left me feeling quite hyper, and I'm worried that my lack of caution will get me into trouble. The first thing I need to do is locate Ian, just in case he freaks out when he sees me and tries to beat me up. I walk down by the bar and notice him by the mirrors in a dark corner, sitting alone with a pint. Usually I'd be straight over to sit beside him, and it feels odd that I should be frightened by my friend. This situation is so fucked up.

I spot Adrienne's DJ-deputy, a short boy in a tracksuit with a blond footballer's haircut. He's dancing near the back with two dark-haired women who look much older than him. I walk across and grip his shoulder.

'All right?' he says anxiously, clearly unsure who I am.

'I need to have a word with Adrienne.'

'What?'

'I need to talk to Adrienne. Can you tell her to come across?'

'But she's DJ-ing.'

'Stand in for her. It'll only take a minute.'

He looks at me again. I can tell he's weighing up how seriously he should take my instruction so I try to look menacing, wanting him to assume I'm some sort of local gangster. The office clothes help me look the part, and after a few seconds of sizing-up he walks back to the podium. I watch as Adrienne makes a big show of removing her ear-phones and leaning down to listen to her friend. As he whispers to her she looks up at me, white light passing across her face.

She nods and passes the headphones across, jumping down onto the dancefloor and coming across to where I'm standing. I smile and she raises her eyebrows at me.

'Yes?'

'Oh good, you're talking to me. I wondered if the restriction would be limited to the office.'

'So what do you want?'

'Alice is coming down.'

'And?'

'I just wanted to check that's OK.'

'It's a club, not a private party. There are no restrictions.'

'Right.'

I stand there. She looks at me.

'Anything else?'

'It's just, well, after the meeting, I said that everything had been sorted out.'

'And what did you mean by that?'

'That we were doing what she'd told us. Talking again and all that.'

'Right, so you want me to talk to you?'

'No. I just don't want things to be awkward. With Ian, I mean.'

'I can't speak for Ian. If you've got a problem, you should talk to him.'

'Will he speak to me?'

'I don't know.' She sighed. 'You don't have any idea what you've done, do you, Dan?'

'Well, to be honest, I thought you might understand. You know how tough things have been for me lately. Especially with my dad and everything.'

She looks at the dancefloor. 'We might have forgiven you. If you'd handled it properly.'

'What else could I have done? You weren't even talking to me.'

'Before that.'

'There wasn't a before that. It happened late on Monday night and I didn't see you again until Thursday morning.'

'You could've told me you were thinking about it.'

'I wasn't thinking about it. The whole thing was entirely spur-of-the-moment.'

'You must've known how we'd feel. Why else didn't you come in on Tuesday and Wednesday?'

'Alice wouldn't let me.'

'She imprisoned you in her home?'

'Not exactly.'

'OK, Dan, let's say I forgive you for starting to see Alice behind our backs. What about the Suggestions Book?'

'I know, that was stupid. But I was angry at you for ignoring me and it seemed a fairly trivial way of evening the score.'

'The thing is, Dan, I believe you are that stupid. It seems perfectly concievable that you would do something as idiotic as that just because you were a bit irritated with me. But unfortunately for you, Ian thinks you're clever. He thinks you've got some scheme in mind and it's going to involve at least one of us losing our job. And you don't need me to tell you how that makes him think about you.'

'So what do I do?'

'You could try talking to him. I'm not sure how much he's had to drink, but even if he's pissed up I doubt he'll get violent. His job means too much to him for that.'

'OK. I'll talk to him. But are things straight between us?'

'I don't know, Dan. I like you a lot. But you're so spineless, and you've got no fucking sense of loyalty. I don't know if I can risk having such a loose-cannon for a friend.'

'Oh come on, Adrienne. I know you're going out with Ian but you don't have to turn into him. You're as much of a liability as I am.'

She smiles. 'OK, you're right, I'm being a cunt. But I do think Ian's right about a lot of things. And I really respect the way he's taken a stance over this. I mean, it's not as if he's done anything bad to you. He's just made it clear you fucked up.'

'Right,' I say, bored of this. 'So if I admit I've been stupid and humble myself in front of Ian, are you prepared to forgive me?'

'I've already forgiven you. I'm just following orders.'

Adrienne returns to the podium and takes the headphones from her stand-in. My stomach feels tight and I go through my pockets, relieved to find I've got enough change for at least one pint. The notes from the last of Adrienne's money are hidden under my side of Alice's double bed, one of the few secret places I could find in her house. I keep thinking I've got loads stashed there, but after the Chinese meal the other night and all the miscellaneous expenses over the last couple of days, it can't be much more than eighty quid. Still, it's not worth having a proper panic until it's all gone.

I go across to the bar and order a pint of Foster's. Then I carry it over to where Ian is sitting, putting it on the table as I slide in beside him.

'All right, Ian?'

He doesn't reply.

'Look, I've spoken to Adrienne and she's told me how you feel.'

'Ade doesn't know how I feel.'

'You tell me then.'

He sips from his pint and angles his head further away from me. I watch his cigarette as he knocks the ash from the tip and brings it back to his lips.

'There's no point.'

'I know I've fucked up, Ian, but you're reading too much into this. There's no big plot, and I'm only fucking Alice because she's an easy shag.'

He laughs. 'Does she know that?'

'You know what I'm saying. I've just been a bit silly, that's all. And mentioning the Suggestions Book to Alice was just a separate bit of pettiness. I'm not saying you're wrong to be angry. Just understand that I've been stupid, not malicious.'

He looks at me and I stop talking, shamed by his attention. Ian's got one of those faces that seem to halt your words after they've left your mouth but before they've reached his ears, sending them back so you can hear them again and realise how stupid you sound. Before this business Ian usually let me off the hook, making some minimal reply which moved the conversation on without being too indulgent. Tonight, however, he has no interest in helping me out and keeps staring at me as if I haven't said anything. I hate the fact that I can't cheapen his integrity, wishing I could remember some terrible act to prove he's not as ethical as he's making out.

'I don't have a problem with you and Alice,' he says eventually.

'Great.'

'But you can't expect me to trust you.'

'Just talking would be a start.'

'All right.'

'Fantastic. Listen, Alice is going to arrive in about five minutes. Can I stay here and wait with you?'

'If that's what you want.'

He looks back to the dancefloor. I can't work out whether our brief exchange has made things better or worse. I'm worried he's only pretending to forgive me so he doesn't have to listen to my pathetic apologies, and that despite the outward appearance of everything being fine, I've slipped even further in his estimation.

After I interrupted her, Adrienne moved out of her acid nostalgia session and is now playing some garage track that's been in the charts lately. (At least, I assume it's been in the charts. It could equally have been on one of the compilation tapes that Ade made for me back when we were still friends. The point is, I recognise it. I don't tend to notice how much music I hear subliminally until I get to The Pentangle and know every second song. It's the way Ade mixes tracks like this with her own more esoteric interests that brings people back to this club, and she is – as I've already explained – brilliant at judging the mood of a dancefloor.) I take another gulp from my pint and look over to the entrance. A girl in a short blue skirt and a white top catches my attention and I follow her path to the ladies toilet. I'm still waiting for her to come out when Ian nudges my arm.

'Alice,' he mutters.

For a moment I forget the current situation and think back to the first time our team leader came into The Pentangle. Then I remind myself that I'm supposed to be pleased to see her and give a half-hearted wave. She's dressed even more badly than

I am, wearing a shapeless brown blouse and the same stretched grey leggings she had on last time she came here. I smile as she approaches our table.

'Vodka and orange?' I ask.

'That'd be nice.'

'Right.' I stand up, then make a big show of going through my pockets.

'Problem?' she asks.

'I don't seem to have brought enough cash with me.'

Ian rolls his eyes. 'I'll get these.'

'No, it's OK,' Alice says, handing me a tenner. 'Use this to buy a round.'

I go across to the bar and order the drinks, watching Alice's and Ian's reflections in the nearest mirrored surface. She puts her bag on the table and moves in beside him. It suddenly occurs to me that I don't know whether there's any romantic history between these two. This is something I haven't even considered, which seems daft now. Normally something like that would be common office knowledge, but both Ian and Alice are pretty secretive, and now that it's occurred to me, their coupling seems a perfectly plausible scenario. That would also explain why Ian's got so angry over something relatively trivial. It's important that I never forget I'm the odd one out here: that no matter how sexually intimate Alice and I become, she's got much more in common with Ian than she'll ever have with me.

The barmaid smiles and takes the money for the drinks. I wait for my change, then carry the glasses back to the table. Alice looks up.

'Have you talked to Adrienne?'

I nod. She looks at Ian.

'And we're all friends again?'

Ian smiles. She puts her arm around his shoulder.

'That's good. I don't like my team fighting.' She looks round. 'Where's Teri?'

'Oh, she hardly ever comes here,' Ian explains. 'I don't think it's her sort of thing.'

'Why not?' Alice asks. 'I think this place is brilliant.'

Ian doesn't reply.

After about thirty minutes of sitting there without speaking, I ask Alice if she wants to dance. She looks at Ian, then nods and stands up.

'You coming?' she asks him.

'No thanks.'

'Suit yourself,' she laughs, and then follows me out onto the dancefloor. I'm holding Alice's hand and it feels as if I'm about to spin her out in front of me and start doing some fifties jiving. Instead of which, we separate and begin shuffling opposite each other.

'What were you talking to Ian about?'

'When?'

'Just now. When I went up to the bar.'

'Nothing much. Ian was surprised about you coming out without any money. He warned me not to let you take advantage.'

'What did you say?'

'I told him I trusted you. So then he told me about the money you'd borrowed from Adrienne and I said I knew about that and you'd soon be paying her back.'

'You told him that?'

'Relax. I didn't say you were getting the money from me. It's good that he knows you can repay your debts.'

'Yeah. I guess so.'

'What's the problem?'

'Nothing. I just haven't told Ade yet, that's all.'

'Never mind. I'm sure she'll just be glad to know she's getting her money.'

'Yeah, you're right.'

I don't say anything more, not wanting Alice to get suspicious. It's not that I'm not going to give Ade the money, just that I wanted to have a couple of days pretending the grand was mine before handing it over.

We carry on dancing through the next few tracks. I know I've been seeing Alice for almost a week now, but I'm still surprised when we do coupley things together. I'm too inexperienced to know whether this is:

1. A natural phenomenon occurring in relationships that begin arse-backwards (i.e. starting with a shag and then expanding into a romance, rather than the traditional gradual escalation).
2. An inability on my part to cope with the change in roles, and a consequent amazement that I should be getting into these situations with my team leader.
3. The standard readjustment necessary when someone who's been single as long as I have finds himself in a couple.

or all of the above.

Nevertheless, I'm pleased that our frugging seems to be working out, especially as this was a source of conflict between Sonia and me. We only danced together on two or three occasions, but I remember getting upset that she wouldn't look at me and feel happy that Alice is maintaining eye-contact.

After the next track fades out, Alice nods in Ian's direction. I shrug and follow her across. Just before we reach his table, she asks, 'Do you think Adrienne's going to come across?'

'I doubt it. She seems pretty engrossed.'

Alice nods. 'Shall we just say goodbye to Ian and go then?'

'OK.'

'You don't mind?'

'No, I'm pretty tired. It's been a long day.'

I wait while Alice slips in beside Ian, exchanges goodbyes, then slips out again. I nod and raise my hand to him, before walking away with Alice. We sneak between the bouncers now relaxing near the entrance and out onto the street.

'Where are you parked?'

'Not far. In the square by the cinema.'

Alice holds her strawberry fob in her left hand and looks both ways before crossing the empty road. A stretch of tattered

Robbie Williams posters curl from the surface of a nearby wall. A dishevelled old man in dungarees and a purple baseball cap walks towards us. I try to ignore him but he stumbles up and grips my arm.

'You found her then.'

'What?'

'The one you were waiting for. Remember?'

'No,' I say, shaking him loose.

Alice unlocks the car and we climb inside. She unclips the crook-lock and throws it on the back seat, then pulls away.

'You didn't want to stay, did you?'

'No, no. I'm really glad to be going home. I don't think I'll wake up until Sunday.'

She smiles. 'Heavy night yesterday?'

'Alice . . .'

'I'm joking. So things turned out OK, right?'

'Yeah,' I admit, 'in the end.'

'And do you think we're OK?'

'I think so. We still haven't had our big conversation.'

'Oh, I can't remember what that was supposed to be about.'

I don't say anything. She looks at me.

'Can you?' she asks.

'Well . . . yeah.'

'Go on then.'

'It was to do with something I've been frightened to ask you.'

'What?'

'This is going to sound crass . . .'

'Just say it.'

'Were you abused as a child?'

'What?' she laughs. 'Whatever made you think that?'

'I don't know. It seemed like something that might have happened.'

'Why?'

'Lots of reasons. The fact that you were such a tomboy at

410

school ... and that your dad's not around any more ... all of that stuff.'

'What, because my parents are divorced and I went through a teenage rebellion, you think my dad had sex with me?'

'It wasn't just that,' I protest weakly.

'No, Dan, I wasn't abused.'

'Good.'

'Anything else?'

'No.'

We don't make love when we get back. My question has made sex inappropriate tonight, and although it seems unfair that she should be so angry about my concern, I understand why she doesn't want me. It's a shame that the evening ended with an argument, but I still feel more settled than I have in ages and hope Alice's good mood will have returned by the time we wake up.

20

I sleep differently when I know it doesn't matter what time I wake up. I know I enjoyed a couple of extended lie-ins earlier in the week, but they were unexpected: my body refusing to meet my demands. Last night was the first time in ages I could sleep as long as I wanted, and in spite of Alice's malicious fidgets, I don't give up her bed until after midday.

I walk naked to the en suite and go through my usual ablutions, then get dressed and find Alice in the lounge.

'Where are the others?'

'Cathy's taken Tim to the video shop.'

'Right. Alice, do you think you could lend me some money to go shopping?'

'I expect so. What do you want to buy?'

'Just some clothes. I'm embarrassed about how little I've got to wear.'

'OK,' she smiles, 'we can go after we get back from the hospital.'

'What?'

'Oh yeah, I forgot to tell you. Claire called this morning to remind you that you promised to visit your dad today.'

'Right. And you're coming with me?'

'If that's OK. I thought it would save you having to get a bus and then that long walk.'

'True.'

'If you don't want me to come, I'll understand.'

'No, that's fine.'

'Do you want some breakfast first?'

'No, I'll just grab an apple and we can get going.'

Dad's still in Ward Eleven. He looks a lot better than the last time I visited, mainly because he's sitting up higher in the bed and wearing his glasses. He smiles lopsidedly at me and I wonder how much his women have told him.

'Dad, this is Alice.'

'I know.'

They exchange a look. I wait, feeling awkward. Then we sit on two plastic chairs next to his bed, I pour two glasses of water from a jug with a white flip-top and hand one to Alice.

'Actually, could I have a glass, son?'

'Course. Sorry.' I quickly fill a glass and hand it to him. He smiles again and takes a long sip.

'So,' he says, 'long time, no see.'

'Yeah,' I answer, 'sorry about that. How have you been?'

'Not bad. The swelling in my leg's gone down but my elbow's still pretty bulbous. Do you want to see the pen marks?'

'No, that's OK.'

Dad laughs, then says to Alice, 'Dan's always been a bit squeamish. Not like my other visitors. They can't get enough of the grisly details.'

She nods.

'So,' says Dad, 'I understand you're homeless.'

'Not exactly. Alice has taken me in.'

'Right. But we don't have the room any more?'

'No.'

'What about my stuff?'

'I've got all your personal belongings, but I couldn't bring the electronic equipment.'

'What about my disks?'

'Yeah, I've got those.'

'But not the computer?'

'No.'

'Or the TV, or the video?'

'No.'

'So what happened? I heard the story from Claire, but I didn't really understand it. Or got the impression that you were holding stuff back. Did you have some sort of fight with Farnell?'

'No, not at all. I wasn't telling the truth when I said I could manage your half of the rent. So I went to Farnell and threw myself on his mercy. His suggestion was that he got someone else in to handle the other half of the rent.'

'You were sharing the room?'

'Yeah.'

'And what happened? Was he a psycho?'

'Not exactly. I mean he wasn't normal, and he had a pretty mental mate called Mavis, but I don't think I was in any physical danger.'

'Mavis?'

'Yeah, but it was a bloke, not a girl. That was his nickname.'

'Right, I think I'm with you. So why did you have to leave in such a hurry? Did you owe him money?'

'No, I just went through this weird paranoid phase. I can't really explain it. Things weren't made any easier by the fact that this guy kept me up all night and kept making me go out so he could shag underage girls and made me watch pornography.'

Dad looks at me. 'Pornography?'

'Yeah. I was just being too sensitive, I guess.'

'So why didn't you take the TV and computer?'

'I couldn't. I didn't move out of the flat and straight into Alice's. There was this long period when I was living in the call-centre.'

'You were living at work?'

Alice laughs.

'Yeah,' I say, smiling, 'I realise that must sound crazy.'

'But you're with Alice now?'

'Yeah.'

'And do you still have a key to the room?'

'Yeah.'

'So you could go back and get the TV and computer and stuff and bring it over to Alice's?'

'Yeah, I guess so. If they haven't sold it or changed the locks.'

Dad laughs. 'I can't see Farnell changing the locks. Do you remember what a song and dance he made about that when we moved in?'

'Yeah.'

'And did your room-mate . . .'

'Kevin.'

'Did Kevin have his own TV?'

'No.'

'Well, he's hardly likely to have got rid of mine, is he? No, I think you should probably go back and pick up my stuff.'

'What if he's there?'

'Just tell him you've come for your stuff. I can't see him having a problem with that.'

'What about Farnell?'

'Farnell's just a common crook. He won't try to stop you.'

'But what about me moving without telling him?'

'Do you owe him any rent?'

'I'm not sure.'

'Well, look, he's got our deposit and someone new in the room. I doubt you're going to have any problems with him.'

He stretches, then looks at Alice.

'You don't mind looking after my computer for a while, do you?'

'No, that's fine.'

'Good.'

I can't help feeling irritated with my dad after this conversation, and say hardly anything to him throughout the rest of our visit. I should've realised his possessions would be all he was worried about. Unlike most men, I've never been that concerned about winning my father's approval, but after all the nice things Claire said to me about how I handled myself after Dad went into hospital, I expected him to be similarly supportive. Of course I understand he's pissed off about losing his computer, but going back to that room could be really dangerous, and I don't think it's fair of him to make light of it.

As we're about to leave, Alice leans over Dad and kisses his cheek. I can't help thinking this is overintimate and feel paranoid again, wondering if they've secretly met before. Last night I dreamt I was in an arranged marriage, and it isn't that much of a stretch to believe my relationship with Alice was planned long before by Dad's group.

'Alice,' says Dad, 'do you mind if I have a quick moment alone with Dan?'

'Not at all.' She looks at me. 'I'll be in the car.'

I watch her walk away, then sit back down. I'm worried Dad's going to want to talk about the stuff I said to Claire about being afraid he was going to kill me. I just can't bear listening to him explain what he really meant in stupid psychobabble, and also don't like the idea of that sort of intimacy between us. Dad's always been a firm believer in voicing taboo thoughts and I know he'll relish such a black conversation.

'Would you like some more water?'

He shakes his head. 'So you've met everybody then?'

'Yeah.'

'What did you think of Claire?'

'She's nice.'

'Good. And they've spoken to you about what's going to happen when I get out of hospital?'

'Sort of.'

'You know they're going to look after me?'

'Brittany said something.'

He raises an eyebrow. 'Brittany?'

'Yeah.' I pause. 'When I met them all together.'

'Oh. Right. So you're OK with that?'

'Let's face it, Dad. I'm hardly going to make the best of nurses.'

He laughs. 'True.'

'Is that all you wanted to talk about?'

'Pretty much.' He looks worried. 'You will come and visit me when I'm with them, won't you?'

'Of course. I'm sorry I didn't see you before, Dad. I was ashamed about losing the room.'

'Don't worry about that, Dan. Just get my stuff back and everything will be fine.'

I leave the back way, going down the rear staircase and cutting through casualty. It's obviously a quiet time for the hospital, and there are no patients with missing limbs or blood gushing from makeshift bandages. I walk across the polished floor and out through the sliding doors.

Alice is sitting in the car, watching me through the windscreen as I emerge between two ambulances and nip across to where she's parked. I open the door and slide in beside her.

'So where do you want to go shopping?'

'I don't mind. Anywhere in the Centre.'

'Burton's, Foster's, that sort of thing?'

'Yeah, although maybe we can go to one of those cheap jeans shops.'

'OK. I'll park behind Argos.'

She starts the engine. I push my fringe out of my eyes and wait for her to manoeuvre out of the space.

'What did your dad want to talk about?'

'Nothing secret. He made me promise to visit him when he gets out of hospital.'

'Where's he going?'

'Didn't I tell you? His group are going to look after him.'

She nods. 'Was he angry you hadn't been in before?'

'Not really. Although he was pretty insistent about me getting his stuff back.'

'I noticed. Do you want to do that after we've gone shopping?'

I look at her, shocked. 'I'm not going there today.'

'Why not?'

'That guy was a total psychopath. God knows what he'll do if he catches me in his room.'

'So what are you going to do?'

'I'll wait until I know he won't be there.'

'Does he work?'

'I think so.'

'So if I give you some time off you can sneak in during the day . . .'

I grin. 'That would be very kind of you.'

Alice parks the car and we go along the ranks of cheap jeans shops. I'm only looking for a pair of black Levi's so it doesn't take long, but we compare prices in all three shops before going back to the first place we tried.

I always used to go clothes shopping with Dad. He was a bizarre dresser, picking out brightly coloured shirts and trousers because he thought they looked funny. I knew he really went for these clothes because he didn't like spending money in the cause of vanity, but he was so good at getting enthusiastic about magenta-coloured jumbo cords that I couldn't allow him this self-deception, and every shopping trip ended with me mocking his false economy and telling him that I was fed up of having a father who looked like a gay painter. He, in return, claimed I was just as deluded, and that it was ridiculous to assume that high price tags were any indication of quality.

My adolescent reaction to Dad's rainbow wardrobe was to start dressing in black. I know this is a not unusual teenage sartorial decision, but I wonder whether other children have come to this choice of colour for the same reason. It was just so reassuring not to have to choose between electric pink and lime green, knowing that no matter how important Dad was making this decision, in reality it was no choice at all.

'Do you want to look for some shirts?'

'Actually, I'm feeling a little peckish. Do you mind if we get some food?'

'I told you to have a proper breakfast. Everywhere's going to be really crowded now.'

'We don't have to go inside anywhere. A hot dog from a van will be fine.'

'OK.'

We walk towards Broadmeads. Alice's cross reaction to my request for food surprised me, and I wonder whether she's more irritated about lending me money than she's letting on. I offer to buy her a hot dog but she says she's not hungry and walks across to the black metal benches.

Not wanting to further irritate Alice, I choose my shirts (one green, the other blue) as quickly as possible, going for something completely casual. My current wardrobe crisis has occurred because everything I own only looks right in an office. These shirts are so informal they'd be inappropriate for anything other than dress-down Friday.

Saturday shopping in the Centre is wearing even with as minimal a mission as mine, and I can tell Alice regrets coming in with me. Not being able to drive makes it hard for me to understand the horror with which drivers regard heavy traffic, but I can tell from the way Alice swings open the car door that she's not looking forward to the journey home.

I try to distract her.

'Thanks for buying me these clothes, Alice. I really appreciate it.'

No response.

'You've been really kind. I know I don't have any money, but I will find a way to make this up to you.'

A laugh, but that's it. I smile at Alice in the rear-view, wanting to prolong this moment of good humour.

'So what do you want to do tonight?'

'I haven't thought about it.'

'A quiet night in then.'

'I expect so.'

Cathy looks up at us as we come in, using the remote to lower the volume on the TV.

'How was your dad?'

'Better.'

'Tim's been waiting for you to get back. He wants you to watch *Schindler's List* with him.'

I sigh. 'Now?'

'I think so. Usually I don't let him take the video into his room, but he was determined to watch it tonight and there's all the Saturday television.'

I look at Alice. 'Do you want to watch it?'

'No. But you go ahead.'

'OK. Come in if you get bored.'

Cathy laughs. 'I think we can entertain ourselves, Dan.'

I cross the hallway to Tim's bedroom. I know I'm in no position to make fun of other people's living arrangements, but I still think there's something peculiar about a bungalow. They were much more popular when I was a child, and I remember my father trying to persuade my mother to live in one. I think he thought it was adventurous, an experiment in modern living. It was up to Mum to point out the practicalities. Unfortunately, she wasn't there when he persuaded me to share a room with him.

There's a plastic danger sign on Tim's door, warning me of the toxic waste within. I knock.

'Come in.'

Tim's sitting on his bed. He stares up at me through his fringe and tugs at his loose football sock. I look round for a chair, then realise there isn't one.

'Sit here,' he says, slapping the mattress.

I do so, pulling the duvet flat beneath me.

'I've fixed it through my stereo so we'll get proper sound.'

'Great.'

'I've already fast-forwarded through the trailers. Did you want to watch them?'

'No, that's fine.'

'Ready?'

I nod. He presses play.

Sitting alongside Tim, I try to remember where I was the first time I saw this movie. I don't go to the cinema often, finding it hard to concentrate even for ninety minutes. But I remember how much I wanted to see this film, and think I also saw *Short Cuts* in the same week. Maybe it was something to do with Sonia. I don't remember. Actually, my memory of the film itself is pretty hazy, and when Liam Neeson first appears it takes me a moment to remember he's the hero. I'd been convinced the main character was Ralph Fiennes. It seems a little evil that I'd made this mistake, but I'm not sure if it's my fault or Spielberg's.

After half an hour I start to lose interest, shuffling round on the bed so I can surreptitiously study Tim's reaction. I want to ask him why he's so interested in the Holocaust, but feel worried about making the boy self-conscious. I don't think I've ever been a specialist on any subject, having no interest in politics, or world affairs, or television or books, or spaceships or dinosaurs. When I was making my way through Dad's library, I felt envious of his intellectual freedom, resenting the way he could move between interests, getting everything he needed from his blue-spined Pelicans. It seems sad that I'm so scared of looking stupid that the only intellectual effort I'm prepared to make is to ironically follow his footsteps, deconstructing his personality before I've had chance to form my own.

I also feel embarrassed about the influence I'm having on Alice's family. Remembering the conversation I had with Cathy about the personalities presented in *Political Ideas*, my attitude now seems incredibly patronising, and I regret answering her as if her questions were stupid instead of admitting my own ignorance. And is it constructive to suggest Tim follows his nine hours of watching *Shoah* with the Hollywood version?

Cathy opens the door. 'Excuse me, boys. Are you ready for dinner?'

Tim scowls at her and stops the video.

'Yes please,' I say, glad of the distraction.

'I thought we'd just have a little buffet meal if that's all right with you, Dan.'

'Fine.'

Her head retreats behind the closing door. Tim looks at me and releases the pause.

Dinner is sliced ham inside slashed rolls, a few lettuce leaves and a packet of salt and vinegar crisps. I eat the rolls and the lettuce but put the crisps to one side, worried my crunching will distract Tim. He doesn't eat anything, but I don't know whether this is because the on-screen atrocities have put him off his food or because he's a purist about his pleasures.

Domesticity has always disturbed me. I've never felt comfortable feeling comfortable and find it hard even taking my shoes off indoors. Eating dinner in Tim's bedroom is an unnerving experience, reminding me of the handful of occasions when I had anything like this with my own family. I can't remember the specifics, but there was this one time when I was very young and I was lying on a mattress with my father eating salt and vinegar peanuts and watching *Play It Again, Sam* on the television. I think we were supposed to be moving furniture but we'd put the bookcase in front of the door so Mum couldn't get in and skived off. It's a very vague memory, but for years afterwards whenever I thought of Woody Allen my mental picture of him was accompanied by an image of my father throwing peanuts in the air and trying to catch them in his mouth.

When the film ends I take my plate back into the lounge and sit down next to Alice. Both women are enjoying the television, but after the last three hours I'm feeling restless and can't concentrate on the screen.

'Do you fancy going to the pub?'

'Not really,' says Alice. 'Why? Do you?'

'No, not especially. I just feel like getting a breath of fresh air.'

Neither woman says anything.

'Do you mind if I go for a walk?'

'No, that's fine.'

As soon as I'm outside I feel angry at myself. This is my life now, I have to adapt to their rhythms. If I don't get used to this now, I'll end up like Dad, staying late at the Casino instead of facing my frustrations at home. What's so terrible about watching TV? It only seems difficult because I'm making it that way, refusing to relax into the programmes and accept them for what they are. It doesn't matter that they're so bland and unengaging. Cathy and Alice probably don't like them any more than I do. They just use the pretext of watching television as an excuse to retreat into their private worlds, freed from the burden of continuing conversation.

I realise this isn't an original observation, and only include it here because this is genuinely one of the first times I've thought seriously about the way people arrange their lives. Oh, I've always known my parents were different, and that in other houses mums and dads didn't get bored at the end of the evening and take their kids on a midnight drive. But I assumed other families had equally unusual ways of killing time, and was never round anyone else long enough to have this illusion disproved.

I cross the road and walk towards the heart of the village. There's something so reassuring about the glow of the streetlights and the scent of the large bushes providing protective walls in front of almost every house here. I love this sort of surburbia, with short tarmac pavements and television light in every living room. There's a group of kids surrounding the church, their bikes propped up against headstones as they sit drinking. I pass them and walk round to the off-licence, thinking that if we are going to stay in,

I might as well attempt to liven up the evening with a few glasses of wine.

Cathy and Alice appreciate my initiative and quickly fetch glasses from the kitchen. After a couple of refills, it's a lot easier to sit still, and although I keep getting the urge to start up a conversation, I manage to resist it and keep my eyes trained on the television. But the best thing about this sort of sit-com living is that it's perfectly permissible to head off to bed early, and at half past ten Alice reaches for my hand and we leave Cathy alone in the lounge.

'That was good wine,' Alice says as she pushes the door closed over the resistive carpet, 'was it expensive?'

'Not really.'

Alice untucks her blouse from her trousers and sits on the bed. 'You didn't mind that I didn't want to go to the pub?'

'No. I'm sorry, I'm just not used to this.'

She frowns. 'What?'

'Normality. Sitting down on a Saturday night and relaxing.'

'I didn't realise you were such a hardcore clubber.'

'I'm not talking about clubbing. I just mean it seems strange that you're so happy spending time with your mother. The first time we talked about our parents you said you found this arrangement really stressful.'

'Did I? I wasn't talking about watching TV. I get on fine with mum. I just meant it pisses me off when she criticises me.'

'What does she criticise you about?' I ask, sensing an opening.

'Oh, nothing serious. I went through a phase when none of my relationships lasted more than a week and she kept saying it was my fault.'

'Why?'

'She thought I was loose, I suppose. Although she likes to pretend she's really liberated so she wouldn't have put it like that.'

I nod, finding it hard to concentrate now she's taken off her bra and is unzipping her trousers. I realise I should get undressed and start unbuttoning my shirt. Alice walks to the wardrobe and takes out a hanger.

'I really wanted you this morning,' she giggles, 'but you refused to wake up.'

'What about now?'

'Not really. Sorry.'

'That's OK.'

'Sure?'

'Yeah.'

She hangs her trousers in the wardrobe and bounds over to the bed in her pale pink knickers. I stand up as she pulls back the duvet, making way for her to slide inside. Then I finish undressing and get in next to her, amazed at how nice it feels just to be holding Alice. I know I'm going to lie awake for the next few hours, but not being alone more than makes up for that. So I have a new life, and despite a few initial frustrations, it shouldn't take me long to adapt.

21

Still, it's a relief to reach Monday morning. I'm beginning to understand the affection other people feel towards the office, and although I'll never be jumping out of bed at seven thirty, I do wake voluntarily in time for breakfast and feel eager to get back behind my desk.

Not that Sunday was all bad. The morning was best, with Alice making up for Saturday night by initiating an hour of long, slow love-making. It was the first time we'd had sex in that lazy, friendly way, and I was surprised at how eager Alice was to ask me questions, enquiring whether I preferred it faster, slower, with her hand, her mouth, like this, like that?

Cathy potters around the kitchen in her dressing gown, making us toast.

'When do you want to do it, then?' Alice asks.

'What?'

'Get your Dad's stuff back.'

'Oh, right. I don't think I should go there before lunch.'

'Why not?'

'I'm fairly certain Kevin used to sleep late. If I go there now I'm bound to run into him.'

'Right . . . so this afternoon?'

I nod. 'If that's OK.'

'I should think so.'

Moving in with Alice has certainly improved my mornings. I've only been here a week and yet I can't imagine going back to the way I used to start the day, staggering out of bed five minutes before the bus and enduring a bleary-eyed morning ride. I think I pretended to like the bus because I couldn't imagine my situation ever changing and thought I ought to make the most of it. Now I have the choice of being driven with the radio playing and my seat adjusted to suit my frame, the bus seems a mediaeval alternative.

There's much less congestion on the road from Keynsham to Quick Kall than there used to be on my old bus route. It also helps speed things up that Alice is free to try alternative roads whenever she reaches a blocked area. The most numbing thing about travelling by bus was knowing that it would inevitably take an hour to cover ground that at any other time could be got through in fifteen minutes.

Alice gets to the Centre so quickly I'm almost disappointed, reluctant to give up this comfort zone and go out into the grim morning. It's only eight thirty and when she lets me out I tell her that I'm going to nip to the newsagents for a paper. I don't really want one, and it's only an excuse not to have to sit in the breaks room for half an hour. She smiles and asks me if I could get her some chewing gum.

After my conversations with Adrienne and Ian in The Pentangle on Friday, I'm looking forward to finding out whether they really have forgiven me and will be prepared to talk to me again. I suppose I should really attempt a reconciliation with Gordon, but I know he won't be prepared to talk to me until he's had the go ahead from Ian. So in the meantime I sit at my work-station and stare at him, waiting for the others to arrive.

Teri turns up next. She's wearing a transparent pink plastic hairband that matches the colour of her lipstick. This seems an unusually girly adornment for Teri, but I get the impression I shouldn't mention it. She puts the tartan bag under the table and sits next to me.

'All right, Dan?'

'Yeah.' I look at her. 'I've managed to sort things out with Adrienne and Ian.'

'Really?'

I nod. 'Yeah, Alice made me go to The Pentangle on Friday and we all had a proper chat.'

Teri smiles. 'So do you think it'll last?'

'I think so. I got a chance to talk to Ian when Alice wasn't there so I think he was being sincere. And Ade was only ignoring me because Ian told her to.'

'What about . . . ?' she nods in Gordon's direction.

'He's still carrying on the campaign, but only because he doesn't realise it's over. Gordon's the soldier left behind enemy lines.'

She chuckles. 'Any idea what's happened to my headset?'

'Probably been swiped. Check the drawer.'

She rolls her swivel-chair further down the table and pulls out the drawer. I look at the pale strip of flesh exposed above her waist as she leans downward. I watch her check through the bits and pieces hidden there and then look up to see Adrienne striding confidently into the office.

'Good morning, Adrienne.'

'Hi, Dan. Good weekend?'

'Not bad. You?'

'OK. Didn't do much.'

Adrienne slumps heavily into her chair and checks her watch. Gordon's been observing our exchange with interest, and looks to Adrienne for an explanation. She pretends not to notice.

'Ian wasn't doing the early shift then?'

'No, he's stopped doing that altogether now. My bad influence.'

All four of us look at each other, lapsing into silence and noticing that according to the neon display above our table, there are already four calls waiting. Even good old Gordon seems reluctant to start work today, and I'm the first person to plug in and take a call.

It's someone on the Car Insurance line, wanting to talk to a qualified adviser. I know I shouldn't be afraid of these calls and if I'd tried dealing with a few instead of always passing them on to Gordon, I might have learned how to handle them by now. It's probably not all that difficult and only seems so because very time one comes through I'm thrown into a panic. It's all on the screen, after all, and if I follow it step by step the computer's menu should guide me through. My biggest failing is to look for short cuts. These programs are designed to turn you into one of those infuriating operators incapable of making the simplest mental jump, having to follow an exact procedure and being prepared to argue the toss for twenty minutes just to get the right information at the right stage.

'OK, sir, bear with me. Before we go any further, the first thing I need is your name and postcode.'

It takes twenty minutes to complete the call. When the caller breaks the connection I feel a real sense of accomplishment. I didn't skip over any stages or guess his response before he said it and I didn't have to go back. I inputted his details correctly so he'll even get the appropriate send-outs. Usually with the complex lines I deliberately fuck up early and then key in any old nonsense safe in the knowledge that it'll never get to them.

A blonde woman approaches our table. It's the karaoke woman, the one I set up with Dennis from the Banks & Building Societies line. She stands by Ian.

'Hi,' she says nervously, 'are you on my list?'

'No,' he says, 'I don't think so. Is it too late to get a ticket?'

Her face lights up. 'No, there's still plenty left. But you'll have to give me the money now.'

'How much is it?'

'Two fifty.'

'Right.' Ian leans forward and counts out the change from his pocket. She hands him a small rectangle of green paper. Ian tucks it into his trousers and she moves on to me.

'I'm on your list.'

'Have you given me the money?'

'I can't remember. Doesn't it say?'

She looks at the list. 'Usually I put a tick by the people who've paid and a star by the ones who've said they're coming but haven't given me the money.'

'What do I have?'

'Nothing, but if you think you're on the list I probably just forgot.'

'So do you want me to give you some money?'

'No, if you think you've paid I'm sure you have.' She laughs. 'You must've distracted me.'

'Guilty as charged. I think I asked you about Dennis.'

'Dennis,' she repeats, 'do you know him then?'

'No, not really. You were telling me how you got some weird phone call telling you to go on a date with him.'

'Oh, yeah, right.'

'Did you ever find out who it was?'

'No.'

'But you're still together?'

'Yeah. Things are going really well.'

'Great.'

She looks at me and bites her lip, as if trying to think her way out of this conversation. 'Are you involved with anyone?'

I nod. 'Do you know Alice?'

'I don't think so.'

I point to reception. 'The woman talking to the guy in the blue shirt.'

'Right. Are you happy?'

'Yeah, I think so. We've only just started going out so I don't know how things are going to develop, but at the moment everything's fine.'

'That's great. Maybe you and Alice would like to go out with me and Dennis one night.'

'I'd like that. Let's talk about it tomorrow night. You can introduce me to Dennis.'

'OK.'

The blonde moves on to Teri. She waits while Teri finishes her call and then asks the same question.

'No,' Teri replies, 'I'm not on your list. I don't think I was here when you came round before.'

'Right. Are you a temp?'

Teri stares at her.

'I mean, perhaps you hadn't started working here when I was selling the tickets.'

'Oh no, I was just out of the office or something. I've been working here as long as anyone else on the team. Probably longer.'

'So would you like a ticket?'

Teri glances at me. 'Yeah, why not?'

The exchange is made, and the blonde woman looks at Gordon. He rubs his chin.

'I'd like a ticket,' he tells her.

'No problem.' She smiles. 'Do you have the two pounds fifty?'

He nods. She waits while he fishes it out. Adrienne glares at her as she hands Gordon his green rectangle.

'No,' she snaps, 'I'm not on your list.'

'OK. And you don't want to go?'

'No.'

Ian looks up. 'Come on, Ade, it'll be a laugh.'

'Yeah. Right.'

'Give her a ticket,' Ian tells the blonde. 'I'll pay for it.'

She looks at Adrienne, who doesn't say anything. Ian gets up to give her the money. The blonde leaves the ticket on the table by Adrienne's computer. Then she smiles broadly at us and walks across to the next team.

It's been decided that if I leave the office at lunchtime, there's no real point in me coming back for the end of the afternoon. Alice has arranged for Cathy to pick me up from the call-centre, drive me to the room, and wait outside while I load up the car. I'm a bit nervous about taking Cathy with me, but I've made her agree not to come into the room and there's no way I'd have been able to transport all that electronic equipment on the bus.

I get Cathy to wait by the twenty-four hour garage and cross the road. I keep near the main wall as I walk down the muddy lane, not wanting Farnell to spot me through his patio doors. When I reach the metal staircase I expect to see John waiting for his chunk of cod. It's hard to get up to the room without a lot of clanking, but I make sure my footfalls are as light as possible, and hold on to the rail as I go up.

Dad was right. Farnell hasn't changed the locks and after two minutes of fiddling, the catch releases and I sneak inside. Stalling, I check the kitchen and the bathroom, as well as trying the doors to the previously uninhabited rooms. Satisfied that there's no one there, I walk up to our room and try the door.

I put my head round, then duck back when I see a shape under the duvet. I hover there for a second, wondering whether I should close the door and make a run for it. But I feel an urge to look again, especially as I'm not exactly sure what I saw.

The duvet looks like a large bandage. In the centre of the bandage there's a patch of red-black blood that's seeped through the material. The sodden bandage is much more disturbing than looking at an actual wound, hinting at the grisly details beneath but still leaving much to the imagination. I've never been the kind of person to confront horrors and I feel no urge to pull back the duvet. At the same time I'm able to stay in the room, and don't feel the way I thought I would feel when confronted with my first dead body. Dead *human* body, that is, and I think the main reason I'm not too freaked out is because it's not that long since I discovered John.

I suppose I should be worrying about the fingerprints I've left on the door frame or all of the other physical disturbances I've made to this crime scene, but for some reason this doesn't worry me. This is partly because although I've seen the most amazing forensic analysis in detective films, I don't believe our local crime unit has equipment of that sophistication and doubt they'll be able to separate this specific set of prints from all the others we've left in this room while we were living there. But even if they could I'd be prepared to explain why I came back, and although I suppose I could get in trouble for not reporting the crime (at least, I'm assuming it's a murder and not a suicide, as people rarely try to end their lives by stabbing themselves in the stomach) I doubt that anything serious would happen to me, and to be honest, getting embroiled in a major police investigation might be just the thing to liven up my life.

I decide I should at least attempt to identify the victim, and with that in mind approach the bed. For a second I feel a silly horror-movie fear that the corpse will suddenly sit up and groan at me, but there's no sign of movement and when I get closer I can discern that the dead body is definitely Kevin. I'd thought that it might be Mavis, mainly because he seemed much more like the kind of person someone would want to kill. Mavis looked like a heavy from a Japanese comic, with his square head and red-tinted glasses; the kind of character with no family and no one to grieve when he gets blown away. Kevin, however, was just an anonymous bloke, even more so now he's no longer breathing. I remember him telling me about his problems with his parents, and wonder whether there was more to his story than he was prepared to share with me.

I take one last look at Kevin's face, then consider what I'm going to do with the television and video. Dad was right again: they hadn't got rid of his equipment. Even the computer is still here, so I definitely know Kevin didn't die in a burglary. There's a tape in the machine. I eject it, examine the label – *Kev's tape* – and put it back into the slot. I'll examine this in greater detail later, see if it gives me any clues as to what happened here.

I disconnect the TV and video. I don't know why I hadn't considered this before, but I'm momentarily perturbed when I realise that getting this stuff out is going to take at least two trips. Possibly even three, as it'll be hard to carry all the different bits of the computer and the printer in one go. Walking past Farnell's windows that many times seems unnecessarily risky.

I wind the wires around my fist and pick up the TV and video together, rocking back so I can take the weight against my chest. I push the door open with my forehead and go out into the hallway. I need a hand free to fiddle with the dropped lock, so I wrap my left arm under the video and around the screen of the television. Holding tightly to the two machines, I jiggle at the sliding bolt, grimacing as I try to get it to slot into place and let me out of the room. When it finally comes free I stagger forward and have to quickly shuffle to make sure everything stays balanced.

I walk out to the top of the metal staircase, looking down over the edge and deciding it's more sensible to take the video and television down separately. Dad would never forgive me if I got this far and then fucked up at the last minute. So I place the video on the square metal sheet at the top of the stairs and heft the television down on its own. I don't want to leave the TV in the mud so I put it in a nearby wheelbarrow, placing it carefully so it doesn't tip up. Then I go back for the video, making sure each movement is as light as possible. Unlike most landlords, Farnell never once complained about the noise (probably because he was worried we could hear the screams from his torture chamber or whatever nefarious set-up he's got down there) so I've got no idea how much sound carries through to where he's living. As the staircase is bolted directly to the side of the house, it seems likely he'd experience at least some vibrations as we traipsed up and down, but maybe he steers clear of that part of the house. Once or twice, usually on a Saturday night, he'd play Bonnie Tyler or Cat Stevens or Starship at full volume, but even then we'd only hear it if we were walking past his windows. Maybe he's done a really good job of sound-proofing.

I take the video and gently step back down the stairs, placing it alongside the television in the wheelbarrow. Then I go back up to the room for the printer and the keyboard, thinking it more sensible to get all the stuff out first rather than carting one load round to Cathy's car and then having to go all the way back. A third trip secures the monitor and computer, which I rest on the garden wall. I go back one last time, pick up

Matt Thorne

a few bits and pieces I forgot when I cleared out, then lock the door.

I considered leaving my keys inside the room, just to ensure a definite end to this episode, but couldn't bring myself to do it. The keys are a symbol of this odd period in my life and I feel an urge to hang on to them. So I put them back in my pocket and return down the steps for the last time. I look at the TV and video in the wheelbarrow and can't be bothered to pick them up, so I take the handles and start trundling it along the muddy path. The path is full of potholes, but fortunately the TV and video are safely wedged so that no matter how much the wheelbarrow gets thrown about they don't fall out. I keep an eye on Farnell's windows as I walk, waiting for him to appear and start screaming at me. When I reach the end of the path I push the barrow up onto the pavement and stop for a few breaths, looking at the short hill I have to cover before reaching Cathy's car.

A woman with a pushchair walks down towards me. She looks at the television and laughs. I smile back, sweeping my fringe from my forehead. Then I pick up the handles again and start my second attack, moving quickly and trying to get the rolling wheel into an even rhythm. It seems much harder to control the wheelbarrow on smooth tarmac than it did on the muddy path, and I'm aware that if it slips over the edge of the kerb everything's going to end up smashed. I remember the times I spent running up here when I was late for work, and feel nostalgic for my old life. I've never really had a set-up that was exactly what I wanted, and most of my adult existence has been spent getting used to my latest privations, but I wouldn't have minded a few more months here.

The slope evens out and I go past the post office, waiting for the lights to change before going over the zebra crossing to Cathy's car. Cathy grins at me from the driver's seat, opening the door and going round to the boot. I push the wheelbarrow up onto the other pavement and then round to where she's waiting, turning it on its side so I have space to lift the TV.

'Is that it?' Cathy asks.

436

'No, there's still the computer to come yet.'

'Do you need a hand?'

'No, it's all right, I've got it under control.'

She nods and stands back as I pick up the TV. I swivel round and put it in the back of the boot, making sure it's wedged safe against some oily blankets. I slide in the video beside it, then pick up the wheelbarrow and start rolling it back.

A silly excitement strikes me as I return for my second trip and I sprint back down the hill, allowing the wheel to jiggle and jump as I run. When I reach the start of the muddy path I'm careful again, keeping my head down so Farnell can't see me. I slow right down and go in close to the wall. There are fewer potholes here and the wheel rolls unhindered until I get halfway down the path and have to stop because the wooden door to Farnell's garden opens directly in front of me.

'Ah,' he says as his face emerges, 'come back to steal my wheelbarrow, have you?'

I've no idea what to say. My immediate instinct is to turn and run, but something inside me believes I can brazen this out.

Farnell squints at me, waiting for an answer. His black beard is shaved back from his cheeks, almost into a goatee, and his face is tanned. I wonder if he's been on holiday.

'I was only using it to get some of my stuff. I'm going to put it back in your garden.'

He laughs. 'That's a weight off my mind. So you're moving out?'

'Yeah. I'm sorry I didn't say anything before, but I can't afford to live here any longer.'

'You found somewhere cheaper?'

'No.'

'So you're on the streets?'

'Shelter.'

Farnell looks away. 'What about the other guy?'

'Dad? He's still in hospital.'

'Not your dad. That other guy.'

'Kevin?'

'Yeah. Is he going too?'

'I don't think so. Why?'

'He owes me rent. Is he up there now?'

I shake my head.

'Oh well. He can't hide for ever.'

He turns his back on me and walks back to his Land Rover.

Once I've got all the stuff in the car, Cathy tells me she needs some petrol and reverses back so she can swing into the garage. I sit and watch the road by the post office, waiting in case Farnell suddenly appears with a sawn-off shotgun.

Cathy comes out of the garage carrying two chocolate bars. She opens the door and drops one on my lap. Then she starts the engine and drives out of the forecourt.

I don't know what I've done, but Cathy's feelings for me have definitely cooled since I went back to work. We're comfortable in each other's company, but she doesn't talk in the same unguarded way she did when we were wasting afternoons together last week. After we get back from Farnell's, I stack all Dad's equipment in the corner of our bedroom, and then we pass time together watching television and waiting for Alice to come home.

When she does arrive, we both spring up. I hide my restlessness by pretending I'm rushing across to give her a hug. She squirms in surprise, then says, 'God, I've had a grim afternoon.'

'What happened?'

'I had my talk with Teri.'

'Which talk? Letting her go?'

She nods. 'And any hopes that she might be mature about it proved to be futile.'

'What's this?' Cathy asks.

'Just some girl in work,' Alice explains. 'We found out that she's been making personal calls so we've had to let her go.'

'So she's gone now?' I ask, nervous.

'No, I've given her notice and everything. I'm being really decent about this. I've given her time to get another job sorted out. Of course she won't, and she'll get into a terrible state and blame it on me, but what are you supposed to do with people like that?'

'Oh, I wouldn't worry about it,' says Cathy, 'you knew when you became team leader that you'd have a few silly situations to sort out.'

'Yeah, you're right, but I just hate that sort of unpleasantness. Especially when it gets personal.'

'How did it get personal?' I ask.

'You know what she's like,' she says, leaning down to slide off her shoes, 'she's had a grudge against me for ages. Everyone thinks she's really innocent because she's small and quiet, but she's actually much more vicious than Adrienne.'

'So she was abusive to you?'

Alice sighs. 'Do you mind if we don't talk about it? I hate bringing work worries home with me and I don't want to let her spoil my evening.'

'Would you like a cup of tea?' Cathy asks.

'Yeah, that'd be nice. Thanks, Mum.'

I desperately want to question Alice further, but know better than to disobey her instruction. She sips her tea with the confidence of someone who knows they're controlling the conversation, and Cathy and I have no choice but to sit there and wait for her to change the subject.

We're still waiting ten minutes later when Tim comes in and starts talking enthusiastically about the A grade he got for his Holocaust essay. Alice smiles but doesn't say anything, balancing her mug on the arm of the sofa. Cathy looks at me and asks what I want for dinner. My stomach feels too tight to eat, but I nod after her first suggestion and then go out to the toilet.

'Are you ready to talk about Teri yet?' I ask later, after a long, boring evening and just before we start undressing for bed.

'I don't really see what there is to talk about. Unless you want a blow-by-blow account of our conversation.'

'No, it's not that. I can just see that it's obviously upsetting you and I thought it might make things better if we talked about it.'

'I don't know, Dan. I don't know what I think about this stuff.'

'What stuff?'

'Talking about work when we're alone together. I worry it'll put a strain on our relationship.'

'Why?'

'Well, Teri's your friend for one, and you're going to have to go in and listen to them saying all kinds of terrible stuff about me. I just think it'll be better for you if you don't feel that you have to defend me.'

I climb under the duvet. 'Fine. But it seems a little pathetic that we're letting work define our relationship.'

'What do you want me to say, Dan?'

'I want you to trust me. I'm your boyfriend. You're far more important to me than my job or anyone at work.'

She kisses me. 'You're being really sweet, but please just let me forget about Teri. I don't want to stay up all night worrying.'

'OK, I'm sorry. I only wanted to be supportive.'

'You're very supportive. Not pressurising me is more helpful than any conversation.'

She walks to the wall and turns out the light. I slide under the duvet and wait until she settles down beside me. I put my arm around her shoulders and she hugs me back fiercely, banishing all thoughts of Teri from my mind.

22

After everything that happened today, it's hardly surprising that I should have a troubled night's sleep. After a couple of scary trailers, the main feature is a paranoia thriller which revolves around me discovering a gutted Teri in a bed not dissimilar to the one in which Kevin met his end. The guilt is unbearable, and I spend most of the dream sobbing. When I wake up Alice tells me my moaning kept her awake most of the night.

We're out of bed a little later than yesterday, and don't have time for a proper breakfast. I snatch an apple from the kitchen and join Alice in the car. She's more talkative than she was yesterday, and now seems to regard Teri as a problem that can be solved as simply as any other office snarl-up.

'Do you think I should talk to Teri again?' she asks me.

'Not unless you're going to offer her her job back. It's not as if you're worried about keeping her friendship.'

'No, I guess not. How do you think everyone else is going to react?'

I look out the window, remembering Friday night and Adrienne telling me that Ian was convinced my plotting would leave them without jobs. No doubt this will confirm his suspicions and result in a return to hostile relations. I realise I sound a lot more flippant about this than I did before, but seeing Kevin's corpse has taken the edge off my paranoia. If I'd suggested to Dad that I could imagine a series of events that would end up with someone dead in our flat, he would've laughed at me. But now I have proof that the threats to my existence aren't just psychological, and can concentrate on the simple arrangements needed to stay alive.

'Ian and Adrienne will think it's my fault.'

'Why?'

I look at her. 'Well, it is, isn't it? I was the one who told you Teri was making private calls.'

'No one else knows that. Don't make them suspicious by acting guilty.'

'I can't help it. I feel guilty.'

'God, Dan, I wouldn't have said anything if I'd known you were going to get like this. If it makes you feel any better I'd already decided I was going to sack Teri before I asked you who you'd seen making personal calls.'

'Really? So if I'd said Ian you'd still have sacked Teri?'

'Of course. Besides, I knew you'd say Teri.'

'How?'

'Because Ian's your mate. I'd already told you that both Ian and Teri had personal calls on their print-outs, so I wasn't asking you to point the finger. You could've said either. I just wanted to see who you'd choose.'

'So the personal calls weren't a factor?'

'They were a factor, but a very small one. It'll act as a warning, and a little office myth to keep people on their toes. But, to be honest, I mean, God knows how many personal calls I made when I was on a team.'

I swallow. 'Teri was making personal calls for me.'

'What?'

'When I went to see Dad in the hospital for the first time, he gave me a list of the people in his group and asked me to call them as soon as possible. Teri overheard me talking to one of the women and said the way I was breaking the news was too blunt. So I asked her to finish off the list for me.'

Alice doesn't say anything, staring at the road.

'And that's why I feel guilty.'

'I see.'

'So now you hate me?'

She laughs. 'Don't be ridiculous. But I am impressed that you've managed to keep that secret.'

'Maybe you should sack me instead of Teri.'

'No, Dan, that's not going to happen. But you're very lucky that I wasn't too specific with Teri. Why didn't you say anything?'

'I didn't know you were going to sack her yesterday. I thought I'd have chance to confess.'

'OK. Teri's already sacked and there's no way she's getting her job back. She doesn't know it's got anything to do with you and as long as you don't say anything that's a situation which is unlikely to change. If Teri and the rest of the team hate anyone it's going to be me, not you, and while you might get a bit of flak for being my boyfriend, I'm sure you can handle it. So don't get paranoid, OK?'

'OK.'

'I mean it, Dan. I've worked hard to sort out your problems with the team, but if you keep starting stuff then it won't matter what I say to them.'

I nod. 'No, you're right. I can stand up to Adrienne and Ian about this one. Although I'll probably need to show Teri a bit of sympathy.'

'Fine. I don't have a problem with that.'

We enter the call-centre together, unconcerned now the rest of the office has had chance to get used to our relationship. I look at our table, eager to talk to Teri as soon as possible. But she hasn't come in yet and the only person logged on is Gordon. I give Alice's arm a goodbye pat and walk over to join my scary team-mate.

'All right, Gordon?' I ask, standing behind him and placing my hands on his shoulders.

He jumps.

'Relax,' I say, as he nervously swivels his head, 'what's making you so jumpy?'

'Nothing,' he says defensively, 'you just took me by surprise.'

'Sorry.' I cross over behind my side of the table. 'You looking forward to tonight?'

'Yeah.'

'Karaoke nights are pretty special for you, aren't they?'

'What d'you mean?'

'You really enjoy yourself, right?'

'I suppose so.'

'Yeah.' I pick up my headset and connect it to the *Aspect*. It's eight fifty-seven and the wait-light's already flashing. I hit *Ready*.

'Hello, Angel Cruises.'

Adrienne's the next to arrive. She's carrying a new leopardskin-print shoulder bag. This seems an unlikely accessory for Ade, and I turn off my mike while I lean across and ask, 'Present?'

'This?' She lifts it from her side. 'Ian got it for me.'

'Nice.'

I stare at her lips, waiting to see if she'll make her real feelings known with a mocking smile. But her face remains straight and I can't decide whether she's simply being loyal or genuinely likes the gift.

Adrienne takes the bag from her shoulder and puts it inside her drawer. I go back to my call, pretending I've been listening all along. It's ten past nine and there's still no sign of Teri or Ian. I tap the caller's details into the keyboard, saddened by the fact that no one's surprised any more that I can get their full address up on my screen just from their postcode. When I first came here callers considered this trick a black magic that reactivated all their primitive fears about technology, and I liked to imagine them contemplating their telephones with an ancient terror.

Ian comes in at quarter past. I regard him carefully as he walks through the office, remembering what Alice said about not appearing guilty. He sits down next to me and I wait for him to work through his complex series of early-morning exhalations.

'All right?' I try.

He nods.

'Late night?' I ask, nodding at the clock.

'Not really. I just couldn't be fucked to get up.'

I weigh his tone for evidence of aggression and decide on reflection that it's best not to broach the subject of Teri just yet. See, I am getting better. Usually I can't cope with unspoken aggression and just weigh right in, which is hardly the most diplomatic way of resolving conflicts. I stand up, trailing my wire around Ian and look for the Breaks Book. Gordon notices my ferreting, picks up the graffiti-covered folder and hands it to me. I'm just about to consult the partially filled black grid when I'm surprised by the appearance of Teri, who shuffles quickly into the office.

She's wearing a grey and black striped top cut in a straight line across her collar bone. It looks very eighties and I wonder if she bought it like that or customised it with a pair of scissors. Her hair is in such disarray she looks like a female Robert Smith, and she's wearing her usual light-pink lipstick. She's also wearing a pair of black PVC trousers. Definitely not office uniform, and it seems unlikely that she's mistaken the date of dress-down day. I wonder whether Alice will tell her to go home and change, but she's busy doing something and hasn't noticed Teri.

Other teams have, however, and there's such a commotion on the other side of the office that I wonder whether another team leader will come over and do Alice's duty for her.

Teri doesn't notice the attention – probably because she's got her back to the gawpers – and walks towards the table, smiling shyly at me. I'm not sure whether this is a good sign, or a prelude to her whipping out an axe and burying it in my chest.

She sits down beside me and starts setting up. I look at the Breaks Book in my hands, then put it down in front of me, unable to decide what to write there until I've spoken with Alice and Teri. Initially I thought I'd have lunchtime to myself today, but now I realise it's important to utilise this time for preserving relationships.

Teri grips my arm. 'Will you look after me today?'

'Of course,' I say, surprised, 'but why do you need looking after?'

'Alice didn't tell you what happened?'

'Yeah. She did. I'm really sorry. I didn't know anything about it.'

She grips tighter. 'Really?'

'Really.'

'Oh, I'm so glad to hear that. I thought that was probably the case, but I needed to hear you say it.'

'It's true. I stayed up half the night trying to persuade her to change her mind, but it wasn't her decision. Orders from above.'

'They had to get rid of somebody. Although I think there were more deserving candidates.'

She nods in Gordon's direction and we both start giggling. I want to put my arm around her but it seems inappropriate, especially if witnessed by the rest of the office. She holds on to me and whispers, 'I had half a bottle of tequila for breakfast.'

I look at her, trying not to appear shocked. 'Really?'

'Yeah,' she grins, 'my housemates thought it was hilarious. Especially when they saw what I was planning to wear.'

'Mmm, it's an interesting outfit you've got there.'

'First I thought I wasn't going to come in. Then I decided I wasn't going to go quietly. They can drag me kicking and screaming from the office.'

I look over to reception. Someone must've had a word with Alice because she's staring at us. Although her face is set in a scowl, I'm not scared about her being angry with me. I told her this morning that she couldn't be cross if I comforted Teri, and to be honest right now I'm feeling much closer to my team-mate than my girlfriend.

I hold Alice's gaze, trying to warn her not to come over, using my lips, eyes and forehead. She goes behind the purple screens. My wait-light flashes. Internal call.

'Hello?'

'What's going on?'

'Nothing.'

'Are you trying to piss me off?'

'No. We talked about this in the car.'

'I can't let her get away with this. The rest of the office will think I'm an idiot.'

'It's not a good idea to start a scene. Leave it for the moment and I'll sort things out.'

'What are you going to do? She's hanging on to you like you're her best mate.'

'I'm trying to keep things calm. She's behind her work-station now. If any clients come in they won't see her trousers.'

'Don't talk about it in front of her.'

'You started it.'

'All right, I'll leave her for the minute. But if anything happens it's your responsibility.'

'I understand.'

'And if anyone else comes up to me I'll have to send her home.'

'OK.'

She clicks off.

I take my breaks with Teri, deciding that it's better to stick with one side rather than do my usual double-agent stuff. She suggests we take off an hour between one and two and make it a liquid lunch. I agree and we go to The Friar. It's probably a risky choice because being Quick Kall's official local, it's frequented by most of the line managers, but I'm in that sort of mood today, and feel eager to be swept up in Teri's madness.

She orders two pints and we take a table outside. I make a small concession to my stomach by asking her if I could have a packet of crisps. She buys me some and I rip them open down the side, spreading the foil into two flaps and leaving them in the centre of the table.

'So are you still going tonight?'

'The karaoke? I wouldn't miss it for the world.'

'Good.' I take a sip from my pint. 'How are you feeling?'

'Not bad. Although I think the tequila's worn off.'

'Oh, I forgot to ask you. How did the revenge go?'

'Pretty much as I expected. It was really disgusting.'

'Did they suspect you?'

'No, they're blokes. They all drink every night and eat crap all the time, except when I cook for them, so their systems are fucked. They made a few jokes about having the squits, but I think they assumed it was the result of a bad curry.'

I laugh. 'So are you going to go out of Quick Kall in the same style?'

'I've got a few ideas.'

'Care to share them with me?'

'Not yet. You'll find out soon enough.'

We get through four pints each during our lunchtime session and I'm swaying on the way back to the call-centre. I didn't find out what time Alice was going to lunch before I headed off with Teri and I'm worried about running into her before I'm installed behind my table. I'm sure I can carry off a convincing impression of sober down a phone line, but a few second's face-to-face conversation and Alice would quickly realise how I've spent the last hour.

Neither of us have remembered our ID cards and we have to wait at the back entrance for someone to let us in. Embarrassingly, the first person to appear is Fat Bastard. He examines me with open contempt, and I worry that he's going to message Alice and tell her he's seen me flirting with another woman.

We enter the lift together. Teri takes my hand. I realise this is simply an extension of the physical fondness she's displayed to me all day, but I still feel a quiet thrill and remember how last time I was in a lift with Teri I desperately wanted to kiss her. I always feel weird when I've been drinking with a woman, especially after everything that happened with Sonia, and don't really know how to behave with Teri. Deep down, I have to admit that I am still a reprehensible, repressed Puritan, but at the same time I hate that side of myself and enjoy conspiring against the sober Dan. I love escaping the critical, snobbish side of my nature, and as Teri and I slowly rise up through the building, I feel so proud that I've chosen to protect my friend.

When the lift stops at the seventh floor we walk through to the call-centre. It's ten past two, but fortunately Alice is out of the office so she can't have a go at me for coming back late. Teri and I cross the office floor together and sit down at our respective work-stations.

I don't know why karaoke should cause such excitement in the call-centre. People seem delighted by the idea of spending an evening with their work-mates, even though most nights they seem eager to leave them behind and get home. I suppose it's the knowledge that it's always on these occasions that any office conflicts are resolved, and the following morning usually sees at least one new relationship, as well as leaving two or three others out of a job. It's also always the source of much more subtle gossip, as feuds become more openly expressed, and eager singles lay the groundwork for later assignations.

Consequently, it's quite hard to concentrate during the rest of the day. Concentration has never been one of my big concerns, but today I become dangerously slack, spending half the afternoon by the water-cooler and the other half in the toilet. OK, that's a bit of an exaggeration, but I don't really settle into anything, keeping the calls short and enjoying several rounds of Connect Four with Teri. I'm sure the drink is the main reason why my eyes keep wandering, but the party atmosphere definitely doesn't help.

I find myself thinking about the blonde woman who sold us tickets yesterday, and how she suggested that Alice and I could go on a double-date with her and her boyfriend. I know she didn't really mean it, but I was touched by the offer, and it made me feel that my relationship with Alice doesn't always have to be illegitimate: a time might come when we are just a normal couple, with a shared circle of friends from the office and a history that no longer concerns either of us.

Someone has given a great deal of consideration about when to start the karaoke evening, kicking off at seven so that most people in the office don't have time to go home beforehand. The most sensible employees go to McDonald's or Burger King and have a few hamburgers to line their stomachs. Everyone else heads down the pub. Most go straight to The Friar, although an adventurous few venture into the Centre. Alice sent a group message round telling everyone to finish a few minutes early so we could get a table, and we find somewhere to sit in the front room. Gordon gets up and offers to buy everyone a round.

I let him buy me a pint. He's only being generous now because he knows that one of us is going to have to get him into a taxi at the end of the evening and he's not yet sure who that's going to be. I'm grateful for the drink, but I'm certainly not going to baby-sit him. I've already done that duty before, and I have more pressing concerns than Gordon's welfare tonight.

I treat myself to another packet of crisps, realising that I haven't eaten properly all day and wondering whether to attack the lunchbox Cathy prepared for me this morning. I quite like drinking on an empty stomach, especially if I can follow up the four or five pints of fluid with a burger or some fish and chips.

'So what are you going to do tonight?' I ask Gordon.

He smiles. 'I haven't decided yet. I thought I might do something a bit different.'

This is extremely unlikely. Gordon always sings 'Wonderwall'. I suppose there's a possibility that he might go for The Verve or Ocean Colour Scene, but I can't see him stretching much further than that. I finish off my bag of crisps and put the foil beneath the ashtray. Alice and Teri are sitting opposite each other, apparently in the middle of a staring-contest. I can tell Alice thinks this form of conflict is childish, and after another thirty seconds she pointedly looks away.

It's always hard to know how seriously to take moments like this.

I'm depressed that soon I'll no longer see Teri at work, but the actual reality of her being absent from my side has yet to sink in. Tonight feels like one of those rites-of-passage moments that mean so much at the time, but are forgotten a few days later. For some reason it seems like it's my last day at work, although I know tomorrow I'll be back at my desk as usual. It's like the end of a love affair, when you want to make grand gestures but ultimately understand that there's no point postponing the inevitable. A time when you wish you were capable of feeling more, of losing your head and beating your breast, instead of waiting calmly for the hysteria to be over.

'I can't believe I'm doing this,' says Adrienne, 'I hate karaoke.'

'Have you ever been?' Gordon asks immediately, which seems surprisingly sparky for him. Perhaps he doesn't like his favourite pastime being denigrated.

Adrienne doesn't bother answering him. I look at the levels of everyone's drinks, waiting for an excuse to leave the table. When they get down to the half-inch mark I stand up and go to the bar. I take a very passive position in the fight to be served, wanting to stay away from the others for as long as possible. At least when the karaoke starts there'll be something to watch. After I've let three or four people slip past me, the barman catches me off-guard and I'm forced to give my order.

At seven o'clock the pub starts to empty and we follow the rest of the office to the Cordon Hotel. The company that provides the equipment and the man who goes with it is called OK Karaoke. When Quick Kall first began staging these monthly events they asked OK Karaoke to install their machines in the breaks room. This only happened twice before they started looking for an alternative location. Knowing how much alcohol gets consumed in the course of a karaoke evening, the manager of the Cordon Hotel was happy to offer the use of his bar.

The Cordon Hotel no longer operates as a hotel. There are beds upstairs, and occasionally the manager will allow one of the regulars to sleep off a funk in one of the decrepit bedrooms, but most of the time it is only a pub. It is a very old-fashioned drinking establishment, one of the few locations in Bristol to escape gentrification. There are older places, with many more features of historical note, but most have been modernised in at least some small way. The Cordon seems as if it's remained exactly how it's always been. Our team stick together and choose a table quite close to the front. I can tell Adrienne's angered by our position, but Gordon is delighted, barely able to remain in his seat.

'It's my round,' says Ian, and checks what everyone wants to drink. I watch the other teams choosing tables, trying to remember who sings which song. Most people stick with their one hit, although there are occasionally some surprising new choices. Temps are the most experimental, usually going for one of the very recent songs whose titles are included on a separate photocopied sheet which comes tucked inside the laminated booklet of the main list, like a list of specials handed out with a restaurant menu.

The MC is always the same tall, smart guy who takes it all very seriously, but nevertheless manages to capture the spirit of the evening. He usually wears a black suit and a shiny shirt and is a fantastic singer, with a voice not dissimilar to Luther Vandross. He begins the evening by doing a couple of tunes himself, while everyone else has another drink and scans through the song-list. I enjoy looking round the room at this point, watching the satisfied way people settle on a song, smirking to themselves and passing the list to their neighbour.

Teri grabs hold of my arm. 'I'm feeling a bit woozy.'

'I'm not surprised. You've been drinking all day.'

'I haven't had that much,' she says scornfully, 'besides, there's been plenty of time for it to get through my system.'

'Perhaps you should have something to eat.'

'No. I should have a lot more to drink.'

Ian hands her her pint and she downs it in one, then belches and starts giggling. Alice is sitting on the opposite side of me and ostentatiously puts her hand on my thigh. Teri ignores her.

'You did promise to look after me.'

'And I will. But what exactly does that entail?'

'Right now it entails getting me another drink.'

'Are you sure that's a good idea?'

'Positive. I'm just on the fringes of being drunk at the moment and that's why I feel like shit. Another couple of pints and I'll be fine again.'

'OK.'

I stand up and walk to the bar. Alice follows me.

'What are you doing?'

'Getting Teri a drink.'

'Don't encourage her.'

'I'm not. I tried to talk her out of it. But she's on a mission.'

'She's just being silly. Tell her you're not going to buy her another drink until everyone else has finished the round.'

'I can't treat her like a child, Alice. Look, she'll just get pissed and pass out. I don't think that's such a terrible thing. After all, she did lose her job yesterday.'

'Fine. But you're taking responsibilty for her.'

She turns her back on me and walks back to the table.

Gordon's the first of our team to get up. His promised surprise turns out to be 'Relax' by Frankie Goes to Hollywood. I have to admit I am taken aback by his choice, and wonder whether Adrienne put him up to it. After all, that track would be the perfect accompaniment to Gordon's Log.

As usual, there's far too much REM. I don't want to be rude about Michael Stipe, but it has to be said that for some reason most middle-aged line managers seem to think they can sing like him. And on the evidence of tonight's offerings their conviction seems to hold weight. Of course, anyone can sound like anyone with the echo on a karaoke mike, but the Stipe impersonations are the most uncanny. I can't work out if he's such a popular choice because people want to be like him, or think they're already like him, or because they think his voice is easily emulated, but he definitely crops up more often than anyone else.

Watching karaoke isn't all that interesting unless you know the person singing, but one thing which does always fascinate me is seeing the illuminated lyrics scroll along the video screen. Most people tend to plump for old favourites and it's always enlightening to discover all the lines you've been getting wrong. Tonight's big surprise is seeing the lines to 'The Passenger' by Iggy Pop. I realise there's not so much you can get wrong with that song, but there's at least two lines I've always misheard and maybe it's just the drink but tonight that seems an incredible revelation.

The blonde woman gets up with her boyfriend Dennis and they do a duet. I look away when the title card comes up so I don't see what song they're doing but it's some old country number with lines about islands and lots of whooping in the chorus. Dennis looks a bit embarrassed to be singing this song and I'm certain the blonde woman must've chosen it. For the last chorus she puts her arms around his waist and everyone cheers, pleased at the first physical action of the evening.

Most karaoke menus have a separate selection of Neil Diamond songs called The Diamond Collection. When the title of the song comes up on the screen there's a computer-generated image of a large diamond with a fearsome point. Tonight the MC makes space in the evening for all the Neil Diamond fans to come up one after the other. Fortunately, there are only three people who fall into this category and two of them want to do the same song so the MC makes them sing together.

A young temp gets up to sing 'Frozen' by Madonna. I take this opportunity to move from my position between Alice and Teri and go down to Adrienne. She's alternating between sneering at the woman singing and staring into her pint. I can tell Ian's pissed off with her and he moves up to let me sit down.

'So what are you going to do?' I ask.

'Nothing. How about you?'

'I don't know,' I say, picking up the song-list, 'what do you think I should do?'

'"Frigging in the Rigging".'

'I thought you liked Madonna.'

'I do, but someone's already done "Frozen" and it would be just so predictable to get up there and do "Like a Virgin" or "Into the Groove".'

'Well, I don't think they've got much of the stuff you like down here. I can't really see you doing karaoke to Spaceman 3 or some stupid drill 'n' bass track.'

'There must be something good.'

'What about "I'm Too Sexy".'

She makes a face.

'All right, I'll give you a choice. You can either do "Ebeneezer Goode" or "Justified and Ancient".'

'Oh, OK, I'll do "Justified and Ancient". Write it down.'

I do so. Teri comes staggering back with two pint glasses. She hands it to me and I take a sip. Then immediately spit it onto the floor.

'God, what's that, it's disgusting. Take it back, there must be something wrong with the pipes.'

'It's meant to taste like that.'

'What d'you mean? What is it?'

'I asked the barman to put a couple of shots in it.'

'Why?'

'To get us pissed, you idiot.'

'I don't want to get pissed.'

'OK, look, give it to me.'

I hand it to her. She puts her other pint down on the nearby table, leans back, and downs the drink in two swallows. Then she starts walking unsteadily back to the bar.

'Where are you going?'

'To get you another drink.'

'No, seriously, I'm fine.'

'Don't be silly. I'll get you a drink.'

She gets away from me and joins the crowd by the bar. Alice springs up and places herself squarely in front of me.

'I know you're trying to be nice to her, Dan, but you've got to tell her to slow down. If she carries on drinking like this she'll end up in the casualty department.'

'And I'll sit with her while they pump her stomach. I'm not going to make her feel any more alienated.'

'Alienated? She's just pissed. Why don't you take her home and fuck her. I'm sure that'll sort her out.'

She lets her anger carry her away from me and struts off to the toilet. I go back to Adrienne. She hands me the piece of paper.

'Take it up then.'

'OK.'

I go up to the podium and leave the paper on the shelf by the MC. The fat man is coming to the end of his tale of Gs and hos, and the MC is already scrabbling around for a replacement.

'Ha,' he says, shuffling through the requests, 'looks like we've got a couple of joke ones here. No, I'm sorry, there isn't a karaoke version of "Bela Lugosi's Dead" or the theme to EastEnders, although we do have "Every Loser Wins" if you'd like to try that instead.' He pauses. 'No? OK, right then, let's have Stacy who's going to sing "Smells Like Teen Spirit". That's one we haven't had for a while.'

I sit next to Adrienne and watch her bite her nails. Ian looks at her and laughs.

'See, karaoke evenings can be a lot of fun.'

'Shut up,' she tells him. 'And you needn't think you're getting away without doing a song.'

'Oh, I never sing. And there's no way you're going to persuade me. It's just one thing I never do.'

Teri returns with my pint. Her steps are hesitant as she approaches our table. Alice is right. Teri is dangerously wrecked. But I'm determined not to moralise, and put my hand on her hip to steady her. She grins at me.

'Here you go. One plain, boring, ordinary pint.'

'That's fine by me,' I tell her, taking a gulp.

Teri sits back down and we watch Stacy's ludicrous impression of Kurt Cobain. It's hard to tell whether she's a huge fan trying to do her hero justice, or taking the piss. Either way, her singing is ludicrously inept, and she seems a shoo-in for the worst singer prize. The people watching seem a little embarrassed, finding it harder to laugh at her than the out-of-tune men. Alice comes back from the toilet and sits next to Gordon. He doesn't seem as bad as he usually does by this stage of the evening, although maybe that's just in comparision with Teri.

'Smells Like Teen Spirit' limps to an end and the MC picks up another piece of paper.

'Thanks a lot, Stacy. Now, can we have . . . let's see . . . Adrienne up here to sing "Justified and Ancient".'

Ian begins a slow applause. Adrienne glares at him but goes up anyway, taking the microphone from the MC and walking down to the video screen. Teri grips my arm.

'I'm going to sing something.'

'OK. What are you going to do?'

'I don't know . . .' she says, slurring her words and looking for the song-list. I hand it to her. She's bound to embarrass herself if she gets up like this, but I don't feel I can stop her. Hopefully it's just an idle ambition and she'll soon get distracted.

Adrienne's performance is very subtle, and she barely moves her lips as she sings. She almost manages to make singing karaoke seem dignified, and I feel proud of her delivery. She makes me want to get back up and do a song I've chosen myself, something better suited to my voice that I could do justice. Neil Young, maybe, or some old growler like Bob Dylan or Nick Cave. Perhaps the balance between your voice and the original singer is dependent on how good you are, because there's certainly more of Adrienne coming through the mike than there was of me. I close my eyes, trying to work out who she sounds like.

Teri jogs my arm. 'I've decided who I'm going to do.'

'Who?'

'Blondie.'

'Right. Good choice. Which song?'

'"Rip Her to Shreds".'

I look at her. 'That's a bit obscure, isn't it? Why don't you do

"Heart of Glass" or "Hanging on the Telephone"? Actually, yeah, do that, people will think you're being funny.'

'No, I'm doing "Rip Her to Shreds". Write it down.'

'OK.' An idea occurs to me. 'Shall I take it up?'

Something in my voice must've given me away, because she says, 'No, I'll do it.'

She takes her piece of paper up to the MC. He winks at her as he takes it. For some crazy reason, I feel jealous. But Teri barely notices his attentions, turning quickly and staring straight at me as she sexily slopes back to our table. The way she looks tonight makes me furious that I didn't make a play for her before I started going out with Alice. It seems crazy that the one time I stayed at her place I was *scared* she might molest me. Maybe Alice is right. Perhaps the best way to end this evening is to take Teri home and fuck her.

'Thanks, Adrienne,' says the MC. 'I don't know what you lot think, but that's definitely got to be a firm contender for best performance of the evening.'

There's some faint applause. Adrienne allows herself a brief smile and then hands the microphone back.

'Now, can we have Greg and Bryan, who are about to break our hearts with their version of "Unchained Melody".'

A huge hoot comes from the other side of the room and I look over to see Fat Bastard and a suspicious-looking man with curly blond hair get to their feet. I watch Alice, wondering what she's thinking about her old boyfriend. She seems just as interested in studying my expression and I know that I daren't risk a smile.

Fat Bastard grins broadly as he faces the room, putting his arm around the shoulders of his suspicious friend and waiting for the music to start with all the confidence of a Vegas entertainer. His friend looks a little more anxious, but Fat Bastard grips him firmly, not about to acknowledge his worry.

They start singing. Fat Bastard's actually got a pretty good voice, and I remember being impressed when I heard him sing before. I wonder whether his relationship with Alice started after a karaoke evening. I guess that would make sense, and he would certainly seem a lot more attractive after she'd seen him up on the podium serenading the office. Perhaps she was just turned on by his position in the office, the ease with which he handles these sort of social occasions.

Teri turns to me. 'Can you get me another drink?'

'If you really want one . . . but you have just downed two pints and God knows how many shorts in about ten minutes.'

'Thanks for reminding me. Look, he'll be calling me up in a minute and I need a bit of Dutch courage.'

'OK. But this is the last one, yeah?'

She nods. 'Get him to put a Southern Comfort in it.'

I stand up. Alice looks at me. I realise she's going to freak out if she sees me buying Teri another drink so I slip a tenner to Ian and ask him to get the round for me. He looks surprised, but gets up anyway, going over to the bar.

Fat Bastard's voice is getting louder as the song builds. He tugs enthusiastically at his friend's shoulder, spreading out his arm as he builds to the climax. I watch Teri, worried by the way she keeps slightly opening her mouth and hoping she's not about to throw up.

Ian gets served swiftly and returns to our table. I take my pint and place it next to the previous one that I haven't finished yet. I'm beginning to feel a bit woozy myself and have to grip on to the table in front of me.

'Thank you, Greg and Bryan. Another fantastic performance. Right, then, let's have Teri who's going to sing the Blondie song, "Rip Her to Shreds".'

Teri makes no movement, and I wonder whether she's heard him. I don't say anything, still thinking it will be much better if she doesn't get up on stage. But then she comes out of her daze and walks across to the MC, eagerly grasping the microphone.

I hold my breath and watch her eyes, surprised she's still able to stand up. She flicks her fringe with her fingers and looks down at the screen in front of her.

She manages about half a verse before giving up. The MC can only see her back and doesn't immediately realise that she's stopped singing. Only when the microphone slips from her fingers and hits the floor does he notice anything wrong. Even then, he stays where he is. This MC is clearly a professional, not one to circumscribe the various types of entertainment that can be found at a karaoke evening.

'Rip Her to Shreds' continues in the background. The instruments and Debbie Harry's voice are audible but faint, as if we're listening to the song on a stereo with inadequate speakers. Teri stands there staring blankly at the audience. Then her eyes seem to focus and she fixes them on me. She winks and I suddenly realise that I know exactly what's about to happen.

Teri takes a second to steady herself and make sure she's got the audience's attention. Then she tugs at the front of her grey and black striped top, pulling it tight against her small breasts. The collar of her shirt shows a small cresent of pale skin and I concentrate on that as she raises and lowers the bottom of it, getting higher and higher with each flutter. The movement is both heart-breakingly innocent and at the same time as skilled as if she did this for a living. It has exactly the intended effect and when she pulls the stripey top high enough to expose the bottom of her black patterned bra, I'm rock hard inside my work-trousers. I lose all sense of the people around me, unconcerned what Alice thinks and feeling that this public performance is really a display just for me. Tonight Teri is my private dancer, and I am her enraptured audience. I suppose despite my hyperbole I must acknowledge that I don't feel completely separated from everyone else in the Cordon Hotel, because if I did believe this was just about Teri and me I would pull out my cock and start wanking, wanting her to see what she was doing to me.

The T-shirt gets higher and higher and I stare at Teri's black bra. I can make out her pale pink nipples beneath the small roses that decorate the otherwise see-thru material, and as she pulls off the shirt completely I can't help thinking that she looks perfect and want to take a million photographs of her. Her wayward hair looks fantastic with her bare shoulders and her drunken gaze makes her seem sexier than ever. I can't believe this is happening and feel that this is a moment I will remember for ever.

She reaches down and quickly unbuckles her black shoes, getting them off with no ceremony as if thinking they have little erotic potential. Her small toenails are painted black and she opens her legs slightly as she steps back. Debbie Harry's voice seems to be growing louder and I look over to the MC to see if he's altering anything. But he seems as transfixed as I am, standing there with an open mouth.

Teri's fingers move down to her crotch and she slowly unzips her black PVC trousers. She pulls back the two sides to reveal a small triangle of her black underwear, which matches her bra. Then she slowly inches the trousers down over her hips, before pulling them up again, repeating the motion four times before letting them fall down to her feet. She steps out of the trousers and stands there, using her fingers to further mess up her bedraggled hair. I want her more than I've ever wanted anyone, and realise that this moment is bringing together so many of my favourite fantasies that I will probably never experience something so sexually exciting again.

She walks forward and then steps back, her movements now less certain, as if she's playing for time before progressing to the next stage. Her fingers go behind her back and she unclasps her bra, holding the material tight and looking straight at me. I feel like crying, begging, doing anything to persuade her to let me see her breasts. I wonder if men who pay to see strippers feel the same sense of supplication I feel now, and for the first time I envy them, wishing I'd spent every night of my life sitting in a bar watching a woman undress.

Teri lets go of the material and her bra falls to the floor. Her breasts look lovely, with small, erect pink nipples that I feel desperate to kiss. This seems so different to how I've always imagined these sorts of moments, with no shouting or wolf-whistling or anything, just everyone sitting in silence, spellbound. Teri strokes her fingers down over her breasts and tummy, not really dancing but definitely moving slightly, a motion that seems to be driven by the balls of her feet.

She slips her fingers under the waistband of her knickers and I fear that my heart will stop if she continues. I stare at her, desperate to see her pubic hair but not wanting the act to come to an end. I want to take a remote control and freeze this moment, slowing it right down and teasing myself over and over again. I blink and stare at her crotch, wanting to savour the experience. She smiles and I exhale. Then, before I can tell what's happening, Teri's head smacks backwards and she falls to the floor.

Someone has thrown a bottle. It looks like it hit Teri square on the forehead, but I don't think it smashed till it landed on the floor. There's a puddle of beer and a mess of smashed glass a few feet from Teri's sprawled body, although I don't think she's been cut. I can hear laughter all around me and I wonder if this noise was happening while she was stripping, and I was just experiencing a temporary deafness brought on by the exposure of her beauty.

The MC is standing behind her, clearly terrified. No one seems about to do anything, so I rush over and pick her up, holding her body in my arms and feel her breasts press against my chest. I look at her forehead, wondering if I should take her to hospital. Staggering slightly as I try to work out the best way to carry her, I then reach down to pick up her clothes and put them on top of her naked stomach.

Alice rushes over. 'What the fuck are you doing?'

'What does it look like? I'm taking her home.'

'What, are you gonna carry her through the streets like that?'

'If that's what it takes, yeah.'

'Fine, Dan. Fuck you. Don't bother coming home tonight.'

I ignore her and carry Teri across to the door. I kick it open and head out into the night.

As soon as I'm away from the hotel, I stumble into a doorway and put Teri's body on the floor as I try to get her into a T-shirt. She makes a long, groaning sound but moves her arms enough for me to dress her. I kiss the ugly red mark on her forehead and whisper that everything will be all right.

It takes me a while to find Teri's house, but eventually I start recognising street names and after a few false turns manage to find what I think is her house. I ring the doorbell and wait. There's no sign of any life inside and I'm worried that I'll have to leave her on the doorstep. Then I finally hear some clicking noises inside and the door draws back wide enough to reveal a shaggy blond head.

He looks at Teri and laughs. 'Had one too many did she?'

'Yeah. I've . . . uh . . . brought her clothes.'

'What happened? Did she pass out on you?'

'Not exactly. She got a little carried away at the karaoke evening.'

'I see. Don't worry, I'll take care of her.'

'Thanks.'

He holds out his arms and I pass Teri across, relieved to be freed of my duty. I know she has fights with her housemates, but they seem the type to be well equipped for this sort of eventuality. I'm sure she must've helped them out after previous drunken expeditions and trust him not to shave her eyebrows or leave her out in the garden. I give him her shoes and trousers and say goodnight.

At first I'd intended to take Alice at her word and go look for somewhere to sleep in the bus shelter. It didn't seem a good idea to hide at Quick Kall tonight and I knew that was the first place she'd look for me. But after a couple of hours I decide that if I go back now she'll proably believe that nothing happened between Teri and me and I'll be able to patch things up. So I get the last bus back to Keynsham, spending the whole journey working out how to flatter Alice into letting me stay.

23

Local newspapers love those lightning-strikes-twice stories. Hole-in-the-heart baby falls down stairs and punctures hole in her throat. Widow's second husband is electrocuted fixing the same television that finished her first. Man hit by car crossing road gets out of hospital only to be killed by bus.

I'm on my first break when I read about Dad's death. The *Evening Post* has never been my favourite newspaper, but I've checked it every day since discovering Kevin's corpse, wanting a head start if the police launch an investigation.

There aren't any customers in the newsagent and the old lady serving is gentle with me, ignoring my attempts at speech and helping me count out the coins needed to pay for my paper.

I leave the shop and walk through to the city Centre, unsure where I'm going but needing at least a few minutes away from Quick Kall. Reaching the Galleries, I go through the top entrance and try to lose myself among the shoppers. When this doesn't work I sit on one of the white wire benches by W. H. Smith's and read the story three times. As I read I speak each word aloud in a newscaster's voice, trying to work out exactly what this information means to me. Obviously it's incredibly upsetting to discover my father is dead, but that sadness seems a luxury I can't afford just yet. I need to think everything through. The first thing I need to work out is who did this to him. Of course, it could be another accident, but it seems too much of a coincidence that Dad should be run down twice. The only thing that stops me suspecting Mum and Doug Smart is the fact that it was a bus that hit him. It's not that I don't believe it's possible for them to infiltrate the public transport system, just that it seems a hard operation to orchestrate.

No doubt Dad's women are already trying to track me down. And perhaps they're not the only ones. What was the name of the man who first knocked over my father? Maybe now my mum's got someone else to finish off that job, he's been dispatched after me. I watch the crowds moving round this upper level, looking for anyone who seems suspicious.

I can't work out whether it's safer to return to work or make a run for it. I know that once Dad's women catch up with me things are going to change drastically, and I'm not sure if I'm ready for that. Taking responsibility seems almost as scary as being killed by one of Mum's hitmen.

I get up from the bench and put the newspaper in a nearby bin. I wish I was able to just accept Dad's death as a tragic accident and begin grieving, but I know with absolute certainty that this is another false ending. I just haven't been looking at the bigger picture, that's all. It was stupid of me to think that this current stage of my life started when Dad went into hospital. The real beginning of this chain of events was Dad running off with Mum's winnings, and just as I didn't worry when he took off because I knew I'd see him again, so I'm convinced his death is only the mid-point in a story that won't really make any sense until I get to the end.

I can't go back to work. Neither can I disappear. Both my parents have, at different times, run away from their lives, but that's never been my style. I go to the nearest bus stop and then back to Keynsham, pleased to find an empty house.

The morning after I took Teri back to her flat I decided it was my duty to return once more and check she was all right. The shaggy-haired guy who'd answered the door the night before had seemed reasonably sympathetic, but after all Teri's horror stories about what her housemates were like (and that morning when I witnessed them in action) I wanted to make sure she was OK.

I had to ring the doorbell five times before getting a response. I suppose this is fairly usual if you go to that sort of household at nine in the morning, but when the shaggy-haired guy opened the door I realised from the music blaring inside that the problem wasn't that they weren't awake, but that they couldn't hear me.

The guy squinted at me like he recognised me but couldn't place my face and then asked me if I wanted to come in for breakfast. I was surprised by the offer, but thought this was probably my best chance of getting any sense out of him and followed him through to the kitchen. The other inhabitants were gathered round the breakfast table just like they were on my previous visit, only this time there was no Teri oiling the pan.

He sat down with his friends and they resumed their breakfast. The sound of spoons raising heaps of soggy cornflakes to lips made me feel queasy and I asked if I could just have a piece of dry toast. He went to the cupboard and took out a slice of white bread. One of the other guys (John, I think) asked me why I had come.

'Oh, just to check on Teri.'

'That bitch,' he said, 'we soon sorted her out.'

'What?'

'Yeah. We all took turns and then got rid of her. If you want to find her you should check the bin-bags outside.'

They all burst out laughing and I realised I was the victim of some tasteless joke. I knew I should play it cool and wait for them to tell me what had really happened to Teri, but their attitude pissed me off and I couldn't be bothered to stay.

'Oh, well,' I said, 'nice seeing you again.'

'What about your toast?'

'Forget it. I've lost my appetite.'

I walked through to the hallway and then out the front door. I was about halfway down the street before curiosity got the better of me and I had to return. I knew thay hadn't really killed Teri, but I thought there must be something behind their joke and wanted to know what it was.

I stopped by the front of their house and looked at the five bin-bags by their front doorway. Although it'd been dark, I was fairly certain the bags weren't there last night. Each bag was only about half full and the black plastic had been pulled into a thick knot at the top. Ordinarily I would've taken the time to carefully unknot the bags but I was pissed off and wanted to get this over with quickly, so I took a key from my pocket and plunged it into the black plastic, dragging it down until I had a big enough slit to look inside.

The first bag was filled with normal household rubbish. There was nothing sinister or untoward about the contents. A few newspapers, crisp bags, baked-bean tins, that's all. I moved on to the second bag. This was filled with rubbish that had clearly been gathered from a bathroom. The insides of toilet rolls, razor blades, that sort of thing. There were many more feminine toiletries than male ones, which, given the division of the household, struck me as a little odd, but maybe Teri had had a separate bin in her bedroom. Then I opened the third bag.

The stuff in this bag was clearly not rubbish. T-shirts, clothes, toys, even a few CDs. I knew these were Teri's possessions and couldn't understand why she would want to throw them away. I looked at the two remaining bags, wondering if it was conceivable that the shapes inside them were a chopped-up human body. Feeling sick, I quickly slashed both. I couldn't stand the suspense of opening one bag, examining what was inside and then moving on to the next. This way the mystery would be solved in one go, and I would know whether it was necessary for me to go and call the police.

The other two bags contained more of the same. Books, letters, all kinds of curious keepsakes. I tore the plastic of both bags wider, wanting to work out the extent of what had been thrown away. It was clear to me now that these bags contained the entire contents of Teri's room. This fact, combined with her housemates' joking, made me distinctly anxious. I needed to construct an explanation for this mass clear-out. As far as I could see, there were three main possibilities:

1. Her flatmates were telling the truth, and had, in fact, killed Teri.
2. After the embarrassment of losing her job and stripping in front of her workmates, Teri had woken up early and fled, leaving her stuff behind, which her housemates – sympathetic to the end – then disposed of.
3. The same as the above, only Teri got rid of her own possessions, filled with self-hatred and wanting to start a new life.

Obviously, I hoped the latter was true, but nevertheless, I couldn't help worrying, and felt an overwhelming urge to help her. The only thing I could possibly do without knowing where she was or what happened to her was to take her stuff back with me. Unfortunately, now I had cut through the bags it was hard to carry them. I walked at least half a mile before I discovered some shopping trolleys outside a small supermarket. When no one was looking, I stole one and pushed it back to Teri's house. I lifted the three bags of her stuff into the trolley and pushed them to the Centre, where I got a taxi back to Alice's. The scale of this operation made me an hour late for work, but everyone was hungover from the night before and even my girlfriend didn't comment.

I stare at the black bags, wondering whether I'm ready to go through them. I didn't have anywhere of my own to hide Teri's stuff so I've just left them in Alice's wardrobe. I haven't told her what's in them or why I'm keeping them, but she hasn't complained. I'm sure she must've taken a quick peek, but if she did realise that these were Teri's belongings she hasn't said anything. Perhaps she thinks I'm going mad.

I slide the door closed. I feel too drained to cope with the mystery of Teri's disappearance as well as Dad's death. There'll be plenty of time for that later. In the meantime, I just need to rest.

*　　*　　*

I get about an hour to myself before Alice appears.

'Hello Dan.'

'How did you know I was here?'

'I didn't.'

'Do you know what happened?'

She nods. 'Claire called.'

'I thought that would happen. I took your phone off the hook. I hope that's OK.'

'Of course. But you know you could have left the ansaphone on.'

'I know, but then I'll have to deal with it. As long as no one can get through to me, I don't have to do anything.'

'I understand.'

'Where's Cathy?'

'I don't know.'

She rubs my back and then gets up, leaving me alone on the bed. I cling on to the mattress, wondering if I'm about to cry. After Dad's accident, I spent a lot of time wondering how I'd react if he died before me. I'd assumed I'd probably piss everyone off by being too stoic. I'm not very good at having the right emotion at the right time, and the small part of me that can still manage to get perspective on this tragedy is delighted that I should prove capable of a genuine human reaction.

Alice comes back with a cup of tea. 'I know you probably don't want this, but I couldn't think what else to bring you.'

'Thank you,' I say quietly, 'you're being very considerate.'

It doesn't take long for the tears to start in earnest. I realise as I wail against Alice's breast that what I'm really mourning for is the last few weeks, the time from when Dad went into hospital. Before that we were as close as a father and son could possibly be (too close, in terms of our living arrangements). OK, so he had a secret life I didn't know anything about, but the more I've thought about that, the more it's seemed irrelevant. I knew my dad, at least in all the important ways. But it was wrong of me not to visit him more often in hospital. I think when he first went in there I felt as if he was leaving me, as if he was passing into a realm where I was no longer needed. Meeting

Dad's women intensified that feeling, and I think that if he had gone to stay with them, our contact would have become less frequent.

When I stop crying, Alice takes off her clothes and climbs into bed with me. Her flesh feels reassuring and I love the way she holds me, offering her body as if it's her only way of putting my loss into perspective. I kiss her shoulders and gratefully fold her up in my arms.

We spend the rest of the afternoon lying together. When Cathy comes home, Alice puts on her dressing-gown and goes out into the lounge to explain what's happened. I can hear raised voices and can tell Cathy's angry with me. There are probably loads of things you're supposed to do when someone dies, and I'm sure this isn't the first time Cathy's had to help with these sort of arrangements. I should be out there taking responsibility, being a proper son.

I've got no idea what Alice says to Cathy, but whatever it is it works, and we're left alone after that. Late in the evening we make love, and afterwards Alice goes out into the kitchen to get us some food. I eat too much and when I sleep I have nightmares, dreaming of hospital porters stuffing Dad's head into a black plastic bag.

The following morning, Alice shakes me awake and asks, 'What do you want to do?'

'I don't want to face it. Not yet. Not today.'

'OK. So what do you want to do?'

'I want to go to work.'

'Are you sure that's a good idea?'

'Yeah. Just let me go to work, just for the morning at least. Then I'll be ready to start dealing with everything.'

'OK, but I'm going to stay here. Just in case anyone calls.'

I nod.

'Right. Well, you'd better get ready.'

I quickly wash and shave, then change into my suit. I stop for a second to examine myself in the mirror, using two fingers to turn my chin. Then I go out to the kitchen.

'Breakfast?'

'I'll just grab an orange. I really want to get going.'

The traffic is especially bad this morning, but Alice doesn't complain, respecting my wishes. She parks in the rear car park and waits for me to get out. I give her a kiss goodbye and she tells me she'll be back to pick me up at lunchtime. Then I walk across the car park and use my ID card to let myself into the building.

I catch the lift up to the seventh floor, then go through the two sets of double doors and walk over to where my team is waiting. I look round at everyone. So now we are four. I wonder if Cordwinder Bird will turn out to be right and this will prove to be a more harmonious team-number.

Gordon smiles weakly at me. I can tell they know about my bereavement and wonder whether someone sent a message out or if they read about it in yesterday's paper. Adrienne looks at me and I can see she expects me to confide in her. Sorry, Ade. I need voices without faces, a sympathetic listener on the other end of a long, long line. I need Moyra, one of Dad's women, hell, even a regular customer will do. I plug in my headset and stare at my wait-light, willing it to start flashing.